To William, Preston, Lukas, and Campbell
who bring such joy to our lives

PROLOGUE

THE KIDNAPPING AND ASSASSINATION OF ALDO MORO

ROME, ITALY, MARCH 16 TO MAY 9, 1978

Note to reader: The Italian terrorist group known as the Red Brigades will be referred to by its Italian name, the Brigate Rosse (BR), in this book.

A SUNNY MORNING IN ROME

A little before nine in the morning on March 16, 1978, sixty-one-year-old Aldo Moro, five times Italian prime minister between 1963 and 1976, emerged from his fifth-floor Rome penthouse apartment on Via Forte Trionfale to be driven to the Italian Parliament for a historic session that would be a crowning achievement in his thirty-year political career.

It was the Thursday before Palm Sunday. Temperatures had been rising the last few days, and Italians had been showing up on beaches to enjoy the warm weather. Spring was in the air.

As president of Italy's largest party, the Christian Democrats (CD), Moro would present to Parliament at ten o'clock his controversial plan to form a coalition to rule Italy called the *Compromesso Storico,* which would include the Communist Party.

Italy would become the first European nation to form a coalition with the Communist Party despite strong opposition from NATO allies and especially the United States. Moro's gamble was to bring unity to Italy, which was grappling with the crippling forces of economic collapse and waves of terrorism.

Moro was Italy's foremost statesman, known for his ability to mediate among political friends and foes alike. As a reward for his long service, he was likely to become president of the Republic in December.

Moro was also a loving father and grandfather. He and his wife of thirty-three years, Eleonora, had raised four children, including two who still lived with them along with their two-year-old grandson, Luca.

Moro had aged in his thirty-plus years climbing the ranks of the CD. His hair had turned gray, and he walked with a slight stoop, but he was still vigorous and healthy. Every morning he lugged briefcases from their apartment loaded with books, pills, government papers, and newspapers.

Waiting that morning in the Via Forte Trionfale courtyard was Moro's bulletproof, dark blue executive Fiat 130. Seated in the front were his driver, Domenico Ricci, and Oreste Leonardi, a Carabinieri warrant officer *(maresciallo)* nicknamed Jude who'd been Moro's body-guard for fifteen years.

In the second escort car, a cream-colored Alfa Romeo, were three more bodyguards armed with Beretta M-12s. It was the first day of duty for one bodyguard, thirty-year-old Francesco Zizzi.

A few minutes after nine o'clock, Moro's two-car motorcade embarked on a route that would take them through the quiet Via Fani neighborhood so Moro could have a few minutes of silent prayer at the Church of Santa Chiara nearby.

The only stop sign along the route was at the intersection of Via Fani and Via Stresa.

Moro's departure that morning had been closely observed by a man wearing a ski cap on a Honda motorcycle. The motorcycle rider rode to Via Fani and looped around, signaling to waiting colleagues that Moro's motorcade was minutes away.

Within the previous hour, a highly organized and deadly drama had been unfolding on Via Fani.

At around 8:20, a blue four-door Fiat 132 had dropped off two men in blue Alitalia uniforms near the shuttered Olivetti Bar. Two other men dressed similarly were already standing beside potted plants in front of the Olivetti. The four men carried briefcases, one with the logo of Alitalia Airlines.

Within minutes, eleven men and one woman had arrived in three Fiat 128s, one Fiat 132, and one Mini Cooper. They parked near the intersection of Via Fani and Via Stresa. All of the vehicles had been stolen recently off Rome streets and equipped with police sirens and flip-over license plates.

The drivers, passengers, and men standing by the Olivetti were all carrying concealed automatic weapons. They waited for Moro's motorcade, which took four minute to reach Via Fani.

Moro was reading a newspaper in the backseat when his driver, Ricci, stopped at the stop sign.

Immediately, the woman in one of the Fiats backed around the corner and blocked Moro's Fiat. Moro's driver tried to make an evasive move but was blocked by the Mini Cooper, which had pulled up behind the escort Alfa Romeo.

The dozen who had gathered that morning sprang into action, pulling automatic weapons from briefcases, bolting from cars, and firing a fusillade of bullets into Moro's stalled motorcade.

The woman and her passenger in the Fiat that blocked Moro's car opened a cross-fire barrage at Ricci and Leonardi in the front seat.

The four men in blue uniforms ran across the street from the Olivetti. Two fired machine pistols at Moro's three bodyguards in the Alfa Romeo. The other two men opened the back door of Moro's car and dragged him out.

The ambush on Via Fani was over in seconds. Moro's driver, Ricci, and bodyguard Leonardi were dead in the front seat, their bodies covered in blood.

Two bodyguards in the Alfa Romeo's front seat were killed instantly, one gripping the handle of his police radio. The bodyguard in the backseat stumbled out, kneeled, and fired two shots. The man on the Honda killed him with one shot to the head.

In twenty seconds, some ninety shots were fired from automatic weapons on Via Fani. Broken glass and spent shells littered the street in puddles of blood. Moro's newspapers fluttered near the Alitalia bag that had carried an automatic weapon.

The four Fiats, the Mini Cooper, and the motorcycle sped away. A minute later, Moro's captors transferred him to a German van on Via Massimo, which sped off and disappeared.

At 9:25 that morning, one of Italy's national radio networks broke the news:

"We interrupt this broadcast to bring you a dramatic announcement that seems almost unbelievable, and though there is no official confirmation as yet, unfortunately it appears to be true. The president of Christian Democracy, the Honorable Aldo Moro, was kidnapped in Rome a short while ago by terrorist commandos. Honorable Moro's escort was composed of five police officers. It is said that they are all dead."

At ten o'clock, a coded teletype alert from the Ministry of Interior ordered Italian police to institute Plan Zero, a secret plan to deal with a national crisis. But Plan Zero had inadvertently never been dispatched to police commanders. It was hurriedly typed, copied, and dispatched around the country. It was a sloppy blunder, one of many that would plague the investigation of one of Italy's most sensational crimes in postwar history.

Roads in and out of Rome were put under surveillance. Airports, borders, train stations, and harbors were alerted. But Moro and his captors were already in a secret location near the center of Rome.

At ten fifteen, telephones in newsrooms in Rome, Milan, Turin, and Genoa received a recorded message:

"This morning we captured the president of Christian Democracy, Moro, and eliminated his bodyguards, Cossiga's 'leatherheads.' A communiqué follows.—Brigate Rosse."

Five thousand police began a house-to-house search around Via Fani. Officials believed that possibly sixty Brigate Rosse members had been involved in the kidnapping: driving cars, obtaining weapons, and maintaining a hideout where they were keeping Moro.

In the police files was a report filed earlier that month by Moro's bodyguard Leonardi about suspicious movement around Moro's home and one of his offices. The day before Moro's abduction, the nation's highest police official had called Moro's office to say that the report had been investigated and that there was no cause for alarm.

The next day, March 17, Brigate Rosse delivered clandestinely their first communiqué to Rome's daily newspaper, *Il Messaggero,* along with a polaroid photo of Moro in front of a Brigate Rosse banner.

The photo had a sinister touch: the double "S" in the word *Rosse* above Moro's head resembled a Nazi swastika. The photo was published in Italian newspapers on Palm Sunday. At noon, the ailing, eighty-year-old Pope Paul VI delivered his sermon at St. Peter's and asked for prayers for Moro, his longtime friend.

Since the turbulent 1960s, Italy had been rocked by hundreds of acts of domestic terrorism known as *Anni di Piombo* (Years of Lead)—bombings, kidnappings, and assassinations committed by right-wing fascists, left-wing Brigate Rosse, and unnamed groups.

The terrorism was concentrated in the northern provinces of Lombardy and Piedmont, the center of Italy's rapidly growing manufacturing industries. From 1955 to 1971, nearly ten million Italians had migrated from poor, southern regions to work in factories and on assembly lines of automobile plants such as Pirelli and Fiat in Milan and Turin.

Waves of migration caused a severe crisis in housing and sanitation. Workers—mostly young, uneducated men from agrarian backgrounds—were forced to live in attics, basements, shacks, and cement buildings with no electricity or running water called Koreas. Squalid housing, low wages, and dangerous working conditions led to widespread protests, riots, kidnappings, and sabotage by workers and revolutionary-minded university radicals.

The year 1969 was a particularly bloody one across Italy. There were 145 bombings, many in public places, such as the University of Padua and the Milan fair, and aboard trains. On December 12, sixteen were killed in Milan's Piazza Fontana (near the Duomo, Milan's cathedral) when a bomb exploded at the Banca Nazionale dell'Agricoltura. The violence led many Italians to fear that the country was on the brink of a violent revolution that could topple the government.

Many terrorist acts were carried out by the left-wing Brigate Rosse, founded by two sociology majors, Margherita Cagol and Renato Curcio, at the University of Trent. Cagol and Curcio married and moved to Milan to mobilize protesters and spread their Marxist-Leninist ideology that capitalism was born in violence and would be overthrown by violence.

Throughout the 1970s, Brigate Rosse *brigatisti* robbed banks, kidnapped judges and industrialists, and dealt in arms and drug smuggling to finance their operations. Their movement grew, and BR cells sprang up in Rome, Genoa, and Venice.

Curcio was arrested in September 1974 for kidnapping an auto executive and was given a prison sentence of eighteen years. But Cagol and a band of *brigatisti* broke him out of prison in February 1975. They went into hiding and began writing a strategic document charging Christian Democracy as being "the enemy of the state."

Three weeks later, Cagol was shot and killed by Carabinieri during a raid on a farmhouse where a kidnapped Italian industrialist was being held. After Cagol's death, Brigate Rosse assassinated Carabinieri, judges, and even lawyers appointed by the courts to defend BR members.

Curcio was recaptured in January 1976 along with four other *brigatisti*. Cagol's death and Curcio's arrest left the BR leadership to Mario Moretti, a union activist and former student at Milan's Catholic University. Moretti's first act as a BR member after he joined in 1971 was to commit a mugging with Curcio. In 1976, Moretti moved to Rome and became the mastermind of Moro's kidnapping.

When Moro was abducted, Curcio and fifteen members of the Brigate Rosse were awaiting trial in Turin. Four days after Moro's kidnapping, Curcio and his Brigate Rosse *brigatisti* were led in chains to a security cage in a Turin court for the beginning of their trial. Curcio asked to read a statement. After the judge refused, the *brigatisti* began yelling, and the courtroom erupted in chaos.

Curcio shouted, "We . . . have Moro in our hands!"

Ten days after Moro's abduction, the Saturday before Easter, BR released its second communiqué. It contained a list of grievances against the Christian Democrats, including a disturbing phrase: "The interrogation of Aldo Moro is under way."

On Easter Sunday, Moro wrote a letter to his wife, telling her he was fairly well, was well fed, and was being treated with kindness. He signed off: "I bless you all; I send my dearest regards to all and a strong embrace."

Over the next few weeks, letters from Moro and Brigate Rosse communiqués were dispatched clandestinely from the "people's prison" to Moro's family, friends, and Christian Democratic colleagues. The letters and communiqués fueled debates in Parliament and were splashed across the front pages of newspapers. They were analyzed by Moro's colleagues, the Vatican, psychologists, and journalists, as well as by an American terrorist advisor, Deputy Assistant Secretary of State Steve Pieczenik, dispatched from Washington. Some read between the lines and believed that Moro was possibly being drugged, tortured, and deprived of food, sleep, and medical care.

From the beginning, Moro's Christian Democrats and the Communist Party forged an intractable position not to negotiate for Moro's release. Their decision was endorsed by the media as if unanimity was a position of solidarity.

As Moro's days of captivity stretched into mid-April, initiatives were made to break the politicians' hard line. These included attempts by Moro's son, Giovanni; the Italian Boy Scouts; Socialist Party leader Bettino Craxi; the Vatican; UN Secretary-General Kurt Waldheim; and Amnesty International.

On April 18, BR Communiqué VII made the shocking claims that Moro had died "by means of suicide" and that his body was at the slimy bottom of Lake Duchessa, in a remote mountain location. The document was proved a forgery, but not before two thousand police and mountaineers trudged on snowshoes to the remote area and Chinook helicopters dropped divers to break through the frozen lake in search of Moro's body.

Two days later, the real BR Communiqué VII announced that Brigate Rosse had launched a grenade attack on police barracks where BR members were held in a maximum security prison. The communiqué confirmed that BR had assassinated a vice commander of Milan's infamous San Vittore prison. Since kidnapping Moro, Brigate Rosse terrorists had also kneecapped the Christian Democrat former mayor of Turin and killed a prison guard where Curcio was being held.

Communiqué VII also included a second polaroid of Moro. This time he was holding a newspaper with the previous day's *La Repubblica* headline: "Moro Assassinated?"

Il Messaggero rushed a special afternoon edition with a banner that read: "Moro Is Alive."

Acrimonious debate by Italian politicians and the media about negotiating a prisoner release of Brigate Rosse for the recovery of Moro dragged on for agonizing weeks. Many believed that Moro's fate had already been sealed by squabbling, indecision, and political treachery by his friends and foes in the Christian Democratic Party and the Communist Party.

In truth, Moro had been doomed from the morning he'd been abducted on Via Fani.

On the morning of May 9, Aldo Moro showered or had a bath but didn't shave. He ate no breakfast and dressed in the clothes in which he'd been kidnapped: dark blue socks and a white shirt with blue stripes and his initials on the pocket. He put on his cufflinks, knotted a blue and white tie, and dressed in his dark blue suit and trousers with suspenders. He put on black moccasin shoes. Inadvertently, he put on his socks inside out.

His wallet, wristwatch, and bracelet were put into a plastic bag. Four BR members walked him to a basement where a red hatchback Renault was parked. They ordered him to get inside. Moro squeezed his five-foot, ten-inch body into the car and lay on an orange blanket.

Moro was shot in the chest eleven times with a .32 caliber machine pistol with a silencer. Seven bullets pierced Moro's left lung but missed his heart. He died from a massive internal hemorrhage.

A few minutes after noon on May 9, a man entered a phone booth at Rome's Termini central train station and dropped two telephone tokens into the slot.

Termini was swarming with tourists and businessmen making travel connections as they did every day. Police and Carabinieri roamed Termini, suspiciously eyeing the homeless, pickpockets, black marketeers selling cigarettes from boxes strapped around their necks, zombielike heroin addicts begging for coins, and hustlers from Naples enticing people to play *gioco delle tre carte* (three-card monte).

It was a hot, hazy summer day. By evening, a dark cloud would hang over the Italian capital, as events would make it one of the most tragic days in Rome's three-thousand-year history.

At 12:10 p.m., Professor Franco Tritto, a friend and teaching colleague of Moro's, answered the phone call from the Termini.

"Is this Professor Tritto?" the man at Termini asked.

"Yes. . . . Who is this?"

"This is Dr. Nikolai."

"Nikolai who?"

"Is this Professor Tritto?"

"Yes, but I want to know who I'm speaking with."

"Brigate Rosse. Understand?"

It was the dreaded call he had been fearing. "Yes."

"All right. I can't stay on the phone very long. Here's what you should tell the family. It doesn't matter that your phone is tapped. You should go there personally and tell them this. We are expressing the last words of the president by informing them where they can find the body of the Honorable Aldo Moro.

"You must tell the family they can find the Honorable Moro's body on Via Caetani. That's the second cross street to the right on Via delle Botteghe Oscure [Street of Dark Shops]. Have you got that?"

"Yes."

"There's a red Renault 4 there. The first two digits on the license plate are N5."

"Dr. Nikolai" hung up and melted into the Termini crowds as police Panther cars sped toward the station, alerted by the tapped conversation.

But police cars became stalled in traffic, and by the time they reached Termini, the caller had disappeared.

Within minutes, political leaders in the Christian Democratic and Communist Parties were alerted about the call. That morning, they had been debating a Brigate Rosse prisoner exchange for the return of Moro.

By one o'clock that afternoon, the streets around Via Caetani were swarming with police and Carabinieri. Christian Democratic and Communist politicians streamed out of their headquarters and ran toward Via Caetani.

By ghoulish design, the Renault was parked equidistant from the headquarters of the Christian Democrats on the Square of Jesus (*Piazza del Gesù*) and the Communist Party on the Street of Dark Shops. Leaving Moro's body in such a symbolic location was a morbid mockery of the politicians who had quarreled for weeks about rescuing their colleague and friend.

Christian Democratic Minister of Interior Francesco Cossiga and Communist Party shadow Minister of Interior Ugo Pecchioli were allowed to cross the police barricade and accompany police to the Renault.

When police looked inside the hatchback, they saw an overcoat draped over a body with strands of gray hair protruding. The hatch was opened and someone lifted the overcoat.

Underneath was Moro's body lying on an orange blanket. His legs were tucked behind, his left arm over his bloody chest, his back against a set of rusty snow chains. His eyes were three-quarters closed.

A Jesuit priest from the church on the Square of Jesus who had known Moro worked his way through the police cordon and administered last rites.

The autopsy on Moro revealed he had not been tortured or bound, and no drugs had been administered to him. In a letter to his wife, he insisted that there be no public funeral. Moro was buried on May 10 with only family members and close friends attending. Burial was in the cemetery of St. Thomas the Apostle in Torrita Tiberina, a village north of Rome where the Moros had bought a farmhouse in the 1950s. In his hands was a rosary from Pope Paul VI that had been given to Eleonora by an emissary from the Vatican.

CHAPTER ONE

MILAN, ITALY, JULY 2011

To most people who knew him, Fabio Cecconi was a young man with a bright future. He was someone about whom Italians would say one day, "I knew Fabio when he was young, before he became famous and influential. He makes me proud to be an Italian."

Fabio was brilliant, well educated, polite, and handsome. People respected him and sought him out for advice. They listened to him when he spoke. He didn't like foolish talk or idleness. Young women fell in love with him and wanted to marry him and have beautiful, well-mannered children.

Fabio was also humble, largely as a result of his widowed mother, who had struggled at menial jobs to raise him and his older brother, Luca. She had cleaned people's toilets, mopped their floors, changed their babies' diapers, and cleaned up after their pets. Fabio's mother had taught him to be respectful and obey the law. He had never been in trouble or been questioned by the police, and he only occasionally got a parking ticket. He was a good driver, didn't drive over the speed limit, and was courteous on the road when driving from his tiny Milan apartment to Università Statale.

When Fabio graduated with honors from Università Statale in Milan, his mother shed tears of joy. Professors and fellow students shook his hand, patted him on the back, and said he had a fine future in politics, teaching, or writing. He would go far in whatever career he chose.

While he worked as a research assistant for a political science professor at Università Statale, Fabio met influential people: members of the Italian Parliament, journalists, authors, and labor union leaders. He fantasized that one day he would become a university lecturer, write books, make speeches, be interviewed on TV, and eventually get elected to the Chamber of Deputies. He believed government should help people get a good education, provide good health care, mandate worker safety standards, and ensure a comfortable pension. He was a socialist. He wanted to help people. What good was one's life unless it helped people?

Fabio's world crumbled the day he was fired from his university position in May 2011. He was so devastated that he went into a depression. He had never been a spiritual person, but he felt his soul had been scarred.

For days, Fabio wandered around Milan, sipping cappuccino in cafés, walking through Parco Sempione, going to the Brera museum, and seeing foreign movies. He wandered alone, crushed by his firing, too embarrassed to tell people he was unemployed, uncertain about his future. He had to create a new life.

With the free time, Fabio stayed up late at night rereading political science and history books and browsing websites about the political and economic crises in Europe since the near collapse of world economies in 2008. After a few weeks, he began to seek out his influential contacts, telling them he was going to become a journalist and write articles about politics and the Italian financial crisis. He interviewed them, took notes, and discussed serious current issues.

The influential people admitted to Fabio that prospects for an economic recovery in Italy were bleak, even hopeless. The Italian political process was paralyzed. There was no financial or political leadership, only confusion and chaos. The times were dangerous, the most perilous since the end of World War II. Civil unrest was right around the corner.

After two months of reading, interviewing contacts, and spending lots of time alone, Fabio began to make decisions about his future. His decisions were more than bold; they were radical, things he had never considered before.

Fabio believed that Italy was ripe for dramatic change. His years of studying the French, Russian, American, Chinese, and Cuban revolutions had proven that insurrections were led by visionaries who were willing to shatter the existing political system to bring about radical changes. Dangerous times called for dangerous measures. History belonged to those bold enough to create dramatic changes, even if it meant personal sacrifice.

But Fabio couldn't create change by himself. He needed a few people he trusted to join him. He would start with a small cell. In time, he could grow the cell after its members had boldly revealed their existence with radical actions—strategic bombings, a political assassination, and eventually hostage-taking. Those radical actions would capture the attention of the world. Italians would learn that they no longer had to tolerate the old ways of political corruption, incompetence, and bribery, which had brought profound misery to millions: the young, unemployed, poor, disabled, and even immigrants.

When Fabio was ready to share his plan with people he trusted, the first person he sought out was his older brother, Luca, whose once-prosperous construction business had collapsed after 2008. Luca was now virtually bankrupt—and very angry.

Fabio rekindled a relationship with a former lover, Vera Pulvirenti, a once-famous Sicilian fashion model he'd met at a bar one night when she had collapsed in his arms from an almost fatal mixture of alcohol and drugs. He had taken her back to his apartment, made her vomit the toxic cocktail, given her coffee, and kept her awake until she was out of danger.

That had begun a four-year passionate affair in which Vera had learned about politics from Fabio. In turn, Fabio had learned about the glamorous but treacherous world of Milanese fashion where vulnerable young women fell prey to predatory men, unscrupulous managers, and financial advisors. Vera's career had ended at age twenty-two after a near-fatal motorcycle accident had left her face scarred.

Fabio had recently met a former demolitions expert, Alfredo Gori, at the bar where Fabio had worked to supplement his meager income from the university. Alfredo was another unemployed Italian full of rage, one of many Fabio knew.

With Luca, Vera, and Alfredo, Fabio planted the seed of a radical political movement. He shared his own views on Italy's dire economic and financial conditions and the mood of despair and hopelessness. He told them that unemployment among young, university-educated Italians was approaching 30 percent. Many were forced to live with their parents while they searched in vain for work. Thousands of small businesses had been forced to close, and some owners had committed suicide when the government had withheld payments on contracts.

One by one, Fabio had asked Luca, Vera, and Alfredo a single question: "Would you join a group that was going to make bold changes in Italian politics, even if it meant using violence?"

Luca had raised a sledgehammer and smashed a cement block that shattered and sent bits of stone and concrete flying around his warehouse yard. "That is what I would do to the Italian government!" Luca had said.

When Fabio had asked Vera, she had pointed a finger like a mock pistol at the TV, where a host was interviewing a scandal-plagued member of the Italian Parliament. "I'd shoot him between the eyes and watch him bleed to death on the floor, writhing like a snake."

Alfredo had smiled at Fabio when he'd asked the question and replied, "Have I told you about the weapons and explosives I stole from the army before they kicked me out? I was a noncommissioned officer in Albania with an explosives and land mine detection unit."

* * * * *

Fabio had not seen his sixty-four-year-old Zio Gino since he'd visited him on his birthday in March at a nursing home an hour north of Milan. Gino was a former Brigate Rosse *brigatista* who'd been arrested and sent to prison after the Moro assassination in 1978.

On a hot Sunday afternoon in July, Fabio borrowed his brother's car and drove to Cesano Maderno to see his Zio Gino. Outside of Cesano Maderno, Fabio drove down a narrow asphalt road in a rural area with olive trees, vineyards, and small farms. When he came to a grove of cypress trees, he turned onto a shaded gravel lane and drove through a narrow valley where hot winds were rustling cypress branches and carrying a fragrance of lavender in the dry, dusty air.

The gravel lane widened into a parking lot in front of a sign: *Casa di Riposo San Donato*. In the center of the parking lot was a fountain, a little larger than a horse trough, drained of water. A statue of Mary was on a raised plinth in the dry fountain, which was littered with twigs and dried leaves.

The Blessed Mother looked tired, her sculpted arms bone-bleached by the sun and streaked with black mildew. Pigeons roosted on Mary's crowned head and strutted along her outstretched arms before flying off over fields of weeds and tree stumps.

Fabio parked in front of a two-story building that housed a clinic run by the nuns. He got out and surveyed patches of dried grass and weeds along stone paths lined with ministatues of cherubs. Fabio watched nuns in white aprons and caps escorting elderly residents in robes and slippers who shuffled alongside, clinging to the nuns' arms.

Fabio walked along the stone path to a courtyard behind the clinic with four one-story stone residences for the sick and elderly. At the last building on the left, an old man was asleep in a wooden chair under an umbrella.

Fabio walked over and stood beside his dozing Zio Gino, whose knobby hands were folded in his lap, clutching a handkerchief. Gino's faded robe was open at the knees, revealing blue veins snaking down pale, bony legs. Yellowed cadaver toes poked from Gino's tattered slippers.

Zio Gino's sunken chest rose and fell, each breath ending in a watery rattle. Corkscrew hairs sprouted from his nostrils, ears, and eyebrows. Wisps of stringy white hair were pasted over his bald head, which was blotched with liver spots and moles.

Fabio put a hand on Gino's bony shoulder, which felt like a stick. "*Ciao,* Zio Gino. *Sono io,* Fabio," he said, leaning down to kiss him on both cheeks. His uncle startled awake, blinking watery eyes, trying to focus.

"*Puu, puu,*" Gino muttered, squinting in the sunlight. "I was dozing," he said, struggling to sit upright. He took a deep breath, making a noise that sounded like a cat being strangled. "You said you'd be here in the morning," he said in a raspy voice. "It's almost time for lunch."

"Sorry, Zio. Traffic was heavy coming out of Milan. Too many trucks and tourist buses."

Gino scowled, scratching his bearded chin with yellowed fingernails, making a sound like nails brushing across sandpaper. "Beh, too many everything . . . cars . . . trucks . . . *motorinos* . . . driving like they're going to hell. *Motorinos* . . . I hate them. . . . They should bury them all in a pit and pour gasoline over them."

Fabio sat down next to him. "It's dangerous to walk in Milan anymore. I saw a woman get run over by one. The bastard never even stopped. Just kept going."

"I never want to leave this place. I'd get mugged or run down by one of those damned *motorinos.*"

"You're better off here, Zio. It's quiet and peaceful."

"Ha! Quiet, all right, like a graveyard. But I'm used to it. I don't want to be around people. You're a professor now, right?"

"No, I don't have a job anymore."

"What do you mean? I tell everyone my nephew is a professor at Università Statale, a smart boy, going to be an important man one day."

"I was never a professor, Zio. I worked for one after I received my postdoctorate degree."

"You worked for an important professor. He was going to get you a good job one day."

"It didn't happen, even after eleven years," Fabio said. "My professor promised me he'd recommend me when a position opened. I worked as his poorly paid assistant for eleven years, waiting for a position to open. But I was broke all the time. I made more money tending bar nights and weekends."

"Terrible. You should be teaching students how to become brilliant like you. You read books, make speeches, inspire people. You're a leader. I don't understand what happened."

"Nothing happened; that's the problem. He paid me eight hundred euros a month to correct exams, read student papers, prepare his lessons, and do his research. I was his chauffeur; I arranged his travel, walked his dog, and took care of his son when he was with his mistress. But he fired me last month without warning. He said I'd been an excellent researcher, but he was hiring his nephew to take my place. He had pressure from his sister; her son hadn't had a job in five years. Now he has my job."

"The bastard! How could he do that?"

"University positions are like everything else in Italy. Rank and promotions are based on who you know or who you can bribe to get a good job."

"That's a disgrace!"

"It is, but I have no way to appeal. A professor doesn't have to answer to anyone."

"Goddamn prick. How could he do that? You're smart, you read good books, serious books. You know politics . . . history . . . philosophy. The smartest one in our family. What are you going to do?"

"I'll tell you later. Are they taking good care of you here?"

"Ha! They think they are, but I'm rotting like an old log in the woods. The clinic is bankrupt. They might have to close and throw us out. Imagine that: old people dumped like sacks of garbage. What kind of country tosses out old people? I have nowhere to go."

"I'll talk to Mamma. Maybe she can help."

"How is my sister?" he asked, looking up with watery, red eyes deep in bony sockets.

"She's fine. I'm going to see her next week. She's working for a family who's taking her to Côte d'Azur for the summer to take care of their children."

"She's still working? She should retire. She's getting old—almost as old as I am."

"She can't afford to retire. After Papa died, she had to work to raise Luca and me. Two jobs sometimes, cleaning rich people's homes, paying for our schooling, sacrificing to put food on the table every night. You know what it was like; you lived with us when you got out of prison. You were good to Luca and me after Papa died. You helped Mamma raise us during those years."

"Your mamma's a saint, always putting other people's needs before her own. Tell her to visit me. She hasn't been here since my birthday. My youngest sister . . . the only other one left in our family. So pretty when she was young . . . beautiful dark eyes . . . full of mischief. I wish I had stayed home more when she was growing up. She always had boys coming to our home to take her to cafés and bars. They were crazy about her, but you should have heard what she said about them: 'He's a scoundrel. He'll do anything to get a girl to spread her legs.'" Gino's laugh ended with a wrenching, phlegm-filled burst.

Fabio squeezed his uncle's bony arm. "I like when you tell me about my mother. You're right; she is a saint."

"When your father came around, everything changed for her," Gino said. "He had a good factory job, was honest . . . hard-working . . . went to mass every morning. I liked him. Oh, how your mother worshiped him. She told everyone she wanted to marry Roberto and give him many sons . . . enough for a soccer team. She loved him so much and then watched him die after that accident at that damned Alfa Romeo factory. He wasn't the only one to die or get crippled back then. People got maimed—crushed arms, broken backs, concussions—or poisoned by fumes: acids, sulphur, mercury. It was a horrible, dangerous place."

"Mamma hated to see Papa go to work in the morning. He'd come home so tired he could hardly eat dinner."

"He was a good man. I miss him."

"We all do, Zio Gino." Fabio reached into his wallet, pulled out a wrinkled piece of paper, and showed it to his uncle. "I still carry Papa's union card. He died making Alfa Romeos for rich people to drive." Fabio kissed it, gently folded it, and put it back in his wallet. Changing the subject, he asked, "How have you been, Zio?"

"Pshaw. . . . No one comes to see me anymore," he said, blowing his nose into the stained handkerchief. "My children don't visit except on my birthday and Christmas. My friends are dead or soon will be. Growing old is hell; don't let anyone tell you different. Die young and you won't have regrets."

"The men in our family do die young, Zio—Papa when he was only thirty-seven, crushed when a beam fell on his chest. Papa's father fought the Nazis as a partisan in World War II and saw Mussolini's corpse hanging in Piazzale Loreto in 1945. He was only forty when he died after the Fascists tortured him in prison. His father, Giuseppe, died in World War I when he was only twenty-seven. He saw his baby son only once before he was killed fighting the Austrians in the Alps in 1916."

"Yes, I remember. Your father told me about the tragic history of his family. Good men, all dying too young. A shame."

"I'll be thirty-seven in November," Fabio said. "If I live six months after that, I'll be older than he was when he died."

"Don't die. I need you. Your mother needs you. Italy needs smart men like you."

"But I came here to talk about you," Fabio said, brushing a hand over his *zio's* sweat-damp head, smoothing the strands of white hair. "How's your health?"

Gino wobbled the hand with the soiled handkerchief. "So-so. . . . If my liver doesn't fail, I could last another year. But who cares?"

Fabio reached over and took his hand. "I do, Zio Gino. I've always looked up to you."

"Ha!" he sputtered. "Why would you want to talk to an old revolutionary?"

"You inspired me, Zio. I admired what you did."

"Ha! You mean, getting arrested and spending ten years in prison? What's to admire about an uncle who spent his best years rotting in rat- and flea-infested San Vittore with murderers and rapists?"

"You did it for a cause you believed in."

"Ha! A wild-eyed terrorist, spouting slogans and hiding in a filthy apartment, afraid the police would come one night and arrest me. Look where I ended up. Rotting like a mangy dog."

"Brigate Rosse was an important part of Italian history. You almost brought down the Christian Democrat government and created a revolutionary state. You were one of them."

"Revolutions!" Gino coughed and leaned over to spit on the ground. "History's crap. Don't let anyone tell you any different. I was young . . . hot-blooded. I didn't want to work in factories anymore. I wanted to be part of something bigger. I was fed up with being a slave on an assembly line. If I'd stayed, I'd have ended up dead like your papa."

"You were a hero to fight the bosses. That's why I admire you. You had the courage to take to the streets for what you believed in: a better life for oppressed people."

"But you didn't come to see a sick uncle and listen to him bitch. Why did you come?"

"You told me stories when you were in the BR. You inspired me."

Gino scratched his chin whiskers. "So long ago . . . forty years. I was crazy back then . . . could have made a good living if I'd become a tailor like my father. He was disappointed when I ran off to join those radicals. They filled my head with Communist dogma . . . going to change the world . . . all the Marxist and Leninist bullshit. I didn't care about that stuff. I just wanted to blow up cars and mug factory bosses. Foolish me, a former altar boy . . . becoming a revolutionary."

"Same as Stalin. He sang in the choir and was going to be a priest But he liked robbing banks to fund the Bolsheviks."

"Stalin wasn't a revolutionary. He was a murderous tyrant! Killed millions of his own people." Gino coughed, a watery rumbling noise that started in his lungs and rose to his throat. He put the handkerchief to his mouth and spit into it.

"Let me get you some water," Fabio said. He got up and walked inside his uncle's building. Inside the lobby, elderly patients in patchy robes were dozing in wheelchairs or on sofas with blankets over their legs. They looked half-dead, hollow eyes staring out the window, lost in memories.

Fabio went to a table with pitchers and water glasses. He poured a glass and brought it out into the sunlit courtyard. Gino grabbed the glass with a shaking hand and gulped several swallows. A trickle of water ran down his chin.

"Thank you," he said, putting the empty glass on the table.

"Tell me more about your days with BR, Zio."

"Why? Are you going to become a revolutionary?"

"Yes."

Gino's eyes widened, the wrinkles around his sockets folding over each other. He held up a bony finger that quivered like a twig in the wind. "Don't do it. You'll end up miserable and alone, like me. You're still young, with your whole life ahead of you. You have a beautiful girlfriend, Vera, wild and a bit crazy. Don't make her a widow."

Fabio wasn't going to tell him that he and Vera weren't lovers anymore; it could confuse him. "Don't worry, Zio. I'm doing this for the people in Italy who have no voice. I don't want to live in a country run by criminals and liars."

"Ha! Criminals . . . liars . . . hoodlums. Throw them all in jail!"

"Tell me why you joined Brigate Rosse. What was it like?"

"Why do you want to know?"

"It's important."

Gino looked into Fabio's eyes. "I knew you'd come one day, Fabio. You were the only one interested in those days. You were different from other children; you questioned everyone. Never satisfied with what was. You were a troublemaker in school, yet you were a good university student. What are you going to do?"

"I'll tell you later."

Gino sighed, poking a withered hand inside his robe to scratch his chest, a mat of white wrinkled hair revealing itself. He looked around the courtyard to see if anyone could hear their conversation. "I know why you're here," he whispered. "You're going to start something. I know it. I can see it in your eyes. You've come here to get a taste of what it was like to be a revolutionary."

Fabio nodded. "Tell me."

Another glance around the courtyard. Gino cupped a hand over his mouth. "Don't make the mistakes we made. We lost popular support with too much violence—assassinations and kidnappings. Too much spilled blood ruined BR. We scared people. Don't make that mistake; you'll regret it."

"I'm starting small with a few people I trust."

"How many?" he said, screwing up his face.

"Just a few . . . I don't want to say any more. Someone might come here and ask about me."

"I won't tell them a word!" Gino sputtered.

"Our cell is small, but we can ignite a larger movement. The time is right; people all over Italy—on the streets, in universities, in bars, in coffee shops, in factories—are fed up with the corrupt Berlusconi government and the financial mess created by European bankers."

"Berlusconi caused this, the bastard," Gino said, spitting out his words.

"He's not alone. His PdL party and its cronies in Parliament are all corrupt. The Popular Democrats and the left wing have been pussy-cats, afraid to confront Berlusconi and bring justice to Italy. They were in power for seven years and did nothing about Berlusconi's blatant conflict-of-interest charges with his TV stations. Communists used to carry banners and promise equality for working people, not just the rich. Now they sail on their yachts, sip wine with beautiful women, and wear cashmere sweaters like movie stars."

"So true. They're as worthless as a dry sow. Berlusconi's a clown—a dangerous clown!" Gino sputtered. "A convicted tax cheat! He paid child prostitutes—for sex! He's a filthy old goat having sex with children! Castrate him! Send him to prison! Throw away the key! Let him rot with the criminals!" Sweat was running down Gino's red, wrinkled face, and the blue veins on his neck were throbbing.

"It's not just Berlusconi. It's the system—judges, lawyers, Parliament, bankers, mayors, journalists."

"Italy is filled with cancer. Things have to change before . . . before the whole country goes bankrupt . . . and there's a revolution. Hopefully, before I die."

"We'll have to do some violent things in the early days, but not as extreme as Brigate Rosse."

"Luca . . . is he in your group?"

"Yes. He and I have been planning this."

"How is his construction business?"

"He's almost bankrupt. The economic crisis in 2008 ruined his business. He used to have thirty workers and made a lot of money, but it's all gone. He gets a small job now and then, but he had to let his workers go."

Gino nodded, studying Fabio's face. "You know how to get people to follow you. You were a leader even back when you were in school. But the police have antiterrorist goons who smash marchers' heads, tap phones, spy on students, and beat prisoners in jail. They're ruthless. Don't think they won't hunt you down and shoot you like they did Renato . . . Roberto . . . Patrizio."

"Tell me why you joined BR."

"I was young. Foolish. Milan and Turin were filled with illiterate peasants from Reggio Calabria . . . Abruzzo . . . Sicily. They came to work in the factories with only the clothes on their backs and the sacks of bread and salami their mothers had packed for them. They lived like dogs in shacks . . . cement blocks called Koreas . . . with dogs, cats, sheep, and goats shitting in the road. You'd have to step over the mounds of animal shit just to get home at night.

"I was in love with a girl from Reggio Calabria, Lorella. We met at a BR meeting. She was beautiful . . . hot-blooded . . . passionate. I loved her. She took me to her village. It was pitiful, people living in cement blocks with dirt floors. They worked at dangerous jobs . . . stamping metal sheets to make Fiat car bodies . . . punching rubber sheets at Pirelli to make tires. So noisy that people lost their hearing. Poisonous fumes were everywhere, and no safety equipment. The bosses worked them like dogs until they got sick, died, or quit."

"I studied labor strikes and BR at the university," Fabio volunteered. "I wrote my thesis on the police hunting down Mario Moretti after Moro was assassinated. Brigate Rosse saw people's misery and organized cells in factories; they handed out leaflets encouraging workers to take over the factories. They kidnapped factory managers, blew up their cars, kneecapped bosses. The police infiltrated and arrested the leaders, but the protests kept going."

Gino nodded. "I know . . . I remember well. . . . The times were crazy . . . and dangerous."

"We want to inspire people to take to the streets and spread protest across Europe."

"You can't start a revolution anymore, Fabio. Italians don't want to overthrow the government; they just want better lives for themselves and their children. Forget all that Marxist crap. It worked in Russia until the people learned that the Bolsheviks were lying to them, feeding them propaganda instead of food. China has become a brothel with whore capitalists pretending to be Marxists. Castro was a dirty joke."

"We're not alone," Fabio said. "England has radicals. So do France, Germany, Spain, and Greece. We'll get their attention and let them do it their way. I just want to cripple the government, bring it down if we can."

Gino's eyes drooped. The afternoon sun was lower in the sky, lighting underneath the umbrella. "I'm tired, Fabio. I had a bad night. I get up to pee during the night and wake up constipated in the morning. I suffer day and night."

"Thank you for talking to me, Zio Gino. You've always been a hero to me."

"Hero. . . . I'm no hero, just someone who sacrificed ten years of my life for blowing up cars and robbing banks. Thank God I didn't kill anyone."

"I'll come back . . . one day."

"I hope you do. I want to see you again. Be careful. I don't want to read in the papers that you've been shot or arrested. Give your old *zio* some peace in his last days. I need it. Bless you, Fabio," he said, reaching out to kiss his hand.

CHAPTER TWO

Palazzo Stoppa-Belgiojoso on Via Cosimo del Fante is one of the prestigious apartment buildings in Milan's Corso Italia section. Neighborhoods around Corso Italia contain homes of wealthy families as well as offices of professionals who cater to the wealthy: architects, high-end real estate agents, accountants, notaries, physicians, boutique fashion designers, and international law firms.

The four-story, burnt orange stucco Palazzo is one of the jewels of the neoclassical apartments preferred by wealthy families to the new, garish glass temples rising in Milan's outer suburbs. The Palazzo has a reputation among real estate agents and the Milanese upper class for its elegant touches: the uniformed *portinaio* who checks identification when he does not recognize a visitor; terraced balconies with pots of geraniums and petunias on balustrades where residents sip wine at sunset; a row of mature oaks pruned, watered, and fertilized by an arborist.

Every morning, Porsche, BMW, and Volkswagen SUVs pick up pampered children in front of the Palazzo, escorted by diminutive, uniformed Filipina nannies, to chauffeur them to Milan's elite private schools, Collegio San Carlo, Sir James Henderson School and Leone XIII.

Half an hour later, another fleet of black and dark blue luxury cars picks up the children's well-tailored fathers, who carry briefcases and morning newspapers, to whisk them off to Milan's power centers of finance, trade, media, government, and technology.

Vera Pulvirenti had been fortunate to buy a first-floor apartment at the Palazzo in 1996, the year she earned her first billion lira as one of Milan's youngest and most famous fashion models.

In those days, Palazzo residents greeted Vera warmly, lavishly praising her beauty and inquiring enviously about parties she attended, celebrities she met, and handsome young men she dated. Every day, residents would notice gifts and vases of flowers delivered to Vera's apartment by admirers and suitors. These items would pile up until Vera returned home at night or from vacations in Switzerland, France, or the Greek islands.

When residents mentioned how fortunate she was to receive so many flowers and gifts, Vera brushed them off and said, "Oh, take them away, please. I get so many . . . they fill up my apartment. I have no more room—and flowers make me sneeze!"

But four years later, fate dealt Vera a cruel hand. In Côte d'Azur, she almost died in a motorcycle accident that killed her Russian boyfriend, soccer star Vladimir Gribov. Two months after the accident, newspapers published photos of Vera leaving the hospital in a wheelchair with bandages around her head; one leg in a cast from a broken hip; lacerations around her neck, arms, and face; and an ugly scar on her right cheek.

After returning to the Palazzo, Vera was initially treated with pity by residents who inquired about her recovery. But soon, wealthy and snobbish women looked the other way when they passed Vera on the street or in the building. Spoiled children mocked her as they dashed in and out of the building. Teenage boys taunted her, calling out as they got on scooters parked in front of the Palazzo, "Hey, Vera, wanna go for a ride? Promise I won't crash."

But the most agonizing humiliation came when Vera's phone didn't ring. Photographers and magazines begged off that they didn't have work for her. Despite plastic surgery, Vera's ugly scar was noticeable. It looked like her face had been peeled off and then stitched back by a clumsy tailor.

As years passed, Vera increasingly retreated into her apartment as a refuge against humiliation and ill fortune. She had three locks installed and removed her name from the metal plate on her door, replacing it with a photo of her Persian cats, Jezebel and Rocketa. For eleven years, she survived by running a small video business, bartending occasionally, and selling her possessions.

One hot July evening, a week after Fabio's visit to his uncle, he and three other men stood outside the gate of the Palazzo and pressed the buzzer to Vera's apartment. When she buzzed the gate open, the men walked through the courtyard into the building and headed down a long hall to her apartment at the end. They heard the clicking of opening locks, and the heavy door swung open.

Vera was holding a glass of wine in one hand. A cigarette dangled from her lips. She was tall and wore designer jeans that bulged at her hips. A tight halter top flattened her breasts and revealed a tummy roll at the belt. Her long black hair was tied back in a head scarf. Antique earrings ending in a loop studded with fake emeralds dangled from her earlobes.

"Fabio! Welcome—" Vera started to say before Fabio shushed her.

"Shhh . . . wait until we're inside."

The men entered and Vera shut the door behind them, clicking the locks to secure it.

"Come in, come in. I've been waiting! Fabio, you bring such handsome men to my apartment," she said, embracing him and kissing his cheeks.

She held his hand as they walked through a dark, narrow hallway into her small apartment. "I've missed you. You never visit me anymore."

"It's been a busy summer," Fabio said. "I haven't seen a lot of friends."

"Aah, just an excuse to keep away from an old girlfriend," she said, turning to his brother, Luca.

Luca was four years older than Fabio, a head taller, and leaner. When they stood next to each other, it was easy to see they were brothers. Both had gentle eyes, broad faces, and almost feminine mouths. Luca looked more like their father; his long, black hair was combed over a high forehead. His face was rugged and bronze-tanned from working outdoors. Fabio more resembled their mother: thin lips, a small chin, and a pale complexion from years spent in libraries and classrooms.

"Luca! You're as handsome as ever," Vera said, stretching up to exchange kisses. "You still have the same girlfriend? Claudia, wasn't that her name? From Pescara, right?"

Luca shook his head. "No, no. That ended a while back. I'm always looking around, though . . . you know me."

"You should always have a girlfriend, Luca. It's good for your blood."

Fabio turned to introduce the other men. "Vera, this is my friend Alfredo that I told you about. You'll like him. He's fearless, a real adventurer. He has climbed the Matterhorn, gone scuba diving in the Canary Islands, and parachuted out of a small plane. He spent two years in Albania with the army."

Alfredo was a tall, good-looking man with broad shoulders and muscular arms with tattoos of Maori designs. His long, brownish hair was combed back like a mane, reaching to his shoulders. He wore a leather vest over a tight cream-colored shirt that clung to his chest like a reptile's skin.

"Ooh, and he's a handsome one," Vera said. She sucked in her breath and looked him over from his head to his brown boots. "Is he married?" She gave Fabio a lascivious wink.

Alfredo let out a husky laugh. "Only once," he chuckled. "A mistake of my youth. She left me to marry a schoolteacher. She thought I was too rough and uncouth. She was right . . . I'm much better at outdoor sports. Not so good with indoor activities . . . making small talk . . . pretending to like people you don't . . . saying nice things you don't mean."

Vera poked Alfredo in the stomach. "You look like you're built for one indoor sport," she said. "Are you rough and uncouth in bed?"

They all laughed nervously, taken aback by Vera's brazenness.

Alfredo eyes widened. "Aah, that's a secret only a few women know."

Fabio cleared his throat. "Ah, Vera, this is Marietto," he said, putting his hand on the smallest man in the room. "He works for Luca. Helps around the warehouse, drives trucks, and does all sorts of odd jobs."

Marietto was a short, wiry man with a slight beard, wrinkles around his eyes, and a sad look.

"Hello, Marietto. Nice to meet you," Vera said, reaching out her hand. He took it but dropped it almost immediately.

"Thank you, Vera," he said demurely. "I'm honored to visit your home."

"I'm glad you're here," she said, taking the cigarette out of her mouth. "I've got wine and pot in the kitchen. I was going to fix a meal, but I'm not much of a cook."

She slapped her hips, which filled out her jeans. "I don't dare eat anymore. Every time I have a meal, I put on another kilo. You should have seen me when I was young and thin. Now I look like a cow."

Vera's living room was long, narrow, and virtually bare of furniture. A straight-backed chair sat in one corner, and the coffee table was cluttered with fashion magazines, newspapers, dirty wineglasses, an ashtray, and a pack of cigarettes. Under the table, two fat Persian cats rested on a fluffy rug, staring warily as if one of the men might be hiding a small dog under his shirt. In a corner, partially covered by a soiled drape, was an overflowing litter box.

An electric chandelier with several burned-out bulbs hung from the ceiling. Three flesh-colored mannequins in stark poses stood in a corner like refugees from Milan fashion week. Two of the mannequins were nude; one was draped in items of clothing and jewelry that looked like they'd been flung from a closet: a strapless red dress scooped low in the back, clumps of gaudy necklaces drooping from the neck, loops of wired earrings, and a rainbow-colored cloth hat on the head.

One wall displayed cover photos from *Vogue, Glamour,* and *Elle* magazines with Vera wearing fashions of the late 1990s. She was very thin and sexy, with long eyelashes, alabaster skin, and full lips painted with dark red lipstick.

"I'm proud of these covers from when I was young and famous," she said, gesturing toward them. "Thanks to them, I was able to buy this overpriced apartment. I wasted the rest of my money on clothes, drugs, travel, and pampering boyfriends. God, was I foolish."

Luca, Alfredo, and Marietto moved to the wall to examine the photos more closely.

"This is my favorite," she said, pointing to a *Vogue* cover on which she was posing with one hand cupped under her chin. Her pose accented her long neck, high cheekbones, and dark eyes. Her hair was swept back like strands of black silk.

"That's stunning," Alfredo said. "You were gorgeous! I wish I had known you then."

Vera puffed on her cigarette and cocked her head like she was admiring a Renaissance masterpiece. "I was so young then . . . twenty years old. I was dating a forty-two-year-old movie star who got me on cocaine. He's dead now, poor bastard. He hit his head diving off a boat at Capri, chasing his twenty-three-year-old girlfriend. He was fifty-six, I think, and died like he lived, chasing young pussy. They couldn't close the coffin at his funeral; he still had an erection."

Alfredo let out a burst of laughter and put an arm around Vera.

The Persians bolted from under the table at Alfredo's loud laughter. They ran for Vera's bedroom, their long, white fur sweeping across the dusty floor.

"We're going to get along well, Vera. I like your spirit," said Alfredo.

She pushed back. "No funny business. I've had enough men to last a lifetime. Isn't that right, Fabio?"

"Vera's one of a kind," Fabio said with a smile. "She's smart, tough, and hard as nails. Don't get on her bad side. You'll regret it till the day you die."

She reached over to pat his cheek. "Fabio . . . one of my favorite men. He rescued me once. . . . I was doing bad things. . . . He picked me up when I was down and taught me to live again."

"A long time ago, Vera," Fabio said. "Those were good years."

"Before I met Fabio, I didn't care about politics. I never read newspapers, only *Cosmopolitan, Glamour, Vogue,* and gossip magazines. He got me reading books and talking about art, music, philosophy, and especially politics. He loves to talk politics."

"He was reading books while the rest of us kids were riding minimotorbikes and playing Pac-Man and Space Invaders in bars," Luca said.

"Fabio is brilliant," Vera said. "He should be a professor and write books. People listen to Fabio. He has ideas . . . good ideas. I love him like a brother."

"You're too kind, Vera," Fabio said. "Thank you."

Vera put an arm around Fabio. "So, when he came to me a couple of weeks ago, I listened to him and told him, 'I'll do anything you want.' We have to do something before this country slides into a swamp."

"I knew you'd want to join us," Fabio said. "We need people like you, who have passion."

"Passion. . . . I haven't had passion in a long time!" she said. "If I can't have it with a man, I want passion to believe in something. And I believe in what he wants to do." She raised her hands and made fists. "Action! I want action. We have to do something to stop the politicians from bankrupting the country and kicking us all into the gutter!"

Alfredo said, "She's good. She's just what we need. No bullshit . . . no whining . . . just tough and determined."

"That's me!" she said. "Hey, enough of this. Let's drink some wine and get loaded. Come into the kitchen."

Vera led them into her small kitchen, where she'd cleared the table and set out four bottles of wine with heavy glasses next to a plate of marijuana joints.

Three pots on the stove held spoons encrusted with dried sauce and strands of pasta. Dirty plates, utensils, and glasses were stacked in the sink. The refrigerator was covered with magnets, postcards, scribbled notes, a calendar, coupons, recipes ripped from magazines, and photos of her cats.

A garbage can in the corner was overflowing with soup cans, empty frozen-food packets, paper coffee cups, dried tea bags, banana skins and orange peels. The air was a mixture of coffee grounds, spoiled fruit, stale bread, and the dirty litter box.

"My kitchen's filthy, sorry," Vera said, opening the refrigerator and taking out a platter of cheese, sliced meats, and olives, which she put on the table. "I'm not much of a house cleaner. I wait until I can't find what I'm looking for, and then I throw everything in the garbage and start over."

The men pulled back chairs and sat at the table, reaching for the bottles and pouring glasses of red wine.

Luca held up his glass and said, "To Fabio. We're going to cleanse Italy of corrupt politicians and judges."

"Alla nostra," they said, clinking glasses. [To our health.]

"I wish it was that easy," Fabio said, sipping his wine. "All we can do is light a spark that will get others to act. We're only five; we'll be the first."

"Talk to us, Fabio. Tell us what you want us to do," Alfredo said, lighting a joint.

Fabio looked around the table. "You know how bad the news is. Italy is facing its worst crisis since the end of World War II—and it may get worse. EU finance ministers are meeting in Brussels again to save the euro. They're pointing their fingers at Greece and Italy as the worst places for government bonds."

"It's terrible," Luca agreed. "Everyone I know is out of work or thinks they'll be fired."

Fabio said, "Revolutions start when people take extreme measures to change history. The last couple of weeks, there've been demonstrations in London, Paris, Rome, even sleepy Brussels. They even protested at the Milan stock exchange last week."

Vera laughed. "I saw it on TV. One protester had a poster of Berlusconi as a clown wearing a crown behind bars with a prostitute on his lap."

"Berlusconi's in his last days," Alfredo said. "He can't survive. Let's push him over the cliff."

"It's not just Berlusconi," Fabio said. "Italy has a cancer of corrupt politicians and bankers they sleep with. Bankers give politicians money for campaigns. In return, politicians don't pass laws to protect small businesses and workers. It's a scandal. They're all to blame."

"Someone should line the bankers against a wall, shoot them, and dump their bodies in the sewer," Alfredo said. He drained his glass and refilled it.

"I hate bankers," Luca said. "They want to take my construction business and throw me into the street. I'm selling a backhoe and dump truck tomorrow to pay my bills. Fabio lost his university job so his professor could hire a nephew in his place. If it was me, I would have beat him and thrown him out the window."

Vera lit a joint and blew smoke over their heads. "How about me? I had to sell my old jewelry, furniture, shoes, and clothes—even one of my cars—just to pay the condo fees. I'm a year behind on maintenance charges. If I don't pay, next winter they'll cut my heating system. I'd sell the apartment, but the real estate market's in the toilet. I'm fed up with Berlusconi and his cronies. He's a buffoon who screws underage prostitutes, cheats on his taxes, bribes judges, and will never spend a night in jail. He should be castrated and hung upside down like Mussolini. *Vaffanculo!*"

"I started working when I was fourteen," Alfredo said, "laying cement, digging foundations, driving a garbage truck, cleaning out sewers. I worked hard and thought I'd always have a good job. During my military service, all I learned was how to shoot guns, blow up buildings, and dig up unexploded land mines. How is that going to help me get a job?"

"Why did you leave the army?" Vera asked.

Alfredo smirked. "Oh, you know how it is in the military. You're around oafish men all day, getting dirty and muddy, sweating like pigs, filthy all the time. You go out drinking at night, get crazy, and curse officers for their stupidity. Month after month. It makes you crazy. One night when I was in Albania, a couple of buddies picked up a farm girl on the road and brought her back to our barracks and . . . well, you know. Things happened . . . and I got kicked out of the army."

"Did you rape her?" Vera asked.

He shrugged. "She got roughed up a bit . . . spent a few days in the hospital."

"Bastard! You shouldn't hurt girls, especially young, stupid ones. There's enough free sex around. You just have to know how to get it."

Alfredo grimaced, turning away from Vera. She reached across the table and grabbed his wrist, squeezing until he pried off her fingers. "I'm sorry. I was young and stupid."

"You can't help being young," she said. "You can help being stupid!" She spit out the word *stupid*. She backhanded him, slapping his tattooed arm.

Alfredo flinched but didn't raise his hand in defense. "I was wrong. . . . I admit it," Alfredo said, lowering his head. "I paid for my sins . . . got kicked out of the army with a bad discharge. I'm Catholic—I know about sin and forgiveness. It's hard to get a job with a bad army record. Thank God, Luca hired me."

"No more arguing," Fabio interrupted. "We're not here to fight among ourselves. We have important things to discuss. Vera . . . Alfredo . . . agree?"

Vera drained her glass of wine. "I just want Alfredo to know he can't be abusive."

"Alfredo . . . enough of this. You and Vera keep away from each other. We can't fight among ourselves."

Alfredo nodded. "I like Vera's spirit. She's good for us. She's tough; I like that."

"Don't make her angry. You'll pay for it."

"I won't. Promise."

"He apologized," Vera said. "Let's move on. We've got serious shit to talk about."

"We have to remember that this is not about us and our woes," said Fabio. "There's a larger issue: a struggle for justice and hope for people who don't have privileges and wealth. All of us come from poor families."

He put his hand on Luca's shoulder. "Our papa died because factories didn't provide safe conditions. A beam fell and crushed him. The factory manager had ignored warnings that the assembly line was dangerous. I was seven years old when Papa died. I cried for weeks. Every day, I think of him and wish he were alive."

Luca raised a fist. "For Papa."

"I also think every day about our Zio Gino, who's dying in a nursing home," Fabio continued. "He was imprisoned after the Moro affair because he was a Brigate Rosse involved in workers' protests in Torino. After prison, he lived with our family, helped our grieving mother, and was like a father to Luca and me. He told us stories about how bad things were in Italy, with the fascists, the corrupt politicians and industrialists, and the struggling workers. I visited Zio Gino last week; I don't think he has long to live."

"Zio Gino is a saint," Luca said, raising his glass. "To Papa . . . Zio Gino . . . and Fabio, who carries on the struggle." They all clinked glasses.

Luca asked, "Fabio, what are we going to do?"

Fabio refilled everyone's glasses and was quiet for a moment. "Here's my plan. Alfredo has made small bombs. He'll set one off at the PdL office at night. A few nights later, he'll set off another at the PD headquarters."

"Why both the PD and PdL?" Vera asked, frowning.

"To confuse everyone. When the bomb goes off at the PdL, the police will think it's a left-wing group. Set off a bomb at the PD office, and they'll think it's a right-wing group. Confuse them right from the start."

"Good idea. I like that," Vera said. "Then what?"

"Then we do something bold. We need to get national attention by doing something big in a public place," said Fabio.

"Like where?" Vera asked.

"How about Stazione Centrale?"

"Oh, that's good," she said. "A million people go through the station every day."

"Not a million, but several hundred thousand," Fabio corrected. "Politicians are always taking the train from Rome to Milan to go to Berlusconi's villa for one of his infamous 'dinners in Arcore.' That place has become the third Chamber of Deputies and is always packed with sluts for the 'after dinners.' We could kneecap one of the politicians when he arrives at Stazione Centrale."

"Great idea, but dangerous," Luca said.

"It will be dangerous, but Alfredo will train us. He learned commando raids in the army. We'll go up in the mountains and train. We'll time the shooting and our escape."

"I'll teach you to become expert shooters," Alfredo said. "I learned from the best."

"Not me. I don't want to shoot a gun. Guns scare me," Marietto said, shaking his head.

"Don't worry, Marietto. You won't have to," Fabio said, patting his arm. "Your job will be driving. Luca said you have quick reactions and are very experienced."

Marietto nodded. "I learned to drive when I was ten years old on our farm. I will drive wherever you want me to go."

"I want to learn shoot better," Vera said. "I had a boyfriend who had guns and took me to shoot targets. I like when the gun kicks and you hear the loud BOOM!" She threw up her hands to accent the *boom*. "We always had wild sex after shooting."

They all laughed, breaking the tension. Fabio refilled their wineglasses.

"I'll teach you to be a good shooter," Alfredo said with a grin.

Luca, Alfredo, and Vera sipped wine and puffed on joints, filling the kitchen with a cloud of smoke that hung over the table.

"Now, the serious business," Fabio said, putting down his glass and looking around the table. "Our lives change starting tonight. We've become a secret cell. No one knows we met tonight or what we're going to do."

They nodded in unison.

"We don't call each other on our personal cell phones anymore. Alfredo has Albanian cell phones with special SIM cards."

Alfredo reached down and picked up a cloth bag from under the table. He dumped five phones on the table.

"Alfredo will show us how to use them. He programmed codes with letters, not names."

"Fabio is A," Alfredo said. "Luca is B . . . . I'm C . . . . Vera is D . . . . Marietto is E."

Fabio continued, "We use these only in emergencies. The police can't tap them like regular cell phones."

They all reached for the phones and turned them over to study them.

"We meet next Tuesday evening at seven at Luca's warehouse," said Fabio. "It's a good location: out of the way, little traffic on the street. Few people will see us coming or going. Luca agreed to let us use it as our hideout. My apartment is too small and on a main street. Vera's is too exposed, and there are CCTV cameras on the streets."

"I've never been to Luca's warehouse," Vera said. "Where is it?"

"Near Bresso Airport, away from the center of Milan," Fabio said. "I'll drive you there next week so you will know where to go. We'll go over the plan to set off the bombs at the PD and PdL."

He looked around the room, and everyone nodded.

"Tuesday evening, we'll discuss our plan for Stazione Centrale. It will be two or three days later, when I know which politicians will be taking the train from Rome. Everything changes in our lives after tonight. We can't go back to our old lives. We're committed to changing the destiny of Italy."

CHAPTER THREE

DAY ONE

MENAGGIO
LAGO DI COMO

Paolo de Matteo loved his ten-year-old granddaughter, Angela, so much that he bought her pistachio gelato every afternoon.

On their daily walks into Menaggio, Paolo and Angela left the family's hillside villa at noon to have lunch along the shores of Lake Como. They strolled hand in hand down Via Sonenga, a narrow, winding road through a neighborhood of modest homes and apartments. A block from their villa, Angela stopped at a small park where her friends, local boys and girls, played soccer and climbed on the playground equipment.

Angela waved and shouted, *"Ciao a tutti!"*

They waved back. *"Ciao, Angela. Come va?"*

"Tutto bene. Ciao!"

Along the route, Angela waved at Italian mothers hanging laundry on ropes strung across patios.

"Buongiorno, signora!" she called out.

"Ciao, Angela. Come stai?"

"Bene, grazie. Buona giornata!"

In the late summer weather, red, pink, and white petunias and geraniums spilled out of flower boxes on balconies and patios. Morning glory vines spilled over fences, and branches of lemon trees drooped to the ground, heavy with fruit. Ripe tomatoes, green bean vines, plump lemon squash, and purple eggplant hung in metal cages, ready for picking. The air was lush with the fragrance of basil, cilantro, oregano, and rosemary, which would flavor home-cooked meals that evening.

One garden had rows of grapevines with branches poking through the slats of a wooden fence. Angela plucked a few grapes and popped them in her mouth, letting the purple juice dribble down her chin.

"Oooh, these grapes are so juicy, Nonno," she said to her grandfather. "I love them."

Five minutes from the de Matteo villa, Via Sonenga merged into Via Monte Grappa, a steep road that led downhill toward Menaggio.

At the base of Via Monte Grappa, Angela and Paolo crossed the street and walked along stone walls of a medieval castle while enjoying the views of Lake Como's deep blue waters and mountains across the narrow channel.

They walked down a narrow cobblestone staircase between stucco-walled apartments, heading to Via Calvi and their favorite café on Piazza Garibaldi. They sat at an outdoor table under an umbrella and ordered from the waiter, who greeted them like members of his own family. Paolo chose his usual: shrimp salad, fresh Italian bread, and a glass of sauvignon blanc. Angela ordered cheese and prosciutto panini, pomme frites, and a lemon soda.

"Whew, it's hot today, Nonno," Angela said, setting her floppy sun hat and beach bag on an empty chair. Angela wore a different hat every day, all acquired by Paolo, who loved to buy her little gifts. "I can't wait to go swimming. Caterina and Maria are waiting for me at the lido."

"It's your last day in Menaggio, sweetheart," Paolo said. "Are you sorry to see summer end?"

"Oh, yes, Nonno. It's been the best summer ever! I love it here. You and Nonna have been so good to me."

"You have your bathing suit and towel in your bag?"

She slapped her cloth bag. "Right here. Do you have your book?"

Paolo patted his shoulder bag. "I always carry a book. I'm almost finished. I can read and watch you swim."

"Swimming in Lake Como's the best, Nonno. I hate our apartment swimming pool in New York. It's small and yucky with chlorine. All people do is swim laps. And no kids. How boring! Swimming in Como is fun."

"It sure is. I learned to swim at camp in New Jersey," he said, taking off his hat and sunglasses and wiping sweat from his forehead. "We didn't have swimming pools in Brooklyn when I was a boy. I couldn't swim until I was twelve years old. And look at you, you swim like a fish—and you're only ten years old."

"Eleven in December, Nonno."

Paolo reached over to pat her hand. "I'll never forget December 8. I was with your dad at the hospital, waiting for you to come into the world. I held you when you were only fifteen minutes old. As soon as you saw me, you cried. I thought you didn't like me!"

She frowned, a playful look in her dark eyes. "Nonno, you always say that! Of course I liked you. I just didn't know who you were. I was just a baby!"

When their waiter delivered lunch on large ceramic plates, Angela nibbled her panini and licked warm mozzarella cheese oozing between thin panini slices. "Oooh, I love cheese," she said, closing her eyes. "It's warm and yummy."

Paolo sipped his wine, savoring the soft citrus flavors rolling over his tongue. "I love my wine. It's yummy too."

"Nonno, you're funny," she giggled. "Wine and cheese are different! Wine is yucky; cheese is lip-smackin' good!"

Paolo chuckled, thrilled by Angela's playfulness. She beamed, delighted that she could make her *nonno* laugh, a jolly "Ho . . . ho . . . ho," a corner of his mouth curling into a Santa Claus grin.

Paolo was a bit like Santa, but more like an Italian version: not a big belly, and taller, with a barrel chest, long legs, and fluffs of curly white hair on his arms and around his neck. His once long, dark hair was stylishly clipped by New York's barbers to accent gray and white streaks that made him look like an aging Italian matinee idol from Federico Fellini's *La Dolce Vita*. Paolo was as generous as Santa, giving Angela gifts, holding her hand on walks, and taking her to Menaggio's lido beach to swim with her Italian girlfriends.

Angela sipped her lemon soda and watched tourists strolling through the piazza wearing colorful short-sleeved shirts, shorts, and sandals, scanning menus posted outside cafés and trattorias. A few yards from their outdoor table, double-decker ferries were crossing Lake Como from Menaggio to Varenna or Bellagio, carving Vs in the deep blue waters. Expensive villas behind gated fences were slotted along the steep mountainsides on both sides of Lake Como.

"Boy, the piazza's really crowded today," Angela said, dipping pomme frites into a mound of ketchup and stuffing them into her mouth.

"It's like this every August, the busiest month of the summer," Paolo said, pushing the olives to the side to enjoy at the end of lunch. "Hotels are full, waiting lines for the ferries, and more tour buses show up every day. A month from now, it'll be quiet and sleepy."

"Can we get gelato after swimming?"

"Of course, sweetheart. We can't go home without gelato."

After lunch, Paolo and Angela left Piazza Garibaldi and strolled along the embankment, where waves from ferries slapped against the stone walls. Angela tore crumbs of bread she had saved from lunch and tossed them to ducks bobbing on the waves.

The lake air smelled of the pizza and pasta being served at outdoor cafés, the rosebushes along the shaded promenade, and the diesel fumes from ferries. Paolo and Angela walked past the elegant Hotel Victoria, where uniformed valets were off-loading bulging suitcases from taxis onto carts and wheeling them into the hotel. In front of the Victoria, fronds of towering palm trees were fluttering in the breeze next to flagpoles with American, Italian, British, and Swiss flags.

The route to the lido followed along the embankment past parks, cafés, gardens, and a monument to Menaggio's women silk-weavers from back in the day when Menaggio had been a village of craftspeople and peasant families.

When Paolo and Angela reached the lido, Angela ran off to the women's locker room to change into her swimsuit. Paolo picked out a lounge chair and umbrella with a view of the beach.

Rows of beach towels were laid out on the lawn. Children and teenagers were sunbathing, laughing, and flirting, suntanned and without a care in the world. Paolo was reading when Angela dashed out of the changing room and dropped her bag next to his chair. *"Ciao, Nonno. Ci vediamo dopo!"* she said, running off with another girl, both speaking in Italian.

Angela's swimsuit accented her long, tanned legs, arms, and bare midriff. She danced across the lawn like a ballerina, her feet barely touching the ground. When the girls reached the beach, their girlfriends jumped up from their towels and hugged them, giggling and energetic as puppies. They sat down on their towels, eyeing young boys diving off a platform and whooping and splashing in the waves.

Oh, the children, Paolo thought. *They're so happy and full of joy.* He envied their youth, knowing that in a few years they would know struggles, disappointments, and frustrations. *Enjoy happy times now, children. Life will get complicated soon enough.*

Paolo marveled at how Angela looked like her mother, Sylvia, when she was her age: stunning good looks, lanky limbs, sensuous dark eyes, and long, silky black hair. Angela would be a beauty—just like Sylvia.

The wine was making Paolo drowsy. He put his book on his chest, took off his sunglasses, and closed his eyes, listening to the children playing, the ferry horns honking, and the waves lapping on the beach.

Paolo loved family vacations on Lake Como, returning to the homeland of his mother and father. After he had made his first million on Wall Street, he had bought his first Menaggio villa, eventually trading up to the present luxurious three-story villa with a wine cellar, enclosed garden, and balcony looking over Menaggio and Lake Como.

After forty years as an investment banker, Paolo was one of the highest-paid executives in his brokerage firm. But he was weary of the grind of long hours, endless meetings, and constant stress. He was ready to retire so he could spend more time in Menaggio and indulge his hobbies of painting watercolors and collecting Italian antiques.

This was a bittersweet day for Paolo. His family would celebrate his sixty-sixth birthday that night. Tomorrow, Sylvia, Angela, and Sylvia's fiancé, Cole, were leaving for Milan and Paris before returning to New York.

Farewells and birthdays were sad occasions for Paolo. Birthdays marked another year passed, and Paolo wasn't sure how many more he would have to enjoy his family. Farewells were sad because loved ones were departing. He and his wife, Harriet, would be alone, a feeling they liked less as they aged and their health deteriorated.

Paolo was also worried about Harriet's health; after they returned to New York, she had a doctor's appointment about her worsening MS. Paolo also had an appointment with his cardiologist in connection with the quadruple heart bypass surgery he'd had two years before.

Paolo was also concerned about Sylvia and Cole's pending marriage. They had met at a New Year's party, had become engaged in June, and were getting married in October. *Too much, too fast.*

Sylvia had been divorced for five years. Cole was also divorced, and his preteen son was living in Chicago with his mother. As a conservative Catholic, Paolo was opposed to divorce for all the stresses and complications it caused families—especially children. Like Angela.

Worries about health and family haunted Paolo every day. Too many situations were out of his control. And Paolo liked control.

CHAPTER FOUR

"Nonno, it's time for gelato!" Angela said, jostling his shoulder. Paolo jolted awake, squinting at the bright sun that had crept under his umbrella, making sweat circles under his armpits and collar. He sat up, rubbed his eyes, and wiped his forehead.

"Uhh, I dozed off. . . . It must be the wine. How are you, sweetheart? Have a good swim?"

"Nonno! You always nap after lunch," she said, swinging her beach bag. Her tanned, wet body glistened like exotic African polished wood. "It's so cute! I'm going to change. Be right back!"

When Angela emerged minutes later, she was running a plastic comb through her damp hair, which dangled in black cords to her shoulders. Her deep tan was accented by her white shorts and pink T-shirt with "I heart Menaggio," which Paolo had bought for her.

"Come on, Nonno. Time for gelato," she said, putting on her sun hat and sunglasses.

"Ooh, won't that taste good?"

They retraced their walk along the embankment to a side street off Piazza Garibaldi, passing a wine shop, children's clothing store, women's handbag shop, souvenir shop with racks of postcards, and trattoria where sun baked tourists were eating pasta and drinking wine in the shade. Near the end of the street, they walked into a *gelateria*, where large plastic cones advertising gelato flavors stood on both sides of the open door.

Angela greeted the teenage girl with a cheery, *"Ciao, Elena. Come va?"*

"Bene, Angela. Signor de Matteo, lei come stai?"

"Molto bene, grazie," Paolo said.

Angela's conversational Italian was excellent, thanks to Paolo buying her toys, stuffed animals, and dolls for Christmas and birthdays to teach her colors, parts of the body, and animal names in Italian. Paolo had enrolled her in a Saturday morning Italian immersion program when she'd started school, and by the time she was in fourth grade, Angela could read Italian fairy tales such as *Pinocchio*.

Angela leaned down to study the trays of creamy gelato in the refrigerated display—apricot, cheesecake, chocolate, lemon, blueberry, strawberry, chocolate mint, and watermelon.

"Mmmm . . . blueberry looks good today," Paolo said in Italian, winking at the pretty attendant.

"My favorite is chocolate mint," the girl said. It was a game they played each afternoon; both knew that Angela always chose her favorite flavor. She pointed at the pale green bin. *"Un cono tutto pistacchio, per favore."*

"You had pistachio yesterday," Paolo said in mock protest. "You don't want to try another flavor?"

Angela shook her head and brushed away the damp hair sticking to her cheek. "Nonno, you know I'm a pistachio girl!"

"Two scoops for Angela. One banana for me," Paolo ordered, pulling out his wallet. The girl scooped pistachio into a waffle cone and handed it across the counter to Angela.

"Grazie," Angela said, licking the swirl. When Elena handed Paolo his cone, he gave her a ten euro note, waving for her to keep the change.

"Ci vediamo domani, Angela?" Elena asked. [See you tomorrow?]

"Purtroppo no! Domani ripartiamo per New York," [Unfortunately no! Tomorrow we are returning to New York] Angela said.

"You mean I won't see you every afternoon?" the girl asked, with a sad look on her face. "I'll miss you and your *nonno. Sei così carina, Angela."* [You're such a sweet girl, Angela]

"I'll be back next summer to see my *nonno* and *nonna."*

"Lucky girl. I'll see you next year."

As they walked out of the *gelateria,* Angela was licking the creamy gelato, forming a green peak at the top.

"Mmm, I love pistachio, Nonno. It's my favorite," she said, taking his hand.

"The best gelato at Lake Como, my dear. You have good taste."

Paolo and Angela leisurely walked among tourists who were window-shopping, licking gelato, and buying postcards, sunglasses, and souvenirs. They passed a children's clothing store where Paolo had bought Angela clothes and hats that summer. "How about a new hat for your trip tomorrow?" he suggested, leading her inside.

"Super!" Angela said. She dropped his hand and walked around the store, going down aisles with racks of stylish and expensive young girls' shorts, tops, scarves, and dresses. Paolo walked to the back wall, where hats and caps were mounted on wooden pegs.

"You like this beret?" he said, taking a tan beret off the peg and handing it to her.

Angela took off her sun hat and put on the beret. She looked in a mirror, turning left and right, cocking her head. "Oooh, I like this, Nonno. It's cool!"

"You look Parisian. Let's get it and surprise your mom."

"She'll love it. Thanks, Nonno."

Paolo paid for the beret. Angela stuffed her sun hat in her bag and put on the beret. They left the shop and strolled down to Via Lestrade, where tourist buses, regional buses, small cars, and noisy motorbikes were crawling along Menaggio's congested main road. They crossed Via Lestrade and passed St. Vincent church where they often went to mass. Finally, they reached the cobblestone staircase to the *castello*.

"I'm going to miss our daily walks," Paolo said, stopping to rest halfway up the steep staircase. "Nonna and I have had a wonderful summer with you."

"The best, Nonno! I love spending summers with you and Nonna. Can I come next August?"

"Of course. You can come every summer."

"Can we ride the ferries again? I love Como ferries. Varenna is my favorite place to go—next to Menaggio, I mean."

"I like Varenna too—more than Bellagio."

"Yuck, too many tourists in Bellagio," she said, nibbling down the cone until there was only a dab of pistachio left.

"We might take a trip next summer."

"Where?"

"How about Florence?"

"Wow, that would be great, Nonno! Will we go to galleries?"

"Of course. We'll see Michelangelo's *David* and Caravaggios and Titians at the Uffizi Gallery."

"Oooh, I'd like that! Mrs. Gillespie will be impressed. I can't wait to tell her."

In addition to introducing Angela to Italian, Paolo had hired an art teacher to teach Angela about using watercolors and pastels. Angela was already displaying a budding talent that Paolo hoped might lead to a career as an artist.

They reached the top of the cobblestone staircase, where stone paths diverged around the *castello*.

"There's our bench, Nonno," Angela said. "Let's rest."

They sat down, and Paolo took off his hat and wiped sweat from his face and neck.

Angela popped the last of her cone into her mouth and wiped her lips with a tissue. "I like resting here. It was hot today, wasn't it? I was so thirsty that I had another lemon soda while you were napping."

"Yes, it was hot. But you're keeping me healthy, walking every day."

Angela giggled, putting a hand over her mouth. "Can I tell you a secret, Nonno?"

"Of course. I like our little secrets."

"Before I came this summer, Mom told me to make sure you got exercise. That's why we walk into town every day."

"A good plan. And it gives us lots of time to talk."

"Our walks are fun, Nonno, especially when we go to the beach and get gelato!"

"It has been wonderful, dear. I'll remember our walks all winter long."

Angela watched Italian mothers carrying cloth sacks of groceries, their children following as they walked up the stone staircase, turning left or right to go home after shopping. Angela sat quietly, twisting a strand of damp hair in her fingers, scuffing her sandals against the smooth stones under the bench.

"Nonno . . . are you happy that Mom and Cole are getting married?"

Paolo held his breath before letting it out slowly. This was the first time Angela had asked him about her mother's upcoming wedding. She'd only made occasional offhand comments since she'd arrived, about Cole bringing his cat to their apartment when he moved in and taking her skating at Rockefeller Center. But she hadn't said anything about how she felt about the wedding.

"Yes, dear. I want her to be happy," he said, hoping she'd express more about her feelings.

"Me too. Mom's happy now, not like when she and Dad divorced."

"That was hard on all of us."

"I'm glad you and Nonna let me stay with you that winter. I was sad at home. Mom was so upset. She cried a lot, and I didn't know what to do. I was only five years old, remember?"

"Yes, I do. That's why we wanted you to spend time with us. We wanted you to know we would always be there for you and your mom."

The rays of the afternoon sun were inching toward their bench, creeping up Angela's tanned legs.

"Andiamo," Paolo said, putting on his hat and standing up. "One more hill and we're home."

They walked along the *castello* to Via Monte Grappa, where they could see the bell tower of the seventeenth-century San Carlo church, one of the most prominent sights in Menaggio.

Paolo loved Menaggio's old Catholic churches, which they passed on their walks. He was proud to be a Catholic Italian American. He had been coming to Italy since his father had brought him as a teenager to meet relatives in the hillside villages around Lago di Piano above Menaggio. He had begun bringing Sylvia to Menaggio when she was six years old, and now he was thrilled to be introducing Angela to the joys of Italian life.

Paolo and Angela walked single file up the steep incline of Via Monte Grappa, moving against the stone wall when a car or truck came their way. They turned onto Via Sonenga, following the winding, narrow road to the playground, where they could see the red tile roof and balcony of the family villa.

"There's home," Paolo said, stopping to catch his breath and wipe his brow.

"Mom's back!" Angela squealed, waving at Sylvia and Cole on the balcony beside Nonna in her wheelchair.

Angela dropped Paolo's hand and dashed up Via Sonenga, waving her beret. "Mom, look! Nonno bought me a beret!"

CHAPTER FIVE

Costanza, the de Matteos' New York cook who had come over with them in August, popped the cork of a bottle of Bolgheri Sassicaia and walked around the patio dining table, pouring glasses.

"We bought this wine in Milan for your birthday, Dad," Sylvia said. "I hope you like it." Sylvia smiled, her face glowing from a deep summer tan. She looked radiant, wearing an attractive light blue and soft yellow blouse, linen shorts, and new sandals. On her wrists were silver and black bracelets embedded with topaz she'd bought in Venice. In her fashionable summer clothes and jewelry, she looked more attractive and stylish than the young, wraith-thin models who strutted down runways at Milan's famous fashion shows.

Paolo put on his reading glasses to read the label. "Bolgheri Sassicaia DOC. Anno 2004. Oooh, this is expensive."

"It's for a very special occasion—your sixty-sixth birthday."

Costanza poured into his glass. Paolo swirled it and held it to his nose. "Mmm, smells delicious. Blueberries . . . black currant . . . a hint of chocolate." He took a sip and closed his eyes. A slow grin spread to his pink cheeks.

"Marvelous . . . subtle and rich."

"Just like you, Dad," Sylvia said.

Everyone laughed as Paolo raised his glass.

"Time for the first toast," he said, raising his glass.

The patio dining table was filled with Paolo's favorite foods prepared by Costanza: risotto with porcini mushrooms; tenderloin with cannellini beans; a selection of strong-flavored cheeses from Tuscany; fresh peas, carrots, and corn from Paolo's garden; and tomato-flavored breadsticks and ciabatta bread from Paolo's favorite *panificio,* Il Fornaio on Via Estrada.

"Not so fast, Dad. This is your birthday," Sylvia said, rising from the dinner table. "We have to toast you first."

Paulo shrugged. "Oh, you know me. I don't like to be on center stage . . ."

Sylvia and Harriet laughed. "Dad!" Sylvia said. "You love center stage. You've been center stage your whole life!" Everyone laughed.

Sylvia, Cole, and Angela pushed back their chairs and stood. Sylvia put her hand on Paolo's shoulder and kissed his forehead. Harriet remained in her chair, nodding toward Sylvia. "I can't wait for this," Harriet said.

Angela was between Paolo and Harriet, wearing a pink dress with a border of pale yellow lace. Lighted candles on the patio railing provided cones of light against the approaching dusk. Across Lake Como, the lights of Varenna and Bellagio twinkled like fireflies.

Sylvia raised her glass. "To Paolo . . . father, husband, and grandfather. One of the great men of Italian heritage. That's a high calling, when you consider that this includes geniuses like Michelangelo, Leonardo, Dante—"

"Whoa, that's a pretty elite crowd," Paolo said with a grin. "They were all Renaissance geniuses. I'm not that old!"

"Okay, how about more recent Italians, like Puccini and Verdi. I'll even throw in Rossellini and Fellini."

"Oooh, still too lofty . . . I am just a lowly Wall Street banker."

"But, Dad, you made money like a genius. The others wrote operas and made classic movies," said Sylvia. "That was your art."

Paolo winked at Angela, his pink face glowing in the candlelight. "I like the gist of this."

"I'll stop there, or I could go on all night," Sylvia said. She cleared her throat. "Let me rephrase my toast: To Paolo, one of the most cherished Italian men of the twenty-first century!"

"Mmm . . . okay . . . I like that," he said, clearly enjoying the fuss and attention.

"Happy birthday! Congratulations!" Everyone cheered and clinked glasses, Angela joining in with a wineglass of lemon soda.

Paolo's round face was flushed from a month of Italian sun and daily walks with Angela. A sheen of sweat dampened his forehead and cheeks in the warm evening air.

Costanza rolled out a cart with a lemon-colored birthday cake with paper Italian flags around the edges. She lit a circle of candles that surrounded two numerical candles in the center, two sixes.

"Oooh," everyone exclaimed, clapping in delight at the decorated cake. "Beautiful . . . beautiful!"

Costanza dimmed the indoor lights so that the candles lit up the patio.

"My, my, look at this!" Paolo said. "What a beautiful cake. Thank you, Costy."

"Blow out the candles, Nonno!" Angela said, standing at his side, her arm around his shoulder.

"Will you help me?" he said.

"You go first, Nonno."

Paolo took an exaggerated deep breath and blew out most of the candles. Angela leaned over and blew out the remainder. Everyone applauded and sang a chorus of "Happy Birthday."

They all sat down, smiling at Paolo.

"Congratulations and happy birthday, Paolo," Cole said. Cole enjoyed the banter Sylvia and Paolo engaged in, playful and endearing.

He was more serious, an academic who thrived on technical discussions with students and fellow academics. He looked like a professor: tall, a bit gaunt, with light blue eyes, thinning brown hair, and a gentle mouth. When he spoke, it was usually with measured cadence, as if he was reading a text.

Paolo looked around the table, his eyes moist. For a moment, he was speechless. Finally, he stammered, "Well . . . I'm a little overwhelmed. This is such a beautiful cake . . . . Thank you all for being here to help me celebrate. And to Costy, it's a very pretty cake. Thank you all."

"You're the best birthday present I could ever have, Nonno," Angela said, kissing his pink cheek. "You're the best!"

Paolo blinked, wiping tears as his moist eyes overflowed. Costanza cut the cake and handed out plates with a paper Italian flag and a candle on each piece.

"Now, where was I before I was interrupted?" Paolo said. "I have a few toasts I'd like to make."

He raised his glass to Harriet. "First, to my lovely wife . . . my life partner, best friend, and loving mother and *nonna*." He took her hand and kissed it. "I love you, dear. You've made me a very happy man for forty-three years."

"Thank you, dear. You've been a wonderful husband."

Paolo turned to Sylvia and raised his glass. "To Sylvia, who has such an exciting fall planned: a gallery show, a new book project, and an October wedding. I wonder how much that will cost me!"

"Don't worry, Dad. Cole and I are paying for most of it."

"Good! Or you'd bankrupt me!"

They all laughed, picked up forks, and began tasting the cake. "Oooh, so good, Costy. You make the best cakes," said Angela.

Costanza smiled, wiping her hands on her apron. "Thank you Angela, and to all of you. I feel so lucky to be part of this wonderful family. You've all been so good to me for all these years."

"You're part of our family, Costy," Paolo said. "Every meal you cook for us in New York is like being in Italy. Isn't that right, Mom?" he said, nodding at Harriet.

"It sure is," she said. "We'll want you with us—even if Paolo retires, which he's threatening to do any day now."

"Really, Dad?" Sylvia said. "Oh, I hope so."

He nodded, wiping his mouth with a napkin. "We've been talking about it all summer, and we wanted to let you know first."

"Wonderful," Sylvia said. "You've got the rest of your life to enjoy whatever you and Mom want to do."

"And we will," he said, "won't we, dear?"

Harriet said, "You've worked hard for many years. I know you want to spend all summer here, not just August. That will make me happy too."

"It's settled. I'll retire in the spring, and we'll spend next summer here. You're all welcome to return and spend as much time as you want."

"Super!" Angela exclaimed. "Summer in Menaggio!"

Paolo raised his hand. "I have another toast: *alla mia stupenda* Angela, the jewel in our family who I hope will carry on our Italian traditions and love Menaggio as much as we have. Have you told them our plans for next year?" He winked at Angela.

"You tell them, Nonno!"

"Next year, I'm taking Angela to Florence, to the Accademia and Uffizi galleries to see the Italian masterpieces. I'm going to arrange art classes with a well-known Florence painter."

"Wonderful!" Sylvia said. "You'll have a great time, Angela. I was about the same age you'll be next summer when I first went to the Uffizi. It was unforgettable!"

Paolo turned to Cole and raised his glass.

"And to Cole, the newest member of our family. We hope he will return to Menaggio for many August vacations."

"Hear, hear!" Sylvia said, clinking another round across the table.

"Paolo, you give such long toasts," Harriet said with a tease. "I swear, it's like you're running for mayor of New York when you have a glass of wine in your hands."

They all laughed and continued clinking glasses, Angela joining in with her glass of lemon soda.

"Mom, you know politics was the career Dad almost chose," Sylvia said.

"That's true," Paolo said. "After law school, I was going to work in the New York District Attorney's office. I've always loved politics. Fortunately, a classmate got me an interview with his firm's broker training program. If I'd become a D.A., I wouldn't have made the money I did, and we wouldn't have this wonderful villa."

"You're a genius at making money, Dad," Sylvia said. "We love you for the things you've done with your money. You've worked hard to give us wonderful lives."

"*Grazie mille,* Sylvia," Paolo said, bowing his head. "This has been special, having Angela with us the whole month. Isn't that right, dear?" he said, turning to Harriet.

"It has been heavenly," she said. "I love my granddaughter so much. Every day we spend with her is special."

"Thank you, Nonna, and you too, Nonno. I like it here in Menaggio. Especially the gelato!"

Everyone raised a glass in another toast. "To Menaggio's gelato, yeah!" Sylvia said.

"Before you leave tomorrow, Angela and I are going to the *gelateria* for her last pistachio of the summer," said Paolo.

Angela beamed. "Nonno, you're the best!"

CHAPTER SIX

Later that evening, a gibbous moon was shimmering on the dark waters of Lake Como as the last evening ferry from Bellagio docked at the Menaggio terminal. Crowds of tourists streamed down the ramp carrying Prada, Gucci, Armani, and Valentino shopping bags and making their way to hotels or restaurants for late dinners.

The night was becoming mellow, with the sounds of crickets chirping, owls hooting, and the familiar refrain of a romantic ballad being sung by an Italian crooner at the Hotel Sonenga, across the road.

Sylvia was relaxing in a patio chair, her bare feet propped on the railing, a cashmere sweater wrapped around her shoulders. Cones of light from the patio candles flickered in the warm breeze.

"Another beautiful night in Menaggio, Dad," Sylvia said, sipping her wine. "I'm sure going to miss this place."

"It's been another great summer, especially having Angela with us all month."

"Cole and I had a great two weeks driving all over. He especially liked Venice and Milan," Sylvia said, patting Paolo on his forearm. "And I got a lot of great photos for my exhibit and new book."

Paolo sipped his Scotch, twirling the glass in his fingers. "We got to know Cole a little better. He's a pleasant . . . dependable fellow."

"Thanks, Dad. He likes you a lot. I think you'll get along well."

He nodded. "I'm sure we will. He's intelligent and well-read. I like that in a man."

"He's very smart. And he grows on you, the more time you spend together."

"You two certainly have a busy fall ahead: your exhibit in September, Cole teaching at NYU, your wedding in October, and Thanksgiving in Chicago."

Sylvia sighed and sipped her wine. "Lots of changes ahead, and you'll have a new son-in-law. You can take care of Angela when we go to see his mother in Minneapolis."

"We'll love it. Every day with her is precious."

"You play an important part in her life, Dad. She talks about you with her friends all the time."

They were quiet for a few moments, Paolo sipping his Scotch, Sylvia her wine, taking in the serenity and memories of their last evening together in Menaggio.

Paolo said, "You and Cole have known each other, what—seven months?"

"Eight, Dad," she said, a touch of irritation in her voice. "I know you're concerned that we're rushing things, but I don't want to put it off. He'll be a good stepfather to Angela."

Paolo nodded. "I see that. She's quite attached to him. I just don't want you to rush. You know me."

"My problem with men, Dad, is that you spoiled me. You should hear stories my girlfriends tell about their fathers. Most were not around much or were cold fish, holding back love and attention. Those behaviors are destructive to women. They end up on the singles bar circuit, picking

up guys, taking them home so they can 'fix' them and get the love they
need. All they get is more heartache and regrets."

"I hope I gave you more than love. I tried to teach you that no one
is perfect. When you're married, you tolerate quirks that all men have,
even if they drive you crazy. If they're good fathers and husbands, that's
all that matters. I liked Charles, even though he had a few shortcomings.
He was good to Angela."

"Maybe I wasn't the most patient wife . . . I was young and high-
spirited. I've matured since then. Cole has taught me patience; he gets
on my case when I'm too emotional. I let him have his way a lot. I've
learned to listen more and react less."

Paolo reached into a shirt pocket and pulled out a cigar. Sylvia
reached over to pluck it out of his fingers. "Dad . . . remember what
Dr. Weinberg said."

He reached over and took it back. "Can't an old man indulge a
little on his birthday?"

"As long as it doesn't involve cigars, rich foods, or too much Scotch."

He grinned. "Now you sound like your mom."

"Dad, don't worry about Cole and me. We've talked through the
important issues: finances, working schedules, making time for Angela.
He's a great dad to his son, and he and Angela get along well. With luck,
his son will join us next year in Menaggio."

Paolo lit his cigar and blew a plume of blue smoke that floated away
on the warm breeze. "That's nice. We'd like to meet the little guy."

"He'll be at the wedding. You'll see that he's a lot like Cole: quiet
and serious."

"Blending families isn't easy. It will take the four of you some time
to adjust and become a family." Paolo sighed. "The older I get, the more
I care about the health and welfare of people closest to me—my family
and a few friends in particular. I used to focus on the big picture: the
economy, the state of the world, my firm, and making New York a better place to live. I've given up on those ideals. Now I worry about a few
people and will do anything to help them. That's why I'm so concerned

about your mom. The hell with New York and the world—I just want her healthy."

Sylvia sipped her wine. "I'm worried about her too, Dad. She's getting more frail. She hides a lot, as she always has, but it's painful to watch her use her cane and walker. She gets so frustrated at not being able to get around on her own."

"She has another doctor's appointment when we get back to New York to look at some new treatments. But I'm worried; she's withdrawing and gets depressed. Sometimes, I just don't know what I can do . . ." His voice trailed off.

They sat in silence, looking at the twinkling lights along the lake. The breeze was turning cooler. Sylvia unwrapped her sweater and pulled it over her head, scooting her chair closer to Paolo.

"I want you to be happy, Sylvia," Paolo said, putting an arm around her shoulder. "Being married is the best part of being an adult. It's the Catholic in me, I guess. Marriage is a great institution, one of the few I still believe in. You need a good husband. And you don't want to be single when you hit forty."

Sylvia sighed. "No argument there. My married friends are happy, even though they struggle with raising kids and managing their money. I was a little concerned that I'd never find a good man. But when I met Cole, I knew we were a good match even though we have different temperaments. I'm more emotional and spontaneous. He's calm and deliberate. I fly off the handle when I get upset; he goes into his study and closes the door. Drives me crazy sometimes, but we're working things out, something that Charles and I never managed to do. We were too young."

"Be patient with Cole. Let him be who he is and don't try to 'fix' him. We'll welcome him into our family as if he were our own son."

"I appreciate that so much, Dad."

Sylvia sipped her wine, wondering if she should tell Paolo that she and Cole had talked about having a baby. Her relationship with her father had grown closer in the last few years, during her divorce and raising Angela as a single parent. He had known of her strong desire to marry again.

Sylvia took a deep breath. "Something else I think you should know, Dad. Cole and I want a child. We might even try the first year."

Paolo's face lit up. "Wow, that's great news! We'd love another grandchild—but that's up to you and Cole."

Sylvia sighed, relieved at his positive reaction. "Thanks, Dad. . . . I'm glad we can talk like this. You know Angela would love to have a baby brother or sister."

Paolo looked over at her, his eyes moist. "Yes, she would. She'd be thrilled." A smile came to his lips. "She's my angel. I'd do anything to make her happy."

"She's happiest when she's with you and Mom. I almost dread going back and starting her school routine, getting up early, taking her to school, studying with her every night. She's so free here, just like I was when I was her age."

"She reminds me of you when you were ten. So full of life. She's got a great sense of humor and makes me laugh every day."

"You should hear her talk about you and Mom with her friends: taking her to the Met to see the Italian masters; watching old Italian movies, *Il Postino*, *Cinema Paradiso*, and your favorite, Fellini's *Amarcord*."

Paolo chuckled and puffed on his cigar. "She loves *Amarcord*, especially the scene with the boys in school peeing under their desks into a tube that lands between the boy's legs in front of the class."

"Oh, God," she laughed. "She tells that story over and over again. She loves the mischievous boys."

"I hope she embraces Italian life like you did when you were young."

"She does; she likes to show off how well she speaks Italian and knows Italian art. That's why we're spending a day in Milan, to take her to the Duomo, La Scala, and maybe the Castello Sforzesco."

"Be careful in Milan. There were a couple of bombings there last week."

"We heard about it at our hotel. One was at a Democratic Party office, I think."

"Another was at Berlusconi's Popolo della Libertà party office. There's scary stuff going on in Italy, with the Euro financial crisis and political scandals. Milan was the center of terrorism back in the '60s and '70s, when fascists and Red Brigade gangs were running around kidnapping, kneecapping, and assassinating judges and politicians. They even killed Aldo Moro, the former prime minister. That was awful—one of the darkest chapters in Italian history. Be careful."

"You know we will, Dad. Don't worry about us."

CHAPTER SEVEN

Later that night, Sylvia and Cole were in bed, propped up on pillows, a sheet over their legs. Sylvia was reading a magazine while Cole tapped on his laptop. A warm breeze was fluffing the curtains of their bedroom window, carrying in the fragrance of lavender and roses from Paolo's garden.

The full moon over Lake Como was shining in the window, lighting up the bedroom with pale yellow light.

"Look at the harvest moon, honey," Sylvia said. "It's so huge . . . orange . . . bright . . . . You could almost reach up and touch it."

Cole lowered his reading glasses. "Yes, it is."

"Don't you love it here?"

"Yes, I do. I also like the effect Italy has on you. You've been so happy the last couple of weeks, almost like a different person than when you're in New York."

"So true. Some of my best times growing up were spending summers here. I had nice friends. They'd take me home to meet their families. I'd sleep over sometimes and enjoy their mothers' cooking. Italian home cooking is the best."

"Now you're talking like Angela! Her favorite phrase all summer has been 'It's the best!' Have you noticed?"

"Oh, yes, and she's been so happy with Mom and Dad."

Cole went on working while Sylvia looked around the room at the family pictures on the wall and earlier ones from when she was in Italy.

"The girl in that picture there was my pen pal," she said, pointing to a framed photo on her nightstand. "Did you ever have a pen pal?"

He laughed. "Nope, never. I heard about them from my parents and thought it was quaint, like something out of the '50s, like vinyl records and dial phones. I don't think I wrote a letter after I got my first computer and started using e-mail."

"When was that?"

"Oh, I was about twelve years old. My dad bought me a used Lisa computer back in the '80s, and I started sending e-mail on CompuServe."

She poked an elbow in his side. "You're such a geek . . . but a cute one."

Cole went back to working on his laptop, and Sylvia leafed through her magazine. But her mind wasn't on reading. She was thinking about their two weeks of traveling around northern Italy. She had shown Cole some of her favorite locations, ones she'd been going to for years, taking photos and documenting life in remote villages where peasant families were maintaining old crafts.

She put down her magazine. "Are you glad we came? I know you had a lot going on, getting ready for classes before we left."

"I'm very happy we came. I'd only been to Rome and Florence as a tourist a long time ago. But seeing Italy with you is like having a professional guide."

"Thanks, honey. We'll come back every summer if you can make it."

"That'll be nice."

"Next year we'll stay around Menaggio if you want. We can hike in the mountains, take ferries around Como, and have Angela with us. I hope Rick can come too."

"It would be nice to have both kids with us."

"Maybe . . . maybe . . . I'll be pregnant. Then I'll need to take it easy. Angela would love to have a little baby brother or sister."

Cole reached over to take her hand. "True, but let's not get too excited. We have a lot of things to work through between now and next summer."

"But I want us to—"

"Please, Sylvia, not so fast. Getting pregnant is serious business. You've been off the pill for months and nothing has happened. We might have to go to a fertility clinic, and that could take months. Let's not get ahead of ourselves. If we're meant to have a baby, we will."

She leaned her head on Cole's shoulder. He set his laptop on the bed and kissed her forehead.

"Okay . . . okay . . . you're right," she said. "I know I have to be patient." She rubbed a hand over his chest. "How do you feel about going back to New York?"

"Well, to be honest, mixed feelings. This is the first vacation I've had in two years. But, like all good things, it must come to an end."

"What about your new job? Are you anxious about starting at a new university?"

"It won't be bad. I know some of the faculty from summer school last year. My teaching load is pretty heavy: six classes and a graduate seminar. I won't have much free time until next summer."

"Except for the wedding and honeymoon," she corrected. "My publisher's booking a tour to the West Coast in the spring. I hope you can come along. We can go to Santa Barbara or San Diego for a few days."

"I probably can't go unless it's over a long weekend. I have to keep up with my classes, and I'll always have papers to correct."

"Won't you have grad students to help you? We have a busy couple of months ahead of us: you starting school, my new exhibit, the wedding in October, Rick with us for Thanksgiving, and then on to Minneapolis for Christmas with your parents. We'll need time for ourselves."

"Don't forget my conference in Chicago in December. I'm delivering a paper and on a panel."

"Angela's birthday is December 8. Will you be there? It will be your first one."

"I'll try. That's a Thursday, and I'm on a panel that day. I'll see if I could switch to another panel."

"Angela will be disappointed if you're not there."

"I'll do what I can."

"Please don't miss it."

"I'll try, like I said."

"I'm counting on you, honey. Better turn out the light. We need to get some sleep. We've got a long day tomorrow in Milan."

They fluffed up their pillows and nestled into the covers. She put her arm around him.

Cole said, "I wish we were going right to Paris instead of taking the extra day in Milan."

"Don't worry. The day will go fast. We'll be back on the train in twenty-four hours. Paris will be fun, seeing Sarah and Bill and eating at great restaurants."

"I'm thinking more of all that's going on as soon as we get home."

"Yes . . . home," she said, her voice fading. "I wish . . ."

"What do you wish?"

She sighed. "I don't know . . . I wish these two weeks could go on forever. I hate to leave."

"But we have to. We both have busy jobs waiting for us."

"I know, I know. Angela starts school on Tuesday, just five days from now. It makes me want to hide under my pillow. I just feel so good here; I wish we could stay forever."

CHAPTER EIGHT

DAY TWO

"This has been the best summer in years," Harriet said, her voice quivering as she looked around at her family in the villa library the next morning. She sat in a sofa chair, a shawl over her legs, wearing a white silk blouse and an antique Italian broach, a gift from Paolo for their thirtieth wedding anniversary.

Harriet stammered and looked up at Paolo, unable to continue. He put his hand on her shoulder and said, "Mom doesn't like long good-byes, but she wanted to say a special thanks for making this summer a very happy one for us."

Harriet took a deep breath and tried again. "I'm not one for . . . long speeches. . . . We can't have two long-winded people in the family, can we, Paolo?"

He smiled and patted her shoulder.

"What Mother means to say is that it was a special time because we had our little angel with us all month."

"Thank you, Nonna. I love you. I want to come every summer and be with you," Angela said.

"You can, sweetheart. If this old *nonna* can have a few more years with you, I'd be so happy."

Sylvia said, "Of course you will, Mom. You don't want to miss her teen years, coming soon. Won't they be fun?"

Harriet's eyes widened and she made a mock look of shock. "Oh, yes. I remember your teen years—a stream of boyfriends coming to our apartment, all the parties, dances, and balls. And you needed a new outfit for each one. My, you certainly liked expensive clothes."

"I still do, Mom."

"I know, honey. I was teasing. You just grew up too fast. But that's the way it is these days."

They said their farewells to Harriet, bending over to kiss her cheeks. Then it was into the foyer and outside, down the marble steps in the bright August sun. Paolo's black Mercedes was parked in the circular driveway, the trunk packed with luggage.

Paolo's garden was in full bloom, with colorful petunias, geraniums, irises, lavender, and lantana around a fountain with a statue of a nymph on a plinth. Around the perimeter, purple, white, and pink bougainvillea grew on lattices up the walls.

"It's sure going to be quiet around here," Paolo said, driving through the gate onto Via Sonenga.

"Don't worry, Dad. Next year will pass quickly," Sylvia said. "You'll retire, and you can come back anytime you want."

"You know, I'm looking forward to that day," Paolo responded. "The firm will have a farewell dinner, there will be a lot of speeches full of hot air, and they'll give me a plaque."

"You'll love every minute of it, Dad. It will be a memorable evening for all of us."

"It's time to let the young bulls take over so this old one can head out to pasture. Here is where I want to spend retirement . . . mornings in the garden, walking into town in the afternoon, and buying Angela gelato every day."

"Hooray! Gelato every day!" Angela said.

"You have a lovely villa, Paolo," Cole said. "Like living in a palace."

"I'm glad you came, Cole. You're always welcome. Just take good care of my girls. That's all I ask."

The bright August sun was blazing down on Lake Como as they drove into Menaggio. Across Lake Como, ferries were sailing from Bellagio and Varenna to Menaggio and Tremezzo. Menaggio's narrow streets were packed with late-season tourists in shorts, sundresses, hats, sandals, and stylish sunglasses, shopping and sipping cappuccinos at cafés along the embankment.

Via Lusardi was, as usual, clogged with buses, motorbikes, and cars creeping through town. Paolo eased into traffic and drove the few blocks to the regional bus terminal. He parked across the street at the Catholic cemetery and memorial park, dedicated to fallen Italian soldiers from World War I and World War II.

Paolo reached into the backseat for a vase of flowers he and Angela had picked that morning from his garden. They got out of the car and walked into the cemetery under a stone arch, passing statues of Mary holding the baby Jesus and saints Peter and Paul.

Paolo turned to Cole. "This is our family tradition. Our last day in Menaggio, we visit the cemetery where our ancestors are buried. My father took me here every summer when I was young. It's a wonderful memory."

The cemetery's walls were lined with marble crypts and gravestones engraved with family names dating back to the nineteenth century. Vases of plastic flowers, dried floral arrangements, and red votive candles with battery-powered lights had been placed at many of the crypts and gravestones.

Fallen twigs, dust, bird droppings, and debris littered the grounds, showing the effects of years of neglect and weather exposure. Photos of the deceased, encased in faded plastic sleeves on grave sites, were cracked, torn, and dusty.

Paolo and Angela walked along the crypts, reading the names of the deceased with birth and death dates. On large gravestones were life-sized statues of Jesus kneeling in prayer and Mary in somber repose, her face turned toward heaven.

Near the corner, they reached a gray marble crypt with *de Matteo* engraved in faded gold lettering. Paolo ran his fingers down the names of his deceased ancestors and stopped at Angela de Matteo, 1914–1976.

"She was your namesake, your great-grandmother, your *bisnonna*. She made me homemade pasta and cookies every summer I came."

Paolo and Angela placed the flower vase on the gravestone. She fluffed the blossoms and stepped back, clasping her hands in front of her.

"Let's get a picture," Paolo said. He moved aside to let Angela and Sylvia stand beside him. Cole took Sylvia's camera and took pictures of them with arms around each other, maneuvering to get the de Matteo name in the photos.

When he was finished, Paolo turned, made the sign of the cross, and bowed in silent prayer. After a few seconds, he turned around and said, "Now . . . it's almost time to get on your bus."

Sylvia and Cole followed Paolo and Angela back to the parking lot, walking hand in hand. In the parking lot, Paolo said, "Angela and I have one last treat before you go."

Angela's face lit up. "Yeah, we're going for gelato!"

Cole and Sylvia sat on benches in the memorial garden. Cole reached into his carry-on bag for a newspaper, and Sylvia got up to walk around the obelisk to read the names of Italian war dead.

Ten minutes later, Paolo and Angela returned, Angela licking a waffle cone. "Mom, this pistachio is so good! I'm going to miss it."

"Don't worry. We can get gelato at our favorite Italian restaurant on the west side."

"But it's not as good as this, is it, Nonno?"

Paolo patted her head. "Menaggio has the best gelato in the world."

Paolo went back to the car and returned with a present wrapped in red paper. "A little something for your trip," he said, handing it to Angela.

She tore off the wrapping paper. "Wow! Another *Harry Potter*! Mom, look what Nonno gave me. I can read it on the train!"

"Another book?" Sylvia said, rolling her eyes. "How many books did he buy you this summer?"

"It's *Deathly Hallows*! We finished *Half-Blood Prince* while you were gone."

"You'll have to tell me about it soon when we see you back in New York," Paolo said, leaning down to hug her.

"Thanks again for everything, Dad," Sylvia said, wrapping her arms around both of them.

"Travel safely. I love my Angela," he said, his eyes tearing.

"I love you too, Nonno."

"I love it when she calls me Nonno," he said, wiping a tear from his cheek.

"That's why she does it, Dad," Sylvia said as they exchanged kisses.

Cole shook Paolo's hand. "Thanks for sharing your home with us."

They wheeled their luggage across the road, where the southbound C-10 bus was waiting. Passengers stood in the shade of plane trees. Men and boys were smoking cigarettes. Women were saying good-bye to friends and family. Two blue and yellow IRTA buses were idling, the southbound C-10 to Como and the northbound C-10 to Colico.

When they boarded, they blew kisses to Paolo across the parking lot. The bus driver pushed a button, the door wheezed shut, and the bus eased out of the terminal, leaving a cloud of diesel fumes in its wake.

Their bus crept south on Via Lusardi to the ferry terminal, where traffic began to ease. Angela waved. "Good-bye, ferries. I'll come back next year."

Sylvia patted her arm. "Yes, you will, dear. We'll be back."

"This is my favorite place in the whole world."

When the bus reached the Menaggio limits, it accelerated on a two-lane highway between Como and elegant hillside villas behind iron gates with gardens and tall trees.

In minutes, they passed through Tremezzo and Villa Carlotta's formal gardens of camellia, azaleas, and rhododendron and a bamboo grove. Angela looked out the window as a ferry from Bellagio docked at the Tremezzo pier.

"Nonno and I took that ferry, Mom. I'm going to miss him. Mom, is Nonna going to be okay? She didn't look . . . you know . . . happy. I think her disease is getting worse."

"MS is a terrible disease. It makes people so frail they can barely walk."

"I wish she could play with me like she used to. But she was tired, so Nonno and I went out by ourselves."

As they passed through Mezzegra, the highway narrowed to one lane between apartments, garages, and shops. Traffic stalled as single lines of vehicles maneuvered and women carrying shopping bags, men talking on cell phones, and teenagers weaved between them. Bus drivers honked horns, glaring through tinted windows at impatient car drivers who made hand gestures before backing into driveways to let buses, cars, farting scooters, and roaring motorcycles pass through.

"Mom, look at those people walking around our bus. Someone could get hurt!"

"Happens every day. Traffic jams along Como are as much a part of life as drinking cappuccino in the morning."

Pillowy clouds hung over the mountains across Como, shading villages and hillside villas. Ferries carved gentle Vs through blue waters, docking at villages to drop off and pick up passengers. It took almost an hour to pass through the lakeside villages of Argegno, Moltrasio, and Cernobbio until they reached the town of Como on the southern shore.

The bus navigated around traffic circles and climbed a hill to the San Giovanni train station. Cole led them off the bus, all of them wheeling luggage into the station. He looked up at the monitor. "Our train's on track number two. Let's get aboard."

"Angela, you're going to love Milan," Sylvia said. "It's an exciting city—fabulous museums, the Duomo, La Scala Opera House, and great shopping."

"I can't wait!"

"How would you like a new pair of ballet slippers when you start lessons next week?"

"Oh, wow, that would be terrific!"

"I know a shop near La Scala. They're expensive, but you'll impress everyone when you show up for class."

CHAPTER NINE

DAY THREE

Sylvia, Cole, and Angela arrived at Milan's Stazione Centrale at four o'clock in the afternoon. They took a taxi to their hotel, near Sempione Park. Sylvia and Angela went shopping along Via Dante. Cole stayed in the hotel room, working on his laptop to prepare for classes the following week.

The three of them had dinner at an outdoor restaurant at Piazza Sempione with a view of the Arco della Pace monument, which was splendidly illuminated by floodlights shining on the white Corinthian columns, the marble arch with Latin inscription, and the statues of horses and warriors on top. Sylvia told Angela that both the wide boulevard Corso and the Arch of Peace were projects begun by Napoleon to imitate Paris's Champs-Élysées and Arc de Triomphe when his army occupied Milan in 1807.

The next morning, the three of them had an early breakfast at their hotel followed by a walk through Sempione Park to the Castello

Sforzesco and then to Via Dante and the Duomo. They spent a half hour walking through the Duomo, viewing the stained glass windows and the paintings hanging along both sides of the narthex.

Sylvia bought Angela a pair of expensive Italian shoes at one of the designer shops in the Vittorio Emanuele arcade, across from the Duomo. After a tour through the La Scala museum, they had their last lunch in Italy at an outdoor restaurant on Via Dante. They splurged on a quattro formaggi pizza, an order of spaghetti con le vongole, risotto Milanese, and an *insalata mista*. Cole and Sylvia shared a half bottle of prosecco, and Angela had her favorite, lemon soda. Dessert was pistachio gelato for Angela, tiramisu for Sylvia, and bowl of fresh fruit for Cole.

They returned to their hotel for their luggage and took a taxi back to Stazione Centrale for their train to Paris. But traffic was heavy around the station, and they arrived only forty minutes before departure.

They carried their luggage and shopping bags through the portico into the main station and up the marble stairway decorated with art deco lamps to the cavernous lobby with high cathedral ceilings. The three of them stopped to catch their breath, standing their luggage upright and rearranging shopping bags.

"Mom, this place is really busy!" Angela said, rubbing her forearms where creases had pressed into her flesh from shopping bags of shoes and gifts for her school chums.

Cole scanned the overhead monitor of yellow lights updating arrival and departure times, platforms, and train numbers for Rome, Genoa, Turin, Venice, Bologna, Naples, Paris, Zurich, Frankfort, and regional cities around Lombardy. The enormous reception lounge was cacophonous with the noise of hundreds of commuters and travelers pushing luggage carts and dragging wheeled luggage through crowds, the screeching of trains entering and arriving on the platforms, and monotone announcements over the station loudspeaker.

"We'd better hurry!" Cole shouted over the din. "We only have a half hour before departure."

CHAPTER TEN

S ylvia, Angela and Cole clustered in a small island in Stazione
   Centrale's turbulent ocean of humanity as tourists, businessmen, families, and immigrants babbling in foreign tongues scurried
from the station into the lobby, meshing with travelers on their way to
departing trains.

Seated in hard plastic chairs in the lobby, travelers scanned the
monitor, counting minutes or hours until departure. Around their feet
were suitcases, backpacks, boxes, sacks, shopping bags, purses, pet containers, and squirming children. The monotonous drone of loudspeaker
announcements was interrupted by the whaa-whaa-whaaing of babies
crying from wet diapers, empty stomachs, or too little sleep. Travelers
clogged the escalators that descended to the first floor, heading for the
fast-food restaurants, the restrooms, and the taxi, bus, and metro stations outside Stazione Centrale.

Polizia Ferroviaria (Polfer) officers roamed through crowds in navy
short-sleeved uniform shirts, black-brimmed caps, gray slacks, and
polished black shoes. Around the waist, each one carried an arsenal of

hardware on a white leather belt: a holstered 9-millimeter Glock machine pistol, flashlight, keychain, handcuffs, radio, nightstick, and pepper spray.

Wiry Italian men in soccer jerseys and running shoes idled by designer windows, scanning the flow for wallet-bulging pockets and dangling purses ripe for plucking. Ebony-skinned Africans of questionable immigrant status hawked colored trinkets, wristbands, scarves, and sunglasses, melting away when Polfers strolled past.

The clash of human babbling and mechanical noise ricocheted off the marble walls and the metal and glass roof arching over the platforms, where sleek, bullet-nosed Eurostar and Trenitalia locomotives rumbled in their steel stalls.

"Wait, wait, wait," Sylvia said, raising her hands in protest. "I want to get some pictures in the lobby. Look at the bas-reliefs and murals on the walls. They're classic fascist style from Mussolini's time."

The events of the next few moments and the memories of their last minute together in Stazione Centrale were to be replayed in the days and weeks ahead.

"Come on, Sylvia," Cole said, his voice rising over the station clamor. "We don't have time. You're not on a photo shoot. We're catching a train for Paris."

"I've been here before, but I was always rushing through. I want photos of the artwork. I don't have any fascist art for my book."

"No time for pictures. Let's go," Cole said, heading toward the platform.

"Just give me ten minutes, Cole. That's all I need."

"No! Come. With. Us. We're getting on the train. Don't be foolish."

Her face reddened. "I'm not being foolish! I just want photos."

"Sylvia, please" he said, rolling his eyes and looking away in frustration. "You have tons of photos already. We're not in a museum. This is a train station!"

"Don't be angry."

"It's risky. We're on a schedule."

"I only want ten minutes. What's risky about that? We have more than twenty minutes before the train leaves."

Cole knew it was useless arguing with Sylvia when her mind was made up. He sighed and looked down at Angela standing between them, one hand on her luggage handle, the other holding shopping bags. "Go, then," he said. "It better be worth it."

"Don't be so controlling. I know what I'm doing."

"I'm not controlling! I'm being an adult. We have a train to catch and a child with us."

"Don't make that face," Sylvia said, scowling. "I hate it when you don't look at me when you're talking."

He looked at her, his face tense with anger. "Then go. Get it out of your system. I'll take Angela. What about your luggage?"

"Angela, I'm putting my purse on your luggage handles. I'll trade for your shopping bags." She hung her purse on the handles of Angela's luggage and took her shopping bags.

"Mommy, please, let's get on the train," Angela said, an anxious look on her face.

"Honey, go with Cole. I'll see you in ten minutes. Promise."

"Mommy, come with us."

"Don't worry. I'll be on the train before you know it." She leaned down to kiss Angela's head. "See you soon, dear."

"Italian trains leave on time," Cole warned.

"Don't worry! I'll be fine. See you!" She turned away, unzipped her camera bag, and took out her camera.

Cole exhaled a breath he'd been holding and reached for his luggage handle. "Come, Angela, let's get on our train."

"Are you okay, Cole?" she asked as they wheeled their luggage into the station. "You're upset. I know you are."

"Don't worry. Your mom gets strange ideas in her head sometimes. No use arguing."

"I know. Thanks for taking me to the train."

A hollow voice droned in a monotone over loudspeakers: *"Il treno Eurocity di Trenitalia proveniente da Venezia Mestre delle ore sedici e quindici è in arrivo al binario 7. Allontanarsi dalla linea gialla."*

Sylvia adjusted her camera bag over one shoulder and her camera strap over the other, rearranged the shopping bags, and began weaving through the crowd, gazing up at the friezes, cornices, and bas-relief on the lobby's walls: busts of helmeted Roman soldiers, shields, swords, crests, and tiled murals portraying medieval cities, villas, and castles.

Sylvia focused on a mural above a marble staircase of a medieval noble wearing a peaked hat astride a horse with a blanket over its flanks and a castle in the background. *Gorgeous texture,* she thought, adjusting the focus to get close-ups and wide-angle photos. The colors were faded, but she would be able to enhance them with software back in her New York studio.

Sylvia stood at the top of the marble staircase and studied the art deco lamps in glass and metal frames on the walls. She loved art deco. She snapped photos, moving down a step at a time. Halfway down the stairs, she lowered her camera and surveyed the layout of the ground floor: stone obelisks, art deco lamps, marble friezes of lions, and zodiac symbols on the walls.

She shot more photos, panning left to right until she focused on tall glass doors at the main entrance. Three people carrying shoulder bags and wearing jeans, dark T-shirts, black cloth caps, and wraparound sunglasses came through the doors, walking abreast and heading toward the staircase. Sylvia refocused and followed them as they mounted the marble steps, with blank faces like fashion models on a runway.

The stockiest was on the left; a tall, thin one in the middle; and the tallest on the right. They ascended the marble staircase like urban guerrillas marching in formation, purposeful and direct. Priceless.

They were twenty feet away when the stocky one looked up as Sylvia snapped her last photo. She turned around and climbed the staircase, excited by the spontaneous shots. She loved capturing dramatic moments in the rush of a busy city setting. The photos would be perfect for her new book, *Italia Ieri, Italia Oggi, Italia Domani,* scheduled for publication the following spring.

Sylvia made her way through the crowd toward the other end of the lobby, glancing up at the monitor. Three more minutes and she'd dash for the train. She raised her camera and shot photos of art deco chandeliers hanging from the vaulted ceiling.

When the three in black wraparound sunglasses reached the top of the staircase, the stocky one grabbed the other two, and there was a hurried exchange of whispered words. The stocky one pointed at Sylvia, who was disappearing into the crowd. He clenched a fist, poked the others in the chest, and fanned his fingers in a gesture toward the station. He clenched his fist again, slapped his chest, and spit out, *"Vai! Subito!"* [Go! Now!]

They separated, the other two hurrying into the terminal while the stocky one rushed toward the area in the crowd where Sylvia had disappeared. He weaved around travelers like a soccer striker racing to shoot at a goal, dodging families pushing carts and dragging wheeled luggage, idlers staring up at the monitor, and lovers embracing before departure. His head swiveled left and right, searching for a glimpse of a woman with black curly hair and a trim figure carrying shopping bags, with a camera and camera bag slung over her shoulder.

"Il treno Intercity di Trenitalia per Ventimiglia delle ore sedici e venti è in partenza dal binario 18. Ferma a Pavia, Tortona, Genova Piazza Principe, Savona, Alassio, Imperia, San Remo, Bordighera. La prima classe è in testa al treno."

The man darted left and right through the crowds, dodging side to side until he spotted Sylvia about fifteen meters ahead, taking photos of the cavernous lobby ceiling. In seconds, he was behind her, maneuvering to grab her camera and pull it over her head.

"Il treno Alta Velocità di Trenitalia delle ore sedici e ventisette proveniente da Roma Termini è in arrivo al binario sette. Allontanarsi dalla linea gialla."

Just then, two Polfers strolled alongside Sylvia and stopped behind her. They looked her over, scanning her attractive figure, expensive shorts and blouse, tanned legs, and stylish hair. They smiled at each other, glanced around a moment or two to show they were on duty, and then once more scanned Sylvia from top to bottom.

"*Il treno Regionale di Trenitalia per Cremona delle ore sedici e diciotto è in partenza dal binario 20. Ferma a Milano Rogoredo, Lodi, Casalpusterlengo, Codogno, Pizzighettone. Il treno effettua solo servizio di seconda classe.*"

In the station, the two in wraparound sunglasses waited between a sunglasses kiosk and a Carpisa store window. Passengers were exiting from the Eurostar train from Rome that had arrived moments earlier on track number seven. As the Rome passengers wheeled luggage and carts toward the station, the two in wraparound sunglasses broke from their vantage point and started walking into their stream.

A quarter of the way down the platform, they spotted three men in business suits carrying briefcases coming toward them. In unison, the two whisked off their wraparound sunglasses, stuffed them into their shoulder bags, and pulled their caps down into ski masks over their faces. They took out Glock pistols.

Fifty feet away, an alert Polfer officer spotted them as they pulled down their ski masks. He grabbed the radio off his white leather belt and barked: "*Attenzione, vedo due soggetti sospetti con passamontagna al binario sette. Mi dirigo verso di loro. Chiedo rinforzi.*"

The officer started weaving through the arriving passengers toward the two men in ski masks.

"*Annuncio ritardo. Il treno Frecciabianca di Trenitalia proveniente da Livorno delle ore sedici e trentadue viaggia con venti minuti di ritardo. Ci scusiamo per il disagio.*"

CHAPTER ELEVEN

Cole looked at his watch. Eight minutes until departure. He sighed, growing restless and angrier. He disliked when Sylvia made impulsive decisions that inconvenienced others, especially Angela. When Sylvia was on a mission, she was deaf to reasoning.

They had argued more than once about her impulsive behavior, but she had held firm: "I'm an artist. Artists respond to intuition and spontaneity, not logic. You're logical—sometimes too logical. See it from my standpoint. I'm visual; when I see something to photograph, I know how I'll get the lighting, angle, and correct focus. That's who I am."

Angela looked up from her *Harry Potter* book and said, "When's Mom coming, Cole?"

Seven minutes until departure. He took a deep breath and looked out the window as late arriving passengers were hurrying down the platform. A conductor on the platform blew a whistle and motioned for passengers to get on board.

"Come on. You're cutting this close," Cole muttered.

"What'd you say, Cole?"

"Nothing, dear. Just talking to myself."

Six minutes. No sight of Sylvia. In the distance, a group of about twenty-five was hurrying down the platform, wheeling luggage and pushing baggage carts. Cole prayed Sylvia was with them.

He sat back down and looked at his watch.

"Is everything okay, Cole? Is Mom coming?"

"I'm sure she is. There's a group headed down the platform. She's probably with them and will get on in a minute or two."

"I like my book. It's really good."

"Good. Read as much as you like. We have five hours before we get to Paris."

"I like trains. They're more fun than flying. Lines at the airport are so long, you always have to wait, and the seats are so uncomfortable."

"That's why we're taking the train. It takes longer, but you get to see the countryside. Italy and France are beautiful to travel through."

Angela went back to her reading. Cole's stomach was churning with the stress of waiting and not knowing where Sylvia was. *Damn, why did she do this?* He'd certainly let her know the effect of her rash decision. Not in front of Angela, of course, but when they were alone, he'd tell her all the reasons her decision was foolish and risky. He hated foolishness and risky behavior; that was who *he* was.

* * * * *

Bang! Bang! Bang!

Three gunshots exploded in the station, ricocheting off the metal and glass ceiling and across the platforms into the lobby. Sylvia jumped, startled by the explosive boom reverberating against the lobby's marble walls and ceiling. The Polfer officers behind her bolted and dashed toward the platforms, unholstering their Glock pistols.

Sylvia looked at the monitor: six minutes to departure. The gunshots scared her; it was time to get on the train. She started to put her camera in the bag when an arm reached around her throat and another grabbed her camera.

Sylvia choked and couldn't breathe. After a second or two, as she struggled to twist away, she felt dizzy and fell backward, losing her balance. The fingers clutching her throat relaxed and grabbed the camera pressed hard against her ribs and chest. Both hands tried to pull it over her head, but her hands still clutched it close.

When Sylvia caught her breath, she gagged and then uttered a weak scream. *"Ai . . . ai . . . aiuto! Aiuto!"* [Help!]

But it was bedlam in the lobby. People were ducking under plastic seats, running down escalators, bumping into each other, knocking over mothers and children, screaming, and running for exits. Sylvia and her attacker were just two more people thrashing in some kind of physical drama that no one else cared about.

Strong arms pulled Sylvia closer and tugged the camera over her breasts. The pain of hard metal against her breasts was excruciating. She tried to scream again, but she only gagged, and spit dribbled from her mouth.

She tried to push the camera away from her breasts, but the gripping fingers were firm and ground the camera deeper. *Oh, the pain!* She thought she was going to faint, but she managed to push the camera to one side. One hand released the camera and slapped her neck. More sharp pain. She reached up and scratched the back of the hand, digging her fingernails into flesh.

"Aaah!" she heard a scream in one ear and felt hot breath on the back of her neck.

The hand jerked away and slapped Sylvia's cheek with force. She felt a hard object like a ring hit her teeth. Another slap, this time striking her lips and front teeth. The sting was like a dentist's drill hitting a nerve without novocaine.

The pains in her cheek, teeth, neck, breasts, and chest weakened her, and she sagged backward, almost toppling over her attacker. Her fingers were still tangled in the camera straps while strong hands tried to wrestle them across her breasts and over her head.

"*Aiuto! Aiuto!*" she screamed. But her cries were drowned out by the noise of people running from the station. Two more gunshots exploded in the station. Bang! Bang!

Sylvia sagged to the floor, the straps of camera bag, camera, and shopping bags entwined around her forearms as forceful hands tugged on the camera. She rolled when she hit the floor, the camera pressed hard against her chest.

Around her feet, wrapped gifts from shopping bags were strewn across the floor. Crowds running through the lobby trampled them, crushing gift boxes and tearing wrapping paper.

Sylvia felt a knee press deep in her side and hands fumble for the camera under her. She kicked; one sandal grazed her attacker's shins and knees, and fell off. A hand slapped her face, and she put up an elbow to shield the blows.

"*Aiuto! Aiuto!*" she screamed, but the crowd ignored her, running to exits. A fist pulled her hair, jerking back her head and twisting her neck. The man hitting her was wearing a ski mask! She screamed but still clutched her camera to her chest.

Stazione Centrale was bedlam. Travelers screamed as they ran like cattle spooked by thunder and lightning. People dropped luggage, bags, and boxes, which tripped other travelers who fell over them or tried to kick them away. A few people glanced at Sylvia pinned to the floor by a man in a black ski mask, but no one stopped to help as panic swept through the station.

There were no heroes or good Samaritans in Stazione Centrale on that hot, muggy August afternoon. It was every man, woman, child, youth, senior citizen, Italian, Swiss, German, French, or American only for themselves.

The two other men in black ski masks ran from the station into the lobby, scanning the screaming crowds, searching for Sylvia's attacker. Back on platform number seven, two bodies in business suits were sprawled on the floor, blood oozing onto the stone.

Sylvia's attacker spotted the men under the monitor, crouched, pistols sweeping around the crowd, their eyes searching for him. Strong arms grabbed Sylvia off the floor and dragged her toward the monitor. As her assailant got closer to it, he hoisted her up, her back pressed against his chest, and scooted both of them toward the staircase.

The three in black ski masks were together again, two of them sweeping their weapons around the panicked crowd as Sylvia's attacker held her as a shield, one arm across her chest, the other pointing his weapon at her head as he dragged her down the staircase. Sylvia's arms were pinned against her chest and entangled with camera straps. Her ankles and heels slammed against the marble steps as she struggled and tried to scream. But her assailant held her so tightly she could barely breathe.

Stunned onlookers on the staircase pressed flat against the walls as the three ran down the steps, yelling at everyone to stand back and sweeping their weapons at the terrified crowd.

Three Polfer guards raced through the lobby and stopped at the marble staircase. They raised their weapons and aimed at the three men and Sylvia, who were on the ground floor moving backward in single file toward the entrance.

One Polfer officer fired two shots, making a deafening noise in the marble staircase. Bullets struck the floor inches from Sylvia's feet, shooting pieces of marble into the air. The tallest man aimed and fired back. The Polfer officer buckled, grasping his chest where a red spot bloomed. His knees hit the floor and his weapon dropped, clattering down the staircase like a falling stone.

CHAPTER TWELVE

Two minutes.

Cole stared at his watch. *She's not going to make it! Why did she do this?* He was furious that Sylvia had risked missing the train to take a couple of damn photos. *How foolish.*

"Where's Mom, Cole?" Angela asked, her lips quivering. "She should be here by now. The train is leaving soon." She nervously kicked her heels against her seat.

Cole stood up. "I'm going to find her. She probably got aboard with that last group. I'll find her and bring her back."

"I want Mom. I want her to read my book with me."

"Keep reading. You can call Nonno and thank him again. He'd like that." Cole rustled her hair and hurried down the aisle. Every seat in their first class car was full, and passengers were relaxing, reading, or chatting with seatmates. *Damn it, how can they be so relaxed when I'm terrified my fiancée is not on our train?*

Cole exited the passenger area and climbed down the steps, holding the railing. In the distance, crowds were rushing from the station into the lobby, bumping and pushing each other like people leaving a burning building. *What the hell was going on?*

Near the front of the train, Cole caught a glimpse of a woman climbing the steps wearing shorts and a blouse like Sylvia's. His heart sank when he saw that she had a purse in one hand and a carry-on bag in the other.

Damn, that's not Sylvia! Her luggage and purse are aboard with us.

"*Signore, salga immediatamente,*" the conductor beside him said. "*Il trano sta per partire.*" [Sir, you have to get aboard; the train is departing.]

"My fiancée . . . I don't see her!"

"*Senta, partiamo fra un minuto. Deve salire sul treno.*" [We're leaving in a minute. You have to board the train.]

"Sylvia!" Cole yelled. "Get on the train!" He felt like a fool, yelling like a worried child at the empty platform. A uniformed guard ran past and disappeared from view. The train whistle blew two short bursts.

The conductor touched Cole's arm. "*Signore, siamo in partenza.*" [Sir, we're leaving.]

Cole climbed the steps, confused by the deserted part of the station that he could see. And the running policeman—*what was going on?*

The conductor pulled up the stairs and closed and locked the door. Cole remained in the foyer as the train jostled and pulled away from the station.

* * * * *

A Polfer officer had run halfway down the marble staircase, his automatic weapon raised. He fired a short burst over the heads of the three ski-masked men and Sylvia, shattering the glass door. Glass fragments flew across the ground floor. The crowd screamed at the gunfire as Sylvia was dragged through the door.

The shoes of the fleeing trio in black ski masks crunched over shattered glass as they ran outside into the sunlight toward a white van parked at the curb with the back doors open.

"Let me go! Let me go!" Sylvia screamed, struggling to escape from the arm across her chest.

Her captor dragged her toward the back of the van. The tall man jumped in the front seat. Sylvia's captor pushed her through the open back doors onto the floor of the van, jumped in, and pulled the doors shut.

One yelled, *"Mettile il passamontagna!"* [Put the ski mask on her!]

Sylvia screamed, *"Lasciami andare!"* [Let me go!]

"Fai tacere quella puttana!" [Shut that bitch up!] the woman ordered.

A pistol butt slammed against the back of Sylvia's head, and she blacked out as the van sped out of Stazione Centrale's parking lot.

CHAPTER THIRTEEN

The Eurostar train to Paris glided out of the station like a log floating down a river. The train picked up speed as it left the terminal
and went through the rail yard, steel wheels clicking over the tracks
like shuffling cards.

Cole was standing between train compartments when he saw three
approaching trains slow and stop before entering the terminal. He was
curious about why they were stopped as his train accelerated past them.

The rail yard was a network of many tracks, switching lines, cement
towers, and posts with metal branches strung with cables and electrical
lines. Piles of broken bricks, tiles, and concrete lay in mounds beside
the tracks amid plastic bottles, torn newspapers, twigs, dried leaves,
weeds, and pigeon carcasses. Concrete barricades enclosed the rail yard
like prison walls. Alongside the tracks, old-generation Trenitalia trains
were abandoned and rusting like relics from an earlier age.

As the train sped through the rail yard, Cole heard the distant
wailing of sirens coming closer: *Wheeeooo . . . wheeeooo . . . wheeeooo . . .
wheeeooo . . .* The sirens faded as the train was shunted from the main rail

yard to one of the many arteries of tracks that extended like tentacles of a metal octopus, heading west, east, south, and north to regional cities and international destinations.

Cole started back to his car, nervous about what he was going to tell Angela. *Where was her mom? What if she hadn't gotten on the train? Had she been swept up in the crowds running in panic?*

He opened the sliding glass door and started down the aisle. Angela was on her knees, looking back over her seat. As he approached her, she blurted out, "Did you see Mom?"

Cole sat down next to her, trying to appear calm. "N-no, I didn't, sweetheart," he stammered. "She's probably making her way back to our car."

Angela whimpered, her face a mask of fear. "Where is she? Go find her, please." She was hyperventilating, her chest rapidly expanding and contracting.

"Our car is several back from the front of the train, where she probably got on at the last moment." Cole cringed, disappointed at how unconvincing he sounded. Angela saw through his feigned attempt at appearing calm.

"Mom knows where we are! I know she does. I want to go back and find her."

"No, stay here."

"Cole, I want to go."

"Sit. Stay. We'll wait here."

"I don't want to!"

"Yes. We'll wait."

Angela sat down, upset and frustrated. She kicked her heels against the seat, staring out the window, tears coming to her eyes.

"Find Mom, Cole. Bring her back."

"Stay here, Angela. I'll get a conductor."

"Bring her back, please," she said, her voice cracking.

A train speeding toward Stazione Centrale on the neighboring track passed alongside with a hurricanelike *whoosh,* causing their train to vibrate. The sudden noise startled Angela. "Aaahh! Oh, oh, oh!"

The train whipped past in a few seconds, leaving dust and dried leaves swirling along the tracks.

"That scared me," she said, shaking.

"Don't worry, honey. That was just a train headed toward the station."

"Find Mom."

Cole got up and hurried down the aisle, exiting their car and entering the dining car, where passengers seated at cramped tables were scanning menus. Uniformed waiters were delivering water, beer, and wine.

No conductor in the dining car. Cole proceeded down the aisle, steadying himself against the rocking of the train by touching the tabletops. He exited the dining car and entered the next car, which was filled with students, tourists, and families. Noisy children were running up and down the aisle, bumping passengers' arms and luggage. Cole moved aside and let them run past. The passengers looked calm and relaxed; Cole wondered if they realized that something had happened back at the station.

Again, no conductor in the car. He entered the next compartment and was relieved to see a conductor checking tickets. He hurried down the aisle. "Excuse me. Do you speak English?"

"Un pochino," the conductor said, holding up a thumb and forefinger to show a small space.

"My fiancée . . . I don't think she made it onto the train."

The conductor looked puzzled. "She is on the train?"

"I don't know."

"Why she is not on train?"

"She was taking photos in the station. She was going to join us. I didn't see her get on."

"Scusi . . . no understand," the conductor said. He pointed toward end of the car. "Is conductor . . . back train more. Speak English."

Cole maneuvered around him and walked down the aisle, opening the doors to a cramped area with stacked luggage and two restrooms marked *WC.* In desperation, he knocked on one. "Sylvia, are you in there?"

An irritated female voice answered, *"Occupato!"*

Stupid! he said to himself. He opened the sliding door into a second-class car and moved down the narrow aisle, looking into glass-enclosed compartments with three seats on each side. Every seat was occupied. High summer season, last weekend in August.

In the last compartment, a conductor was doing paperwork, with a cell phone, timetable, and seating charts on the table. Cole rapped on the glass, and the conductor slid open the door.

"Do you speak English?"

"Yes, a little."

"I'm worried. My fiancée isn't on the train. She stayed in the station when we boarded, and I don't think she got on."

The conductor frowned. "I don't understand. Why didn't she get on?"

"It's a long story. She's a photographer, and she wanted to get photos at the station. Can you call the station and see if she's there? Her name is Sylvia de Matteo."

"Sir, there was a problem at the station as we left. Some kind of emergency."

"What kind of emergency?"

"I don't know. I heard a message as we were leaving Stazione Centrale. Let me inquire if your fiancée is there."

"Sylvia de Matteo's her name," Cole repeated.

The conductor punched a number on his cell phone and began speaking rapidly. Cole wished he could understand what the man was saying, but the only Italian phrases he knew were perfunctory: *prego, buongiorno, buonasera,* and *grazie.* Sylvia was fluent in Italian, and she had done all the conversing on their vacation.

The conductor mentioned Sylvia's name twice and Cole waited anxiously for a positive response. Nothing. The conductor listened, nodding his head *"Sì . . . sì . . . sì . . . sì."*

The conversation went on for what seemed like several minutes, the conductor's eyes darting left to right, his lips pressed tight. He nodded several times, avoided looking up at Cole, and then repeated, *"Certo . . . certo . . . certo,"* and signed off with, *"Capito. Grazie."*

The conductor put down the phone and looked up at Cole with a strained look on his face. "Sir, there was . . . an incident at the station as we left."

"What kind of incident?"

"A shooting."

"A shooting?" Cole said, not believing what he was hearing.

"Yes . . . police are there. It's an emergency. People were injured. The station has been blockaded so police can investigate. A government official was shot, plus two or three police."

"What about my fiancée? Did you learn anything?"

"I'm sorry, no. The incident is still going on. It's an emergency, and information is not complete. I told them her name. They will try to locate her."

"You're not telling me everything."

"Sir, where are you sitting? I will find out and come find you. Please return to your seat."

"My fiancée's daughter is there, and she's very worried. What shall I tell her?"

"Sir, I don't know. Just return to your seat, please."

Cole handed him his ticket, and the conductor wrote down the seat and car number.

Cole's imagination became a tornado of terrible scenarios; *had Sylvia been swept up in the chaos at the station? What kind of shooting? A terrorist attack? A robbery? Was she in danger? How could they get in touch? Where was her cell phone? Should he call Paolo?*

He walked unsteadily back to their car, his confusion upsetting his balance. He almost fell, but stuck out a hand to grab a door handle to one of the compartments.

As he steadied himself, his mind began to clear. He had to see if Sylvia left her phone in her purse or had it with her. If it was in her purse, he would call her and see if she was OK. Oh God, I hope she's safe!

He reached their compartment and looked over passengers' heads to where Angela was seated. What was he going to tell her? She was already upset, crying, and hyperventilating. He was afraid that she would be able to tell that he was worried, which would make her even more upset. He couldn't lie; Angela would see through it. He'd say that there had been an accident, but not a shooting. She'd be terrified. He'd calm her down and reassure her that they would all be together soon. But how? Where? When?

He slowly walked down the aisle, steadying himself as the train rocked gently from side to side.

Angela saw him from three seats away. "Where's Mom? Did you find her?"

"No, not yet. I'm sorry."

Her eyes were red with tears. "Cole . . . where is she? I want her here!" Angela's *Harry Potter* book was facedown on the seat across, on top of Sylvia's purse. Their seatmate, an elderly French gentleman, looked confused and apparently didn't speak English.

Cole sat next to Angela and took her hands. "I talked to the conductor. He called the station to find her, and he'll get back to us. There was an accident there, and some people didn't make it to their trains."

"What kind of accident?"

"I'm not sure."

"Tell me, Cole. Tell me. I want to know!" Angela pleaded.

He shook his head. "I really don't know."

"Can we get off the train and go back and find her?"

"No, we're not going to do anything until we find out more from the conductor."

Her little chest was moving in and out in panicked breathing. "Cole . . . I want Mom," she pleaded. "I want to go back. Please, let's go back." She kicked her heels against the seat until Cole put his hand on her knee.

"Angela, be calm. I know you're worried. We'll find your mom, and everything will be okay."

"Promise?" Tears were streaming down her cheeks.

He reached across to Sylvia's purse and dug for her cell phone. He found it. No calls had come in. He put it into his shirt pocket.

How could he get in touch with Sylvia to see if she was safe? His feeling of panic was paralyzing; he felt numb like his nerves had been cauterized. After a few seconds, he realized he had been holding his breath; he breathed in and out slowly, regaining some composure. He couldn't let Angela know how terrified he was.

Ten anxious minutes later, the conductor was standing in the aisle. "Sir, could I speak to you?"

Cole bolted from his seat. "Angela, I'll be right back. The conductor is going to help us find your mother."

Angela looked up, her eyes red from crying. "Okay," she said weakly, looking out the window, kicking her heels against the seat.

The conductor led Cole out between the cars and shut the sliding glass doors. It was noisy in the cramped area, with the clicking of wheels over the tracks beneath them.

"Sir, police blocked off the station. No one can get in or out. Your fiancée is probably there. It is a very serious incident. Police are investigating. Trains are being held back from entering or departing the station until the emergency is over."

"What about my fiancée? Did you ask about her?"

"I gave them her name. They will call when they locate her. The police are questioning witnesses. They are restoring order and get trains moving. Please be calm. I'm sure everything will turn out well."

CHAPTER FOURTEEN

Sylvia's head was throbbing as she started to regain consciousness. The back of her head felt like she'd been hit with a hammer. The terror of the last minutes in Centrale flashed through her mind—being grabbed, dragged, and thrown into the back of a van and smashed on the head.

She struggled to breathe; something was over her face, a cloth that smothered her breath when she exhaled through her nose. Something else was jammed into her mouth, making it difficult to swallow.

She moved her head, but it made the pain worse. She was lying on her side on a floor, knees tucked in a fetal position, something tied around her wrists in front of her. She opened her eyes but all she saw was a black mesh. She squirmed and made muffled noises through the cloth in her mouth.

"Falla respirare," [Let her breathe] someone said. A hand reached under the cloth, felt around her face, then lifted it above her mouth and nose. She snorted to take in air, her chest heaving to get oxygen into her lungs. God, she was so uncomfortable and in pain all over her body.

The vehicle was moving through traffic, slowing down, speeding up, turning a corner. She heard horns honking and traffic noise outside. Muffled voices were speaking Italian in tense outbursts. Although she spoke Italian, she couldn't understand everything they were saying.

She tried to wiggle to get more comfortable, but a knee was pressed into her side. Her chin was against the floor. Every part of her body ached—the back of her head, her neck, her face where she had been slapped, her arms from when she had been grabbed and dragged, her ankles and heels from slamming against the staircase. The pain was everywhere. She'd never hurt so much in her life; it was like she'd fallen off a mountain onto a slab of stone.

The car was not moving fast; its driver was apparently obeying traffic signals and speed limits. She heard traffic noises, horns honking, jack-hammers at a construction site, dogs barking, and the blare of car radios.

Then the scream of a siren! Police were coming to rescue her! *Please pull over the vehicle and rescue me!*

The siren wailing was speeding toward them, getting louder by the second: *wheeeooo . . . wheeeooo . . . wheeeooo . . . wheeeooo.*

Oh, please, God, get me out of here!

The vehicle slowed. A harsh male voice in the front cursed. Then the vehicle stopped abruptly, jostling Sylvia forward. Were they being pulled over? She was going to be rescued! The siren was beside them . . . so close she could almost feel the vibration. Then it passed behind them and moved in the opposite direction. The police weren't going to rescue her! Damn! *Help me. Dear God, someone help me!*

Another siren was wailing on a nearby street, but it also moved behind them.

An outburst of Italian curses exploded in the vehicle, *"Non troppo veloce!"* [Not too fast!]

"Fermati. Cazzo, è rosso!" [Stop! Damn it, the light is red!]

"Non di qua. Gira di lì." [Not here. Turn there.]

"Minchia, sono troppo vicini!" [Fuck, they're too close.]

The vehicle drove slowly away from the sirens, accelerated to a constant speed for a minute or two, and then made a series of turns, left, right, left again, changing lanes, but constantly moving.

Sylvia struggled to get comfortable, adjusting her neck and moving an arm, but a foot or knee was still pressing into her side.

The car made a sharp right turn, went straight, decelerated, and turned left.

More voices. . . . She heard a woman's voice. . . . Her heart skipped. . . . They were talking about her. . . . What were they saying? What were they going to do with her? She strained to hear, but the voices were low and muffled. The knee or foot in her side eased, and she could breathe easier. Thank God. But she still ached all over, especially her head and neck.

The vehicle kept moving. Muffled voices were arguing; words were spit out in bursts of short phrases.

"Cazzo facciamo adesso con 'sta qua?" [What the fuck do we do with her?]

"Bella situazione di merda!" [What a shitty situation!]

"Ammazziamola subito." [Let's kill her now.]

"Che cazzo dici?" [What the hell are you saying?]

"Abbiamo già fatto secco il porco, questa qui cosa c'entra?" [We have already killed the fat pig. What has she done?]

"Minchia di una minchia!" [Fuck, fuck!] It was the female voice, angry and loud.

Were they going to kill her and dump her in a ditch? Sylvia squirmed, again trying to adjust to a more comfortable position.

The vehicle accelerated and turned right, then left, and then went straight. The sounds of traffic were subsiding; an occasional car passed by them, no honking or sirens. The vehicle made a sharp left turn, slowed, went over a small bump, moved a short distance, and stopped. Sylvia heard something like a metal door being shut behind them.

The van's side doors opened, and the vehicle shifted as if people were getting out. Sylvia heard more voices outside the vehicle. Excited . . .

angry . . . cursing. The voices went on for a minute or two. What was happening? Where were they? If only she could see.

The vehicle's back doors opened, and Sylvia heard more voices. Another argument, curses, doors slamming shut. She didn't hear street noises. They were in a park or someplace remote. She wiggled her feet to get circulation where the pressure had been.

"*Ma chi cazzo è questa?*" [Who the fuck is she?] she heard someone say. "*Cerca di capirlo!*" [Find out!]

A hand fumbled around her breasts to her waist and into her pockets. She felt fingers digging into her front pockets. They pulled out coins, nail clippers, and a receipt from lunch on Via Dante.

Everything else—wallet, cell phone, driver's license, business cards, passport, address book, notebooks, makeup—was on the train. With Angela and Cole. *Oh, my God, what about them? Do they know what happened to me?* Her heart beat faster as she recalled the terror back at the Centrale when her world had gone seismic.

Hands fumbled with the straps of her camera and camera bag, which were pulled off her shoulders and over her head.

"*Portala dentro. Muoviti!*" [Take her inside. Move!]

Two hands grabbed her arms and pulled her backwards. Someone said, "*Alzati.*" [Lift her up.] She remained limp. Where were they? By the side of a road? *Are they going to kill me here?*

Hands dragged Sylvia out of the vehicle, and her feet hit the ground. Her knees were wobbling, and she was off-balance as a hand gripped her biceps and dragged her across a rough surface. Dirt and rocks. Were they in the woods? Were they going to shoot her and dump her body among the trees?

She struggled to stand, but her knees wobbled from being in a cramped position. She couldn't stand by herself, and her head was throbbing with pain. She wanted to cry out, but the fabric in her mouth made her gag.

"Don't kill me!" she screamed, but only muffled moans came out.

Someone said, *"Non le parlare. Portala dentro."* [Don't speak to her. Take her inside.]

Hands at both elbows pulled her along as she stumbled, wearing only one sandal and unable to see.

She heard a door open, and someone said, *"Tienile su il passamontagna. Portala sul retro."* [Keep her mask on. Take her in the back.]

Sylvia stumbled forward as a strong hand pulled her along the rocky surface. A door opened, and she was taken through. It was cooler. The faint light coming through the mask dimmed. She was inside someplace. It was quiet. A home? A shed? A warehouse? A farmhouse? Were they in the country?

She smelled a dog. A guard dog? The dog barked; it sounded like a German shepherd. Someone said, *"Fallo stare zitto, portalo via."* [Shut it up. Move it away.]

Sylvia heard the dog muzzled and pulled away, claws dragging across the floor.

She was led across a surface like concrete or stone tiles. She smelled food; something had been cooked. A dusty smell. Cigarette smoke.

Arms turned her left. A door opened, and she was pulled through. She heard a click, and a faint light came through her mask.

Hands pulled rings from her fingers: a sapphire ring from her father, the diamond engagement ring from Cole. Her wrist was lifted, and her watch was pulled off.

People were going in and out of the room, speaking in low voices. It was hard to hear under the mask. A female voice. Two, three male voices, one husky and rough.

The female said, *"Falla sedere lì."* [Sit her there.]

She was pushed down on a chair. Fingers reached under the mask and pulled the cloth out of her mouth. Sylvia gagged, coughed, and spit out bits of fabric.

"Dove siamo?" [Where are we?] she screamed, her voice breaking. *"Chi siete? Cosa volete? Sono una cittadina americana."* [Who are you? What do you want? I am an American citizen.]

"Taci, troia," [Shut up, bitch] the female voice spit out. *"Stai zitta! Niente domande."* [Be quiet. No questions.] The woman's voice was harsh and tense.

No answer. How many people were around her? *Is this it? Are they going to kill me?* Her stomach tightened with fear.

"Chi siete? Cosa volete da me?" [Who are you? What do you want with me?] she said, her voice cracking. *"Lasciatemi andare!"* [Let me go!] Sylvia screamed and started crying.

"Stai zitta, ti ho detto! [Quiet, I told you!] *O ti ammazziamo."* [Or we'll kill you.] The female voice was chilling. Decisive.

This was it—she was going to be killed! Sylvia was so terrified she wet herself.

"Help me!" she sobbed. "Help me! Help me! Dear God, help me!"

CHAPTER FIFTEEN

Cole returned to his seat next to Angela, deeply concerned how she would take the news that her mother was probably back in Milan. His relationship with Angela was warm but merely an extension of his relationship with Sylvia. He'd rarely been alone with Angela and never in a traumatic situation like this.

He cared about Angela and would do anything for her. He had helped raise his son during his divorce before his ex-wife moved to Chicago. But that was trivial compared to the trauma of Angela worrying about her mother missing with no way to contact her. He had to take responsibility for Angela and keep her calm.

He took Sylvia's cell phone from his shirt; still no phone messages. He was certain she would have called if she was safe and able to find a pay phone at Centrale.

"Does the conductor know where Mom is?" Angela asked, her face ashen.

"Not yet, he doesn't. He's called the station, and they're looking for her. We have to be patient. She may have been lost in the station, and she may call us to let us know she's all right."

"Is she all right?"

"Yes, dear, I'm sure she is. Would you like to go to the dining car and order a pizza?"

She shook her head and started crying. "Cole, I want my mom. I don't want to be here . . . I want to go back. Can we go back . . . please?"

The miles were clicking away as the train sped farther from Milan by the minute. They had zipped through small towns between Milan and Turin and were coming into an industrial corridor east of Turin, with stretches of manufacturing, heavy machinery, construction, warehouses, parking lots, apartment blocks, and shopping centers.

Cole wondered if they should get off in Turin and get a return train to Milan. If there was time, he'd ask the conductor and arrange to disembark.

He picked up Sylvia's cell phone and scrolled to Paolo's Menaggio number. "Angela, I'm going out to get some fresh air. Stay here."

She nodded, staring out the window.

Cole went out into the corridor and pressed Paolo's number. Paolo picked up on the fourth ring. *"Ciao, tesoro. Come va?* [Hi, sweetheart. How are you?] How's your journey? I was out on the patio, like we were on my birthday. How's Angela? Did she enjoy shopping in Milan?"

"Sir, it's me, Cole. I'm calling on Sylvia's cell."

"Well, hello, Cole. How are my girls?"

"Sir, there's a problem."

"What? What problem?"

"Sylvia's not on the train."

"What?" he said, his voice straining. "What do you mean, she's not on the train?"

"We were at Centrale station. She saw some murals she wanted to photograph. She stayed in the station, and I took Angela onto the train. Angela's with me, but Sylvia didn't make it onto the train."

"What? She stayed in the station to take pictures? That's crazy! Why did you let her?"

"I told her it was risky, but she said she'd only be gone ten minutes. I looked out the window as we were pulling away but didn't see her."

"Damn foolish. Why would she do that?!"

"Sir, there's another problem."

"What?"

"There was an incident at the train station. Some kind of shooting. The police blocked off the station. Maybe that's why she didn't get on. I heard sirens speeding toward the station as we were pulling away."

"God damn it, why did she do that! She's so impulsive sometimes; it drives me crazy. And now something like this. What are you going to do?"

"I'm not sure. We might get off in Turin and go back. But I'd be worried she'd catch another train and our paths would cross; we'd be heading to Milan, and she'd be on her way to Paris. I'm going to talk to the conductor after we finish. He told me about the shooting."

"You're calling on her cell phone, which means she doesn't have a way to contact you. Or me."

"That's right."

Paolo let out a deep sigh. "Let me think . . . give me a minute . . . I doubt there's another train tonight for Paris. . . . She could call from a public phone or get one of those cheap cell phones. She has her numbers programmed into her cell phone but doesn't know them without her phone."

"Probably right, sir."

"My number here isn't listed, and there's no way she could get it unless she called my New York office. But she probably doesn't know that number either. Damn! How's Angela taking this? Is she upset? What have you told her?"

"She's worried but holding up as well as expected."

"Damn. What can we do?"

"I don't know, sir."

"First priority: Take care of Angela. Don't let her out of your sight."

"I'm outside the compartment so she can't hear our conversation."

"Good . . . good. No reason to get her more upset. I'm going to make some calls and see if I can find out anything. I'll call you back in ten minutes."

"I'm waiting for the conductor to come back. Maybe he'll have more news."

Ten minutes later, Sylvia's phone rang while Cole was sitting next to Angela, who was slumped in her seat, staring out the window. It was Paolo. "Yes, sir. I'm here with Angela."

"Cole, God, this is terrible. Worse than we expected. I don't want Angela to hear this. Go out of the compartment. I'll hang on."

"Yes, sir," Cole said, moving into the aisle. "Honey, I'm going out to take this call from Nonno. I'll be right back."

Angela nodded, looking sleepy, leaning her head against the window.

Cole went into the corridor between cars as the train slowed coming into the Turin station. It was too late now to get off and head back to Milan. Cole's stomach was churning, partly from hunger but mostly because of worry and fear.

Cole shut the sliding glass door, still keeping an eye on Angela. "I'm outside the compartment now, sir. It's okay to talk."

"Cole, this is bad news. Really bad. I'm watching an Italian news station. They're reporting from Centrale. They say it was a terrorist act. Some government officials were shot."

"Terrorists! Oh, God. The conductor just said there was a shooting, nothing about terrorists. What the hell does that mean?"

"I don't know . . . the reporter keeps repeating the same information. It's not much. They're outside the train station. Police cars are all over, sirens and lights . . . ambulances . . . fire engines. It's chaos. The piazza in front of the station is taped off. Helicopters are circling. TV stations are broadcasting live. Police are keeping crowds away from the station. Reporters are saying police are interviewing witnesses inside the station. God damn it, Sylvia's probably in that mess! A TV camera with a telephoto lens is focusing on the entrance. Lines of police are keeping people behind tape."

"Sylvia is probably inside and can't get out."

"Probably. Let's hope she's okay. Wait . . . wait . . . they're playing a video . . . hang on."

Cole heard the volume increase on the TV. A reporter was speaking rapidly in Italian, almost shouting. Then Cole heard Harriet scream. "Paolo, look! They're dragging a woman!"

"What the hell is going on?" Paolo yelled.

"What is it, sir? What's happening?"

Paolo came back on the line, his voice quivering. "Cole . . . the TV is showing a cell phone video. It's grainy . . . blurry . . . pandemonium . . . men in masks dragging a woman downstairs. They're playing it again . . . it's only a few seconds long . . . wait . . . wait . . . there! *Oddio, oddio . . . oh, mio Dio!*" [Oh, my God. Oh, my God!] Paolo screamed.

"What is it, sir?"

"Cole—you can see her legs . . . her shorts . . . one of her sandals . . . it's Sylvia! They're dragging Sylvia down the steps! *La mia* Sylvia . . . *Hanno preso la mia bambina!*" [They took my baby!]

Harriet wailed, "Oh, God, please . . . no! Sylvia! . . . Sylvia! . . . Sylvia!"

CHAPTER SIXTEEN

Giorgio Lucchini, director of Milan's law enforcement agency DIGOS (General Investigations and Special Operations Division) at the Polizia di Stato, cursed when he bumped his head climbing out of his unmarked Alfa Romeo police car and saw traffic jams surrounding Stazione Centrale. *"Ecchecazzo!"* [What the fuck!}

Lucchini grimaced, rubbed his head, and yelled into the backseat: "Let's get out and walk, or we'll never get there!"

Lucchini slammed the car door and cursed again, "Damn. Damn," as he turned sideways to weave between taxis and cars backed up on the streets leading to Stazione Centrale.

Lucchini's deputy, Antonella Amoruso, scrambled out of the backseat and ran to catch up with him, followed by Lucchini's bodyguard, who adjusted his Beretta M-12 submachine gun to point the barrel up. Behind their car, three plainclothes officers from Milan's Polizia di Stato Scientifica forensics team similarly bolted out of their unmarked car and ran to catch up, carrying briefcases with tools and cameras.

Curious pedestrians, drivers, and idlers had been observing the urban drama as emergency vehicles had raced toward Stazione Centrale with sirens screaming—white Croce Rossa ambulances, blue Milan police Alfa Romeos and Fiats, black Carabinieri Iveco vans, and BMW motorcycles. When their vehicles were forced to brake and stop along Piazza Duca d'Aosta, officers jumped out and ran toward Stazione Centrale, carrying unholstered Beretta pistols and M-12 submachine guns.

Milan's media, alerted by police scanners, were not far behind. Paneled vans with rooftop antennas and logos of Milan's TV stations—RAI, Mediaset, La7, Sky, and Telelombardia—were speeding toward Stazione Centrale, adding to the congestion.

"Traffic's a mess!" Lucchini said to Amoruso, who was a step behind him. "Police cars can't even get close."

An ear-shattering noise like machine gun fire startled them. They turned and looked up as two black Polaria police helicopters flew low over office buildings on Via Vitruvio toward Stazione Centrale, their whirring blades making a jarring racket of *whoopa-whoopa-whoopa-whoopa-whoopa*. From open panel doors, helmeted Polaria scanned with binoculars the traffic as the helicopters circled Stazione Centrale, black plumes of exhaust floating down like dirty, smelly snow.

Lucchini looked at his watch. "Twenty minutes to get here from Linate," he shouted, referring to Milan's city airport, seven kilometers away, where a squadron of Polaria was stationed.

"The Fiorino's off the streets by now . . . tucked away in a garage!" Amoruso was taking two quick steps to one of Lucchini's strides, hurrying to stay close. "What the hell took so long? We made it here before they did."

Twenty minutes earlier, Lucchini and Amoruso had been in his office at Milan's Questura when the first Polfer alert had come in over their COT radios. Lucchini had grabbed his coat, and they had run down the corridor and taken an elevator to the courtyard where Lucchini's unmarked car, driver, and bodyguard had been waiting with the engine running. Behind his car, the Scientifica forensic team had been piling into their car.

The drivers had slapped magnetic flashing lights on their roofs, had driven out of the courtyard onto Via Fatebenefratelli, and had turned on sirens. When they had reached Piazza Cavour, they had accelerated toward Piazza della Repubblica, changing lanes as cars had pulled to the side to let them pass. When they had reached Via Pisani and could see Stazione Centrale ahead, traffic had slowed to a crawl.

In the best of times, Lucchini was impatient; when events interfered with his duties, his temper erupted. "Damn! Run over those cars! Let's get there!" Lucchini's vehicle had swerved out of stalled traffic and had jumped the curb along Duca d'Aosta. His intense dark eyes swept across the piazza like a general surveying a battlefield.

"How many shooters, you think?" he said to Amoruso.

"Not sure . . . could have been three . . . four," she gasped between gulped breaths. "Arrived ones or twos . . . different entrances . . . came together to attack . . . escaped."

"Split up . . . after shooting," Lucchini said, breathing hard as he ran. "One or two might have gotten away . . . undetected . . . didn't leave in Fiorino."

"Hope . . . Polfer . . . capture one . . . make jobs . . . easier. . . . What think? . . . Robbery . . . terrorists . . . Mafia?" Amoruso puffed as she ran to stay within a step of her boss.

The late August afternoon heat was baking the tiles of the piazza and reflecting off glass and steel office buildings.

"No robbery . . . shoot and run . . . don't think . . . mafia shoot in public place . . . gun down . . . rival . . . remote . . . dump body in river . . . down abandoned shaft," said Lucchini.

"What . . . terrorists . . . anarchists . . . old Brigate Rosse . . . fascists?"

"God . . . hope not . . . terrorists," Lucchini responded, slowing to a fast walk as his team reached the crowds near Stazione Centrale's main entrance. "Already financial crisis . . . political scandals . . . failed government . . . too many . . . crises."

The massive edifice of Stazione Centrale loomed ahead like a mausoleum: seventy-two meters high and two hundred meters wide, with tall white marble columns, crests of lions and swords above the arches, and larger-than-life statues of gladiators and stocky horses looking down on the piazza.

Lucchini stopped to give his team a few seconds to catch their breath. He took out his police ID, held it above his head, and started moving through the crowds.

"*Permesso . . . polizia . . . fate passare . . . polizia . . . fate passare.*" [Excuse us . . . police . . . let us through . . . police . . . let us through] Travelers turned and momentarily glared until they saw Lucchini knifing through the crowds, followed by Amoruso, the armed bodyguard, and a forensic team.

A path cleared to the red and white *zona di rispetto* police tape in the portico. Shards of broken glass were scattered across the marble floor. Polfer crime scene investigators were photographing the broken glass and beginning to carefully pick it up with instruments and drop into plastic bags.

Lucchini turned to his forensic team. "One of you stay and get to work . . . the rest, follow me."

A young Polfer agent cradling a Beretta 12 submachine gun recognized Lucchini and motioned for the crowds to let them pass. "*Dottor Lucchini, il Comandante mi ha chiesto di accompagnarla di sopra.*" [Dr. Luccini, the Commander asked me to escort you inside]

Lucchini and his team ducked under the tape and followed the officer into Stazione Centrale and up the escalator to the lobby. On the escalator, they had a moment to catch their breath after sprinting across the piazza. Amoruso reached into her bag for a tissue to wipe sweat from her face.

A trail of police tape had been strung from the portico into the entrance with its shattered glass doors, up the marble staircase, and into the lobby. Lucchini's team got off the escalator and followed the Polfer agent into the noisy lobby. Polfer agents were shouting orders at travelers to stay behind the tape and to keep moving toward the platforms.

A gaggle of reporters and TV cameramen spotted Lucchini and his group walking through the taped corridor. Camera strobes flashed, and bright TV lights focused on Lucchini and Amoruso. Reporters shouted at them, stretching over the tape to aim microphones in their direction. Polfer agents rushed over and pushed the reporters out of the taped corridor they had invaded.

"*Dottore*, who did the shooting?"

"How many victims? Is the *sottosegretario* [political official] dead?"

"Have you received a claiming of responsibility?"

Lucchini grimaced; he knew Milan's rapacious media wanted immediate and gory details, the bloodier and more graphic, the better. Hell with them for now. He'd give them a minute later, but not now. He had to do his job first. There would be little that he would learn in the next hour that he'd tell the media before discussing it with the Questore and with the prosecutor appointed to the case. He waved in the reporters' direction to acknowledge that he'd seen them, and he followed the Polfer agent into the station.

The shouting followed them: "Capo, can you give us a minute?"

"Have you found the shooters?"

Lucchini ignored them and followed the officer, who led him to a tall, heavyset man wearing a blue *dirigente* Polfer uniform with ribbons on his chest and gold stripes on his sleeve.

"*Salve, Dottor Lucchini. Sono Salvatore Greco, primo dirigente della Polfer,*" [Greetings, Dr. Lucchini. I am Salvatore Greco, director of the Polfer] he said to Lucchini, shaking his hand. "Your office said you were on the way; we've been waiting."

"Sorry, we were stalled in traffic; it's a mess out there. My forensic team and deputy are with me. Please take us to the crime scene so they can get to work."

"This way," said Greco. "We're collecting evidence on the platform where the *sottosegretario* was shot. Here is the path the shooters took when they ran into the lobby—where a woman was taken hostage—and the staircase where they escaped."

Polfer investigators were photographing and examining pools of dark blood, the contents of briefcases spilled on the platform, newspapers, and chalked outlines where victims had fallen.

"How many were shot?" Lucchini asked.

"Two government officials, two Polfer, and three civilians hit by stray bullets."

"Any dead?"

"Not yet. One of our officers was shot on the platform," Greco said pointing to an area where Polfers were photographing the taped outline where a colleague had fallen. Nearby were three white circles where bullet casings had been found. "Another was shot on the staircase; he's the most seriously injured, a bullet in the chest. He was unconscious when our ambulance took him away. Both are in the hospital."

"What weapons did they use?"

"Glock 9 millimeter. We've collected nine bullet casings."

"We'll take them to the Questura to run tests."

"Yes, sir. We have them ready for you."

"Tell me about the shooting."

Greco walked a few paces to the marble arch leading to the lobby. He pointed to a row of designer store windows. "Two shooters were in the shadows between the Carpisa and Benetton stores, wearing sunglasses and caps. They walked through the crowds when the Rome train arrived and passengers were going into the lobby."

Greco walked back to platform fourteen and pointed. "The shooters stopped here and fired four shots, wounding the *sottosegretario* and his aide. Our officer spotted them seconds before they shot, and he ran toward them. One turned and shot at him twice, hitting him once in the shoulder."

Lucchini walked over to look down at the white tape where the bullet casings had fallen. He turned to calculate the distance from the platform to the marble arch that led to the lobby.

Amoruso went over to the side of the platform. She got down on one knee to examine the gravel and debris around the cement ties. When she stood up, she asked, "Have you searched the tracks for possible evidence? Maybe one of them dropped something."

"No, *dottoressa,* we haven't," Greco said. "Not while the trains are in the station. The train from Rome and the other are both empty."

"When will they depart?"

"The general director of *Ferrovie dello Stato* is waiting for us to give the word."

"Have them move to another platform. You might find something down there."

"Yes, *dottoressa.* I'll give the word. No one's been allowed on the trains since the shooting."

"You've interviewed witnesses from the Rome train?"

"Yes, *dottoressa.* They're in our office giving statements. We have names of all passengers and the seating."

"Good. We'll want to read your reports."

"Yes, of course."

"Can we see the CCTV tapes?" Lucchini asked.

"This way," Greco said, motioning him to follow. Lucchini and Amoruso walked behind the *comandante* to the Polfer headquarters at the side of the station beyond platform twenty-four. A Polfer officer cradling an automatic weapon was standing guard.

They entered the Polfer reception area, where an officer was behind a desk. On the wall across from him was a map of Stazione Centrale and an electronic monitor of train timetables.

Greco led them down a corridor past offices and conference rooms where witnesses were being interviewed by investigators. At the end of the corridor, two open doors led into the command center, a large, windowless room brightly illuminated by racks of ceiling lights. A dozen uniformed Polfer agents in teams talking on headsets were stationed at computers, telephone banks, and video monitors. They were exchanging information among themselves, speaking in low tones, their voices tense with emotion. Some of them were relating information from Polfers patrolling in Stazione Centrale and from operators viewing monitors of CCTV cameras throughout the station, while others were analyzing tapes of the shooting.

Ceiling fans swirled air from air-conditioners, making the room cold. Several Polfer agents wore jackets over their uniforms.

Greco cleared his throat and rapped his knuckles on the door. *"Attenzione, sono arrivati il Dottor Lucchini e la Dottoressa Amoruso della DIGOS."* [Attention. Drs. Lucchini and Amoruso from DIGOS are here]

The agents looked over and started to stand in respect to the stature of the DIGOS officers. Lucchini and Amoruso were the only civilians in the room. Lucchini wore a dark suit, blue silk tie, and white shirt. His black hair and sideburns were streaked with touches of gray. His frame was short and husky, like that of a former soccer player.

Amoruso's dress and manner commanded respect. She wore a navy pantsuit, a white silk blouse, a triple strand of pearls around her neck, and bracelets on her wrists. She was attractively formal, more like a mid-career finance executive than a high-ranking DIGOS officer. Her black hair was combed in a wave below her ears. She had a dark complexion, a small mouth, and a delicate chin.

Lucchini motioned for the agents to remain seated. "Please, stay at your stations. We're here to observe and coordinate."

Greco took them to a console where operators were analyzing videotapes from the shooting. "Show us the sequence from the beginning."

"Yes, sir." The operator pushed buttons, and a tape in color began running on a monitor in the center of the console. The date, hour, minute, and second were running at the bottom of the screen.

"Here is the Fiorino driving into the station," the operator said. "We can't read the license plate; they put tape over it."

One person got out of the passenger side of the Fiorino. Two more emerged from the back door. They wore sunglasses and black caps pulled down over their foreheads. All three clutched shoulder bags to their sides. When they disappeared under the portico, the Fiorino turned and departed from the station into traffic. Eight seconds had passed.

"What happens to the Fiorino?" Lucchini asked.

"It returns in seven minutes. The driver knew when they would be back."

Amoruso asked, "Did they use cell phones?"

"Not that we can see. No sign of cell phones on any of them."

The operator pressed more buttons, and monitors showed three angles as the trio entered and walked toward the staircase. "Here they're coming through the main entrance," he said. Four seconds later, as they were ascending, one monitor showed a woman near the top of the staircase photographing them. She looked encumbered by a camera strap around her neck, a bulky camera bag over one shoulder, and two shopping bags dangling from each forearm.

"This is the woman who was taken hostage," Greco said. "We have tape of when she's grabbed. Watch when they get to the top of the staircase."

The three stopped momentarily at the top of the stairs, put their heads together, and separated. Two moved toward the station, with the third disappearing off the monitor.

"Here's the shooting."

Three monitors from different angles showed the two in sunglasses and caps in shadows against a store window. As crowds streamed past from the platform, the two moved out of the shadows and began weaving among arriving passengers. When they reached the fourth car, they made a series of rapid moves. Simultaneously, left hands pulled ski masks over their faces; right hands took off their sunglasses, put them in the shoulder bags, and came out holding pistols.

They fired at two men in dark suits carrying briefcases coming toward them. The victims fell, sprawled on the platform. One shooter pumped two more shots into the legs of one of the men writhing on the platform. Then the shooters turned and ran toward the lobby. A Polfer agent with gun raised appeared at the left of the screen. Three shots were exchanged. The agent fell and rolled over, his weapon still in his hand.

The shooters dashed under a marble arch, arms raised, holding their weapons. Frightened crowds started running in all directions.

One monitor showed a sea of people running through the station. Another showed a man wearing a black ski mask grabbing a woman with a camera and shopping bags from behind. She resisted and they struggled. Their arms became entangled, with the man trying to pull the camera over her head. Crowds almost tripped over them, but people veered off and kept running. The woman's knees hit the floor. The man was still over her back, his arms reaching around her chest.

After a few seconds of struggling, the man jerked her up and dragged her toward the staircase. The shopping bags fell to the floor. The woman's arms were entangled in camera straps, and she flailed with her legs to kick her assailant. One sandal fell off her foot.

The three in masks reunited at the staircase and went down backward. Two of them were sweeping their pistols to keep crowds back. The woman's captor was holding her tight against his chest with one arm and pointing a pistol to her temple with his other hand. The woman's eyes and mouth were open; she was screaming and thrashing to get away.

Monitors followed them down the staircase. Two Polfer agents appeared at the top of the stairs. One, then the other, shot. Glass in the entrance door shattered and sprayed the crowds; people were running into each other. One of the Polfer agents was shot in the chest; he dropped to his knees, his gun falling down the steps. The three departed the station with the woman, who was last through the doors, her feet kicking.

"That's terrifying," Amoruso said. "She could have been killed. Who is she?"

"We don't know," Greco said. "No one identified her. She didn't have luggage, only a camera, camera bag, and shopping bags."

"Why no luggage? Did she leave it someplace? Was someone with her luggage? Or was she alone?"

"Sorry, *dottoressa*, we don't know. We're searching earlier tapes to find when she comes in."

"Let's see close-ups of the shooters," Lucchini said.

The operator again pressed buttons, and the monitor showed a frozen frame of the three entering the station.

"Hard to identify anyone," Lucchini said. "The sunglasses are wraparounds, and the caps hide most of their foreheads. All we can see are noses, mouths, chins, and necks. Simple clothes—jeans, T-shirts, running shoes. Half the people in the station dress like this."

"Let's see them closer up," Amoruso said.

The monitor zoomed in on the three faces. Strands of dark hair under the caps. Wraparound sunglasses covered eyes, eyebrows, and tops of cheeks.

"The one in the center is a woman," Amoruso observed, pointing to the monitor. "Small cheekbones, soft chin, thin lips, dark. What's on her cheek? Is that a scar?"

The screen zoomed to a small jag that started under the sunglasses on the right cheek.

"If that's a scar, it might help identify her," Amoruso said. "We'll check our data bank for women with a facial scar on the right cheek. A woman assassin . . . who was our last woman assassin?"

"Don't remember," Lucchini answered. "Let's see close-ups of the others."

The monitor zoomed to the one on the left, the hostage captor. "Light beard . . . sharp chin . . . big nose . . . prominent cheekbones . . . looks about forty years old. He might be the leader if he broke off to grab the woman," said Lucchini.

The screen moved to the taller one on the right. This time, Lucchini observed, "Long face . . . heavier beard . . . longer hair . . . cleft on chin. Looks strong, like a weightlifter or manual laborer. Maybe mid thirties, but that's just a guess. Damn, I wish we could see their eyes."

Greco said, "Those are the best views of their faces before they pull down masks. They moved quickly; they knew they'd be taped."

"These aren't amateurs," Amoruso said. "They knew surveillance cameras would be all over them."

"We're loading cell phone videos and photos into our database," Greco said. "It will take time until we can see them together." He turned to the operator. "What have you seen so far?"

"They're blurry or from a distance," the operator replied. "We have one from ground level, five meters away at the entrance. Can't tell much with ski masks, but we're enhancing them."

Amoruso said, "I want to download all that we've seen to take back for our forensic team to analyze. They'll work on identifying key facial features. Your tapes automatically erase, don't they?"

"Yes, *dottoressa,* every two hours. We've downloaded these to study. I'll get you hard disks before you leave."

"Let's go back to the crime scene," Lucchini said. "I want Amoruso to go over it again. She's in charge of the investigation and will be coordinating with the prosecutor."

"I'll take you to the lobby where the woman was grabbed," said Greco. "Her shopping bags spilled on the floor. And we have her sandal."

"So, who is she? That's what I want to know," Amoruso said. "A mystery woman. I hope they don't kill her. Any word on the Fiorino?"

"Nothing yet," Greco said. "They're off the streets by now."

They left the Polfer office, and Greco led them back to the platform. Trains on tracks thirteen and fourteen were still in the station, but trains were entering and leaving from other platforms. Crowds were moving in an orderly fashion outside the red tape lines. A loudspeaker was droning arrival and departure announcements. A degree of normalcy was returning to Stazione Centrale.

Lucchini took Amoruso's elbow. "I'm calculating that it took less than a minute to shoot the *sottosegretario,* his aide, and the Polfer agent; run into the lobby; and find the one who took the woman. Thirty seconds to run down the staircase and out to the Fiorino."

"Rehearsed like a military operation," Amoruso said. "They came to the station to pace distance and time from entering to escaping. They drilled someplace remote, paced off distances, ran through it until they had it timed to the second so the Fiorino would know when to be back."

"Lightning-fast and professional," Lucchini said. "Amateurs would blunder, trip over each other, make a wrong move, or shoot too much and delay escape. They knew what they were doing."

Amoruso paused and looked up at Lucchini. "Except for the hostage. That wasn't in their plan. They huddled at the staircase to modify their plan so one could get her camera. It wasn't a random grab for a human shield. Too many things could go wrong: the hostage struggles, slows the operation, someone in the crowd pounces on the assailant. Taking a hostage was risky."

Lucchini's police radio squawked, and he put it to his ear. "*Dottor* Lucchini, we have a call from the Stazione di Polizia in Menaggio. An American called and said his daughter is the hostage at Stazione Centrale."

"What? How does he know?"

"He was watching TV and saw a cell phone video of the woman dragged down the steps."

"Who is he?"

"A New York banker. His daughter, her fiancé, and his granddaughter were with them in Menaggio two nights ago."

"What? Where are they? No one has come forward to identify her."

"They're on a train for Paris. The fiancé didn't see her get on the train."

"Why were they on the train and not with the woman? That doesn't make sense."

"He says she stayed to get pictures of Stazione Centrale. They got on the train, and she stayed in the station."

"Strange . . . why would she do that?"

"*Dottore,* he wants to come to Milan to talk to the police and identify her."

"Let him come. I'll meet him at the Questura."

"Right, sir. Menaggio police said they would drive him here."

"I'll return to the Questura when I finish here. Probably an hour or so. Amoruso will stay; she's in charge of the investigation."

Lucchini and Amoruso followed the *comandante* to the lobby, where Polfer investigators were snapping pictures of the contents of the shopping bags that had spilled on the floor. Next to one of the shopping bags was a black Prada flat-heeled woman's sandal with golden hardware and an adjustable ankle strap.

"Before you pick anything up, we want to see," Lucchini said to the investigator.

"Yes, sir."

Amoruso knelt to study the contents of the shopping bags, two from La Rinascente. Inside were a Dolce & Gabbana miniskirt; two Diesel sleeveless polo shirts, size XS; a pink butterfly-shaped Pupa makeup set; a set of pens and pencils from the Teatro alla Scala shop; a Vergelio bag with a pair of expensive Tod's shoes, size thirty-five; and a pair of Porselli ballet slippers, same size.

When Amoruso stood, she said to Lucchini, "Those are new sandals, just a few scrapes on the sole. The label is Prada. She bought them recently. Some of these gifts look like what a young girl would buy."

"The woman's daughter was with her fiancé on the train."

Amoruso sighed. "Oh, that poor child. I wonder if she knows what happened? How old is she . . . not too young, maybe an adolescent."

"Don't know. The father is coming tonight; he'll tell us. We need to hear his story. He can identify the hostage."

"*Per la miseria* . . . I hope they don't hurt her," Amoruso said, her face twisted in anger. "A mother . . . how sad. I don't like this . . . . Those shooters are bad, bad, bad. I'm going to check to see if the hostage might have been released. Or worse, shot and dumped on the road."

She got on her radio. "This is *Dottoressa* Amoruso at Stazione Centrale. Any word on the woman hostage? Has she been found or released?"

Her radio squawked. "Checking. . . . Nothing so far. Let me call around and get back to you."

"One shooter took her as a human shield; she had a camera they wanted. He tried to get it over her head, but couldn't and dragged her down the steps. Now she's a hostage."

"Right. I'll get back to you."

Amoruso and Lucchini started back into the station. The crowd of media saw them and began firing questions as TV camera lights shined on them.

In a low voice, Lucchini said, "I have to say something to them. I'll keep it short. Stick around."

Amoruso let Lucchini walk toward the media behind the tape, where the cameras and lights focused on him. He stopped about five meters from the tape, took a deep breath, and put his hands behind his back to signal he would take questions. With the bright lights on him, he had to squint to see the shouting reporters, each trying to be louder than the others:

"How many died, *Dottor* Lucchini?"

"Have you arrested the murderers?"

"Are they terrorists?"

"Who's the hostage?"

Lucchini paused a moment, deciding to make one or two statements rather than get trapped in answering questions in detail. The cameras were clicking like frenzied insects. He cleared his throat and spoke distinctly, like a judge issuing a decision from the bench. "I'm reviewing the crime scene and am confident that the Polfer are conducting a thorough investigation. We're working closely with them."

"Who are the shooters?"

"I don't have identification at this point. We've alerted police agencies throughout Milan and Lombardy. We're reviewing evidence, caring for the injured, and conducting an intensive search for the criminals."

"When do you expect to make arrests?"

"Was one of the victims a politician? What's his name? We need his name."

"I can't release names at this time. We are contacting families to notify them. Once we have, we'll release names."

"When? We're live. When do you expect to arrest someone?"

"Sorry, I have nothing more to say at this point. I will be at the Questura press office tonight. I'll release information when we have it. Thank you."

He turned around and walked back to Amoruso, taking her arm to lead her away from the reporters, who were still shouting questions.

"I hate this," said Lucchini. "We're investigating a multiple shooting . . . a woman hostage . . . Polfer and innocent victims in the hospital. All they care about is meeting a damned deadline."

"I don't want your job," said Amoruso. "I'd rather deal with criminals than talk to the media."

"Vultures, every one of them. I hope from tonight on, the prosecutor and the Questore will deal with the press. I'm fed up with them."

CHAPTER SEVENTEEN

Vera locked the door where she'd left Sylvia in a small room in Luca's warehouse. When she turned to face the others in the corridor, she could read the look on Fabio's face; he was angry, his eyes narrowed, lips pressed tight.

"*Tutti fuori,*" [Let's go outside] he muttered, motioning with his head for all of them to follow him outside. The door was still open from when they had brought Sylvia into the warehouse.

They followed him into the late afternoon sun and stood beside the Fiorino, which was parked at an angle behind trucks, old cars, and *motorinos* against the back wall. Luca's warehouse was enclosed by four stone walls on a quiet street in a mixed neighborhood of car dealerships, convenience stores, middle-class apartments, playgrounds, and nondescript office buildings.

Fabio slammed the Fiorino's rear door, which had been left open after they'd dragged Sylvia out. "*Perché cazzo—*" [Tell me why] he started to say, when the jarring *whoopa-whoopa-whoopa* of low-flying helicopters interrupted him.

The noise startled all of them, and they turned their heads to look west. Two black helicopters were flying low toward them about two kilometers away, maneuvering in search patterns, turning a few degrees to the north and south, coming together, then veering off to make aerial surveillance of industrial parks, office buildings, and traffic moving on the streets below.

"Get the Fiorino in the garage!" Fabio shouted, pushing Marietto toward the vehicle. "Police helicopters!"

The Fiorino was behind one of Luca's trucks, which was parked under the metal roof of a cinder block garage with no doors. Marietto jumped into the Fiorino, put it in gear, and tried to drive it in next to the truck. But the space was cluttered with construction materials, tools, lumber, and fuel containers.

He shouted out the window, *"Non ci passo. C'è troppa roba davanti!"* [Move that stuff. I can't get in!]

Fabio, Luca, and Vera ran into the garage. They grabbed tools, lumber, and barrels and hauled them out, dragging them across the warehouse's unpaved back lot to a corner pile of trash with mounds of garbage bags, broken pipes, wooden slates, tiles, and cement blocks. They tossed the items onto the trash and ran back to remove more debris, looking over their shoulders as the helicopter rumbling grew louder.

Their second trip to the trash pile had cleared sufficient space for the Fiorino. Marietto eased it under the metal roof.

"Nascondetevi!" [Out of sight!] Fabio yelled as they ran back, almost tripping over each other as they stumbled into the garage. They pressed their backs against the Fiorino to shield it from view, panting from the fear of being seen and the physical exertion of running and carrying the tools. They gulped air in the shadow of the garage, watching the helicopters bank away from the warehouse and come a hundred yards from them.

"Sono bassi . . . troppo bassi," [Close . . . too close] Fabio gasped. The helicopters changed their flying pattern, separated to fly wide loops to the south, and then flew back together, one facing north, the other

south. They hovered in place, circling slowly, revealing police agents with binoculars scanning industrial parks and office buildings near the Bresso corporate airport.

Vera grabbed Fabio's hand and squeezed it against her chest. *"Oh, Dio, fa che non ci vedano!"* [Oh, God, please, don't let them see us.]

"Stai zitta!" [Quiet! Don't talk!] Fabio gasped.

The helicopter descended to fifty meters above ground, as if they were about to land. But they continued to hover in place. In the distance came the sound of a siren. Then another. And a third. The helicopters hovered, pivoting in a full circle.

"They're searching the car dealership," Luca whispered. "They keep hundreds of vehicles in a back lot."

The sirens merged near the hovering helicopters. Police agents in the side doors made hand signals, pointing at something below them.

"Another helicopter," Fabio whispered, pointing to a lone helicopter flying from the center of Milan toward the other two.

The three helicopters came together, hovered for a minute, and then, one by one, ascended and flew in formation over Bresso airport, banked, and flew south over the Sesto San Giovanni section of Milan. After making several passes over Sesto San Giovanni, the helicopters turned and flew back toward the Bresso airport, searching roads in the area of Bresso industrial parks and office buildings.

"They're following your route," Fabio said. "If you were still driving, they'd have spotted you."

Luca cursed. "Damn police, too close. How did they know we drove here?"

"Maybe they didn't. They could be searching all over the city."

"Oh, God, I'm scared. We almost got caught!" Vera said, wrapping her arms around Fabio. The helicopters broke formation again and separated, each flying in a different direction, to the east, west, and north. One was flying straight toward them.

"Coming back!" Fabio said, his voice cracking. "Throw something over the back of the Fiorino!"

Luca ran to a pile of tarps against the warehouse wall and grabbed one. He and Fabio pulled it over the Fiorino to cover the rear and stood alongside, securing the tarp to the roof so it wouldn't slide off.

The helicopter's noise got louder.

"He's going to fly over us!" Fabio shouted over the noise. Seconds later, the menacing black fuselage and swirling blades appeared thirty meters above the trees on a course that would take the helicopter directly over the warehouse. They could see the pilot wearing a bulbous black helmet with a visor that covered his face.

"*State giù!*" [Get down!] Fabio shouted. He and Luca lowered their bodies but held the tarp in place while Vera and Marietto squatted beside the Fiorino, hands over their ears, as the helicopter flew thirty meters over the warehouse and swirled up clouds of dust, leaves, and dirt. The deafening noise rattled the windows and lasted several seconds. Everyone coughed in response to inhaling dust and dirt.

"*Oddio, aiuto!*" [Oh, God, save us!] Vera cried, gasping and retching.

The noise diminished but was still loud as the helicopter flew away.

Fabio, Marietto, and Luca ran out into the cloud of dust and dirt and watched the helicopter turn east, climb to a hundred meters, and fly to meet the others that had returned to Bresso. When the three helicopters united, they turned and flew in formation to the east, climbing and disappearing in low-hanging clouds.

The growl of their engines faded, and the neighborhood was quiet again. Birds in the trees behind Luca's warehouse started chirping again. The sound of traffic on the streets returned. Honking horns. Screeching tires. Children playing in a park. A door slammed. A woman across the street called out from an apartment window for a child to come home.

"Thank God, they're gone," Fabio said, exhaling a breath he'd been holding. "We're safe now," he said, brushing dust off his clothing. He put his arm around Vera, still wheezing for fresh air. "Let's get inside . . . I want to hear about the hostage."

They stumbled into Luca's warehouse, speechless from the terror of the helicopters flying so close to them. They stood in the corridor, still gasping for fresh air, wiping dust and dirt from their clothes, looking nervously at each other, reliving the panic of the last few minutes.

"*Vacca boia, mi sono cagato in mano,*" [Damn, I shit in my hand.] Luca gasped, wiping sweat from his forehead. "That was . . . too . . . close."

"Let's go . . . into . . . your office," Fabio said, still panting. "That was . . . frightening. Marietto . . . bring us . . . beers."

Marietto went into a kitchen across from the office and removed beers from a refrigerator. He opened them, brought them into his office, and passed them around as they each took a chair. One by one, they put the bottles to their lips, tipped their heads back, and let the cold beer slide down their parched throats.

Sweat ran down their faces, which were lined with dust and dirt. They looked around at each other, no one speaking for several moments. Luca and Vera reached for cigarettes and lit up, coughing as they inhaled.

Luca had partitioned the warehouse for an office, an apartment for himself, a modest kitchen, and four rooms with a communal bathroom and shower for workers from southern Italy, Eastern Europe, and North Africa who couldn't afford apartments in Milan. Sylvia was locked in one of the rooms with a sink, bed and small desk.

Luca's office was a shambles of used furniture: desks, some with chairs, filing cabinets against the walls, an old TV on top of one, a desktop and two laptop computers, a printer and table stacked with blueprints, files, binders, and days-old newspapers. Wastebaskets were overflowing with crumpled papers, plastic coffee cups, and the contents of ashtrays.

Taped on the walls were photos of Luca's completed construction projects around Milan: apartments, offices, schools, homes, resorts, and sports complexes.

Fabio broke the silence. "I'm going to have nightmares about those damn helicopters . . . I've never been so scared."

They all nodded, sipped their beers, smoked, looked at each other, elbows on knees. Vera ran her hands through her windblown, dusty hair. She put down her beer, put her hands to her face and started to cry, first whimpers, then a sob. She bent over, shaking her head, and broke down.

"Minchia, quanto odio la polizia. . . . Li ammazzerei tutti . . . tutti . . .
tutti!" [Oh, God, oh, God, I hate police. . . . I want to shoot them all!]

Fabio went over and ran a hand over her back, then stroked her
hair. "Go ahead, cry. Get it out. We're all . . . scared. But we did what
we did for a reason."

She sniffled, lifted her head, and wiped tears from her face. "I
know . . . . I'm sorry . . . . I just lost it. I'll be . . . all right. I'm strong."

"Yes, you are," Fabio said, running a hand over her head.

He looked at the table where three black shoulder bags were lying
on stacks of newspapers and files. He raised the flap on one of the bags
and carefully lifted out one of the Glock pistols by the grip.

"Alfredo, get these out of here. I don't like guns. Lock them up
where you have the others."

Alfredo collected the three bags and carried them down the corridor
to the storage closet, where Luca had installed a metal locker under the
floor for the weapons Alfredo had stolen during his army days or bought
on the black market.

Fabio said, "Turn on the TV. Let's see the news."

Luca took the remote from the cluttered table and turned on the
TV to an RAI station broadcasting from Centrale. A scroll at the bottom of the screen read: *"Sparatoria a Milano in Stazione Centrale. Ucciso*
un Sottosegretario del Ministero delle Finanze, due agenti Polfer feriti
gravemente. Gli assalitori sono scappati in un Fiorino bianco." [Shooting
at Milan Stazione Centrale. Finance *sottosegretario* and two Polfer shot
by terrorists. The shooters escape in a white Fiorino.]

The TV was rebroadcasting footage taken that day. A camera inside
the station panned the lobby, focusing on a Polfer agent escorting a man
and woman in dark suits to the train platforms.

Reporters yelled out: *"Dottor* Lucchini, who was shot?"

"Have you found the murderers?"

"When do you expect to arrest someone?"

The man in the dark suit waved and kept walking past them. The
TV reporter spoke excitedly: *"Dottor* Lucchini from Milan's DIGOS has

just arrived, apparently to confer with Polfer agents investigating this afternoon's shooting. Several victims have been taken away in ambulances. We don't have names of victims or how many were shot, but we have unconfirmed reports that one victim was a *sottosegreterio* from the Finance ministry."

Fabio picked up the remote, muted the sound, and tossed the remote back on the table. "They'll be broadcasting all night. We need to talk about what happened. Why do you have a hostage—and a woman?"

"We had to, Fabio!" Luca said. "She took our pictures at the station."

"How do you know?"

"Her camera was pointed at us on the stairs. I heard it click twice. I was going to call off the mission, but she disappeared in the crowd."

"Then what happened?"

"When we got to the top of the steps, I told Vera and Alfredo I was going to grab her camera. I sent them into the station; we were only seconds away from carrying out the mission. I was going to find the woman and grab her camera. When I found her, Polfer were following, staring at her ass like dirty little boys. Filthy bastards. I wanted to shoot them."

"You should have ended the mission and left. When you divert from a plan, you risk the mission."

"But you weren't there, Fabio!" Luca protested. "I made a quick decision—if I could get the camera, the mission could succeed."

"So why didn't you steal her camera? You didn't need the woman, just the camera."

"If I grabbed her camera and the Polfer saw me, they would have arrested me. I was carrying a gun. I'd end up in jail, and they'd want to know why I had a pistol in the station. Then what?"

"All right, all right. But you could have left the station."

"Vera and Alfredo were in the station already. How could I find them in the crowd? Everything was happening so fast. When they heard gunfire, the Polfer agents ran into the station. I grabbed the camera, but my hands got tangled in the straps of her camera and bags. People were running over us. She was fighting me and fell down. I had to move fast."

"Fabio's right," Vera said, coughing as she lit another cigarette and took a deep puff. "We can't take risks. I wanted to shoot her in the car and throw her on the road."

Fabio shook his head. "No. Bad idea. We don't murder civilians. If you shot her and dumped her body on the street, somebody would call the police, and they might find evidence from the car. They'd know your escape route. You were right to bring her here."

Vera took another deep drag from her cigarette, exhaling a cloud of smoke. "Let's kill her now and dump her body someplace at night."

"Absolutely not," Fabio said. "She's innocent—at the wrong place at the wrong time. We don't shoot innocent people."

"She's not innocent. She took our pictures," Vera said, flicking ashes on the floor.

"We're not going to kill her. Forget it. We'll find a way to get rid of her so she can't identify us. I need to think. . . . We'll keep her locked up tonight and release her tomorrow far away. Drug her so she doesn't remember anything."

Luca nodded. "I agree. You're right; we can't kill civilians."

"Where's her camera?" Fabio asked.

Marietto held up the camera and bag by the straps. "I have it."

"Let's see her pictures."

Fabio took the camera and turned it over in his hands. "Professional camera. Canon D-4. A 35-millimeter lens." He depressed the power button, and a blue light came on. He examined the buttons on the back and pressed one. The monitor displayed the last photo Sylvia had taken, a stone crest on the station wall. He viewed her photos in reverse order—stone friezes, murals, gladiator busts, marble steps—and a six-photo sequence of the three entering the station and walking up the steps.

Fabio held the camera so the others could see the photos as he scrolled back and forth. "Damn. Six pictures. The last two show your faces under your caps and sunglasses. If you hadn't grabbed this, your faces would be on every news broadcast."

He handed the camera to Vera. "Put the photos on the computer. I want to see them all."

Vera dug into Sylvia's camera bag and pulled out a USB cord, plugged it into the camera, and took it to Luca's desktop computer. She plugged in the other end of the USB cord. The icon of an external device appeared on the monitor and flashed, "Loading 2,400 pictures." It took almost five minutes for the photos to upload.

Vera clicked on the thumbnail with the current date. The file started with photos of the Duomo, La Scala, lunch at an outdoor café, and a series of Centrale landmarks. She ran through the pictures, stopping at the sequence of the three of them entering the station and ascending the stairs.

"Enlarge those," Fabio said.

Vera clicked on one and toggled the enlarge link. The photo doubled in size. The three were looking ahead, wearing sunglasses and caps.

Luca whistled. "*Vacca boia . . . queste foto ci portano dritti a San Vittore.* [Damn . . . those pictures could send us to prison.] Destroy the camera—get rid of the woman."

Fabio shook his head. "No . . . not yet. Why was she taking your photos?" He looked in the camera bag and saw a business card inside a plastic sleeve stitched into the upper flap. He took it out. "She's American. Sylvia de Matteo. From New York. A professional photographer. She has a website. Look it up."

He handed the card to Vera. She typed the URL into a search engine and up came Sylvia's webpage with the logo of her studio and photos of Italian landmarks. Vera clicked on links that showed Sylvia's professional bio, a list of awards, a press release about her forthcoming book, *Italia Ieri, Italia Oggi, Italia Domani.* One link was titled "Where I'm working today." Vera clicked on it, and the screen showed a photo of a woman with a young girl and a handsome man in front of a fountain in a flower garden. The caption read: "Our family villa in Menaggio on Lago di Como. Back in New York next week."

"Interesting," Fabio said slowly, bending over Vera's shoulder to study the photo. "Find out more about her. She's American . . . a professional photographer. Maybe we won't let her go."

He looked up at the clock on the wall. "What food do you have in the kitchen, Luca?"

"Not much. Beer, wine, a little cheese, ham, sandwich bread, canned soups, and beans."

"What?" Vera asked. "What do you mean? Are you hungry?"

"I'm thinking of the woman . . . Sylvia de Matteo. We have to feed her."

"You're crazy," Vera said. "Why do you want to feed her? She could have gotten us all in prison!"

"No. We might keep her hostage a few days. We have to take care of her. Get some soup, cheese, and bread, and take it to her."

CHAPTER EIGHTEEN

"Cole, I'm going to hang up!" Paolo screamed into the phone. "I've got to call someone and get help! I'll call you back. God damn it, they've kidnapped Sylvia!" Cole heard a click.

Cole was shaking so much that he had to sit down. He pushed open the door into the WC and flipped down the toilet seat. He sat down, staring at Paolo's name and number on Sylvia's cell phone, his hand trembling so much he thought he might drop the phone. His eyes welled up with tears.

A tornado was tearing through his life, uprooting so many things he held dear—Sylvia, their future, Angela, the ailing Paolo and Harriet.

An hour before, Sylvia had been with them at Centrale, looking forward to a couple of days with friends in Paris, the City of Lights, Cole's favorite city.

But Sylvia had been grabbed by criminals and dragged down steps—and had vanished! Where was she? When would police rescue her? And how?

It had happened so fast. A relaxing breakfast yesterday with her family in Menaggio, a busy day shopping in Milan, and now he and Angela were speeding toward Paris alone. How could life spin out of control so fast?

Cole's mind was reeling with the disastrous consequences of Sylvia's impulsive decision to remain at Centrale. How absurd! She had taken a thousand photos already in Italy. Why had she needed more—especially under tight time constraints? Why hadn't he insisted more vehemently that she get on the train? Everything would have been fine. They would have been on their way to Paris, safe and happy.

Cole didn't know what to do. He could still hear Paolo yelling into the phone about the grainy cell phone video. The image kept playing over and over in his head. He took a deep breath and let it out slowly, feeling his galloping heartbeat slow down a bit. His hands were no longer trembling, but they were damp with sweat. He had to return to Angela.

He put Sylvia's phone in his pocket and turned on the faucet, splashing cold water on his face until his shirt collar was damp. He looked in the mirror. His eyes were red and puffy, hair mussed from running his hand over his head while listening to Paolo. Drops of water trickled down his neck onto his shirt. He dried his face and neck with a paper towel, tossing it in the dispenser.

He had to get back to Angela. Find the conductor and get off at the next station.

An older woman was waiting outside when he unlocked the door and stepped out. She recoiled like she was seeing a ghost, confirming what he'd seen in the mirror. He looked a mess.

"*Scusi,*" Cole muttered. When he opened the sliding glass door to their compartment, Angela was staring out the window, her face drawn and pale. She was a trouper, resilient for a ten-year-old. She looked up at him.

"What's wrong, Cole?"

"Ah, it's okay, dear. Sorry, I had a sneezing spell. Couldn't breathe for a couple moments. We're going to get off the train and go back to Milan."

"Oh, yes! Yes! I want to go back. Thank you. I want to find Mom." Cole could hear the relief in her voice.

Their train was speeding through the Italian countryside, passing orchards, pastures, vineyards lush with ripening fruit, and small farms with stone barns. A stream of cars, buses, and trucks sped along the *autostrada* parallel to the tracks.

"Stay here, Angela. I'm going to find the conductor. Do you want to go into the dining room? Are you hungry?"

"I'm thirsty."

"I've got bottled water." He reached up for his luggage and retrieved two bottles of water, handing her one. She opened it, took a long swallow, and wiped her chin.

"I'm okay now. When are we getting off the train?" she asked.

"Let me find out. Stay here."

The elderly Frenchman sitting across from them had been watching the drama, looking puzzled. He said something in French, which Cole didn't speak.

"Do you speak English?" Cole asked.

The man shook his head. "No, sorry."

A young English woman in the row behind stood up. "I speak English," she said with a British accent. "Can I help? Your little girl looks worried. You look shaken. Is everything all right?"

Cole was relieved. "We have . . . an emergency. I need to find the conductor. Would you please keep Angela company for a few minutes?"

"Of course. I have a little girl myself. Let me sit with her."

"Wonderful. I need to arrange to get off the train and go back to Milan for her mother."

The woman looked puzzled. "Is she all right?"

"She . . . she missed the train. We have to go back for her."

The woman left her seat and sat down next to Angela. "I understand. I'll sit with Angela. Don't worry. Take your time. We'll be fine."

"Thank you. That's so kind," Cole said, relieved that he was getting help for Angela. He hurried down the aisle, passed through the dining car and two other cars, and reached the conductor working in his cubicle. The conductor opened the door when he saw Cole. "Please come in."

The conductor's face was firm. "I talked to my supervisor at the station. A very bad thing has happened. Apparently terrorists shot several people and have a woman hostage."

"My fiancée is the hostage."

"What?! How do you know?"

"Her father in Menaggio was watching news about the incident. They had a cell phone video of a woman being taken hostage. Her father thinks it was her—my fiancée. I want to get off the train and go back to Milan. When do we come to the next station?"

The conductor looked at his watch. "In about fifteen minutes. We stop at the village of Modane, just inside the French border. I will call the station and tell them."

"Can I get a train back to Milan?"

"I'm sorry, no. There are several tomorrow, one in the morning—nine-thirty, I believe."

"I need to get back to Milan tonight. Can I rent a car there?"

"I don't know. Modane is a tourist town, mostly hotels and ski resorts. They might be able to help you."

"Can you find out?"

"Let me try." He picked up his cell phone, punched in a number, and spoke quickly in Italian: *"Sì, poveretto, è un'assoluta emergenza . . . la situazione è tremenda . . . dice che vuole una macchina a noleggio. . . . Ah . . . allora sì, una doppia per stanotte . . . sono padre e figlia . . . certo . . . certo. . . . Grazie mille. . . . Va bene, glielo dico . . . grazie . . . grazie."*

When he hung up, he said to Cole, "There are several hotels not far from the station, a couple kilometers. My supervisor thinks some hotels have rental cars. But it is late; the offices may be closed for the day. Maybe you'll have to wait until morning."

"How long would it take to drive back if I can get a rental car?"

The conductor shrugged. "I do not know. It's a long drive back to Torino, down the mountains, then the *autostrada* to Milan. Milan suburbs are difficult to drive through. Centrale is in the center of town, and there is much traffic. Do you know Milan?"

"No."

"Aah, too bad."

"How about a taxi?"

"A taxi to Milan? That would cost many euros."

"How many?"

"Several hundred possibly. I do not know."

Cole didn't like the options. He could pay a lot of money, get to Milan late at night and find a hotel. But Angela was already exhausted and frightened. Putting her through the stress of riding in a taxi at night was not a good idea. It had been a long and traumatic day, and they both needed a good night's sleep—if possible.

"Just get us off the train. I'm going back to be with my fiancée's daughter. She's only ten years old and very worried."

"Would you want a woman conductor to sit with her?"

"No, there's an English woman sitting with her."

"Good. I will come to your compartment." He looked at his watch. "We only have ten minutes. Get your luggage, and I'll meet you at your seat."

Cole hurried back through the cars and was relieved to see the English woman reading the *Harry Potter* book with Angela, who was still nervously kicking her feet against the seat.

"I'm back. Angela, how's my little girl?"

"Are we going back to get Mom?"

"Yes. I'll get our luggage ready. The conductor is having someone meet us at the station."

"Can I help you?" the woman asked.

"Please. Can you help Angela get her things and walk to the exit with us?"

"Of course. Come, Angela. Let's get you ready to get off and go back for your mother."

Cole got down their luggage, looping Sylvia's purse over his shoulder, not caring what anyone thought of a man carrying a woman's purse.

The train was slowing, jostling side to side as it approached Modane. Cole took his and Sylvia's luggage and carry-on bags into the corridor between the cars. The English woman followed, holding Angela's hand and wheeling her luggage.

The train brakes screeched as the train pulled into the station. Outside, the landscape had changed to a mountain hillside with apartments, hotels, and shops. Above the town were green hills with empty ski lifts and long green trails through forests.

The conductor arrived and waited for the train to stop so he could open the doors and lower the stairs. "The station manager is waiting. I will help you get off."

The train stopped with a jolt. The conductor opened the door, stepped down, and helped Cole get their luggage onto the platform.

A tall man with dark hair in a blue uniform was waiting, holding a clipboard and cell phone. The badge on his coat looked almost like a military insignia.

"This is station manager Benoit Joubert. He will help you get a hotel."

"Thank you," said Cole. "I appreciate what you've done for us."

"And a good evening to you, sir. I hope your return to Milan is safe and all is well with your fiancée. My best wishes to you."

The train whistle blew. The conductor climbed the steps, looked up and down the platform, and signaled toward the engine. Another whistle, and the train moved slowly out of the station. In a minute, it rounded a curve and disappeared.

* * * * *

Three hours later, Cole and Angela were in their fourth-floor room in a ski resort hotel. After a quick dinner in the restaurant, Cole had taken Angela upstairs, where she had collapsed on her bed, exhausted from the day's journey and traumatic events.

Cole was also exhausted. He doubted he would sleep well, worrying about Sylvia and wondering where she was tonight. He turned on the TV after Angela had gone to sleep and watched Italian news broadcasting from the station, with the sound muted.

The piazza in front of Centrale was lit up with streetlights, TV lights, and rotating red and blue lights from ambulances, police cars and vans. Reporters were interviewing people, gesturing at Centrale in the background. Live broadcasts were interspersed with cell phone videos and pictures shot inside Centrale earlier in the day, showing crowds running after the shooting, armed police keeping people behind tape, investigators picking up evidence, and two plainclothes police officials talking to reporters. Cole watched for an hour, horrified by the grainy videos of men in black ski masks dragging Sylvia down the marble staircase, over broken glass, and outside. Over and over the videos played, making him nauseous.

He sat on the edge of the bed, putting out his hand to touch the TV screen when the video focused on Sylvia's legs, shorts, and one of the sandals she had bought in Bellagio the week before.

It was definitely Sylvia. Cole shuddered, imagining the terror she had gone through, dragged by a masked man down the stairs, her heels slamming against the marble steps, a large pistol at her head.

Where was she tonight? Was she still alive?

When he finally turned off the TV and collapsed into bed, he closed his eyes and rolled over several times, trying to fall asleep. But all night his memory replayed the grainy video over and over and over.

CHAPTER NINETEEN

P aolo arrived in the Menaggio police car at the Hotel Cavour on Via Fatebenefratelli at 10:30 at night. While the police officer drove the car to the Questura a block away, Paolo went into the hotel, carrying a cloth briefcase and one piece of luggage he'd packed hurriedly at his villa.

It had been a long, frustrating day in which Paolo's life had been thrown into turmoil when he'd recognized Sylvia being dragged down the steps at Centrale. He'd switched TV channels during the afternoon, looking for other stations broadcasting from Centrale, his heart racing as he had become convinced it was his daughter, a belief corroborated by Cole's saying she had not made it onto the train.

Paolo had left Harriet in Menaggio in the care of Costanza after calling a doctor to come and give her sedatives to calm her anxiety. Paolo had called the police and then rushed to his bedroom to throw a few clothes into a suitcase. He'd sipped a Scotch while waiting for the Menaggio police car to arrive. The sun had been descending over Como, and puffy white clouds had been touching the mountaintops.

It had been dusk by the time the police car had pulled through his gate to pick him up.

Paolo had talked feverishly to the Menaggio police officer as they drove down the lakeside road to Como, sharing his family background; details about the trip Sylvia, Cole, and Angela had made to Italy and about their one-day visit to Milan; and Cole's story about the events at Centrale.

The police officer had listened, asked a few questions, and told Paolo that he would be meeting the DIGOS officers at Milan's Questura who were investigating the shooting. It was recommended that he stay at the Hotel Cavour, a short walk from Questura.

After they had talked for half an hour, Paolo had tried to relax as the officer navigated the *autostrada* to Milan. Paolo felt the weariness of the day mixed with anxiety of what he would learn in Milan. He was pumped on adrenaline and fear, and he knew he'd be miserable if he stayed in Menaggio, apart from Cole and Angela. God willing, they'd be reunited with Sylvia shortly.

In his heart, he prayed the trauma would be over soon, maybe even that night. Or tomorrow. Or the day after. He was determined that Sylvia would be safe and reunited with the family as soon as possible. Paolo would do whatever he had to, talk to any official, pay for any services, bargain with anyone with influence over events, overcome any hurdle to have his daughter returned safe and secure.

He wouldn't be stopped in achieving his goal; that's who he was, a man of action, intelligence, and perseverance. Nothing mattered more to him than the people he loved—his family and closest friends. He hadn't reached the heights of his career and wealth without resolve to let no obstacle stand in his way.

He had learned this lesson in life from his father, who had left Italy as a poor, uneducated teenager and arrived in a strange country where he didn't speak the language and knew no one. Paolo's father had worked hard, made many sacrifices, raised his family, loved his wife, and left a legacy of children who were well educated and professionally employed. He had died a happy man, surrounded by family and friends at his death, including Paolo, Harriet, and baby Sylvia. On his deathbed, Paolo's father had whispered, "I'm the happiest man in the world seeing all the people I love with me." That experience had motivated Paolo his entire life to have the same satisfaction and pride that his father had had, a sign of a life well lived.

Paolo walked up to the reception desk. "*Buonasera.* I'd like a suite, please, two bedrooms and a living room if possible."

"Welcome to Hotel Cavour, sir," said an attractive middle-aged woman in a stylish light brown hotel uniform. "Let me see what we have." She put on reading glasses to check the hotel's computer. "How many nights, sir?"

Paolo shook his head. "I don't know; three or four maybe. I'll be joined by two family members tomorrow. My future son-in-law and my granddaughter."

The receptionist continued scanning the reservations. "We're in luck. We had a cancellation earlier today. We have a two-bedroom suite on the fourth floor. Three nights or four?"

Paolo shook his head. "I don't know, to be honest. Make it four. I'll also want to talk to your manager."

The receptionist handed him a registration form, took his passport to copy, and pressed a button under the desk. While Paolo scribbled on the form, a distinguished-looking gentleman with grayish white hair combed back over his head came to the desk.

When Paolo slid the form across the desk, the gentleman spoke. "Good evening, sir. Welcome to the Hotel Cavour. I'm the manager. May I help you?"

Paolo pulled out his wallet, removed his credit card, and handed it to the receptionist. "My name is Paolo de Matteo. I'm from New York. I have a villa in Menaggio, and I am in a very distressed position. You probably heard about a shooting at Centrale today?"

"Yes, of course. A dreadful event."

"My daughter was taken hostage. The Menaggio police drove me here. I'm going to the Questura as soon as I drop my luggage in my room."

The manager was shocked. "Mr. de Matteo, I'm very sorry. How can I help you?"

"Tomorrow my future son-in-law and my granddaughter will be checking in. My granddaughter is ten years old. She's very upset, as you can imagine, with her mother missing."

"Yes, sir, I'm sorry. How can we help?"

"I want to arrange for a woman—a guardian, a caretaker—I don't know the right term . . . someone who can be with my granddaughter when my future son-in-law and I are away from the hotel."

"Of course, I understand. I have recommendations."

"What are they?"

"We get such requests from our guests from time to time. We have women who look after children when their parents leave the hotel. We check backgrounds, referrals, and credentials for security purposes. Tonight we have a female student from Bocconi University staying with two children in the family's room. An older woman, a former nurse and mother who raised three children, is taking care of another family's young child."

"I like the nurse. I'll come down tomorrow morning and would like to meet her."

"Yes, sir. Just call and I'll arrange for you to meet." He handed over his business card, which Paolo slipped into his pocket. The Menaggio police officer came in and waited behind Paolo.

"Let me drop off my luggage," he said to the officer. "I'll be right down."

Paolo was back in five minutes. The officer led him outside and down Via Fatebenefratelli. The night air was warm and humid. Across the street, people were drinking wine and listening to jazz at an outdoor café. Couples were strolling down the street, holding hands, looking in shop windows. "The Questura is close, just two minutes away," the officer said as they crossed a street. "The DIGOS capo is waiting to meet you."

In the middle of the block, two Milan police officers were stationed at an arched entrance of a three-story, yellow stucco building. Streetlights bathed the building, illuminating a large red, white, and green Italian flag and a blue European Union flag with five stars. Fiorino police vans were parked facing each other at Questura, with police officers holding automatic weapons standing alongside, eyeing passing cars and occasional pedestrians.

"The Questura's on high alert tonight," the Menaggio officer said as they walked under the arch at 11 Via Fatebenefratelli. Two Milan police stood blocking the Questura courtyard. The Menaggio officer handed his identification to one of the courtyard officers, who took it to a glassed guard station. Paolo looked around the courtyard, where blue police Fiats and Fiorino vans were parked with drivers standing by.

The officer returned and led them to a door that opened onto a corridor. They followed the escort to an elevator that clanked and jostled as they rose three floors. When they exited, the escort took them down a narrow corridor, through an arched doorway, and into another building with different dimensions and floor patterns.

The escort turned a corner, and the group came upon a vaulted door with the DIGOS logo inscribed over the entrance. He punched a code on a panel, picked up the phone, and gave his name. There was a metallic click, and the door opened.

The escort handed them off to two DIGOS plainclothes officers, who took them down a brightly lit corridor. They passed offices, most of which were empty, but in a couple of them there were men in street clothes working at computers and talking on phones. The offices were cluttered with papers, files, and folders on crowded desks, as well as posters, flags of soccer teams, family photos, and children's crayon drawings.

Toward the end of the corridor, a group of men were leaning against doors to empty offices. They were short or medium height.

Their muscular chests and biceps filled out faded jerseys and T-shirts of Italian soccer teams, liquor brands, sports cars, motorcycles, and Milan nightclubs. Most had short, clipped hair and were partially bald, their pates shining in the corridor lights. A few had scruffy beards, stringy hair, or drooping mustaches. Their arms were folded across their chests, their pistols holstered on their wide belts. Their eyes followed Paolo as he walked past.

One of the men caught Paolo's eye and lowered his head in a discreet nod. The corners of his mouth flashed a half-smile. For a brief second, Paolo imagined the men knew who he was.

The DIGOS escort led them to an office with the name plaque and emblem of the DIGOS commander. The office door was open, revealing a man in a dark suit behind a desk talking to a woman in a navy pantsuit and to two men seated beside her.

The man stopped talking, looked over, and waved for the escort to enter. He stood and put out his hand to Paolo. *"Buonasera, sono Giorgio Lucchini, Primo Dirigente della DIGOS. Entri pure, la stavamo aspettando."* [Good evening, I'm Giorgio Lucchini, director of DIGOS. Please come in. We've been waiting for you.]

The two men got up and left the room; the woman remained. Lucchini motioned for Paolo to take one of the empty chairs.

"I'm Paolo de Matteo from Menaggio. Thank you for seeing me," Paolo said, his voice breaking. "Could we please speak English? I speak Italian but don't do well when I'm nervous. I'm very upset. . . . They have my daughter."

"Of course, sir. I understand. We both speak English. Let me introduce you to my deputy, *Dottoressa* Antonella Amoruso. She's in charge of the investigation. We were at Centrale when we got the message about you from the Menaggio police."

Paolo shook Amoruso's hand and sat next to her. The Menaggio officer sat down in the empty chair.

"Mr. de Matteo, could you tell me more about your daughter being at Centrale?"

Paolo quickly told them about the two weeks Sylvia and Cole had been in Italy, and he added that Angela had spent August at the family villa in Menaggio.

"Do you know where Sylvia is?" Paolo asked. "Have you found her yet?"

"No, we haven't," said Lucchini. "And we don't know who took her. Or why they shot a government official and one of his aides. They also shot two Polfer agents. One is in serious condition with a bullet in his chest. The other is in a hospital with bullet wounds in his arm and shoulder."

"Who did this? And why?"

"Sir, we don't know. The motive appears to be political, but we don't know who they are or why they shot the government officials."

"Are they terrorists?"

Lucchini pressed his lips together. "Sir . . . we just don't know. My deputy and I have been reviewing evidence, testimony from witnesses, and videotapes from Centrale. Terrorists usually are quick to take credit when they commit a heinous crime. They usually make a phone call to the newspapers or leave a message someplace. We haven't heard a word. It's unusual. We were discussing that when you arrived."

Paolo's chest sagged. "Can you find her and bring her back safely?"

"Sir, police agencies all over the country are investigating. We have alerts at airports as well as at bus and train stations. But we don't have a photo to help them know who to look for."

Paolo reached down to his cloth briefcase and took out two framed photographs. "I brought these." He handed them across to Lucchini, who looked at them and handed them to Amoruso.

One photo was of Sylvia and Angela at a beach, wearing sun hats and swimsuits, smiling at the camera, their faces touching. The other was a family photo taken at Paolo's New York apartment in front of a Christmas tree. The family was dressed in holiday clothing, Harriet, Angela, and Sylvia in red dresses with festive accessories, Paolo in a dark suit with a red and green tie.

"We can crop this family photo and get a close-up," Amoruso said. "That's the best one."

"Sir, could you please help us with the events that led up to her being at Centrale? We need to have precise information so there are no misunderstandings."

"Of course. They had been with us two nights ago in Menaggio. Yesterday, Sylvia, her fiancé, and her daughter left to spend a day shopping in Milan, intending to leave this afternoon for Paris."

"And why were her fiancé and daughter on the train, yet she remained in the station?"

Paolo sighed. "My daughter's a commercial photographer. She's writing a picture book about Italy. She showed us photos when she was with us. Her fiancé said she wanted to get photos of Centrale for her book."

"I see. . . . I see," Lucchini said, looking puzzled.

"Sir, it seems unusual that she would risk missing a train to take photos with so little time. We checked the timeline; she was taken hostage only four minutes before the train departed." Amoruso said.

"Yes, I suppose. But she's a very determined person, spirited . . . sometimes she acts impulsively. Like this," he said, shaking his hands in frustration.

Lucchini and Amoruso looked at each other.

"What did you see on the video that convinced you it was your daughter?" Amoruso asked.

"We were together in Menaggio two nights ago for my birthday dinner. I remember what she was wearing. When I saw the video, I recognized her clothing: blouse . . . sandal . . . tan shorts."

"You remember her sandals?"

"Yes. Sylvia sat next to me on the patio that night after my birthday dinner. She had her sandals propped up on the railing."

Lucchini looked over at Amoruso. She got up, went in to an adjoining office, and returned in a few seconds. "Sir, is this her sandal?" she asked, showing the sandal to Paolo.

Paolo gasped. "Yes, it is! She was wearing it at my birthday party. . . . She put her feet on the railing. . . . I saw them from a couple of feet away. I told her how fashionable they were. She bought them in Bellagio earlier this week."

"Mr. de Matteo, this sandal was taken from Centrale, where your daughter was taken hostage."

Paolo cried out and clutched his chest. "Oh, yes. Oh, yes." His face sagged. "It's definitely hers."

Amoruso reached over and put a hand on his shoulder. "I'm sorry, sir." She spoke softly. "Mr. de Matteo, could you look at the credit card receipts we recovered from her shopping bags? You could verify her signature."

Amoruso looked over at Lucchini and said, "I'll call Prosecutor Moretti immediately, now that we're positive about the identity of the hostage. He should be the first to know."

"Yes, yes. These are Sylvia's signatures," Paolo said, leafing through the receipts. He started to cry. "Oh, Sylvia . . . oh, Sylvia. . . . I want you back. Please! Please!" he sobbed.

CHAPTER TWENTY

DAY FOUR

Sylvia was abruptly woken from a troubled sleep the next morning by a sharp rapping on the locked door of her dark, windowless room.

"*Sveglia!*" [Wake up!] The woman's voice commanded.

Sylvia bolted up in bed, rubbed her eyes, and recalled the terror of the previous day and night. A sliver of light under the door reaching a few inches across the cement floor was the only illumination in the cramped room.

"*Siediti!*" [Sit on the chair!] the woman's harsh voice said. "*Se fai la brava ti diamo la colazione. Se no, ciccia. Capito?*" [Obey, we give you breakfast. Disobey, no food. Do you understand?]

"Yes, *capisco,*" Sylvia said, her voice weak. She slid off the bed, her body aching, and sat on the chair, groggy and listless from a sleep-disturbed night.

A key turned in the door. It opened a few inches, streaming light on dingy plaster walls, Sylvia's rumpled bed, a sink, and a desk. Two figures at the door wore ski masks, their bodies backlit by a harsh ceiling light.

The shorter person came in, went behind Sylvia, and pulled a woolen cap over her face.

"Stay!"

"Who are you?" Sylvia asked. "Let me go! Why are you keeping me?" She clenched and unclenched her fists on her lap, a futile defensive reaction as she anticipated that she was going to be beaten.

Vera raised a fist, but Fabio grabbed her wrist and squeezed until she winced.

"Please let me go," Sylvia said, starting to rise.

"Sit down or I'll hit you!" the woman screamed, her mouth inches from Sylvia's ear. Sylvia flinched. The woman's voice was as sharp and cutting as broken glass. Sylvia smelled cigarette smoke on the woman's breath, and it made her nauseous. Her stomach was empty, and bile rose in her throat.

"Don't cause trouble," a man said, his voice flat and calm. "We will give you breakfast if you answer questions. Do you understand?"

"Yes," Sylvia said weakly, terrified at her powerlessness. The nausea was making her dizzy; she feared she was about to vomit.

"Who are you?" Fabio asked.

She took a couple of slow breaths, inhaling and exhaling noisily, choking down the bile. "You . . . you . . . know who I am. I'm an American." Her heart was thumping, her stomach churning. She felt so many strong emotions—anger, terror, frustration, despair, pain. Her head throbbed from the blow in the car, her shoulder was sore from being wrenched, and her feet were swollen from being dragged down the steps.

The night had been a nightmare, spent locked in a tiny room that was like a prison cell. When she had been left alone, she had laid down on the hard bed, crawled into a fetal position, and sobbed, her tears dampening a thin pillow that smelled of sweat.

She had cried for a long time, reliving the terror in the station and the agony of missing Angela and Cole. She'd never been so afraid in her life. After a long spell of crying, she had sat up, wiped tears from her face onto her blouse, and strained her eyes to look around the room. Dark as a cave.

The air was stale and sour, like a closet containing soiled clothes. Sylvia had felt nauseous and had laid back down, but painful memories had kept running through her mind. A wave of exhaustion finally had swept over her. She'd closed her eyes and tried to sleep. Just as she had been about to drift off, she had been jolted awake by the memory of the terrifying episode at the station. And the memory of watching Angela and Cole walk away from her toward the train. If she had gone with them, they'd all be in Paris now, with friends, eating great food, drinking wine, and laughing long into the night. Oh, why had she insisted on staying in the station to get a few photos? How foolish she'd been! The terrible situation she was in was her own fault . . . and she could die for her stubbornness.

Sylvia had rolled over and tried to get comfortable in the hard, lumpy bed. She'd had no concept of time. Was it daytime or evening? She had stared in the darkness, trying to imagine what the room looked like. She had run her hands over the plaster wall, her fingers touching small cracks and lumps.

Her right hand had reached the corner, where the walls met. She had run a finger up and down the corner.

When her hand had touched the bedpost, she'd touched something as soft as silk. A second later, something like a feather had raced over the back of her hand and up her arm. Fast, light. Not a feather, but several. They weren't feathers, but insect legs.

Oh, God, a spider! She hated spiders!

Sylvia had screamed and jumped off the bed. She had brushed her other hand over the arm where the spider had run, brushing and brushing down her arm and then down her blouse in case the spider had jumped and was tucked in a fold of her clothing. Her heart had been beating so fast that a wave of dizziness had come over her, and she had felt like she was going to faint.

She had sat on the edge of the bed, continuing to brush her arms and body, breathing deeply until the dizziness went away. She couldn't feel the spider but didn't know where it was. She had swept her hands over the bed to brush it away if it was there. She had been unable to see anything; the spider could have been anywhere. She had run her hands all over her body, from her hair and face down her arms, blouse, shorts, and legs.

She had stopped for a moment to see if the spider was on her, and then she had repeated her frantic brushing, from head to foot. When she had finished the second frantic brushing, she had sat on the edge of the bed, put her head in her hands, and cried. A long time.

Sometime later, an hour or two or three after she'd been locked in the dark room, she had been startled by a knock at the door.

"*Sdraiati. Ti ho portato da mangiare. Non ti alzare o non avrai niente.*" [Lie on the bed. I have food. Don't get up, or you won't get anything to eat.]

Sylvia had followed orders and had turned on her side, facing the wall, terrified that the spider was still on the bed. A key had turned in the lock. The door had opened, and a faint light had illuminated the room. Someone had entered, set something on the bed, and departed. The key had turned and locked the door, and Sylvia had been back in darkness. She had sat up and reached toward the end of the bed until her fingers touched a tray. Her fingers had discovered two plates and a glass. Some kind of bread on one plate.

She had nibbled even though she hadn't been hungry. She'd picked up a piece of fruit and sniffed it. An orange. Her stomach had been too queasy for an orange. She had lifted the glass and sniffed. No odor. She had tipped the glass, and her tongue had felt a cool liquid. A sip. Water. She had taken a drink, then another, and emptied the glass. She had been thirsty. It had been hours since she had had anything to drink.

She had put the tray on the floor and laid down, feeling more lonely and lost than she'd ever felt before. More images had run through her mind: shopping with Angela and Cole that morning in Milan, having lunch on Via Dante, and rushing to the train station, before her world had been thrown into a tornado.

Who had grabbed her and thrown her in a car? Why had they taken her? What did they want? Who were they?

She had pulled the sheet back, gotten back in bed with her clothes on, and laid back down, finally falling asleep. But she had been awakened repeatedly by nightmares, some of the station, others of bizarre things happening to people in her life.

$$* * * * *$$

And now they were back. Two people in ski masks. The woman with cigarette breath. The man whose voice was calm. She had to find out who they were and why they had taken her hostage.

"Tell us why you were at Stazione Centrale," the man said, his voice measured and direct, like a teacher quizzing a student.

"Let me go!"

"Why were you at Stazione Centrale?"

Sylvia knew she had to cooperate if she was going to survive. She had to learn who they were and why they had taken her. And how she was going to be set free. She had to get free!

"We were going to Paris," she said, trying to appear calm. "I wanted some photos. I'm a photographer."

"Who is 'we'?"

She took a deep breath, thinking about her answer. Should she tell them about Angela and Cole? Would that put them in danger? She couldn't imagine how, except in some "prisoner" exchange, but that didn't seem likely. "I was with my fiancé and daughter," she answered.

The man waited a few moments before he asked his next question. "Where are they now?"

"Why do you want to know?"

"Tell us. Where are they?"

Sylvia exhaled, balling up her fists. "They were on the train when . . . when . . . you grabbed me."

"Answer the question. Where are they?"

Sylvia sighed. "I have no idea where they are. How would I know? You've had me prisoner for a day. Let me go back to my family," she begged. "Please, let me go."

The man ignored her. "Why were you taking photos in the station?"

"I'm a commercial photographer. I take pictures. Scenery. Statues. Monuments. People. I'm writing a photo book about Italy." The questioning session was making her weary. She was tired, sore, and hungry.

"Why did you take pictures of us on the steps?" the woman asked.

Sylvia flinched. She didn't want to talk with the woman but didn't want her to know how much her voice irritated her. "I took pictures of three people walking up the steps," Sylvia said, keeping her voice neutral. "A minute later, someone grabbed me. Knocked me down. Tried to get my camera. Dragged me down the steps and threw me in the car. And hit me! My head hurts, my shoulder is injured. My knee is wrenched. I'm in pain. Let me go!"

"Why did you take pictures of us?" the woman demanded.

Sylvia smelled her cigarette breath, smoky and foul. "Who the hell are you?" she said bitterly. "I don't know who you are! I don't care! Let me go! I'm in pain."

The woman was making her lose control. Sylvia was tired of the interrogation. She started to cry, her words coming between sobs. "I don't . . . know . . . who . . . you are . . . or why . . . you grabbed me. . . .Why? . . . Why?"

Fabio nodded at Vera and motioned with his head toward the door. "Enough for now," he said. "We're leaving. Remain in your chair. We have food for you."

Vera went outside, picked a tray off the floor, brought it in, and set it on the desk. On the tray were a cup of *caffelatte,* some slices of sandwich bread, ham, cheese, and an orange.

The two departed, and Sylvia heard the click of the lock turning.

Fabio and Vera took off their ski masks and walked down the narrow corridor to Luca's office, where he, Alfredo, and Marietto were smoking and sipping cappuccino, listless from fatigue.

The previous day had been stressful for them: the drama of the shooting, the helicopters searching for them. They had spent the previous night drinking wine, smoking, and talking about their hostage and their next attack. It would be another bombing; there would not be another shooting until they saw the ramifications of their Stazione Centrale attack.

They had watched the TV news late into the night, which was still being broadcast from Stazione Centrale, until they were all exhausted, the color in their faces drained from fatigue.

A reporter was broadcasting outside the station. The scrawl at the bottom of the screen read: *"In diretta: aggiornamento sulla sparatoria di ieri nella Stazione Centrale di Milano. Oggi la Questura renderà noto il nome della donna presa in ostaggio."* [Reporting from Stazione Centrale, scene of yesterday's bloody shooting and hostage taking. Questura will reveal name of hostage today.]

"What are they saying?" Fabio asked.

"The same rehash," Luca said, flicking cigarette ash into a full ashtray on the table. "They keep replaying the interviews of witnesses yesterday. . . . The Questura is slowly responding to questions. . . . Polfer agents are recovering in the hospital. . . . *Sottosegretario* Pallucca is having another surgery on his legs."

"Turn it off. We need to talk," Fabio said.

Luca grabbed the remote, muted it, and tossed it back on the table next to wineglasses, bottles, and plates with cheese, lunch meat, and stale bread from the previous night. "What did the woman say?" he asked.

Fabio poured two cups of coffee for him and Vera from the large moka on the stove and added two tablets of aspartame for Vera. Luca poured himself a small glass of cheap grappa. Vera lit a cigarette and tossed her package and lighter back on the table. Alfredo grabbed the package and took a cigarette for himself, while Marietto took the last of the coffee and mixed it into his cup with a shot of grappa.

"She's angry, tired, and afraid," Fabio said. "But she's not hysterical. Leaving her in the dark for the night probably calmed her down. I don't think she'll cause trouble."

"How long are we going to keep her?"

Fabio looked over at Vera, who was smoking nervously, her eyes bloodshot from fatigue.

"That's what we need to decide. Our plans must change now that we have a hostage. Vera and I learned a lot about her last night. She's not just a random hostage but someone who can help us with our overall mission."

"How can an American photographer help us?" Alfredo asked, frowning.

"It's not what she does as a profession. It's her family. We looked through her pictures last night, the last with her family in Menaggio. There was a birthday party for her father. He had a birthday cake with *'Buon compleanno, Paolo.'* We did a Google search of Paolo de Matteo and found out he's a Wall Street investment banker."

Alfredo cursed. *"Figlio di troia!* Ah, one of those fat American bankers who caused the financial meltdown. Criminals. Those bastards caused all the trouble in the world."

Fabio said, "We kept searching and found a government website where American bankers have to release information about their salary, title, and position."

"What is his salary?" Luca asked.

"Last year he made three million dollars."

Everyone groaned. "Three million dollars—for what?" Alfredo said. "To spread misery around the world? They get rich, and everyone else gets poor?"

Fabio continued. "His bank received millions from the US government so it wouldn't fail. When one American bank, Lehman, failed in 2008, it spread across the rest of the financial world. The American government didn't want more banks to fail, so they gave them money to keep the markets and economy functioning."

"Why did the American government do that?" Luca said. "They should throw the bankers in jail along with the thieves, rapists, and murderers. That's where they belong. Isn't that what we're protesting, the crooked politicians and greedy bankers?"

"The American government is as corrupt as the Italian!" Alfredo said, slapping his hand on the table, almost tipping over the ashtray. "The bankers who cause the trouble hire fancy lawyers, bribe judges, and never go to prison. Just like Berlusconi, Ligresti, Gaucci. Bastards. Criminals! They've always starved the proletariat to fatten up their wallets. I would hang them upside down, all of them!"

"So, Fabio, how does this help us?" Luca asked.

"We get a ransom for his daughter."

"Make him bleed if he wants to see her again," Vera said.

"How much ransom?" Luca said.

"Three million euro," Fabio said, looking from one to the other to notice their reaction. One by one, they nodded, the fatigue melting from their faces. Everyone except Vera.

"Make it ten million. No, twenty million!" she said, stubbing out her cigarette and reaching for her packet on the table. "Take every penny and make him live on the street like a feral dog."

"No, we have to be realistic," Fabio said. "He probably has three million in an account, maybe in Milan, for all we know. That amount he should be able to get to us quickly."

"Make it five million," Alfredo said. "Make him squirm like a pig."

"We don't have time to argue. If we want a ransom, we need to send a letter and a photo of his daughter."

"How will you do that?" Luca asked.

"Brigate Rosse sent communiqués and letters from Moro when they had him in the 'people's prison.' Left them outside newspaper offices in phone booths or garbage cans. They were published, and that's how the whole world knew about Moro in the people's prison."

"Are we going to do that?" Alfredo asked, lighting another cigarette.

"I need to think about the details. But first we need to take care of our hostage."

"What do you mean?"

"She needs to be isolated while we carry out our plan. But not in that tiny room. Luca, clean out your apartment. Remove anything that could identify you. We'll move her there. She'll have a bathroom, lights, more room. I want her more comfortable."

They looked at each other, nodding, all except for Vera. "No!" she spit out. "Keep her where she is. She's our prisoner!"

Luca said to Fabio, "I can do that. My personal things are in my apartment in town. I just sleep here when it's late and we have to be at a job early the next morning. Same with Marietto."

"Good. Then can you cut a hole in the wall between the apartment and kitchen so we can talk to her? Install a blurred window so she can't see us. Put bars over it so she can't break it."

Luca nodded. "I've got tools and glass in storage. Marietto and I can do it this morning."

"Good. I want to move her this morning. One more thing. We want to limit what she knows about us. No one talks to her except Vera and me. I'll hint that our group has many resources and members."

"Good thinking," Alfredo agreed.

"She needs clean clothes," Fabio continued. "She slept in hers last night. If she's more comfortable, with clean clothes, food, books, and magazines, she'll be easier to deal with. Vera, buy her clothes today—toiletries, shoes, whatever a woman needs for a week."

"Buy her clothes?" Vera protested. "Fabio, you're treating her like one of Berlusconi's bimbos! She's a tramp, a Wall Street millionaire's spoiled brat daughter. Treat her like one!"

Fabio raised a hand. "No . . . think about it, Vera. If we treat her well, she'll be easier to deal with. We need time to arrange the ransom. If she were trapped in a small room for a week, she could cause problems, have a breakdown, become hysterical. Treat her like a guest who's going to get us three million euros. Get her what she wants to eat and drink—wine, beer, prosecco, anything."

"That's absurd! She's our prisoner. She should live like a prisoner at San Vittore," Vera fumed. She stood up and walked toward the door.

"Cooperate or you won't be able to talk to her. I need a woman to deal with her, to know what a woman would want and need. Don't be so emotional. You need to get some sleep."

"You know what I want to do with her, don't you, Fabio?" Vera said, her eyes ablaze.

He nodded. "I do. But you're not going to. She's too valuable; she's going to get us a three million euro ransom. Think about that before you explode again."

CHAPTER TWENTY-ONE

Paolo stood outside the Hotel Cavour the next morning, waiting for Cole and Angela's taxi to bring them from Stazione Centrale. They had talked several times that morning. Cole and Angela had taken a train from Modane to Milan and then had gotten a taxi at Stazione Centrale to bring them to the hotel.

When the taxi pulled up to the hotel, Angela was waving at Paolo from a half-opened window, "Nonno! Nonno!" she yelled gleefully.

Paolo opened the taxi door, and she jumped into his arms. "Nonno, I'm so glad you're here. Is Mom with you?"

"No, dear, not yet," Paolo said, trying not to show his distress. They hugged again, and she squeezed him tightly. "Will Mom be back today?"

"I hope so. How was your train ride?"

"Super! We ate breakfast in the dining car. I had a Nutella croissant and a latte *macchiato* with real coffee. Everyone was so nice. I spoke Italian to the waiter and the people next to us."

"Wonderful," Paolo said, releasing her from their hug and greeting Cole. They shook hands and then embraced. "Thanks for getting back so soon," said Paolo. "I was worried about you; could hardly sleep last night."

"I didn't get much sleep either. But Angela slept better—fortunately." Cole's hair was mussed, he hadn't shaved, and his shirt looked like he'd slept in it.

Paolo took Cole's arm and Angela's hand and walked to the hotel entrance. "Come on. I have a suite for us: separate bedrooms, living room, and balcony on Piazza Cavour. They brought up a bowl of fresh fruit this morning."

"Are we going to see the police today?" Cole asked.

"Yes, at two o'clock at the Questura, right down the street. I hope they have good news. I've been watching the news all morning and reading the papers. They released the names of those shot, but nothing about Sylvia. The news shows are questioning why the police haven't found her yet."

Valets retrieved Cole's and Angela's luggage from the taxi and wheeled it on a cart into the hotel and up the elevator to the fourth floor. Paolo led Cole and Angela down the hall and unlocked the door.

The door opened into a foyer that led to a small living room with a sofa, chairs, a coffee table, and a TV on the wall. The room was elegant, with a glass chandelier and prints of Milan's landmarks on the walls. A vase of fresh lilies and a bowl of fresh peaches, apricots, bananas, and kiwis were on the table.

The valets set down the luggage, and Paolo handed them a crumpled pack of euros for a tip.

"Angela, let me take you to your bedroom," Paolo said, picking up her suitcase and leading her down the hall. Angela followed him. She walked around the room, ran her hand over the dresser by her bed, and went over to the window to pull back the drapes to look out on Piazza Cavour.

"I like it, Nonno. I even have my own TV."

Cole carried his and Sylvia's luggage into the second bedroom and put hers in the walk-in closet. The room had two queen-sized beds, matching dressers, a table, sofa chairs facing the window, and a TV.

When Cole returned to the living room, Paolo was hanging up the desk phone after asking for Angela's caretaker to come up.

"Angela, could you please come into the living room?" Paolo said. She returned to the living room and sat next to him on the sofa. He took her hand. "Honey, I know you're worried about what happened to your mother, but we're going to stay here until she comes back. I'm confident she'll come back soon so you can all return safely to New York."

"When, Nonno? I want Mom back," she said, her eyes tearing. "I really miss her. . . . I'm afraid. . . . I cried last night."

"I know you did. So did I. Nonna too. We all did. But we have to be strong the next couple of . . . days . . . until she's back with us."

"Why can't the police find her and bring her back?"

"They're doing all they can. I went to the police station last night and talked to the chief of police, a very nice gentleman who's working on it along with all the police in Italy. Cole and I are going back this afternoon."

"Can I go too?"

"No. I have a nice woman who's going to stay with you while we're gone. She's a mother, a nurse, a kind, sweet lady. She's coming to our room in a few minutes to meet you."

"A nurse? Why do I need a nurse?"

"You don't, but I thought it would be good to have someone who's cared for people."

Angela shrugged and wrinkled her brow in a nonchalant way. "Well, okay, I guess. How long will you be gone?"

"Not long. Then we'll come back and go out to lunch at a nice restaurant."

Ten minutes later, there was a knock at the door. Paolo answered it and led in a tall, distinguished woman dressed in pale blue trousers, a white polo shirt, a white light sweater over her shoulders, and brown leather sandals. Her wavy blonde hair was tightened up into a bun. She wore light makeup and no jewels except for two small pearl earrings.

"Angela, this is Clelia."

Angela looked up at the woman without any show of emotion.

The woman bent down to look Angela in the eye. *"Ciao,* Angela. *Come stai?"*

"Bene," Angela said softly.

"I like girls your age, Angela. I had two daughters who were your age once. Tell me, what do ten-year-old American girls like to do?"

Angela shrugged her shoulders and looked away. "I don't know . . . read books . . . watch TV . . . go to ballet."

"Oh, you dance ballet? I love ballet. My girls took lessons when they were your age. My husband and I used to take them to La Scala to see the Nutcracker, Giselle, and Swan Lake."

"What are their names?"

"Vittoria and Carolina. They're mothers now and gave me three grandchildren. They're just babies, not grown up and pretty like you. Two of them don't even have a single tooth yet."

Angela looked over at Paolo as if she were seeking approval. He stood to the side, nodding, pleased that Angela was warming up to Clelia. He winked at Angela, who returned a half-smile.

"Your *nonno* told me you spent the summer with them in Menaggio. I'll bet you had a lot of fun. You have a great tan. Did you go swimming?"

"Yes . . . Nonno took me to the lido so I could swim with my friends. And we rode ferries a lot."

"He said you love gelato."

Angela grinned and looked over at Paolo, whose smile widened. "Pistachio. I only eat pistachio."

"Oh, it's my favorite flavor too. Shall we have them bring us pistachio gelato to the room?"

"Can we? Nonno? I haven't had pistachio since yesterday."

* * * * *

Cole and Paolo left for the Questura at noon and walked down Fatebenefratelli. The street was more crowded than it had been the previous night. Polizia di Stato vans were still parked facing each other in front of the Questura. A half dozen agents wearing bulletproof vests and holding machine guns were patrolling in front of the arched entrance, eyeing passing cars and talking on radios.

A police escort took them through the headquarters and up the elevator to the vaulted DIGOS area. The hallways and offices were mostly vacant or quiet. Only two plainclothes agents were in their offices talking on the phone.

Lucchini was in his office, reading a stack of papers from files on his desk. His suit coat was hung loosely on a clothes rack in the corner. His face was drawn, and his eyes looked as if he hadn't slept. His tie was loosened, his shirt winkled. He stood up when he saw them at the door. He managed a half-smile, which vanished quickly.

"Please come in. Have a seat."

Paolo introduced him to Cole. "*Dottor* Lucchini, this is my future son-in-law, Cole Boylton. He brought back my granddaughter, Angela, from France this morning."

"Thank you for bringing him along, Mr. de Matteo. I'm glad you both came. We have questions to ask Mr. Boylton about your daughter. I'd like an agent to come in and take notes."

Lucchini made a quick call, and within seconds a plainclothes DIGOS agent was sitting behind them. Cole related the events of their day in Milan: shopping, taking a taxi to Stazione Centrale, and Sylvia insisting on staying to take photos in the station.

"Did you have any contact with Sylvia after you separated?" Lucchini asked.

"No. Her cell phone was in her purse, which I had on the train, along with her luggage. She had her camera, camera bag, and a couple of shopping bags."

"Did you see her talk to anyone in the station?"

"No. We turned and walked toward the train. I turned once and saw her photographing murals on the walls."

"Did she have contact with any suspicious people on your vacation?"

Cole shook his head. "No, not at all. We traveled like tourists. She talked to several people for her work, all professionals—artists, architects, historians. Her Italian is very good; she spoke to them all in Italian."

"Did she exhibit any . . ." he looked around, struggling for the right word, "unusual behavior at any time?"

"No, she was herself the entire time we were in Italy. Happy, excited to show me around. She's been to Italy many times, as I'm sure her father has told you."

"Yes, he has. Let me bring you both up to date on our investigation. We released Sylvia's name and photo to the media. They want more information, but we are withholding it until we have talked to you.

"Any news about Sylvia?" Paolo asked.

"Not yet. Investigators all over the country are on alert. They have her photo and name. Our detectives are contacting sources—some very sensitive, as you could imagine—in the Mafia, in radical political groups, and among known criminals, to see if they have information that would help us. Our command center is taking 113 calls from around the nation from people who think they have leads. We've received thousands of calls already, and it's taking time to follow up."

"When will we learn what they've done with her?" Paolo asked.

Lucchini shook his head, the wrinkles around his face showing his frustration. "We don't know. We're puzzled as to why her captors have not released any information. That's unusual. Typically, when there's a kidnapping or hostage taking, the captors contact the police or media, stating their demands. They have an agenda, and they want publicity for their cause. And it helps us narrow down our investigation. But we don't know their objectives—why they shot the *sottosegretario,* much less why they took an innocent hostage. It's been almost twenty-four hours. We should have heard from them."

"Do you think . . . they might harm her?" Cole asked.

Lucchini shook his head. "I really don't know. If she was a planned hostage, they would have an objective in taking her. But it appears she was grabbed randomly or because she took photos. I don't think there was any political motivation in kidnapping your daughter. She just happened to be in the wrong place yesterday afternoon."

"Would it help if I issue a message through the media asking for her release?" Paolo asked.

Lucchini nodded, straightening his tie. "Possibly. Let's wait to see how our investigation goes. If we hear from them today or tomorrow, we'll learn their intentions and motives. We have artists drawing their faces without sunglasses and caps. When we release those drawings, we'll have thousands more calls from people who think they recognize them. That could break open our case and help us find her."

CHAPTER TWENTY-TWO

S ylvia was lying on the bed, staring toward the ceiling in the dark, fearing spiders were in the room, crawling around the bed, or waiting in a web, preying on insects. There had to be insects in the room; otherwise, spiders would starve. What kind of insects? Oh, God, she was losing her mind, obsessing about spiders and insects.

When she wasn't worrying about spiders, she was recalling the terrible events at Stazione Centrale . . . which led her to think about Cole and Angela. Her conscious mind was a roller coaster of horrible memories, painful thoughts, and deep longing for her family.

Where were Cole and Angela? Were her father and mother still in Menaggio? What did they know about her situation?

Her aches were subsiding. She still felt a dull pain in the back of her head, but sometimes she could forget about it. Her feet were not as sore as on the previous day. Her shoulder didn't ache now; it was just sore when she moved it a certain way. She was grateful she hadn't torn a muscle or ligament.

A rapping on the door startled her. *"Alzati!"* [Get up!] the woman's voice ordered.

Sylvia's heart skipped. She hated the woman's voice and feeling her anger. Were they going to interrogate her again?

"Siediti sul letto e metti il passamontagna. Ti spostiamo." [Sit on the bed. Put on the mask. We are moving you to another room.]

Sylvia did as she was ordered; she sat on the bed, pulled the woolen cap over her face, and waited. The lock turned and the door opened. She heard a faint shuffle of feet coming in. They were moving her to another room—what did that mean? Would it be smaller, darker, more depressing? A basement dungeon?

A hand grabbed her arm and lifted her off the bed. She stood uneasily as the arm led her out of the room. She shuffled awkwardly along, wearing her one sandal. She counted nine steps before a hand touched her back, turned her to the right, and gently pushed her forward.

"Ancora qualche passo," [A few more steps] the man's voice said, apparently the one whose hand was on her back. She counted six steps forward until the hand on her arm braked her movement. The hand on her back fell off. She was standing alone. Where was she? It had been only ten or fifteen meters, not far from where she had been. Was this an apartment? A home? A basement? Someplace in the country?

A door behind her shut. A lock clicked. She remained standing, waiting for the next command. She wanted to take off the mask but feared someone was behind her, the terrible woman, who would hit her like she'd threatened to do before. Was it day? Night? She'd slept fitfully over the last many hours and had lost concept of time. She needed bearings—time, place, day, night. She felt her sanity would erode if she didn't get some bearings.

The man's voice came from her left but was muffled, as if it was behind a door. *"Togli il passamontagna."* [Take off the mask.]

She pulled off the woolen cap and looked around, squinting as she adjusted to the sudden brightness. She was in a larger room with a light burning overhead. She could see again!

Her eyes darted around the room to examine her surroundings. A desk and chair in front of her. A larger bed against the wall to her right. A table with magazines and newspapers. An open door in the corner that looked like it connected to a bathroom. She walked over and looked in. It *was* a bathroom! There were a sink, toilet, shower, and cabinet. And it was clean! She smelled a deodorizer or liquid cleanser. They actually had cleaned the bathroom for her.

She'd been able to use the toilet only three times since her arrival, a dreadful experience each time. The woman had announced her presence with a loud knock and a command to get up. Sylvia had been escorted with a mask over her head to a cramped room with a dirty toilet, a dingy shower with a moldy plastic curtain, and stains on the walls.

Sylvia had dreaded the possibility that she would be forced to use that shower with mold in the cracked plaster, and have to step onto the filthy cement floor with the hair-clogged drain. The sink had had grunge around the basin and a dried sliver of soap in the dish. A dirty towel had hung from a rack.

Her new quarters were austere, like a trailer. Basic, no frills, but much better than the dark cell. Old prints hung on the walls of popular Italian vacation destinations: Amalfi, Lago Maggiore, Portofino, and Costa Smeralda. A bare wall across from the bed had a square hole covered with blurred privacy glass and metal bars, like in a cheap hotel bathroom. What was that for? She couldn't see out; hopefully, no one could see in.

Sylvia's eyes fell on three shopping bags on the bed. She reached into the first, from Oviesse, and took out three tops, two pairs of shorts, panties, bras, sandals, and walking shoes. The second bag was from a drugstore, Essere & Benessere; it contained makeup, a comb, a brush, a toothbrush, toothpaste, mouthwash, tampons, a razor, a bar of soap, shampoo, conditioner, and aspirin.

She reached into the third, also from Oviesse, and pulled out two fluffy bath towels and face cloths. All of the goods still had price tags. No receipts in the shopping bags.

They were buying her clothes, toiletries, and towels? What did this mean? It was like she was a guest and not a prisoner. She was puzzled by her sudden change of circumstances. Why had they moved her into a more spacious room and supplied her with all these things?

But her main concern was to take a shower. She really needed to feel clean again. She took the towels and toiletries into the bathroom, shut the door, took off her clothes, and took a long, hot shower. She shampooed her hair and shaved her legs. She relished the sensation of the hot water running over her body. It felt wonderful!

When Sylvia emerged from the shower, she toweled off, feeling fresh and clean after too many hours of living and sleeping in the same clothes. She felt the best she'd felt since that afternoon at Stazione Centrale. She put a towel around her and went into the room to get fresh underwear and clothes.

While she'd been in the shower, someone had come into the room and left a tray with food on the desk. Glasses with orange juice and water. A paper cup of coffee. Plates with mozzarella, *bresaola,* sandwich bread, a kiwi, and an orange.

Sylvia held the towel around her and ate some bread with mozzarella and *bresaola,* and she sipped the coffee. She felt hungry for the first time since she'd been a prisoner. They were feeding her healthy food. Why?

She returned to the bathroom to dress, put on makeup, brush her teeth, and swirl mouthwash. She took her time, enjoying the effects of having had a hot shower, clean clothes, and a little food. Her hair was clean and combed. She felt better with a little makeup. Her mouth was fresh from brushing and using mouthwash. She felt like a vibrant woman again, not a prisoner in a cell.

When she emerged from the bathroom, she was more relaxed. As soon as she saw the privacy window, she was reminded that she was still a prisoner, not a guest. She'd had twenty minutes of luxurious pampering when she hadn't relived her kidnapping—the first reprieve from her imprisonment.

Sylvia sat at the table, ate the rest of the food, and sipped the coffee. She closed her eyes, relishing the hot, bitter liquid sliding down her throat. Her stomach felt warm and satisfied.

Sylvia remained confused about the time and day. She thought it had been two days since she'd been grabbed. Her only framework was two periods of restless sleep and nightmares.

A rap on the privacy window startled her.

"Sylvia. It's time to talk." The man's voice. He knew her name.

"Yes, I'm here."

"Are you comfortable?"

"Yes, I am. Thank you for the clothes and food. I feel better. But I still want to go. When will you release me? I want to see my family."

"In good time. Be patient."

She couldn't see his face, just a shadow behind the privacy glass: the shape of a head and neck, like a dummy in a department store window.

"Why not now?"

"Impossible. Don't ask anymore; it won't help. We want you to be more comfortable."

"I am, but I want to leave. My family is waiting for me. They're worried about me. I want to see them. I don't know why you took me. I'm a prisoner; you kidnapped me. That's a serious crime. When they find me, you'll go to jail."

"I don't need warnings, Sylvia. It won't help your situation. Just obey and you won't be harmed."

It was eerie, being alone in a locked room, talking to someone through a blurred window, speaking like a concierge and hotel guest. The shower and clean clothes had improved her mood, but her situation hadn't changed. At least she didn't feel like she was going to be beaten, raped, or tortured.

"Tell me again why you were at the station."

"Like I told you, I'm a photographer writing a book about Italy. I take pictures around the country and publish them in a book."

"I saw some of them from your camera."

"Why did you look at them?" she asked, not sure if she was pleased or irritated. "Those are my pictures. I don't want you looking at them. They're personal."

"I need to know your motivation for taking pictures at Stazione Centrale."

Sylvia felt irritated, not at a flashpoint, but angry that they had looked at her pictures. How many had they seen? She and Cole arriving in Menaggio and spending a few days with her parents. Relaxing around Como. Driving to Venice, Bologna, Parma, Padua, and Vicenza to shoot photos. Returning to Menaggio. She had at least a thousand pictures in her camera. Had he looked at all of them?

"Do you have any connections to the police or government, Italian or American?"

"Of course not! I'm a private citizen, a commercial photographer, a mother. I resent you thinking I might be a government spy."

"You have a daughter. What's her name?"

"No! I'm not going to tell you. It's none of your business. Let me go. I hate being locked up like a prisoner. I didn't do anything wrong. You're criminals for kidnapping me. You're going to be arrested and thrown in jail. It's just a matter of time—"

"Stop it, Sylvia. I don't want to hear any more. This conversation is over."

The privacy window lightened; the shadowed face was gone. She put her ear to the bars to see if she could hear anything. A faint mumbling of voices, low and muffled. A door shut. It was silent behind the window.

Who had she been talking to? Was he the one who had grabbed her and dragged her down the steps? Or one of the other two who had waved guns at the crowds? What had happened at the station? She had heard shots and running. Had they murdered someone?

She was confused as to why they had improved her confinement conditions. An hour ago, she'd been in a dark cell, hungry, thirsty, sore, sweaty. Now she'd had a shower, put on new clothes, brushed her teeth and hair, and had something to eat. And she could see around the room.

With these few nice things, her attitude had improved. What was next? When would the man talk to her again? She was going to give him a name . . . someone who had a calm voice and tried to soothe her with a few kind words.

Mr. Rogers! She'd call him Mr. Rogers, from the children's TV show *Mr. Roger's Neighborhood*. Angela had loved Mr. Rogers when she was younger.

Was she going a little crazy? To think of something so silly as recalling Mr. Rogers and giving her captor his name? She was a prisoner, living in a cell, forced to be away from her family, and she was thinking of a children's TV show.

CHAPTER TWENTY-THREE

DAY FIVE

Fabio was sipping coffee and eating toast with apricot jam the next morning in the kitchen, reading the Sunday newspapers, while Marietto was preparing breakfast for Sylvia.

La Repubblica read: *L'ostaggio della Stazione Centrale ha un nome.* [The hostage in Stazione Centrale has been named.] *Identificata la donna presa come scudo umano: è la fotografa americana Sylvia De Matteo. Paura per la sua incolumità.* [The woman taken as a human shield has been identified. She's an American photographer, Sylvia de Matteo. Fear for her safety.]

Il Giornale read: *Il Sottosegretario Pallucca ancora in pericolo di vita.* [*Sottosegretario* Pallucca still in danger of death.] *I terroristi di sinistra autori della sparatorio tengono in ostaggio un'americana. Berlusconi preoccupato.* [The left-wing terrorists are keeping an American woman as a hostage. Berlusconi is very concerned.]

Corriere della Sera read: *Identificata la donna ostaggio: è americana.* [The woman hostage has been identified: She's American.] *La fotografa Sylvia De Matteo è nelle mani dei killer da ieri. Non ci sono rivendicazioni.* [The photographer Sylvia de Matteo is in the killer's hands from yesterday. No claims of responsibility yet.]

Sylvia's photo ran below the headlines with her name, age, and New York hometown.

Corriere della Sera continued: Polizia di Stato released the name and a photo of the woman taken hostage Thursday afternoon at Stazione Centrale. She is Sylvia de Matteo, 37 years old, a New York commercial photographer. Ms. de Matteo was waiting to board a train to Paris before returning to New York from a vacation with her 10-year-old daughter, Angela, and fiancé, Cole Boylton. Ms. de Matteo's daughter and fiancé were on the train when Ms. de Matteo was seized by gunmen in a dramatic scene witnessed by hundreds of horrified travelers.

Three assassins were involved in the violence, which lasted less than three minutes. They shot and seriously wounded sottosegretario Adriano Pallucca and two Polfer agents. One assassin seized Ms. de Matteo, dragged her out of the station, and pushed her into a white Fiorino, which sped away.

Witnesses say the Fiorino drove north on Via Melchiorre Gioia, but police cars arrived too late to pursue the vehicle in heavy traffic. Police are searching suburbs and industrial parks in northern Milan and the autostrada.

Questura released CCTV photos of the three terrorists, enhanced by forensic artists. One woman and two men were wearing wraparound sunglasses and caps that disguised their appearance.

Police officials have released little information about the shooting and hostage taking. A nationwide alert is in force at airports and train and bus stations.

Anyone with information about the Stazione Centrale shooting is urged to call 113. Police are investigating tips already received but are releasing no information.

Police agents are going door to door in neighborhoods, coffee shops, bus stops, and newspaper kiosks along the Fiorino's escape route to inquire if anyone saw the vehicle after the shooting.

The enhanced photos of Luca, Alfredo, and Vera ran across the middle of the article. The lower half of their faces were taken from the CCTV cameras. Their eyes, noses, and foreheads were illustrated, looking almost lifelike but not fully accurate.

Alfredo's forehead appeared higher than it was in real life, his eyes widely spaced. His half beard made him look like a criminal.

Luca's forehead was mildly distorted, wider, and the cheekbones were too prominent.

Vera's was more lifelike, including the small scar on her right cheek. Her eyes were smaller and more deep-set in the illustration. Her face was bloated, not attractively lean like when she was a model.

The enhanced photos made it feasible that someone could recognize them. If so, it was only a matter of time before police would investigate leads and track them down.

Luca, Vera, and Alfredo would be arriving soon after spending the night at their apartments. They would have to go underground to prevent police from finding them and locating the warehouse.

Marietto tapped Fabio's shoulder and pointed to the breakfast tray he'd set next to him. They maintained silence in the kitchen so Sylvia could not hear conversations from the next room.

Fabio went to the privacy window and rapped twice. "I have food for you," he said, his voice neutral. "Go into the bathroom. Shut the door and don't come out. A tray will be brought to your room. Do you understand?"

A shadow appeared on the other side. "Yes. I'll do what you say."

Fabio put on a ski mask, took the tray to the apartment, unlocked the door, went in, and set the tray on the table. He returned to the kitchen and waited until he heard the bathroom door open. A shadow behind the window revealed that Sylvia had sat down at the table.

"Thank you . . . I'm hungry."

Fabio and Marietto left the kitchen and went down the corridor to Luca's office, where Marietto got busy cleaning up the dirty plates, silverware, food containers, wine bottles, glasses, and ashtrays from the previous night.

Fabio turned on Luca's computer, opened the file with Sylvia's photos, and scrolled through them, picking up where he'd left off the previous night. The earliest photos, dated mid-August, were taken around Lago di Como. The first sequence included family pictures at a villa with a garden, a fountain, and benches shaded by stucco walls. Fabio identified Sylvia's father, Paolo, the Wall Street banker; her mother, who used a cane; Sylvia's daughter; and Sylvia's fiancé.

Photos inside the villa showed expensive furniture, a spacious dining room that opened into a living room with a plasma TV, a wet bar, a piano, modern art, and Chinese vases. A wine cabinet held a couple hundred bottles of wine. Her father was wealthy and had expensive tastes.

Most pictures inside the villa were of Sylvia and her father toasting each other, having animated conversations, smiling and laughing, and working in the kitchen wearing aprons while helping an older Italian woman who was cooking pasta and making a salad. The last photos were of the de Matteo family around a dinner table, glasses raised, smiling at the camera. Sylvia's fiancé had apparently taken most of the photos.

Another sequence was from the upper deck of a ferry on Lago di Como. Sylvia, her daughter, and fiancé looked tanned, happy, and relaxed. Most of these photos were of Sylvia and her daughter, smiling, shielding their eyes from the summer sun. One photo was most poignant: Sylvia behind her daughter, hands clutched over her daughter's chest, their faces radiant, eyes bright, smiles warm. They looked very happy.

Fabio studied a sequence of Sylvia and her fiancé together. They stood close, not always touching. Sylvia was inches away, her fiancé's arm over her shoulder, her hands folded in front of her. Sylvia's smile was formal, her fiancé's expression more serious. Fabio interpreted the body language, sensing an emotional distance between them. They were close, but not intimate. More like friends than lovers.

* * * * *

Meanwhile, that same morning, Cole and Clelia took Angela for a walk in the fresh air. They emerged from the hotel into the bright sunlight on Via Fatebenefratelli. It was a hot and muggy day, with dark clouds over the northern lakes and mountains.

"It looks like we'll have rain this afternoon," Clelia said, squinting in the bright sun. "The weather has not been as hot as usual."

Clelia recommended that they walk to Piazza Cavour to take Angela to shops and clothing stores that she would enjoy. Cole took Angela's hand as they crossed busy intersections and walked down Via della Spiga.

At noon they had lunch at Luini's, near the Duomo, each ordering a Milanese specialty, *panzerotto,* a baked dough with various vegetable, meat, and cheese fillings. Angela loved hers, slicing into the soft dough and tasting the warm filling of tomato, mozzarella, spinach, and mushrooms. "Oooh, this is sooo tasty. . . . I love it. I want to bring Nonno here. He loves food like this."

After lunch, they strolled into a shopping mall on Corso Vittorio Emanuele. Cole bought Angela a new hat, like Paolo had done in Menaggio.

By early afternoon, dark clouds were moving toward Milan. The three started back to the hotel, passing a large park, the Giardini Pubblici Indro Montanelli, with shade trees, benches, and a playground.

"Do you want to stop in the park before we go back to the hotel?" Cole asked Angela.

"Oh, please. I miss playing outside. It's boring being in the hotel all day," she said, dropping his hand and running through the gate into the park. She chased a squirrel up a tree, greeted young children in a sandbox, and joined others her age on a swing set. Cole and Clelia sat on a bench nearby and watched Angela as she kicked to gain height on the swings and spoke Italian with the other children.

"It's nice to see her having fun again," Cole said. "She needs to escape for a few minutes and just be a kid."

"Yes, she does. She gets bored in the hotel without other children," Clelia said. "She seems to be making the best of a difficult situation."

"The first day was very traumatic for her," Cole said. "She cried on the train and the night we spent in Modane. The next morning, I tried to boost her spirits, saying we were returning to Milan to reunite with her mother. We said a prayer for her safe release. That made her feel better. Paolo has also been reassuring her, telling her not to worry, that everything is going to be normal soon and we can go back to New York."

"You can see how much love they have for each other," Clelia said. "I'm impressed how emotionally secure she is."

"Sylvia has taught her to be confident. You can see it when she talks to adults. On the train back to Milan, we met a couple from Toronto who had a granddaughter her age. She asked if their granddaughter liked Harry Potter. When they said she did, they talked for half an hour about their favorite characters and how they loved the movies. Before you knew it, we had arrived in Milan. She hadn't worried the whole time."

"That's nice to hear, Cole. She's lucky to have you with her during this traumatic time. Not every man would be so patient."

"You've been a big help already, Clelia, spending time with her when Paolo and I are away."

They left the park and walked toward the hotel, stopping at a *gelateria*. While they were waiting, TV vans and taxis pulled up in front of the Hotel Cavour, letting out reporters and photographers carrying cameras, tablet computers, tape recorders, boom microphones, and lights.

Doors slammed, horns honked, and reporters shouted at each other, jostling for position near the hotel entrance, talking on cell phones, puffing cigarettes, and tossing the butts into the street. A valet came out, asking them to clear a path for guests. But they ignored him, standing two and three deep in front of the entrance.

By the time Angela, Cole, and Clelia walked out of the *gelateria*, the media scrum had taken over the sidewalk and was spilling onto the street. Clelia saw the crowd in front of the hotel when they turned the corner onto Via Fatebenefratelli. She grabbed Cole's arm. "I don't like what I'm seeing. I think we should turn—"

A reporter spotted them at the curb. "Hey, there they are!" he shouted. He ran into the street, lifted his camera, and snapped pictures. Clelia, Cole, and Angela froze when the throng dashed toward them. In seconds, TV lights lit up the intersection, and reporters began shouting.

"Cole Boylton, can I have a word with you?"

"Is that Angela, Sylvia's daughter?"

"Are you worried about your mother, Angela?"

The swarm swirled around them, cameras clicking, TV lights blinding them, boom mikes hovering over their heads.

Cars braked as the street filled with the swarm. Drivers honked and leaned out their windows, swearing at the reporters to clear the intersection. They ignored them, elbowing to get closer and shouting more questions. Pedestrians stopped to watch the throng that was shoving to get close to Cole, Angela, and Clelia.

"Cole, let's run for the hotel!" Clelia said, taking Angela's arm. The media scrum pushed back, not letting them through. Cole put his hand in front of one camera and others snapped his action.

"Hey, don't do that. We need photos!" a reporter yelled.

"Cole, how are you dealing with your fiancée's situation?"

"Angela, have you heard from your mother?"

"Have the police told you where she is?"

"How are you dealing with the crisis, Angela?"

Angela held up her hand to keep the lights from blinding her. A reporter stumbled and bumped her arm, spilling the gelato down her front. It smeared her blouse and plopped on her shoe.

"Get away!" she cried, leaning against Clelia.

"Are you worried about your mother?"

"Get out of here!" Clelia said, pushing through them. "You're pests. Leave us alone!"

"Are you Sylvia's mother? Do you know where she is?"

"Angela, are you going back to New York, or will you wait for your mother to be freed?"

Cole was about to strike a reporter when Clelia grabbed his arm. "Keep walking! Ignore them. Get to the hotel!"

The reporters moved back reluctantly, making them inch across the street. A valet pushed through the crowd, clearing a path to the hotel.

"Out of the way! We have a child with us!" Clelia shouted, pushing through the crowd, an arm around Angela.

The crowd opened enough to let them go through single file, Cole trailing, scowling at reporters, poking his elbows out to keep them away. The swarm followed, cameras clicking, lights shining, as Clelia, Angela, and Cole reached the hotel. Pedestrians moved aside to let them enter.

The reporters slinked back into the street, grumbling, lighting cigarettes, and taking out cell phones to call editors with breaking news. TV reporters stood in front of cameras, sputtering impromptu, emotional statements, claiming to have encountered the hostage's family at the hotel and to have witnessed their grief, with Sylvia's daughter in tears. Taxis continued to pull up and disgorge more reporters and photographers.

The hotel manager took Clelia's arm and led them through the hotel to the elevator. He escorted the three of them all the way up to their room.

Paolo was on his cell phone with Harriet when Cole unlocked the door to their suite. Angela ran to him, throwing her arms around his neck. "Nonno! Nonno! Those people scared me! They pushed me—spilled gelato down my shirt. It fell on my shoes! They're ruined!"

"What the hell?" Paolo's eyes flared, his face reddening with anger. "Harriet, I'll call you back. Angela just came in crying about something that happened on the street." He put down his cell phone and held Angela. "What the hell happened, Cole?"

"We were coming back when a mob of reporters in front of the hotel ran at us. They surrounded us and said rude things that upset Angela. I was appalled."

"I hate the media," Clelia said. "They sensationalize everything, turn a tragic event into a circus. It's dreadful how they treat people in a crisis. They put them in the spotlight and treat them like dancing monkeys. It's pathetic."

The manager was shifting his weight from one foot to the other, looking first at Paolo, then at Clelia, then back to Paolo, waiting to have a word. "Sir," he said, clearing his throat and standing erect. "I apologize for what happened to your family. I'm calling the police to have them disperse the rabble. We'll have security guards at all entrances and keep them out."

"Don't let this happen again," Paolo said, his eyes flashing. "They assaulted my granddaughter. I'm disgusted by their rude behavior. It's totally unacceptable!"

Paolo sat Angela next to him and picked up his cell phone to call Lucchini. He was put on hold until Lucchini was located and came to the phone. Paolo gave a summary of the incident, fuming as he told Lucchini about the assault on Angela. He restrained himself from swearing because she was next to him.

"How did they know we were at the hotel?" he asked angrily. "They have no right to invade our privacy. I'm appalled at their rudeness."

"Sir, I apologize," Lucchini said. "Someone from the press may have discovered where you were staying. You're staying at the hotel closest to the Questura. They could have bribed someone on the staff. I'm very sorry."

"They assaulted my granddaughter! If I knew who it was, I'd file charges against them."

"Our press office will call the newspapers and TV stations and warn them to respect your privacy or face assault charges."

As soon as Paolo rang off with Lucchini, his cell phone rang. It was Harriet.

"Paolo!" she blurted out. "I'm frightened. Reporters are knocking at the door! Have they found Sylvia? How do they know where we live? I wish you were here . . . I'm so upset . . . I don't know what to do."

CHAPTER TWENTY-FOUR

DAY SIX

Antonella Amoruso sipped a *caffelatte* as she toweled off from her morning shower at her Porta Venezia loft apartment. She had clicked on the TV as soon as she had awakened and had propped herself up on pillows, switching channels to see how each station was broadcasting the morning news. They all led with the photos of Sylvia and her captors and with clips from the incident outside the Cavour hotel.

The host for RaiNews on the all-news RAI channel led with: "Sylvia de Matteo: *Ancora nessuna notizia dai sequestratori.*" [Sylvia de Matteo: Still no news from the kidnappers.]

TGCom Mediaset all-news channel reported: "*L'angoscia della famiglia de Matteo per la sorte di Sylvia.*" [The anguish of the de Matteo family on Sylvia's destiny]

SKY Italia led with: "*Attentato alla Stazione Centrale: la polizia brancola nel buio. Nessuna notizia della donna rapita. Il Sottosegretario Pallucca e gli agenti della Polfer ancora in prognosi riservata.*" [The attack at Stazione Centrale: The police still grope in the dark. No news about the kidnapped woman. *Sottosegretario* Pallucca and Polfer agents still in critical condition.]

Mattino Cinque, a Mediaset morning show, reported: *"Sylvia ancora nella mani dei sequestratori. Il pianto di Angela, 10 anni: 'Voglio la mia mamma.'"* [Sylvia is still in the hands of her captors. Angela, ten years old, cries, "I want my mommy."]

The previous night, Antonella had laid in bed watching the evening chat shows. Vapid hostesses and breathless hosts acted shocked and angered by the Stazione Centrale events and then wallowed in the pathos of Angela crying in front of the Cavour. They ended the story by questioning why the Questura had not been able to rescue Sylvia and reunite her with her daughter and fiancé.

Antonella was slipping on her underwear when her cell phone rang. It was her husband, Carlo, calling from Zurich.

"Buongiorno, amore," [Good morning, love] he said, sounding alert and buoyant. "I trust you had a good night's sleep?"

"Could have been better," she said, not wanting to admit she'd tossed and turned all night, wrestling with the turmoil of the last three days and the so-far fruitless investigation. "How about you?"

"Oh, yes, like a baby. I had dinner last night with a Zurich Air executive and have a meeting at their office this morning. Then a quick trip to Helsinki tomorrow, and I'll be home Friday. Do you want to plan anything for the weekend?"

"No, I don't want to plan anything. I never know what's going to happen hour by hour. I've cleared my calendar to work on the shooting investigation, the biggest of my career. My sister was coming this weekend. I asked her to postpone."

"How's the investigation coming along?"

Antonella sat on the bed, keeping one eye on the TV. "I wish I could say we had leads, but not much has developed. We're still searching for the Fiorino, getting calls on the 113 line. Photos were released to the media yesterday."

"They were in the papers here, too. This story is on front pages all over Switzerland. Big story, a well-off American woman with a daughter and fiancé left at the train station. Lots of soap opera material. How's the Italian media playing the story?"

"Grrr. They make me so angry. All news is soap opera to them. They're *oozing* empathy. They're so unctuous, I want to throw up. Now they're criticizing us for not breaking the case, and it's been only three days. Secretly, they want the story to drag on longer so they can milk every bit of juicy gossip and innuendo about the poor de Matteo family. They love crime stories so they can exploit the pathos of the poor families who are victims."

"Do you think the de Matteo woman is alive?"

"I can't say. We haven't heard a word from the kidnappers. That's disturbing. If they murdered her, they wouldn't announce it. The longer this goes on, the less optimistic I am. So many things can go wrong when a victim is held more than a couple of days."

"Good luck. I'll call tonight. I love you."

"Yes, I love you too. Have a good day."

Antonella put the phone on the bed and went into her closet to choose her wardrobe for the day. She ran her fingers over the hangers of dresses, pantsuits, and blouses.

She loved the mornings in her luxurious bedroom with its window seat. She had decorated the room with photos, artwork, pillows, bedcovers, lamps, and ceramics. It was a sanctuary, a quiet hour before she commuted to her office, where the serenity of her bedroom turned into bedlam, with constant phone calls, scheduled and unscheduled meetings, agents bringing her up-to-date on investigations, and the constant bickering and politicking that went on at all levels of the Questura.

Most mornings, Antonella was alone. Carlo's travel schedule took him away almost every week. He would return for the weekend, when they'd go out to dinner or visit friends. Some mornings, she felt like a single woman even though they'd been married fourteen years. Would it ever change?

She selected a favorite outfit: a taupe pantsuit with faint white stripes, a beige blouse, and tan shoes with low heels. She tossed the clothes on the bed and went to her dresser to choose jewelry for the day. She selected a necklace Carlo had given her on their last vacation to Nice. Two years ago—for one week. That's all the time Carlo could get away, except at Christmas, which was spent with her family in Naples or his in Piacenza.

Antonella took off her bathrobe, sat on the bed, and slipped on her pantsuit, trying to remember the last time she'd been with people she loved, having long talks that lasted into the night, drinking wine, eating good food, and celebrating the rewards of years of hard work, devotion, and sacrifice.

Antonella enjoyed her job because of the drama and excitement, and she loved bringing justice to the world. But the job came with a cost: constant stress, a demanding schedule, and the tension of knowing that her phone could ring at any hour of the day or night, sending her on a chase or to a stakeout, often for hours.

Every waking hour, she was thinking about criminals: murderers, Mafia hoodlums, and terrorists. Throughout the day, most people thought about weather, politics, careers, friends, families, movies, food, travel, and sex. Mostly about sex. But since she'd been a cop, she had become preoccupied with understanding the twisted minds of criminals.

Antonella's preoccupation with the criminal mind affected how she related to people. Even when she had lunch with a friend and listened to her talk about her life, career, family, and husband, Antonella found herself listening for clues. Clues that could mask lies. People told lies every day, but police weighed every word in conversations, looking for where the words did not match up with what was known about the person or the situation.

When Carlo called from the road, Antonella listened carefully to his words, almost expecting to hear the hint of a lie. Who did he have dinner with? How many beautiful women did he encounter each week? Was he having clandestine affairs? Did he have secret lovers in Helsinki, Zurich, Munich, Paris, and London, where he traveled most often?

Carlo always professed faithfulness, by words and actions. But was he faithful? Would he come home one day and drop a bomb, saying that he wanted a divorce?

She hated that part of her job: having to weigh every word, looking for a hint that might be a hidden lie. Criminals were often bad liars; you could see it in their eyes, furtive glances away, shifts in body position, facial tics, sweaty hands, or changes in voice inflection.

Antonella envied her sister, Marianna, owner of an art gallery in Bologna. Marianna bubbled over with a love of life. But Marianna had two lovely children and a devoted husband. Her job was interesting with little stress, other than the gallery finances, exhibits, artists, collectors, and attendance. How quaint, worrying that not enough people would come to a splashy opening.

Maybe if she and Carlo had children, she wouldn't be so suspicious. She would never know. She couldn't have children; her Fallopian tubes were constricted. An expensive operation with no guarantees. And, at thirty-eight, she was coming to the end of her ability to have a healthy child.

Would she have been a good mother? She loved kids, especially other people's kids. But she was grateful she didn't have to take care of them when they were sick, crying, and waking up in the middle of the night. Did she have the patience to have been a mother?

* * * * *

Giorgio Lucchini was on his cell phone when Antonella walked into his office half an hour later. He was watching the same morning news programs she had seen earlier at her apartment. He muted the news and closed his cell phone. "Morning. Come in. I've been waiting. Would you like coffee?"

"Yes, please."

"Good. I'll call the bar across the street and have them deliver." Giorgio made the call and put down his cell phone. Antonella liked their morning meetings. Giorgio was all business. Open and respectful—a good boss. He listened to her. Asked good questions. No bullshit or wasted small talk.

"Anything new from last night?" he asked.

"Nothing," she said. "Patrols are out in the neighborhoods along Via Melchiorre Gioia, fanning out, showing photos of Sylvia and the shooters to shopkeepers, people in markets, and parents picking up their kids from school. They've been tracking down owners of white Fiorinos to find out who was driving them the day of the shooting. There are thousands of Fiorinos in Milan, so it will take time."

"Keep looking. You have to do it. Many cases are solved by the long slog of going door to door. What else?"

"They've blanketed the main streets and are working side streets. They're looking in garages and stopping at gas stations, repair stations, parking lots, and rental car outlets. They're showing photos and asking if anyone saw anything unusual that afternoon. Nothing yet."

"How about 113 calls?"

"We're sifting through them, mostly related to the Fiorino. Some callers saw men acting suspiciously. Those are all over the city. It takes time to follow up, but we're working through them."

"How about suspicious cell phone traffic?" he asked.

"We've contacted the telecommunications companies to investigate cell phone calls around Stazione Centrale beginning the morning of the attack. We're looking for repeated calls near the station before and after the attack and cross-checking to see if any calls were made to suspects involved in terrorist attacks."

"Good work," Giorgio said. "That might turn up a good lead." He leaned back in his chair, put his hands behind his head, and crossed his legs, the position he took when he wanted to probe into an investigation.

"I'm expecting something's going to break soon," he said. "This is a major crime. A high-profile hostage—an American woman, even—and we have no leads. If these were seasoned criminals, you'd expect that someone would want them busted and would leak information to us.

But we don't have anything to work on. Maybe they're a small group with no criminal past. They've lucked out so far, but something's going to break in our favor soon."

"The photos we released are critical," Antonella said. "Someone's going to recognize them and give us a name. Then it's just a matter of time."

"People even turn in their friends, especially if it's a terrible crime like this."

"I think they're amateurs who got a hostage dumped in their laps," said Antonella. "Now they don't know what to do. That's why we haven't heard from them. They have to figure out their next move."

Giorgio nodded. "If this was a standard terrorist group, we'd have heard from them already—a communiqué with demands, a screed of right-wing or left-wing ideology. If it was a standard kidnapping, we'd have a ransom note. Kidnappers are impatient; they want to get their hands on a ransom as soon as possible."

"Let's talk about motive," Antonella said. "There may be two, one for the shooting and another for the hostage."

"I think you're right. Shooting a midlevel finance official is blatantly political. Maybe an old grudge, revenge for a past misdeed."

"Or," Antonella said, raising an eyebrow, "something tawdry. A jealous lover. A disgruntled former aide. An old political grievance. Gambling debts. Politicians are not pure; they all have skeletons in their closets and enemies who want to get back at them. They don't get political plum jobs by being altar boys. They've stepped on a lot of toes climbing the ladder to Silvio's circle of close friends."

"Shooting Pallucca in a public place elevates the significance," Giorgio said. "They want to expose him and embarrass the government. We're already looking into his past. Quietly, of course. We can't risk pissing off the PdL."

"The PD would love another juicy scandal to embarrass Berlusconi," Antonella said. "His plate is full already: the sex scandal with the teenage prostitute, the tax-evasion charges."

"He's getting ravaged by the papers every day," Giorgio said. "The euro crisis, government debt, high unemployment, his sleazy cronies. Maybe the terrorists think they can topple Berlusconi from his throne."

A knock at the door. A uniformed Milan police officer was standing outside with a covered paper tray. Giorgio waved him in, took the tray, and handed over a cup of coffee to Antonella.

When the officer left, Antonella said, "Let's not forget about the bombings last week."

"You think there's a connection?"

"Possibly. The first was at the PdL. Was that a left-wing plot? Then the second at the PD. Was that retaliation by some right-wing faction?"

"Don't forget the fringe groups—anarchists, Black Bloc, and No TAV. They've all got crazies who could do something radical to get attention," Giorgio pointed out.

"But no claims from any of them," she responded. "We don't know who did those things or why. No communiqués from any group that claims responsibility. That's puzzling. For the sake of argument, let's say the Stazione Centrale shootings are linked to the bombings. These things happen over a few days according to a plan: throw a couple of bombs, shoot a *sottosegretario*. What's next?"

Giorgio nodded. "I've thought about that. My fear is that this could lead to another *anni di piombo* period. Madonna, I hope it's not a new dangerous group of terrorists. This country isn't stable enough to withstand another group raising hell with bombings, assassinations, kidnappings, and bank robberies. That would create chaos throughout the country."

"Exactly. I'm afraid of what might happen next."

"That's why I wish we'd hear from them, so we would know who we're dealing with."

Antonella asked, "You've talked to Interpol?"

"Yes, a couple of times," Giorgio said. "The Questore has contacted the American consulate as well. The prosecutor has requested from Interpol information on the de Matteo family back in New York. They want to know more about the father, his background, his career, and Sylvia's as well—anything that might give us something to go on. We have taps on Sylvia's and Mr. de Matteo's cell phones in case the kidnappers call. I've told Mr. de Matteo to keep them on the line if they call."

"I'm going into the field today," Antonella said. "I'll be in a patrol car driving around, asking questions. I've got a map in my office of all the streets they've been to and the Fiorinos they've checked out."

"Good. Let me know how it goes."

"I spent ten years in Rome as a street cop before this job. Now I sit behind a desk all day, taking phone calls and telling agents what to do. I miss street action; it makes you feel like a real cop. You never know what's going to happen when you knock on a door or pull over a car."

"I wish I could do more of that myself. But I'm trapped here all day, a prisoner in the Questura. I'll write about that when I create my memoir."

"Do that," she said with a smile. "But make sure you let readers know you couldn't do your job without hundreds of officers and undercover DIGOS on the streets every day. They're the ones who bring in the criminals and make you look good."

Giorgio grinned for the first time that morning. "I'll do that. You can write that chapter." He got up, walked her to the door, and placed a hand on her shoulder. A small crowd of plainclothes DIGOS were outside his door, waiting to see him. They nodded respectfully, moving aside to let her pass.

"I'll have my radio," Antonella said. "Call if something breaks."

"Could be your lucky day, Antonella," Giorgio said. "Be safe."

"You too. Stay at your desk; that's where you do your best work."

* * * * *

It was nine fifteen that evening by the time Giorgio made it home to his Brera apartment. It was the third night he'd been late since the shooting. His wife, Giulia, poured him a prosecco while he took off his coat and went down the hall to spend a few minutes with their two sons, who were playing videogames. He asked about their day at Milan's American school, what they'd done with friends, their homework, and their soccer practice. He said a few sentences in English to test their learning, and he had to make only one correction. He was pleased; they'd be nearly fluent by the time they went to university, a very important skill for professionals in all fields.

After ten minutes, he patted their heads and said in English, "Don't stay up too late. I'll come in to tell you goodnight after I have dinner."

"Good night, Papa," they both said in English, with a slight Milanese accent.

Giulia had reheated dinner and set it on the corner table in the kitchen, where they often ate late meals while looking out at the lights of the Castello Sforzesco. Giorgio sipped a glass of Vermentino wine while he ate lasagne al pesto and a salad with smoked salmon, crème fraîche, fennel, and dill.

Giulia told him about her workday as a patent attorney. These intimate evening dinners were when they often had important conversations about their careers, their boys' progress in school, and other family news.

"How's your big case going?" Giulia asked. "I've been watching the news."

"Not much to say. No word from the kidnappers. The father is upset about the media jumping on his daughter and Sylvia's fiancé outside their hotel yesterday."

"I saw it. So sad. That poor family. Do you think Sylvia is safe?"

"Madonna, I hope so. She's a mother with a young daughter. So much life ahead for both of them. She's from a nice family. It would be tragic if they hurt her."

"My heart breaks when I see a family in crisis. One day their lives are perfect. The next, they're victims of a terrible crime. They didn't do anything wrong, and now they're in the hands of ruthless criminals."

After dinner, Giorgio went into his library with his glass of wine. He put on the CD of Puccini's "Turandot," went over to the window, and looked out over Milan. Such a beautiful city at night, with bright lights that stretched in all directions. He gazed at the red taillights of cars driving down Via Ponte Vetero and at the neoclassical columns and beautiful communal garden of the nineteenth-century building in which he lived.

Giorgio took out his cell phone and called Paolo. "Good evening, Mr. de Matteo. This is Giorgio Lucchini calling. I know it's late. I just wanted to check and see how you are."

"Thanks for the call, Mr. Lucchini. I've been watching the news all night. CNN and the BBC are covering this. Sylvia's photo was on the front page of the *New York Times* today."

"My press office is getting calls from all over the world for updates. How are you managing?"

"Fine, under the circumstances. I'm alone. Cole went out for a walk and dinner. Angela is spending the night with her caretaker, whom the hotel arranged. Angela likes her very much. She had her two married daughters come to her apartment so Angela could play with her young granddaughters. It's better for Angela to be there than stuck in a hotel all night."

"That's nice. I hope to meet Angela one day."

"Of course. She's sweet, very personable."

"I'm sure she is."

"Any news about Sylvia?"

"Nothing, I'm sorry. We have patrol cars all over the city searching for her. We're coordinating with Interpol and the American consulate. Thousands of officers are on the streets day and night doing their jobs to bring her back safely. Officers follow up on thousands of leads that eventually lead to a break."

"I understand. It's just hard when it's your own daughter who's the victim."

"I want to be honest with you, Mr. de Matteo. It's unusual for us not to have heard from the criminals. It's puzzling, not knowing why they did what they did."

"Waiting is taking a toll on all of us," Paolo said with a tone of exasperation. "I can't sleep, read, watch a movie, be with my wife—any of the things that relax me. Call me the minute you have news."

"Of course. Maybe tomorrow we'll get a break."

"Let's hope so," Paolo sighed. "I don't know how long I can hold up with all the stress. It's terrible for all of us."

CHAPTER TWENTY-FIVE

A stack of morning papers had been piling up in Luca's conference room, and the TV had been on all day. Luca had driven off in the Fiorino the middle of the previous night and had ditched it in the basement garage of an abandoned construction site several miles away. He'd returned with Marietto, driving one of his trucks. Luca and Alfredo had shaved their beards and gotten haircuts. In addition, Fabio had advised them to wear floppy hats and sunglasses during the day.

"Tomorrow Marietto will deliver the communiqué and cell phone photo to the RAI station near Corso Sempione," Fabio told them as they sat around the table later that afternoon, drinking wine and eating kebab sandwiches.

"Why not *Corriere della Sera*? That's the best newspaper for us," Luca said.

Fabio shook his head. "It may be, but it's around the corner from the Questura on Fatebenefratelli. I don't want to risk anything; if someone sees Marietto put it in the trash bin, they might remember and report it. It's too risky."

"That would be risky," Luca said, nodding. "There's plenty of newspapers and TV stations where we can drop off the package."

"One of the telejournalists from RAI Tg3 has been reporting more objectively than the trashy journalists from RAI1 and RAI2 or those pitiful so-called reporters at Berlusconi's Mediaset stations," said Fabio. "His name is Pietro Besana. I heard about him when I was in high school. A very passionate leftist who went to Università Statale. He studied political science, and we had some of the same teachers when I attended ten years later. He's become a good journalist."

"I watch him too," said Vera. "He's not a Berlusconi lackey like so many others on RAI and Mediaset."

"I'll address the envelope to Besana and call him in the morning from a public phone that can't be traced. I'll tell him he has fifteen minutes to retrieve it before the trucks drive by at ten thirty to pick up trash.

"Marietto will put the envelope in a trash bin at ten o'clock in the morning on Corso Sempione near the Agip gas station, about fifty meters from the RAI. I've already warned him that the Guardia di Finanza commissary is close to the RAI headquarters. He'll make sure no one is watching when he puts the envelope in the trash bin."

"What if police check fingerprints?" Luca asked.

Fabio held up a paper sack and dumped out a pack of envelopes in a plastic wrapper. "Vera bought these envelopes this morning. When I open the package, I'll wear rubber gloves. Same with handling the communiqué and the cell phone photo of Sylvia holding up yesterday's newspaper. Marietto will wear rubber gloves when he handles the envelope as well."

"Good thinking," Vera said. "What about the ransom?"

"We'll give her father three days to come up with the ransom."

"How will we get the money?" Alfredo asked.

"Last month when I was thinking about our plan, I anticipated that we might take a political hostage and negotiate a ransom. One of my classmates at Università Statale, a trusted friend, works at a charity and handles its finances, sending and receiving wire transfers from various offices around Italy and some outside the country.

"His political views are the same as ours. I asked if he would be willing to help us. Not only is he willing, but he shared with me how this could be done even under police surveillance."

"Really? How would he do this?" Luca asked.

"Our ransom demand will be for three million euros, to be deposited to the account of Casa di Marta e Maria, an international charity that aids abused women and children. The amount will remain there for a few days, but then portions of it will be wired to clinics and group homes that take care of women and children. Some of these monies will sit in dummy accounts until the home or clinic has been approved for receiving funds. My friend can open an account, close it in a few days, and eliminate any records with a few computer keystrokes. He took an accounting course and learned how the Mafia launders money from drugs, prostitution, and extortion and puts it into legitimate businesses like restaurants, resorts, and hotels.

"The police will be monitoring accounts once the ransom is delivered, expecting it to be wired into an account, leading to our arrest. After a couple of months, my friend will get us a card to withdraw money from an account, but not in large amounts that would attract attention."

"I like that. I hope it works," Vera said, exhaling cigarette smoke. "I want some of that money. I earned it."

Fabio shook his head. "No. We have to be patient. This money will be used to support our cause, get us vehicles and places to stay, and buy more weapons if Alfredo wants them. This money won't end up in our pockets but will support what we do in the future."

Everyone nodded, understanding Fabio's reasoning.

"So, we go on with our lives?" Alfredo asked.

"Yes, but we have to make changes in our daily lives. For the next couple of weeks, we'll be underground. Stay in your apartments at night; don't go out to bars or restaurants, where you could be seen. Keep away from crowds. The enhanced photos are close enough for people to identify you. Be only with people you know and trust. If anyone questions you about the photos, just laugh and say they look like half the people you know. Don't act suspicious. Especially you, Vera."

"Don't pick on me. I'm a loner, anyway. My few friends are all in Sicily."

"Maybe you should go there until the heat is off. Stay a couple of weeks until I call you."

"I might do that. Then I won't have to wash Sylvia's laundry or shop for her. You're spoiling her, *quella ricca troia borghese."* [That rich, bourgeois bitch]

Fabio shook his head. "I understand your anger, but we have to keep focused on our goals. We need to get the ransom and release Sylvia while we're getting ready for our next operation. Until then, we have to treat her well to get what we need. If she has what she needs, she's less likely to cause problems. I needed her to write that letter to her family, which we'll deliver with our communiqué and her cell phone photo. If we hadn't treated her well, she might have refused. Let me deal with Sylvia. She's compliant."

* * * * *

After the others had left for the evening, Fabio rapped on the window. "Sylvia, do you want to talk?"

Sylvia got off the bed and went over to the blurred window. "Yes. I don't like being alone all the time. It's driving me crazy."

This was the second time Fabio and Sylvia had talked that day. Earlier in the morning, he'd informed her that he needed her to do two things that would get her released.

She'd listened to his requests and agreed to cooperate. Fabio had wanted a cell phone picture that would be delivered to the Italian media. When she had agreed, he had put on a mask, gone into her room, given her a newspaper, and taken a picture on his cell phone of her holding the newspaper with the headline of her capture.

When he had taken the photo, he had left a tablet for her to write a letter to her family, to be delivered along with the photo.

"Thank you for cooperating and writing the letter," Fabio said to her shadow behind the glazed window. "It will be delivered tomorrow. Your family will know you're being well taken care of and in good health."

"You could let me go, no questions asked. They want me back. I want to leave as soon as I can. This is terrible; I'm a prisoner cut off from my family. I want out of here."

"Be patient."

"You're asking a ransom from my father, right?"

"Like I told you, yes."

"Bastard. You'll end up in prison for this. Kidnapping is a serious offense all over the world."

"We're taking good care of you."

"Feeding me, giving me clothes and magazines, but I'm still a prisoner in this miserable place. I hate it; it's the worst experience of my life."

"It may be over soon. Then what will you do?"

"That's a stupid question. I'll go back to my family, fly to New York, and have a normal life."

"Your story is big news in America. The *New York Times* has reported it on the front page."

"I don't care. I don't want that kind of publicity. I never did."

"You'll get offers to write a book and maybe a screenplay."

"That's ridiculous. I'm not that kind of person. I don't want to be a celebrity because of a crime you committed."

"They'll tempt you with a lot of money."

"Money's not important. Family and friends are what I value."

Fabio contemplated her statement. Her defiance was to be expected, but she was managing to restrain her emotions and not be belligerent. She was a mature, sophisticated woman keeping her senses so she could make the right decisions to save her life. "What was your life like before this?" he asked.

Sylvia was puzzled. Why was he asking these questions, appearing to care about her and to want to know about her life? He was a criminal, a kidnapper, and yet he acted like someone you'd meet at a party. She didn't know what to tell him. *Doesn't he have more important things to talk about than my life?*

"I have a good life—a very good one. I have a busy career, many friends, a loving family. What more could a person want?"

It took Fabio a minute to answer. When he did, he asked a question that surprised her.

"How will your life be different when you return to New York?"

It was a thoughtful question, implying concern and empathy. "I . . . I really don't know," she answered. "Maybe . . . I'll be more careful . . . more patient . . . slow life down a bit. I've been terrified here . . . in this horrible, terrible place. I don't even know how many days I've been here—three, four, maybe five."

She was somewhat touched by his questions, wondering what he was looking for. She wanted to turn the tables.

"How have . . . the last few days changed you?" she asked, holding her breath.

Fabio was surprised by the question. Sylvia was right; maybe he had changed somewhat. But he didn't know what to say. "I'd have to think about it."

"You have time," she said, surprised by how bold she sounded. "Neither one of us is going anywhere that I can tell."

He took his time before answering. "True, we'll be here . . . longer," he said not wanting to say more.

Sylvia was intrigued. It seemed he wanted to talk more. But why? She thought about what she should say next that wouldn't end the puzzling conversation. She considered several questions that seemed lame and then simply said, "Tell me about yourself . . . what you can."

Fabio leaned back in the chair, pondering what he should say. He obviously could give no details that the police could use to identify him.

He had to keep it short and unrevealing. "I come from a small family. My father died when I was very young."

Two short sentences. But to Sylvia, they revealed much. Losing his father at a young age probably had been very traumatic for him. Perhaps he was a loner, not a crazy maverick. She wanted to know more but veered away from his personal life, since he would likely shut down and the conversation would be over.

"Your English is very good, I must say. How did you learn to speak so well?"

He was quicker to answer this time. "I started early in school. I've been to America twice, once for . . . a long time."

"Do you know many Americans?"

"A few I met when I was there. We don't keep in touch, but I think about them often. They were good people—friendly, warm. They took me into their homes, and I met their families."

"Were you a student?"

"More or less. But I traveled too."

"Can you tell me where you traveled? America's a big country."

"I . . . I'd rather not say."

"Okay. I understand. I like that you met nice Americans."

"I like most Americans I've met. They're . . . almost like Italians."

CHAPTER TWENTY-SIX

DAY SEVEN

Ablue Milan *polizia* car raced down Via Melzi d'Eril with blue lights flashing and siren wailing, forcing buses, cars, and taxis to pull to the right lane. The speeding *polizia* car turned the corner at Corso Sempione and drove two blocks to the RAI TV station. People on the sidewalk stopped to follow the drama, wondering if there'd been a shooting at the station. The 150-meter-high RAI tower was a prominent landmark in that area of Milan, rising above Parco Sempione and the four-lane boulevard Corso Sempione.

A four-meter-high fence was the first line of security around the heavily guarded RAI compound, where one of Italy's major government TV stations broadcast news.

The *polizia* car slowed at the RAI entrance, where a team of security guards waited in a guardhouse inside the fence. A guard came out and opened the gate as Antonella emerged from the front passenger seat and flashed her DIGOS badge. "We're here to meet Pietro Besana," she said. "He called twenty minutes ago. He knows we're coming."

The guard assumed a rigid posture of respect for Antonella's commanding presence. She was dressed in a black pantsuit and crisp white blouse. She held her head high, and her eyes swept around the immediate area of the entrance, taking in the people staring at her and at the *polizia* car with the flashing lights. The guard glanced down at Antonella's waist and saw her weapon clearly visible on her belt, ready to be drawn and aimed in a split second. DIGOS had the reputation of being the toughest and most experienced police agency in the country. She was the first DIGOS the guard had ever encountered; she looked fearless and dangerous. The guard would have a gripping anecdote to share about DIGOS with his colleagues after he'd escorted her into the building and taken her to Besana's office.

"Yes, of course. We were notified," he said, stepping aside to allow her to pass. "You may enter the compound. *Dottor* Besana is waiting in his office. I will escort you."

Antonella walked quickly through the open gate. She hurried up the steps, followed by the escort and a Milan *polizia* officer who had emerged from the backseat. The escort rushed ahead and opened the glass double doors into the station and then led them through the lobby. An elevator was waiting, because the guardhouse had called when the *polizia* car had arrived.

When they exited at the fourth floor, the escort led them down a carpeted hall. Administrative offices were around the perimeter of the fourth floor. The spacious center of the floor was a large open area behind glass. It contained recording studios, rows of reporters' desks with computers, and more than a dozen TV monitors broadcasting news from Telelombardia, Mediaset, RAI, La7, Sky, CNN, BBC, and Deutsche Welle.

Everybody in the enclosed glassed area was busy. People were working, tapping at computer keyboards, congregating in twos and threes to talk and sip coffee, and keeping an eye on the TV monitors for breaking news from around the world.

The RAI junior staff were dressed informally in slacks, jeans, casual shirts, and blouses. They looked to be recent university graduates, attractive and poised, eager to show they were cut out for the highly competitive world of telejournalism.

On-air reporters and readers appeared to be a few years older and were dressed more formally. The men had stylish haircuts and wore dark suits with white shirts and dress ties. The women looked like fashion models: long hair, makeup, fashionable dresses, silk blouses, and too much jewelry. They lingered around three partially lit sets with backdrops of props and station logos. The set was crowded, with sound, light, and camera technicians wearing headsets and circling on-air reporters or readers who were attended by people briefing them about news content from the editorial staff, brushing imaginary specks off their clothes, dabbing on makeup, and combing back strands of loose hair.

The escort led Antonella and the Milan *polizia* officer to a corner office with Pietro Besana's name and title on a plaque outside the door. Besana's door was open, and his office was lit with natural light coming through corner windows that looked out toward Corso Sempione and, in the distance, the white marble arches of the Arco della Pace at the entrance to Parco Sempione.

A tall, handsome man dressed in an expensive sport coat and slacks pushed back from his desk and stood when the escort knocked on his open door. His dark, wavy hair was touched with streaks of white that made him look like a model or an actor. He smiled at Antonella, his eyes warm and gentle.

"I'm DIGOS Deputy Antonella Amoruso, in charge of antiterrorism," she said, flashing her badge at him. "The Questura received a call that you had received a communication from the Stazione Centrale terrorists."

"Welcome to RAI. We've been waiting," Besana said, reaching across his desk to shake her hand. He motioned for her and the Milan *polizia* officer to sit down.

A shorter, much older man who looked like a lawyer or an accountant was sitting off to the side. With his sad, drooping eyes, paunch, and partially bald head, he certainly would not be appearing before TV cameras. He stood and introduced himself. *"Buongiorno, Dottoressa Amoruso. My name is Gianfranco Massarini. I am Pietro's director in charge of news at Tg3. Welcome to our station."*

Antonella shook his hand and then looked down at Besana's desk at a wide white envelope, two sheets of paper, and a color photo printed on paper.

"Is this what was in the envelope?" she asked, leaning over to examine the items.

"Yes. I received a call at ten fifteen this morning instructing me to go to the waste bin on Corso Sempione to pick up an envelope about the American woman hostage."

"Tell me about the caller. A man or a woman?" she said, leaning lower to look at the photo of Sylvia.

"A man. It was a very short message stating I should get there before the trash truck picked it up."

"What else did he say?"

"Just that a package was there from the people who had Sylvia de Matteo."

"Did he give a name?"

"No, just the message. Then he hung up."

"Any distinctive tone to the voice? Was it a young man? An old man? Any stutter or voice tone you could describe? Was it an accent from Milan, or any strong accent from a recognizable part of Italy?"

"I think he was Milanese. The call didn't last more than fifteen or twenty seconds."

"Did you ask who he was?"

"Yes, I did. He ignored me, repeated his message, and hung up. I was puzzled, of course, and thought it might be a prank. But I didn't have time to think more about it. I immediately left the building and asked a security guard to accompany me. We found the trash bin by the Agip gas station. The envelope was buried under discarded coffee cups and paper wrappings."

Antonella looked closer at the white envelope to see if there were any identifying marks. "Did you open it on the street or bring it back to your office?"

"I picked it up by one corner and brought it back to the building. I didn't open it until I was in my office. I thought it might contain explosives, but the security guard said it was too thin. Bombs come in heavier packages or boxes, sometimes with bulges. He said he learned that in a training course."

"There are letter bombs," Antonella said, "but they are bulkier than this envelope. The guard gave you good advice. Then what did you do?"

"I shut the door to my office. The security guard was with me. I called *Dottor* Massarini. I wanted them both as witnesses. I opened the flap and let the papers fall on my desk. I moved them around with a pencil so I wouldn't leave fingerprints. The documents appeared real, especially the photo of Ms. de Matteo. I'd been on her webpage and looked at her photos. She has several pictures of herself on her site."

"Why didn't you call us immediately?" Antonella asked. "We would have picked it up and saved you the trouble."

"I didn't want to bother you if it was a hoax. You know how people are—practical jokers, people looking for publicity. Someone might have been shooting a video when the envelope was picked up, with the intention of putting it up on a website as a practical joke. We get a lot of crazy people trying to get publicity for themselves."

"How soon did you call us after you read the documents?" Antonella asked, skimming Sylvia's letter and the communiqué. Sylvia's letter was handwritten on notebook paper. The communiqué was typed and printed. Antonella's hands were behind her back, one hand still holding her badge.

"Probably ten minutes. *Dottor* Massarini and I discussed when we would broadcast about the documents, either on my noon news show or on a special broadcast. I told him I wanted to call the Questura before we reported the news. I said we should cooperate with the Questura, figuring it might help us in the future when you uncover information and want it reported."

"You made the right decision. I'll report what you said to my boss," said Antonella. She picked up her cell phone and called Giorgio. "Sir, I'm at RAI. The documents and letter look legitimate. There's a photo of Sylvia de Matteo, a handwritten letter to her family, and a communiqué with ransom instructions, typed and printed. Besana says he hasn't touched the documents or the photo. He hasn't reported this yet."

She waited a few seconds then answered. "Yes, I've read them. I'll put them back in the envelope and bring them to the station immediately."

Antonella was quiet as she listened to what Lucchini said. Then she looked at Besana. "Did you make copies?"

He nodded. "Yes, we did. We used tweezers to pick up the documents by the corners. No one touched them with their fingers. We want to get approval to report this as soon as possible."

Antonella repeated his message to Giorgio. She shook her head when she heard his response and then spoke to Besana. "No, not yet. Please cooperate with us. We want a news blackout until we study these further."

Massarini stepped closer and pointed at the documents on the desk. "We will cooperate up to a point, *Dottoressa* Amoruso. We are a serious news organization. We report breaking news. This is a major story."

"I understand your position, but this is a serious crime we're investigating." She picked up the tweezers from the desk, lifted each of the documents, and slipped them back into the white envelope. She looked up at Besana. "Why do you think they sent this to you?"

Besana shook his head. "I really don't know. I'm as surprised as anyone."

"What about your background? There must be a reason they called you."

"I don't know why," Besana said, shaking his head. "I'm a serious journalist and have been for twenty years. I was with Telelombardia before I won the public concourse to join RAI."

"Do you know any radicals from your past . . . university days . . . traveling abroad . . . people you met socially or professionally?"

"No, not at all. I don't socialize with people I report on. I rarely go to parties or social events with politicians. My best friends are journalists or friends of my wife. She works for Comune di Milano as a tourist guide. Before our son was born, she was a freelance media planner. Our lives are quite boring, actually. We spend time with old friends, our parents, and friends we've met through our son's school."

"What is your wife's name?"

"Laura Beolchi Besana. I will give you her number if you want."

Antonella took out a notebook and wrote her name and phone number. "Does she have any radical friends from her past?"

Besana smiled. "Not at all. Her family was well-to-do, and she went to private schools. All her friends are from the upper class."

"Anything else I should know about you?"

Besana knit his brow and thought a moment. He felt like he was being interrogated. As a journalist, he was usually the one asking hard questions. "I don't think so. I'm a good Catholic. I go to mass occasionally. I went to a public school, Liceo Classico Beccaria, and graduated from Università Statale twenty years ago with a political science degree."

"We'll check into your background," Antonella said. "There must be a reason they contacted you."

"Please do. I'm a serious, unbiased journalist. I want to be the first to report this story. It's breaking news, the biggest story we've had in Milan in many years."

"Not until you hear from me. I'll call you after we study the documents and photo. My boss at DIGOS will make the decision about when you can report."

Massarini said, "I repeat, *Dottoressa* Amoruso. We're a news organization. Our job is to report news that comes to us. Our lawyers want to get approval in the next hour or so, before other stations or newspapers find out and report first."

"I'm well aware of your job, *Dottor* Massarini. But a woman's life is at stake. These are ruthless criminals who shot several people at Stazione Centrale. They're dangerous, and our job is to protect victims of crimes."

* * * * *

Fifteen minutes later, Antonella and Giorgio were in his office surrounded by police officers and technicians studying the documents laid out on his desk. Photographers were taking pictures of the documents, turning them over with tweezers so no fingers touched them.

"Our first break in the case," Lucchini said, leaning over his desk and looking at the documents through his reading glasses. "I want the prosecutor to see these immediately. Let's check for fingerprints. The photo appears to be of Ms. de Matteo, but photos can be altered. Call *Dottor* Besana and tell him to hold off on reporting until they hear from us."

"They know. I told them I would call this afternoon. They want this for their afternoon broadcast."

"I already got a call from Gianfranco Massarini, director of Tg3. He's contacted the prosecutor, the Questura press office, the Questore, and the Capo di Gabinetto of the Questura. Massarini is putting pressure on everyone to let them report the story within two hours. If we don't give them approval, he hinted it would be leaked in a way that would make our office look bad, like we're trying to strangle the media. We don't want that, so we have to analyze the documents and verify Ms. de Matteo's photo as soon as possible."

"Yes, sir. They're working on that now. They know there's a deadline."

"Call Pietro Besana at RAI and see if there's a chance they could get the phone number from the call. It might have come through a switchboard, and they might have a record."

"I'll call him right away."

* * * * *

Giorgio sat at his desk, his head in his hands, his eyes poring over the documents and photo. Antonella was by his side, rereading the pages that had been copied at the Questura.

Antonella picked up Sylvia's photo and studied it through a magnifying glass that a forensic analyst had brought in. "Sylvia's fingernails appear a bit long. She probably had a manicure before she left New York. I don't think she had one in Italy. It's been three weeks."

"Interesting," Giorgio said. "Anything else you noticed?"

Antonella continued studying the photo with a magnifying glass. "Mmm. Her hair looks a bit long and not well combed. Every woman has a favorite comb and brush she uses every morning after she showers. She probably has a comb, but maybe a cheap one or a man's comb. I see loose strands around her neck and ears that most women would comb through before they leave for work in the morning. She probably doesn't have a hairbrush."

"Very observant," Giorgio said, leaning back in his chair and watching her as she studied the photo. "Keep going."

"She has on little makeup. No blush. A trace of lipstick. She isn't smiling. Her lips are together. It's hard to keep your lips tight. It's an expression of distress. She has tiny wrinkles around her eyes like she's looking at something in the distance."

"Maybe whoever is taking the photo."

"Probably so. Did you notice how she's holding the newspaper?" she asked.

"No, I didn't, just that you see her hands."

"Look at her fingers. One hand is underneath the paper with two fingers pointing up. Her left hand is holding the paper by the side with three fingers showing."

"Let me see," he said, reaching for the photo and looking at Sylvia's hands holding the newspaper.

Antonella said, "What are the first two letters of the English word *help?*"

"H and E," he said.

"Right. Her right two fingers form an H with a shaped slant. Her left hand has three fingers extended, like the letter E."

"Amazing. You're right!" he said. "I never noticed. Do you think she did that on purpose?"

"I don't know. Maybe we'll have a chance to ask her one day."

"Let's hope so. How about her letter? Do you read anything significant in how she worded it?"

Antonella picked up a copy of the letter and reread it. "It's very personal, also reassuring. She's most concerned with letting her family know she is making the best of a very bad situation. No hint of anger. She doesn't say anything to make them more fearful. She's writing as if she knows they'll be reunited and she'll be safe. It's a sign of maturity and hope. She appears to be a strong woman, secure in her emotions. I'd also say she's a bit confident, like she's holding her own with her captors. They probably talk to her, give her orders, let her know her life is in their hands. But she doesn't cower like an animal in a cage. She probably argues back and tries to use her wits to earn their respect."

Giorgio smiled. "You'd make a good psychologist."

Antonella laughed. "We're all amateur psychologists. You have to be in this job. Every time we talk to a suspect or a criminal, we're trying to get into their heads."

"And keep one or two steps ahead of them," he said. "I'm always thinking of the next question or two when I'm interrogating a suspect. It's second nature for being a good cop."

Giorgio handed Antonella the communiqué. "How about this? Put on your psychologist hat and let me know what you read between the lines."

She read through it for the fourth or fifth time.

"It was written by someone with a good education, obviously," she said. "It's worded almost like an academic exercise. Angry, of course, even belligerent. You could read something like this any day in letters to the editor. Their position is a grudge. They're really pissed off and dangerous enough to act. They have an elevated sense of their own power. They expect others to follow them, a sign of arrogance. Or self-deception."

Giorgio nodded. "I think this is the real thing," he said. "It's direct, forceful, angry, like you'd expect them to be."

"I agree," she said. "So what do we do next?"

He leaned back in his chair, taking off his reading glasses and rubbing his eyes. "I'll call the prosecutor when we have the fingerprint report and our lawyers have reviewed the documents. Then I have to call Mr. de Matteo. He has to know. The ransom note is intended for him."

He got up and went over to close his door. "Before you leave, I want to share something." He went back and sat in his chair, picking up the documents and photo and putting them in a small pile. "I'm worried. Worried about what might come next."

"What's that?"

He patted the copies of the documents. "This reminds me of the Moro affair. BR sent several communiqués. Moro wrote numerous personal letters to his wife, the Pope, and his Christian Democrat party members. One of the communiqués had a polaroid photo of him holding a newspaper with a headline about his kidnapping. Just like we have here."

"I remember well," she said. "I studied the Moro case when I was in law school."

"And they call themselves Nucleo Compagni Combattenti. That's chilling. It's a militant name. They might have a connection to the old Brigate Rosse. If that's true, we may have a new major terrorist group planning more dangerous acts."

* * * * *

At three thirty that afternoon, Paolo and Cole were in Giorgio's office. He told them about the documents and photo that his office was studying. Paolo was visibly shaken, his face almost sunburn red. Trickles of sweat were running down his cheeks; he had rushed over from the Cavour minutes after he had received the call from Giorgio.

Cole looked anxious and ill at ease. His face was pale and drawn. He blinked nervously, as if he had dust in his eyes.

"Wh-when can we see them?" Paolo asked. "I want to see the photo to see if it is Sylvia."

"It appears to be," Giorgio said. He lifted an open file. Underneath were the documents and photo. Paolo grabbed the photo and held it close to study it. "It's Sylvia. No doubt about it," he said, his voice quavering like he was about to break out in tears. He handed it to Cole, who took it, his hands shaking.

After a couple of moments, Cole said, "I don't recognize the blouse she's wearing. It looks cheap, not like something she'd buy. This isn't what she was wearing the day we went to the Stazione Centrale."

"Thanks for telling us," Giorgio said. "I'll mention it to my deputy. Maybe they bought her new clothes."

Paolo picked up Sylvia's letter and read it quickly.

Dear Papa,

I know you, Mamma, Angela, and Cole are very worried about me. I am a prisoner of people who want a ransom before they release me. They are treating me well. I'm not being tortured. I'm being fed well. I am in a small room with freedom to move about. I'm not being mistreated except for being isolated.

I think about you all day—morning, noon, and night. I miss you all so much and want to be back with you. I want my life back as soon as I can get it. I don't know what else to say other than that I love you all from the bottom of my heart.

This is a very difficult time for all of us. But I hope and pray we will be reunited soon. Please tell Angela how much I love her and miss her. I dream about her every night and know I will be able to hold and kiss her again.

I know they want money from you, Papa, a lot of money. I hope you will do what they ask to allow my safe return.

My deepest love and respect to all my family.
Sylvia

The communiqué read:

We are the Nucleo Compagni Combattenti, a committed group of patriotic Italians who want justice and equality returned to our beloved country. For too long, corrupt politicians, judges, the media, and lawyers have put their greedy interests before the needs of common people, the people who work hard and want justice for all and a better life for their children.

Italian people must take their demands to the street, lead demonstrations, and make politicians and judges accountable to the people. Judges and politicians must stop fattening their wallets with illegal bribes, payoffs, and criminal extortion.

The people of Europe are suffering because of the greed of filthy bankers and their political cronies who allow them to get rich off the misery of common people.

We call on patriotic people in England, Germany, Greece, Spain, France, and Portugal to take to the streets and wrench back the people's democracy, which has been stolen from them illegally. We are willing to take extreme measures to return their rights. We call for a European revolution where people's rights will be honored and never be abused again.

We are the Nucleo Compagni Combattenti, calling on patriotic people to take back their governments and throw out the criminal politicians and greedy bankers who have stolen from the common people.

Wall Street banker Paolo de Matteo is one of the financial criminals who caused the Euro financial crisis that crippled the Italian economy and threw people's lives into misery and despair. Unemployment in Italy is criminally high. We call on banker de Matteo to give three million euros to people in need, the abused women and children of Italy who are suffering the most in our country.

Banker de Matteo must give the charity three million euros if he wants to see his daughter, Sylvia, alive again. In three days, his payment must be in the account of Casa di Marta e Maria.

We are the Nucleo Compagni Combattenti.

CHAPTER TWENTY-SEVEN

DAY EIGHT

Marietto burst into the office, his eyes wide, waving his arms and stammering. "F-Fabio! *C'è la polizia, vogliono entrare qui! Orco Giuda, cazzo facciamo?*" [Police are outside! They want to come in. What should I do?]

Fabio jumped up from the computer where he'd been reading online international news about the communiqué and photo reported by the RAI station the previous evening.

"Police?" he said, his voice shaking. "How many are there? What do they want?"

He thought quickly about his options. Luca had a pistol in a file cabinet. Alfredo's weapons were locked in a floor safe in the storage closet. *Are they here to arrest us? Or is this a routine search?*

He wasn't going to overreact. He needed to find out what they wanted. Maybe it was routine, a theft in the area they were investigating. Or a stolen car.

"They want to come into the warehouse! They're investigating the shooting! Come out and talk to them. I don't know what to say!"

Marietto was agitated, shifting his weight from one foot to the other, wringing his hands, his face twisted in fear.

"Calm down. Stay here. I'll find out. If they come in, get busy doing something. Don't say anything. Understand?" He put a hand on Marietto's shoulder and looked him in the eyes. Marietto stopped fidgeting and nodded. "Okay. Okay. Stay away. Don't talk. I'll work in the kitchen—straighten the shelves."

"Good. Don't say a word. I'll take care of everything." Marietto hurried into the kitchen and started opening drawers and cabinets.

Fabio went outside to the parking lot and walked around the corner toward the front gate, which was partially open. Through the opening, he saw the profile of woman in a dark pantsuit and a uniformed Milan police officer standing beside a blue *polizia* car.

Fabio pushed open the gate. Amoruso turned to look at him. "Hello. My name is Fabio Cecconi. Can I help you?"

Amoruso flashed her badge. "I'm Deputy Amoruso from DIGOS, investigating the Stazione Centrale shooting last week. We'd like to ask a few questions. A white Fiorino was reported coming into your facility last week. Can you tell me about it? Who does it belong to?"

Amoruso's voice was firm. Her black hair was pulled back over her ears, accentuating high cheekbones, a sharp nose, and a small chin. Sunglasses rested on top of her head. Her dark eyes were penetrating, like a black laser. She was attractive but had the presence of someone who didn't want to be challenged or provoked.

The police officer behind her was silently observant, peering over Amoruso's shoulder at Fabio, looking him up and down. His right hand was on the holster at his side.

"I'm not sure. This is my brother's construction warehouse. I work for him part time. He has workers who come and go between jobs."

"Where is your brother? What's his name?"

"His name is Luca Cecconi. I help with paperwork and scheduling."

"Where is he? I want to talk to him."

"He's out at a job over in Paderno d'Adda. He won't be back until this evening. Can I help you?"

"Can we come in and look around?"

Fabio's mind was racing with possibilities. *Act calm. Make this seem like a routine questioning. Don't show anxiety or fear. Act as normal as possible.*

"Of course. I'll open the gate so you can drive in."

"Don't bother," Amoruso said. "Our driver will stay in the car. I'll come in with my fellow officer."

Fabio pushed open the metal gate. Amoruso and the officer followed him through. They walked across gravel to a paved walkway between the warehouse and the three-meter-high stucco walls.

Amoruso's eyes scanned left and right, taking in the dimensions and condition of the yard: patches of weeds, piles of masonry, slabs of tile, long boards, wheelbarrows, and tools leaning against the walls. Fabio followed behind to the parking lot, where a truck, three cars, and Marietto's *motorino* were parked against the back wall. Amoruso and the officer looked at the vehicles, then back at the three buildings: the warehouse/office and two cement structures, one for storing vehicles, the other for equipment and storage.

Amoruso stepped off the cement walkway and moved toward the far corner, where trash bins stood and construction debris was piled. She looked over the trash and came back to face Fabio. "Is this where the Fiorino was parked?" she asked.

"Ah, I really don't know. Some workers park their vehicles here when they are out at work sites. My brother drives them in his truck."

"Who drove the Fiorino?"

Fabio shook his head, trying to remain calm. "I really don't know. It could have been one of his workers. Or someone making a delivery. Supply stores bring equipment or parts almost every day. Sales reps show up trying to sell him something. Men show up every day looking for work. It's hard to remember who drives what vehicle. Sometimes I never see them. They knock on the office door, come in, and leave in a few minutes."

"I need to know who drove the Fiorino."

"I'll ask my brother when he comes back. Maybe he knows."

"When will he be back from the work site?"

"Hard to say. Probably early evening, seven or eight o'clock. He's working over in Paderno d'Adda today. It's about thirty kilometers from here."

She turned from Fabio and walked past the open buildings, where construction gear, cement mixers, tools, and loaders were stored. She went inside both buildings, looked around, and then came back.

"What's this building?" she asked, pointing to the partially open door.

"It's my brother's office. There's a conference room, kitchen, and storage. That's where I work."

"Can we go in?"

Fabio tensed. Sylvia was about fifteen meters away. If he let Amoruso in, Sylvia might hear strange voices and say something. But he couldn't refuse Amoruso entrance; she'd grow suspicious and things could get bad very fast.

"Yes, of course," Fabio said, his heart hammering in his chest. *Act calm. Behave normally.* He walked around Amoruso and pushed open the door.

She walked in, looking left and right, scanning the open area and the hallway. She looked in the conference room.

"What's this room?" she asked.

"Ah, the main office. My brother keeps records here—blueprints, invoices, bills, computer, printers, phones, and file cabinets. It's cluttered, sorry. We work here all day."

Amoruso walked around and surveyed the room. Open files were on the conference table along with coffee cups, ashtrays, and dirty plates with crumbs and stale bread from breakfast. The top newspaper on a stack reported the communiqué, Sylvia's letter, and the photo that had been sent to RAI the previous morning.

Amoruso glanced at the newspapers and walked around the table, examining the computer, printer, and file cabinets. The TV was tuned to the RAI news channel, which showed a photo with a crawl that said that Onorevole Adriano Pallucca had just died.

"Turn up the TV," Amoruso said, looking at the screen. "I want to hear what they're saying."

Fabio grabbed the remote and increased the volume. The reader reported:

"We have a breaking story. The Presidenza del Consiglio dei Ministri has announced that Onorevole Andriano Pallucca died earlier this morning. The distinguished politician was shot last week at Milan's Stazione Centrale mass shooting, along with two Polfer agents who are still hovering between life and death in the hospital. Prime Minister Silvio Berlusconi has called for a press conference in an hour to share the nation's grief about the tragic death of Pallucca, who was a close aide to the prime minister and was working to resolve the Euro financial crisis."

Amoruso shook her head. "I knew Pallucca wasn't going to make it. His wounds were too severe. Now the terrorists face murder charges. The media has been obsessing about the fate of Ms. de Matteo, treating the shooting of Pallucca and the two Polfer agents as side stories. Maybe Pallucca's murder will get more attention now."

Fabio was very uncomfortable. He felt chilled when Amoruso accented the word *murder,* reflecting her anger as she narrowed her eyes at the TV.

She clenched her jaw and turned to Fabio. "Okay, let's continue. What goes on in here?" she asked, waving her hand around the room.

Fabio forced himself to appear calm. "Ah, this is where I work. It's messy, sorry."

She made another pass around the conference table, this time slower. She looked at the computer screen, which showed the *Corriere della Sera* online news reporting the death of Pallucca. She passed in front of Fabio and walked out into the hallway to the kitchen and looked in. Marietto was on his knees, cleaning out the grease trap underneath the sink.

Fabio was quick to stay a few steps behind Amoruso. "This is Marietto. He helps around here with chores and cleaning." Marietto looked up, managed a weak smile, and then ducked his head back underneath the sink.

"We make coffee and sandwiches here," Fabio said. "We feed the workers a light breakfast and coffee in the morning before they go out. We make sandwiches for them; many work sites aren't near cafés."

Amoruso walked past the microwave oven, refrigerator, sink, and cabinets, passing by the glazed window to Luca's apartment, where Sylvia was imprisoned. Amoruso looked at the glazed window and then moved on, passing a cabinet with shelves where bread, crackers, food and soup cans, pasta, wine and beer bottles, and spices were stacked. She walked out and went down the hallway, stopping at Luca's apartment. "What's in here?"

Fabio's heart was thumping against his chest. He hoped that his face wasn't revealing his extreme anxiety. He kept his hands at his side, fists clenched. "Ah, that's my brother's apartment. He sleeps here some nights after a hard day working. I don't have the key, sorry."

It was quiet in the apartment. Fabio desperately hoped Sylvia couldn't hear the conversation outside the door. If she could, she probably thought it was routine: a female voice and his voice, both parties speaking in low tones, something she had heard before. *Please,* he thought, *don't make a sound, Sylvia.* If she said anything or made a noise, it would be all over. Amoruso would want to know who was in there and why the door was locked.

Amoruso pushed on the door, but it was locked. She nodded and kept walking down the hallway.

"We have small sleeping rooms down the hall for young workers who can't afford apartments in Milan," Fabio said, moving behind her. "Only one of them is being used now; business has been very slow. My brother had to lay off most of his workers."

Amoruso walked to the end of the hall and pushed open a partially open door to the storage room. She flicked on a light and the room brightened, showing brooms, pails, shovels, waste bins, laundry soap, and stacks of trash bags. Alfredo's floor safe with their weapons was covered by a sheet of flooring. Fabio held his breath while she looked at the ceiling and around the shelves. Then she turned out the light.

Amoruso came back to Fabio and pulled out her notebook. "I need your name and phone number. Also your brother's."

"My name is Fabio Cecconi. My brother's name is Luca." He gave her their cell numbers.

She jotted down the information and then returned down the corridor, looking in the kitchen and conference room one more time before walking outside, followed by her fellow officer.

Amoruso stood outdoors and scanned the parking lot, the trash area, and the open buildings again. Then she turned to Fabio. She reached into a pocket and pulled out the *polizia* Identi-Kit–enhanced photos of Vera, Alfredo, and Luca. She handed them to Fabio.

"Do you know any of these people?"

He looked at the photos. "No. I've seen these on TV and in the newspapers."

"They were taken at Stazione Centrale before the shooting. We're trying to identify them. Does anyone look familiar?"

Fabio kept his eyes on the photos. "I don't recognize anyone. Sorry." He handed them back.

Amoruso stuffed them back into her pocket and looked around the yard one more time. "Thank you for letting us look around. Someone from the Questura will call your brother and ask who owns the Fiorino. If he gets the message, have him return the call immediately."

"Yes, of course I will," Fabio said. "He'll cooperate with the Questura."

* * * * *

When Fabio returned to the conference room, he was sweating. His body was tense from the confrontation with Amoruso and the *polizia* officer. They had walked just a few meters from Sylvia, locked in Luca's apartment. If she had spoken or made a noise, their cover would have been blown.

Fabio glanced up at the TV monitor. The screen read: *Prime Minister Silvio Berlusconi is about to speak to the nation. Stand by.*

The screen showed a hallway in the Palazzo Chigi. Berlusconi walked out of a door, holding the hands of two children, a boy about eleven years old and a girl about eight years old, dressed in black. A step behind him, a plump, short woman in a black dress and hat followed. They walked to a small stage with a podium and three ornate chairs alongside.

Berlusconi led the others to the chairs. He leaned down to kiss the children on their foreheads, patted them on their heads, and touched their shoulders to have them sit. He hugged the woman and patted her on the back. He led her to the third chair, waited until she was seated, and then stepped over to the podium. He lifted a hand to his right eye and, with a knuckle, wiped away an imaginary tear.

Berlusconi faced the camera. The lights shining on his slicked-back, dyed black hair and his suntanned face made him look like he'd spent a great deal of time before the press conference with his makeup artist, not with Pallucca's inconsolable widow and children.

"Today is a sad day for the people of Italia," he said, his voice breaking. "One of our most valued public servants, Onorevole Adriano Pallucca, passed away this morning from severe wounds after he was tragically shot by terrorists at Stazione Centrale. We grieve with Onorevole Pallucca's family today and hold them in our arms to comfort them."

A TV camera panned the room, showing long faces of Berlusconi's political servants, who were applauding weakly, squirming in their seats, and wishing they were still on vacation instead of having been encouraged to show their allegiance to Berlusconi by filling the room for the nationwide broadcast.

Berlusconi turned around to look at the children on one side and then at Pallucca's widow, who was crying and dabbing her eyes with a white handkerchief clutched in her hands.

"I lost a close friend today. Italy lost a patriotic hero," Berlusconi continued, raising a hand to wipe another imaginary tear from his eye. "We will not rest until the terrorists who committed the terrible attack on innocent people at Stazione Centrale are brought to justice."

Berlusconi raised a hand dramatically to his mouth, held it there for a second, and then lowered it. "A few minutes ago, I spoke to the Questore di Milano and to the prosecutor in charge of the investigation. They both reassured me that DIGOS's highly trained agents will capture the criminal terrorists soon. I take comfort in knowing that the Questura will make that promise come true so the gentle people of Milano will be able to sleep in peace once again after those terrorists are locked up in jail and face trial for their heinous crimes."

Berlusconi lowered his head as if in prayer, the lights shining on his dyed, slicked-back hair. When he raised his head, his eyes were damp. He walked over to Pallucca's widow, who stood, and they went hand in hand to the children, who also stood. They turned their backs to the camera and walked down the carpeted hallway, one of Berlusconi's arms around the widow Pallucca and the other holding the children next to his side. The applause from Berlusconi's political servants followed them until they disappeared behind a door where uniformed guards stood at attention.

* * * * *

Fabio was in the conference room reading online news and reflecting on Berlusconi's maudlin performance, which had been watched by millions of Italians who probably had wept on cue from the Prime Minister's histrionics. *Typical Berlusconi,* he thought. *Tugs at people's heartstrings, panders to their deepest fears and emotions, and keeps the country distracted while he pushes laws through the Parliament that make him the richest and most corrupt politician in modern Italian history.*

Berlusconi was pitiful, a national embarrassment. He already had been convicted of tax evasion, bribing judges, and paying prostitutes to attend "bunga bunga" sex parties at his villa in Arcore, Brianza. When Berlusconi's teenage prostitute girlfriend, Ruby Heartstealer, had gone on television to tell Italians that they should be proud of Berlusconi and that he was an honorable man, it made Fabio, a lapsed Catholic, sick. Berlusconi had cheapened everything in Italy. He was a cancer that had to be removed.

Fabio was surprised at how smoothly he had handled it, being courteous and not betraying his fear.

After Amoruso and the officer had left, Fabio had walked around the compound to vent his nervous energy. Then he had left the compound to walk in the neighborhood. He had stopped at a park where children were playing on swings, kicking soccer balls, laughing and screaming, and enjoying life as only young children can before the reality of adult life hits them with choices, often tough choices dealing with difficult people, sometimes parents or relatives.

Fabio had taken deep breaths to ease his tension, which had reached a critical level when Amoruso had been just meters from Sylvia. He had escaped a near-disastrous encounter with the police. Would he be as lucky the second time?

When he had returned to the warehouse, he had let Marietto go for the day and spent time on the computer until he heard the faint rapping at the glazed window.

"Hey, I want to talk. Are you there?"

Fabio jumped up and ran into the kitchen.

"Is anyone there? I want out."

Fabio sat beneath the window. "Yes, Sylvia. I'm here."

"What's your name?" she demanded.

"Um, call me . . . Mario. That will do."

"That's bullshit. You're not a Mario. I knew a Mario once and didn't like him. I'm going to call you Leo."

Fabio said nothing.

"Let me go. I'm fed up with your silly political charade. You're in over your head. The police will find you and throw you in prison. It's just a matter of time."

Fabio was quiet. *Let her vent her anger until she settles down.* She had a bit of Vera in her; she would blow off steam, say nasty things, try to get an argument started, yell, swear, and make accusations. If Fabio didn't reply, she would settle down, and then there was the possibility of a conversation. He didn't respond to hysterical women.

Sylvia was impatient to talk, growing more frustrated when Fabio did not answer. She hated that. It made her angrier when Cole would not engage her when she was upset. She tried again. "Talk to me! Don't play games. I hate that!"

"I'm here," he said calmly.

"I want out of here. I hate being here. Let me go."

Fabio was quiet for several moments. Then Sylvia said, "I read the *Corriere della Sera* you slid under the door this morning. It was terrible, your communiqué, just a bunch of Marxist bullshit. You'll never get away with it."

Fabio remained silent. Sylvia continued. "My father won't pay your ransom. He's smarter than you."

Silence. She banged on the glazed window.

"Don't do that, Sylvia. Keep it up, and we'll come in and tie you to a chair. You'll have to beg to go to the bathroom. We'll tie you in bed at night. There won't be a second warning. We have people here who want to send you back to the room with the small bed and no light. Do you want to go back there?"

"No, I don't."

"I'm the only one you can talk to. You're testing my patience. Don't push."

When she answered, her voice was softer. "How much longer will you keep me here?"

"That depends upon your father."

"I don't think he can come up with three million euros in a short time. If he does pay, will I be released?"

"We'll find a way. It depends upon him."

"I want to leave. I'm losing my mind being locked up. I haven't talked to anyone but you in a week. I'm going crazy. Do you understand?"

"Yes, I do, Sylvia."

"Then help me!" she pleaded.

"How can I help you?"

"Talk to me. I need to talk."

"What do you want to say?"

"I'm . . . I'm lonesome. I miss my daughter. I miss my father and mother. I miss my fiancé."

"I understand."

"I want my life back."

Fabio didn't respond.

"I don't know if I can even go back to my old life," she said, her voice lower.

"Why not?"

"I . . . don't know. I feel traumatized . . . stripped of everything I believed in. Hope. Future. Even . . . love. I don't know what I can believe in anymore."

"You're a strong woman, Sylvia. You'll recover and have your life back one day."

"I can't take this much longer. I mean it."

Fabio paused before answering: "You sound like people I talk to every day, Sylvia. Your feelings are what most Italians are going through. They've been beaten down, lost jobs, lost hope. They can't pay for medical care for their children. They can't buy books for their children in school. Pensions are being cut from people who worked their whole lives, believing they could have a safe retirement. It's all gone. Everything they believed in has been stripped from them by corrupt politicians, judges, and greedy bankers who robbed their future."

Sylvia made a sniffling sound and started to cry. "Oh, please, let this end. I want it over. I want to go home."

"Most Italians don't have the comfortable life you enjoy, Sylvia. Their families are suffering every day with no hope that things will get better. Times are desperate for Italians. You are one of the lucky ones; you live in America, and your family is wealthy. Most Italians are not as fortunate. Their futures are bleak. They won't get better unless significant changes come to Italy. Our country is very sick. It has terminal cancer. We want to give people hope that things will get better. That's what we believe."

"I read your communiqué. I understand what you want, but you're what, a few people who commit violent acts? How is that going to help?"

"You believe in a fairy-tale Italy, a mecca for rich tourists. They visit the Vatican, see the Sistine Chapel, go to Florence to see Michelangelo's *David,* ride gondolas in Venice, go to Positano and drive along the Amalfi Coast, and shop at designer stores in Milan. That's what rich tourists come to Italy for. They're blind to the poverty and lost hopes of generations of Italians. They'll go home and brag to friends what a wonderful country we have. They don't see that Italy is impoverished, that politicians are corrupt and evil, and that bankers have made Italy and the rest of Europe bankrupt. Our government bonds are worthless. The media is foul and polluting the minds of young children. You wouldn't want to raise your daughter here, Sylvia. Italy is sick and dying; it will be a painful death unless we change the system."

CHAPTER TWENTY-EIGHT

DAY NINE

Later that evening, Giorgio punched in Paolo's number on his cell phone. "Good evening, Mr. de Matteo. I was just calling to tell you I'll be leaving shortly to go home for dinner. My wife and I can have a regular dinner for the first time in several days."

"Good for you, Mr. Lucchini. You and your team have been working hard. I appreciate how you've kept me informed. It means a lot to me. I feel isolated in the hotel, but your calls and our meetings at your office have meant a great deal to me and my family."

"Thank you, sir. I'm glad you're close by, allowing us to keep you informed. I also wanted you to know that we may have another break in the case."

"Wonderful! Tell me about it."

"We may have an ID on the woman who did the shooting. She's a former fashion model who had a motorcycle accident years ago that scarred her face and ended her career. The scar on her cheek was recognized by several people who called our command center and gave us her name. We know where she lives, but we haven't found her at her apartment. We're searching for her now."

"That is good news. I hope you find her soon. Thanks for letting me know. By the way, would you want to stop by for a drink before you go home? I promise I won't keep you long. I'm here alone. Cole went out for dinner, and Angela is with her caretaker, spending the night at her apartment again. She's been wonderful with her. She keeps Angela's spirits up, and that's a blessing."

"I have time to stop by for a drink. I'll be there in fifteen minutes."

Paolo had on a new sweater when he opened the door for Giorgio. "Come in, *Dottor* Lucchini. I'm glad you could stop by. I get bored at night. All I do is watch the news on TV and talk to my wife. I went shopping this afternoon to buy some clothes. I got this new sweater, a pair of slacks, and a couple of shirts. I brought only a few clothes from Menaggio. It seems ages ago."

They went into the small living room in the suite, and Paolo went over to the bar. "What would you like? Scotch? Bourbon? A glass of prosecco?"

"Scotch would be wonderful," Giorgio said, sitting on the sofa. "I rarely drink Scotch at home. It's not as common here as in the US."

Paolo poured three fingers of single malt for Giorgio and added a splash to his own drink. He brought the glasses over and handed one to Giorgio.

"You mentioned you've been to the US," Paolo said, sitting on the sofa chair. "How many times?"

"Several times, actually. Twice when I was a student," Giorgio said, sipping his Scotch. "Since I became a cop, I've been there more often. I went to training at the FBI in Quantico, Virginia, and have attended several meetings at the FBI and Homeland Security headquarters in Washington. I like Washington—such a clean, historic city. I've been to the Smithsonian and took tours of the Capitol, the White House, the

Pentagon, and the State Department. Your federal officials have been very helpful in keeping us informed about the latest techniques and methods for investigation and surveillance."

"Nice to hear my taxes are going for a good cause," Paolo said, sipping his Scotch and reaching for a box of cigars. "Do you like cigars? I bought some Cubanos today. I have to smoke them before I return to New York. We still have an embargo against Cuban goods, and we can't bring back cigars. Too bad; I love Romeo y Julietas.

"Can we smoke in the hotel?"

Paolo winked and got up. "I go on the balcony when I light up. Care to join me?"

"Sure. I haven't had a cigar in years."

Paolo took two cigars and the ashtray he had purchased, and he went over to pull back the drapes and open the sliding glass doors. On the small balcony, two chairs and a small table looked over Piazza Cavour. "The hotel doesn't know my little secret. I flush the ashes down the toilet," he said with a smile.

They sat on the small chairs. Paolo struck a match and lit Giorgio's cigar and then his own. They both took puffs and blew out clouds of blue smoke. "Mmm. Cubanos smoke so smooth. I love them," Paolo said, sipping his Scotch.

"Yes, it is good. Quite mild."

"So, has your family joined you on trips to America?"

"Two years ago, my wife and two young sons flew to New York, and I met them after I finished an FBI course in antiterrorism. We had four nights there. Went to Broadway plays, museums, and art galleries. Walked in Central Park and had several good meals in Greenwich Village."

"Wonderful city, isn't it? I'm glad you enjoyed it. I can't wait to go back when this dreadful mess is all over. I really miss Manhattan."

"You're lucky to live there. So much to do and so many interesting people. It's one of the most exciting cities in the world."

"Did you travel any more in the US?"

"Yes, we drove up to Buffalo so our boys could see Niagara Falls. Then we went to a resort on the Finger Lakes for two nights. We had a wonderful time. We saw several movies. My sons like American movies, especially those starring Brad Pitt, Robert De Niro, and Sylvester Stallone."

Paolo laughed. "Like all boys, they love action movies. What actors do you like?"

Giorgio took another puff and continued to nurse his Scotch. "Hmm, let me think. Liam Neeson, although he's not American. Billy Crystal is very funny. Danny DeVito and Stanley Tucci; they're both Italians."

Paolo smiled and puffed his cigar. "They're all great actors. I met DeVito at a charity event one time. He's very funny. He tells long stories about actors and funny things they do. He keeps everyone laughing. He's a real character."

"We also like American food, even New York pizza. My favorite meals in New York were rib eye steaks. You have good beef in America."

Paolo smiled. "I love prime rib myself. We do raise good beef in America, especially from Texas and the Western states. You need to visit the American West sometime: Denver, San Francisco, Los Angeles—all great cities with lots to do and see."

"We'll do that when my boys are a little older. They love American hamburgers, which are much tastier than what they get at McDonald's here."

Paolo laughed. "Hamburgers win over all foreign tourists. They eat them by the truckload, drenched in ketchup with mounds of French fries. *Patate fritte.*"

"I like California wines as well, especially from Napa and Sonoma," Giorgio said. "They're fruitier than Italian wines."

"I agree. If you come to New York, I'll show you my wine cellar. I have more than two thousand bottles, mostly American and a few classic French burgundies."

"I'd like that very much. You're like most Americans I've met. They're friendly and they make good conversation. I always learn something new when I meet Americans."

Paolo twirled his cigar in his fingers. "Nice of you to say, and thank you. I think you'll find most New Yorkers to be friendly—and we certainly love to talk. The city gets a bad rap as cold and ruthless, but I don't agree. If you make it back, I'll take you around to meet some friends."

Giorgio glanced at his watch. "Mr. de Matteo, I think I should be leaving. Thank you for inviting me, but my wife is waiting for me. I don't want to disappoint her by being late."

"Of course, and please call me Paolo. I'm glad you stopped by," Paolo said, putting out his cigar in the ashtray. Giorgio did the same and said, "This has been most enjoyable. And please call me Giorgio."

"I should tell you that I called my brokerage firm, where I have all my money," Paolo said. "Much of my holdings are in real estate in Menaggio, New York, and Vermont. The rest is invested in securities. I didn't have three million in cash to convert to euros, so they sold some of my investments. It takes three days to settle.

"But a bigger problem is wiring the money. You probably know about the Patriot Act, enacted by US Congress after 9/11. The federal government has regulations about wiring money internationally, mostly to prevent money laundering for the illegal drug trade, but also for funding terrorist groups. Lawyers in my firm are talking with the Treasury Department. Paying a ransom to terrorists is illegal, as you know. The lawyers say this is going to a charity, not to terrorists. I'll have to wait a few days to see if we get their approval."

"We have a similar law in Italy. It's called *blocco dei beni,* which prohibits payments being made to kidnappers. It's been on the books for a couple of decades."

They got up and went through the sliding glass door into the living room. Giorgio put his glass of Scotch on the table and said, "To repay your kindness, I'd like to invite you for an evening in Milan. Once our investigation is over and we have rescued your daughter, my wife and I would like to invite you to an opera at La Scala. I need to check the program for September. I hope there is something by Verdi or Puccini."

"La Bohème—I'd love to see it again," Paolo said. "I've seen it at the Met, but I can never get enough of Puccini. *Tosca* and *Madama Butterfly* are my two other favorites. Italians write such great operas. They'll last forever: one of the greatest accomplishments of Italian arts."

As he walked Giorgio to the door, Paolo said, "So tell me. How do you think the investigation is going? I hope you find Sylvia soon and bring her back safely. I can't sleep at night, and when I do I am having bad dreams. I wake up and pace around the hotel. My wife is having an even tougher time. She's on medication to help her sleep. We talk several times a day. I have to keep her calm."

"I'm sorry. I know this would be especially hard on a mother."

"I'm driving to Menaggio this weekend to see her," Paolo said. "Fortunately, our New York maid has been with us in Menaggio and is taking care of her. Relatives of my deceased father who live nearby are stopping in. Such friendly, warm people. In the past, I helped them out, paying for appliances and fixing up their apartments or homes. It's one way I can repay them for the honor of being Italian."

"I'm sure they appreciated your kindness."

"Before you leave, is there any more you can tell me about the investigation?" Paolo asked.

"The calls we received about the woman could be the break we need to locate the group, arrest them, and return your daughter."

"God, please bring her back soon, I pray. How long will that take?"

"Impossible to say," Giorgio said. "We have to find the woman first. We went to her apartment today, but she wasn't there. Neighbors say she comes and goes at odd hours. She may be at a hideout. We have a warrant to enter her apartment and search. We'll probably find clues there that will help us locate the group and arrest them all."

CHAPTER TWENTY-NINE

Fabio and the others were in the conference room that night, drinking wine and eating pasta Marietto had prepared. They were watching the evening RAI news, their faces grim. The mood in the room was somber. Their weeks of planning, training, and executing the Stazione Centrale attack had led to a crisis: Vera had been named as a suspect.

The backdrop above the RAI reporter's head was a panel with a photo of Sylvia and the enhanced photos released by the Questura of Vera, Luca, and Alfredo. Vera's photo was circled in red with her name spelled out below. The reporter read, "Questura has released the name of a woman possibly linked to the Stazione Centrale shooting that claimed the life of Onorevole Pallucca. Her name is Vera Pulvirenti, a onetime fashion model who was on the cover of *Vogue* magazine at the age of eighteen."

The screen showed the magazine cover of the thin, sultry teenage Vera, her face turned to the camera, chin almost on her shoulder, lips slightly downturned in a pout. The sideways pose accented Vera's lean body and the slinky, sleeveless black dress that fell three inches above her knee. Vera's long black hair was swept behind her ear and came down to her shoulders. She wore dark lipstick and heavy eye makeup that accented her large, black eyes, arched eyebrows, and long lashes. She looked a worldly, sexy thirty but was a dozen years younger.

"In 2000, Ms. Pulvirenti was in a serious motorcycle accident with her boyfriend, Russian soccer star Vladimir Gribov, in Côte d'Azur. Gribov died in the accident. Pulvirenti was hospitalized for three months with injuries to her head and face that ended her fashion career when she was one of Italy's top models. Pulvirenti is being sought for questioning because Questura photos taken at the Stazione Centrale shooting revealed one of the terrorists to be a woman with a scar on her right cheek."

Vera stared at the TV, her face tense, smoking a cigarette, her fingers shaking. "God damn TV. They dig up that cover to show me when I was young and sexy. That was a trashy cover. I hated it."

"That cover made you famous, Vera," Fabio reminded her. "You made hundreds of millions of lire that year and bought your apartment."

Vera's eyes misted. She made a fist and put it under her chin as if she needed to prop up her head. "I was so . . . young . . . foolish. . . . If the accident hadn't . . ." She stopped and wiped away the tears running down her cheek.

"This is bad news, Vera," Fabio said. "You've got to disappear."

Vera dragged deeply on her cigarette, letting out a long stream of smoke. "How the fuck do I disappear?" she asked.

"Go to Sicily. Ask relatives or friends to hide you. They'll cover for you. Find a remote village where you can say you were on vacation. Your alibi is you've been in Sicily the last two weeks on vacation. You didn't read newspapers or watch TV and didn't know about the shooting."

"Vuoi liberarti di me, stronzo?" [Want to get rid of me, asshole?] she grumbled, scowling. "You'll be alone with Sylvia. Is she your new girlfriend? You've got the hots for her, treating her like a princess, buying

her new clothes, feeding her like she's at a resort. Pretty soon you'll have her in your bed."

"Stop that, Vera. This is serious. If they find you in Milano, they'll arrest you, interrogate you aggressively, and threaten you. They'll play with your emotions. You'll get angry and fight back."

"You're a bastard, Fabio. You don't think I can handle myself. I won't say a thing, even if they torture me. Cops are stupid pigs. I'll fight back and never cooperate!" She took another long drag on her cigarette, blowing the smoke over his head.

Fabio leaned over until his face was inches from hers. Vera pulled back but Fabio kept his eyes locked on her. "I know you, Vera. We spent years together. Even when we were lovers, we battled almost every day. The Questura has psychologists who know how to break down a person's resistance. They'll toy with you, get you irritated, get you confused and frustrated, and break you down. In the end, they'll get the information they need, and we'll all end up in prison."

A wave of fear washed over Vera's face. She looked from Fabio to Luca to Alfredo and back to Fabio. "I . . . I don't want to go to prison. I'd kill myself. I could never stand to be locked up in a cage. I'd rather die."

"Then do what I say," Fabio said. "Go to Sicily. Get your family to hide you and give you an alibi. That's your only choice. You have to leave Milano. Immediately."

Fabio looked at Luca. "Can we give her some money?"

Luca nodded. "I keep some in the safe. How much do you want?"

"If you have it, a thousand euros. She can't use an ATM in Milan. They'll have a record. She'll need cash to buy gas and food."

Luca went over to the door, closed it, and opened a wall safe. "The Questura left a message for me today about the Fiorino," he said. "I didn't call them back." He took out an envelope, counted out several worn bills, slipped the rest back into the safe, and locked it. He dropped the pile of worn euros on the table. Vera scooped them up, counted through them, then stuffed them into her battered bag on the table.

"You want me to leave now? Just like that?"

Fabio managed a weak smile and reached over to put a hand over hers. "I think it's best, Vera. Drive a few hours tonight, pull off the *autostrada,* and get a hotel room in a small town. Sleep during the day and drive at night. Don't use credit cards when you travel. The police will be able to check. Call me on your Albanian cell phone when you get to Sicily."

Vera looked at Luca and Alfredo, who stared at her in silence, then back at Fabio. "So this is it? We break up and go our own ways?"

"Until the heat is off. The police will search for you for several days, and when they can't find you, they'll go on to something else. We all need to go undercover until the story is off the front pages and the daily news."

CHAPTER THIRTY

DAY TEN

Giorgio had been at his desk the next morning only a few minutes when his cell phone rang. The ID said it was from Paolo. He answered it, hoping it would be a short call. He didn't have time for socializing at work.

"Good morning, Paolo. Thank you for inviting me over last—"

Another voice interrupted him. "Sir, this is Cole, Sylvia's fiancé. I'm afraid I have bad news. Paolo had a heart attack last night. Fortunately, I was sleeping in the same bedroom. The hotel had an ambulance come quickly. They took him to the Fatebenefratelli Hospital, which is where I'm calling you from. I've been here since four this morning by his bedside."

"Oh, my. How terrible," Giorgio said. "I was with him just a few hours ago. We had . . . a nice conversation on the balcony."

"Yes, sir. He told me about it after I got back from dinner. He was so happy you came over."

"What is his condition?"

"I'm sorry to say it doesn't look good. His doctors said he may not live long. His heartbeat is very weak, and they have him on drugs. He had heart surgery two years ago and takes medication every day. But the stress of the last several days was too much for him. I could see it; he wasn't sleeping well, up in the middle of the night, not eating right. He likes his Scotch and cigars, neither of which is good for someone with a heart condition."

"I'll be there in half an hour."

* * * * *

Giorgio went to the security office at the hospital to get permission to enter the intensive care unit where Paolo was. When he arrived at Paolo's room, Cole was seated next to Paolo's bed. The bed was covered with crisp, white sheets that reached to Paolo's upper chest, where patches were taped and attached to monitors.

Paolo's eyes were closed. A clear plastic oxygen mask was over his mouth and nose. Intravenous lines led from his arms to plastic bags hanging on metal stands. Electronic monitors beside the bed were beeping. Jagged lines moved across the screen, and tiny blue lights blinked as Paolo's blood pressure, pulse rate, oxygen levels, and heartbeat were monitored. A nurse and a young doctor were by his bedside, looking at the screens.

Giorgio introduced himself. "I'm Giorgio Lucchini, primo dirigente at DIGOS. I'm investigating Mr. de Matteo's daughter's kidnapping."

The young doctor wore wire-rimmed glasses and a white lab coat. "Yes, *Dottor* Lucchini," he said. "Mr. Boylton said you were coming. You may stay a few minutes, but we have to make a decision soon if we're going to take him into surgery."

"May I speak to him?" Giorgio asked.

"Only for a moment. He's heavily sedated with morphine and epinephrine."

Giorgio moved to the side of the bed and put a hand on Paolo's pale fingers, which looked like pieces of chalk. He leaned over the bed and said in a soft voice, "Paolo, it's Giorgio Lucchini."

Paolo's eyes opened halfway and blinked several times. He opened his mouth and spoke weakly. "Hello. . . . Thank . . . you . . . last night . . . enjoyed . . . was . . ." Then he shut his eyes.

"You'd better leave now," the doctor said. "He needs rest. We're monitoring his condition and will make a decision in the coming minutes about surgery."

Cole and Giorgio went out into the hall, the door shutting behind them soft as a whisper. It opened again and the doctor and nurse left. Cole said to Giorgio, "I called Clelia, Angela's caretaker. They'll be coming soon. It will be hard for Angela. She's very close to her grandfather. But I think she should be here and know his condition, even as bad as it is."

Giorgio's face was grave. "Yes, I suppose you're right."

"I have to call Mrs. de Matteo in Menaggio," Cole said. "She needs to know. I may get someone to drive me there so I can tell her in person. I wish Sylvia was here. She'll be devastated if he dies. God, I hope he doesn't. The family has had enough crisis in recent days. And now this."

"Yes, it's truly unfortunate. I'm so sorry. I like Paolo. He's a sincere man who loves his family and would do anything for them. Such a tragedy."

"What about the press? Will they find out?"

"This is an extreme situation. If he dies, I can have the Questura press office enforce a news embargo prohibiting the release of the information. I will demand at least forty-eight hours before the media can report. I'm worried about what might happen to Sylvia if the terrorists find out."

"I'll stay around until I hear from the doctors," Cole said. "Then I'll decide about going to Menaggio to see Mrs. de Matteo."

"That's a wise decision. She's already grieving about Sylvia. Paolo told me about her last night. He was very worried about her. And now this—it's tragic. The poor family. I feel so sad for them."

* * * * *

Paolo watched Cole and Giorgio go out the door, followed by his doctor and nurse. He was alone; he hated being alone at any time. He was drugged and not thinking clearly, but he knew how bad things were. He looked around the room: sterile, metal equipment; everything white and lifeless. He heard the beeping and whirring of monitors beside his bed and watched the jagged lines, graphs, and blue and red lights flashing his vital signs. *It's all bad,* he thought. *Otherwise, I wouldn't be here.*

He looked down at the tubes in his arms, snaking up to plastic drip bags. The oxygen mask over his nose and mouth felt strange: oxygen flowing to his nose and mouth, little hoses giving him life. What life was left?

He was dying. Alone. His hope had always been to die like his father had thirty years ago, surrounded by his wife, children, grandchildren, close friends, and doctor. Fate had finally dealt him a cruel hand. He wouldn't have what his father had for his final reward, his loving family surrounding him during his last moments on earth.

Paolo lifted his head from the pillow and tried to cry out, but the oxygen mask muffled his words. No one heard him. He started to cry, tears welling in his eyes, rolling down his cheeks, and pooling in the oxygen mask.

A sudden pain in his chest shocked him. He tried to breathe, but his lungs felt like a stone was pressing on them. He gasped, tried to suck in air, laid his head back on the pillow, and closed his eyes.

Then he died.

CHAPTER THIRTY-ONE

V era drove out of the warehouse parking lot, spinning gravel as she reached the street, and sped off into the night. Seconds later, there was the sound of tires squealing and car horns honking. Then came the roar of a car accelerating, the squeal of tires, honking, and the sound of the speeding car muffled by the apartments and buildings.

"Porco Giuda, quella guida come un cane ubriaco, speriamo che non vada a sbattere," [She drives like a drunken dog. I hope she doesn't hit something] Luca said. "She'd swear at the officer, get arrested, and we'd all end up in jail."

Fabio sighed. "I'm worried about her. When I asked her to join us, she was enthusiastic. I hadn't seen her in a few months, but I thought she would be an asset. I didn't know how frustrated she was with her life. She's not making money with her video business. She's still bitter about how her fashion career ended. She made a fortune for a couple years; then it all went up in smoke. Her friends are avoiding her, and she doesn't have a boyfriend. She's going through a rough time in her life."

"Vera's too emotional," said Luca. "It's hard to have a serious discussion without her exploding. I'm glad you cut her loose. We can work better as a smaller group."

Fabio sighed again. "Let's go back inside. We've got lots to talk about, but I wanted to wait until she left."

They walked back into the conference room. "Marietto, get us more wine," Fabio said.

Luca and Alfredo watched the evening news, smoked cigarettes, and changed channels to see if any stations were updating news about Vera. Marietto brought in bottles of Lambrusco, filled their glasses, and left the bottle on the table. He went to get plates of cheese, olives, mortadella, sliced salami, and crackers.

Fabio went down the hall to one of the sleeping rooms and brought back a small suitcase. "Any more news about Vera?"

"No, just the same as we saw on RAI," Alfredo said.

"Then turn it off. We've got serious business to discuss."

Luca turned off the TV with the remote, and Alfredo poured more wine. They snuffed out their cigarettes, their faces drawn.

Fabio took a deep breath and let it out slowly. "Things have changed in the last thirty-six hours. The police showed up and looked around and asked about the Fiorino. That DIGOS woman was giving me looks that she was suspicious."

"That's the way they are," Alfredo said. "They're suspicious by nature. Don't make too much of it."

Fabio shook his head. "I'm not taking any chances. I wouldn't be surprised if they come back. They may bring a search warrant and want to enter Luca's apartment. They'd take Luca's computer too." He looked at Luca. "Take it home tonight and bring in another one."

Luca nodded. "Sure. I'll bring my old laptop tomorrow."

"The more serious issue is the Questura identifying Vera. Sending her away will buy us time, but they'll probably pick her up in a few days. If she reveals the warehouse, they'll be crawling all over here. We have to move Sylvia."

"Where will you take her?" Alfredo asked.

"Cornalba," Fabio said.

"Good choice," Luca said.

"Where's Cornalba? I've never heard of it," Alfredo said.

"It's north of Bergamo. It's our mother's home village. It's remote, in the mountains. Just a few homes. Only one road into and out of the village. Nothing ever happens there."

"Where will you keep Sylvia?" Alfredo asked.

"Our mother inherited the family home when our *nonno* died. She vacations there sometimes—drives up on weekends. But she's in France for another month. I have the key. Luca knows the place well. We spent summers and vacations in Cornalba when we were children."

"It's as quiet as a cemetery," Luca said, smiling. "More pigs and chickens live in that valley than people. Mamma's house is at the end of a dirt road that ends at a forest. A perfect hiding place. Is the old Cornalba bar and restaurant still open? Remember going there when we were teenagers?"

"I sure do," said Fabio. "I stopped in when I was there in June helping Mamma with her garden. The old bartender died; his brother is running the place now. He looks like he's ninety years old too."

"How long will you stay?" Alfredo asked.

Fabio shook his head. "I don't know. I just want to get there tonight. Marietto bought me food to last two or three days: wine, bread, cheese, pasta, fruits, and vegetables. There are markets in nearby villages. I can get more food if I stay more than a few days."

Alfredo asked, "How will you get Sylvia there?"

"Luca's Stilo has tinted windows; no one can see in. Come out and we'll show you how we'll keep Sylvia secure. She won't be able to open the car door or break a window."

"How about when you get to Cornalba? Where will you lock her up?" Alfredo asked.

"We have that planned. After our Zio Gino got out of prison, he lived with us in Cornalba. He tore down an old chicken shed and constructed a stone cottage to live in. He put in a bathroom, installed electricity, added a bedroom, and lived there for two years. He even put bars across the door and windows in case hooligans tried to break in when no one was there. I'll lock Sylvia in the stone cottage."

"Have you told Sylvia?"

"This afternoon. She was surprised but glad to get a new location. She's bored, living in the same room for over a week."

"When are you going?"

"Tonight. It'll be easier driving at night, less traffic. I'll be there after midnight. Come out to the car. We'll show you what Luca did to confine Sylvia."

They went out to the parking lot to Luca's black Fiat Stilo. Fabio opened the back door. Four plastic cords and a pair of gloves were on the backseat.

"We'll put her in the backseat, tie plastic cords around her wrists and ankles, and tie them together. She won't be able to move more than a few inches. The door and window will be locked, and we'll put sunglasses on her that Luca painted over with black paint."

"Hmm," Alfredo said, picking up the cords and twisting them. "Strong. Impossible to break. The police and the army use plastic handcuffs when they detain suspects."

Fabio looked at his watch. "It's ten thirty. Let's get Sylvia into the car so we can leave."

They went into the kitchen, and Fabio rapped on the glazed window. "Sylvia, we're ready. Put on the ski mask and have your clothes and toiletries on the bed."

He turned to the others and whispered, "Don't say a word when we're in the apartment. Vera's and my voices are the only ones she's heard. The fewer she hears, the better. Let her think there are a dozen of us."

They went into the corridor, and Luca unlocked the door. Sylvia was seated on the bed with the mask over her face. Her few clothes were in a small pile next to her toiletries in a plastic bag. Fabio motioned for Marietto to pick them up.

"We're taking you to the car," Fabio said. He and Luca took Sylvia's arms and led her out to the hallway and then outside. She stepped gingerly, stumbling when her sandals hit the gravel in the parking lot.

When they reached the Stilo, Fabio said to Sylvia, "The backdoor of the car is open. Get in. We're tying cords around your hands and feet. They won't hurt."

Luca put his hand on her head and gently guided her into the backseat.

"Put your hands in front of you," Fabio said. He and Luca tied the cords around her wrists and ankles and then looped another cord connecting them.

"Turn your head to the right and close your eyes," Fabio said. "I'm taking off the mask and putting sunglasses on your face."

Sylvia followed his directions, and Fabio adjusted the darkened sunglasses. When he was finished, Marietto opened the other back door and slid sacks of groceries, her clothes, and her toiletries onto the seat next to her.

"I'm shutting the door. I'll be back in a minute," Fabio said before closing the door.

Fabio motioned for the others to go back to the warehouse. When they were inside, he glanced at his watch. "It's getting late. I want to get on the road. It will take at least two hours. Mountain roads are tricky at night."

They looked at each other, not saying anything for a few moments. Alfredo and Marietto were a step behind Luca and Fabio, who faced each other. Luca wrapped his arms around his brother, and they slapped each other's backs. "Be careful, little brother."

"You know me. I drive like a pensioner."

Luca laughed. "I know. It drives me crazy. Be careful in Cornalba. I wrapped the Glock in a towel and put it under your seat."

Fabio shook his head. "I hope . . . I don't have to use it. You know I don't like guns."

"You might need it in an emergency. I put a box of ammunition in the glove box," said Luca.

"Luca's right. You need to protect yourself and Sylvia. Don't be afraid to use it," Alfredo said.

"I hope it doesn't come to that," Fabio said. "Cornalba's a safer place than here for the next couple of days."

"It is," Luca agreed. "Mamma's neighbors will think you're up for a few days with your girlfriend. Just wave at them, ask how they are, and act normal."

"I'll feel more secure in Cornalba," Fabio said. "Remember when we were kids? We hiked every trail, knew every stream, knew almost every tree in the forest. We had secret places and caves where we hid from Mamma and Zio Gino."

Luca smiled. "I remember well. I miss Cornalba. We had wonderful summers there."

"Join me in a few days," Fabio said. "But for now, you need to be here. Show the police around if they come back. If they arrived and the warehouse was vacant, it could look bad for us."

Luca said, "I have enough small jobs to keep me, Alfredo, and Marietto working another week. Nothing after that. We can join you then."

Fabio shook Alfredo's hand. "This is temporary. I'll probably just be gone a few days. If the ransom comes through, I'll have a plan worked out to release Sylvia."

Alfredo said, "Good luck, Fabio. Call us on your Albanian phone when you get there."

Marietto reached out to shake Fabio's hand. They embraced and then broke quickly. Marietto ran out of the parking lot to the front gate.

Luca and Fabio embraced one more time at the car. Then Fabio got in, started the engine, and drove slowly to the metal gate Marietto had opened.

Streetlights were illuminating the tree lined neighborhood when Fabio turned onto the quiet street. No one was walking on the sidewalks.

A few lights were burning in apartments. A car drove around a round-about and came toward him. Fabio drove slowly to the roundabout, took the left exit, and three blocks later reached the ramp of the A4 *autostrada* to Bergamo.

* * * * *

"We're on our way," Fabio said, accelerating to one-hundred kilo-meters per hour on the *autostrada*.

"Where are we going?"

"I can't say. It's about two hours from here. We'll be there about one in the morning."

"What kind of place are we going to? A home? An apartment? A farm?"

"Something like that. You'll find out soon."

"Why are you doing this?"

"For safety."

"Whose, mine or yours?"

"Both."

"Oh, I see," she said sarcastically. "If police come to that place, they'll shoot it up and kill people, possibly even me."

"Don't let your imagination run wild, Sylvia. You're going to be safe. It's quiet where we're going."

"What'll be different? It'll be another prison, just like where I've been. Why don't you just pull over, untie me, and let me out? I don't want to be here . . . with you . . . riding in some car . . . taking me someplace I don't want to be."

Fabio drove without talking. He didn't want to engage in a tense discussion that would end up making them both angrier. He had a long drive ahead, and he didn't want distractions.

"These sunglasses make me feel like I'm blind. I don't like them."

"It will only be for a couple of hours. Relax. It will be easier for you."

"Easy for you to say," she said, biting off each word.

Fabio ignored her.

Traffic on the *autostrada* was light, mostly heavy trucks traveling between Torino and Venice. Fabio glanced left and right and looked in the rearview mirror to see if *polizia* cars were on the highway. One passed going the other direction.

Fabio kept driving at the same speed. He looked in the rearview mirror again and saw the right side of Sylvia's face. She had turned toward the tinted window as if she could see through her sunglasses, possibly seeing dim lights from passing trucks and cars.

"This is boring. You're driving, and I can't see a thing," Sylvia said. "Turn on the radio. Find some music."

He turned the radio to a classical station. When she heard a symphony, she said, "That's better. What is it?"

"Debussy."

"You know music?"

"Yes, a little."

"How did you learn?"

"I liked music as a child. My mother listened to classical music and opera all the time."

"Where is your mother?"

"I . . . I'd rather not say. It's not important."

"Are you close to your mother?"

"Yes, I am."

"Ha, I'll bet, like most Italian men. Italian men live with their mothers, who do their laundry for them, cook their meals, and pamper them like little boys."

"Not all Italian men. You get that from reading magazines and watching trashy TV shows."

"Do you live with your mother?"

"No."

"Are you married? Do you have children?"

Fabio ignored her questions. He concentrated on driving. He passed the exit for Agrate followed by a sign indicating Bergamo was forty kilometers ahead. He scanned in both directions for patrolling *polizia* and maintained his speed of one-hundred kilometers per hour, letting faster cars zoom past and speed ahead, their red taillights disappearing in minutes.

Fabio enjoyed driving at night, even though he rarely did so. It let him collect his thoughts, analyze decisions he'd have to make, and ponder the consequences. He'd been in the warehouse for days, and the stress and boredom had made him tired and listless. He'd had many dark moments, fearing the police would discover them and arrest them. He'd worried about all the things that could go wrong, even questioning if they had made the right decision to shoot Onorevole Pallucca and take Sylvia hostage. He felt the weight of sending Vera away and moving Sylvia. Was he doing the right thing? He wished the ransom would be wired so they could release Sylvia and start planning their next move, perhaps another bombing at a bank or at one of Berlusconi's TV stations or real estate holdings. He would write another communiqué about their movement and try to inspire others to take action.

Sylvia broke his concentration. "Why won't you talk to me?"

"I'm busy driving. I don't like to be distracted."

"How much longer?"

Fabio glanced down at the car clock. Eleven forty-five.

"An hour, maybe more."

"Where are we going?"

"I told you, I can't say."

"What kind of place will you put me in?"

"It's in the woods, quiet. The weather will be cooler."

"That's nice," she said. "It was hot in that room. Stuffy. The air was stale. The walls were closing in on me."

Fabio thought over what he was going to say next, wanting to ease her anxiety and give her something to look forward to. "I might let you out for walks to get fresh air."

"Really?" she said, her voice rising. "Oh, God, I'd love fresh air. I've been cooped up like a rat in a cage. I hated it."

Fabio was quiet, wanting to hear what she'd say next. Her anger had subsided; the rest of the drive would not be as tense as the beginning.

They drove without talking for several minutes until Sylvia broke the silence. "I'm worried about my family. I know they're worried about me." She sighed heavily. "Especially my daughter. She's so sweet and innocent, never had a tragedy in her life. I don't want her to be emotionally scarred by . . . what's happened."

Fabio continued driving, but in silence, enjoying listening to Sylvia talk when she was not angry.

"My mother's health is not good," she continued. "She has a muscular disease and can barely walk. She used to be active, but now she needs a cane or walker just to get around the house. My dad has heart problems; he had surgery a couple of years ago, a quadruple bypass. That's pretty serious; I worry about him all the time. He takes heart medication and is on a low-fat diet. But he's so hyperactive," she chuckled, "and so am I. We're so much alike. We both work all the time, too many late-night hours. He's crazy about my daughter. They laugh and have their private jokes. It's so cute. She stayed with Mom and Dad a lot when I was getting my divorce. They helped her during that rough time in our lives."

Fabio looked at the clock. He wanted her to keep talking. Knowing what she was thinking was better than her being silent with him wondering what she was thinking.

"I wonder where they are," Sylvia continued. "Are they in Menaggio? Did they go to Milano? Do they have someone with them? Mom and Dad have friends from New York who might fly to Milano to be with them. The Culbertsons . . . the Morrises . . . even the Gaudys. I'll bet someone is with them."

Fabio reached Bergamo's ring road. He exited at Dalmine on a circular ramp, drove a couple of kilometers, and exited on another roundabout to get on SS 470 for eleven kilometers. When SS 470 merged with Strada Provinciale 27 at Nembro, he saw a sign for several villages before Cornalba: Ponte San Pietro, Alme, Ambria-Spino. Traffic was even lighter on the regional highway, which started climbing the foothills of the Alps alongside the Serio River. The road was dark, with few cars, and Fabio drove through pine forests where jagged mountain peaks blocked twinkling stars.

"You're slowing down. Where are we?" Sylvia asked.

"We're climbing. The road winds for several miles," he said, watching for the turn to Strada Provinciale 30, which would take them to Cornalba.

"You're not talking. It's boring, sitting here tied up."

"I'm concentrating on driving. I'm a careful driver. I don't want an accident."

"Of course not. You'd get arrested for kidnapping, and this farce would be over. Part of me wishes you would have an accident."

Fabio ignored her comment.

"Sorry. That wasn't nice," she said after a minute of silence. "I didn't mean to upset you. I was talking about my family a few minutes ago. That makes me feel good, but also sad. I miss them. God, I miss them."

It was quiet in the car for some time.

"I'm curious about you," she said finally, breaking the silence.

"Why?"

"Well . . . you almost seem like a . . . decent person. You speak well, almost politely sometimes—not what you'd expect from a criminal. You're a kidnapper, but in certain ways, you've been kind to me." She waited a moment then softly said, "Thank you."

After Fabio drove through the village of Ascensione, he reached the tortuous hairpin turns that climbed the mountainside. Each turn was almost one hundred and eighty degrees, so sharp that he had to slow to ten kilometers per hour. As a boy, Fabio had loved those hairpin turns, sitting in the backseat with Luca, sliding from one side of the car to the other as their mother or Zio Gino made the twisting climb. "Whee! Do that again! It's fun!" they'd scream, giggling and tickling each other.

"These are sharp turns," Sylvia said. "Are we near Lago di Como?"

"Can't say, sorry. There are mountains in Lombardy."

"Yeah, north of Milano, I know. We might be getting close to Menaggio. I've been going there every summer since I was ten years old."

"That must have been nice for a New York girl."

"See, you're being kind to me. I like that, Leo."

* * * * *

Half an hour later, they pulled off Highway 30 into the village of Cornalba. The few lights in the village were from living rooms of modest homes or from the neon signs outside the single bar and restaurant, Bar Ristorante Vico. Fabio took a sharp right turn and drove up a steep hill, passing several darkened homes.

Most residents of Cornalba were elderly, went to bed early, and rose at dawn to feed chickens, pigs, or a milking cow. Yard lights illuminated gardens with staked tomato plants, bean vines strung on lattices, and patches of herbs. Fabio drove slowly until he reached a clearing where moonlight fell on pastures and on dark farmhouses with trucks, tractors, and old cars parked in the driveways.

In his headlights, Fabio saw a small home against a hillside with tall pine trees behind. He slowed as the headlights illuminated a modest house with a porch, stone steps, and a fenced garden.

He stopped, opened his door, and said, "We're here."

CHAPTER THIRTY-TWO

DAY ELEVEN

"Can you believe RAI releasing Vera Pulvirenti's name without authorization?" Antonella said, her voice tense, eyes bulging in anger. "How did they get that? Somebody leaked. How the hell can we do our work if sensitive information is leaking like a sieve to the media?"

"Don't worry. We can't do anything about it now," Giorgio said, looking over his reading glasses at her. "It might have been one of those who called in to ID her. There were eight—people she'd worked for, and even friends. Can you believe that—a friend turning you in to the police? Not much loyalty there, but I'm glad they called."

Antonella was twisting a handkerchief in her hands, making a thin rope, unwinding it, and twisting it again.

"What are you doing with that handkerchief?" Giorgio asked, looking down at her lap.

"Just a nervous habit," she said, stuffing it in her pocket. "I need something to distract me when I'm angry. Otherwise I'll go back to smoking."

"Don't start smoking again."

"I came close this morning. I asked one of our agents to give me a cigarette in the garage. He lit up, and I grabbed his pack of cigarettes and put one in my mouth. But he wouldn't give me a light, the bastard!"

Giorgio laughed. "So, did you light up?"

She rolled her eyes. "No, I couldn't. He grabbed the cigarette and threw it on the ground. He was one of my smoking buddies when we had to go outside to smoke. He shook his finger at me and said, 'Don't you dare. I'll tell the boss!'"

Giorgio laughed. "Good for him. Who was it? Volpara? Esposito? They still smoke."

"I'm not telling you. That's my secret."

Giorgio smiled. "I'll find out."

She nodded and rolled her eyes. "You probably will, damn it. I won't tell you any more secrets."

"Don't take up smoking, even if this case is driving you crazy. I remember how hard it was for you to quit. You'd snap at me if I asked a simple question."

"It was the hardest thing to do. I thought I had willpower, but I didn't when it came to cigarettes. But this case is getting to me. I'm not sleeping well. I'm eating bad foods—drinking sodas during the day, and eating a pint of gelato at night. I've put on five pounds in the last week."

"I'm the opposite," Giorgio said. "I skip meals and spend more time in the gym. I've lost weight since this started. Let's wrap this case up and get back to a healthy lifestyle."

"Deal," she said, rapping her knuckles on his desk. "As mad as I am, I think things are going to go our way soon. I'm furious about the Vera leak, but at least we have her name. I was with the patrol that went to her apartment yesterday. We knocked on her door, but there was no answer. We didn't expect to get lucky and find her at home. We went to the apartment manager and told him we're putting the building under twenty-four-hour surveillance. We have webcams in the hall in case she gets in or is hiding in another apartment. We've tapped her cell phone and are getting records of her ATM and credit card activity."

"How about her car?"

"It's a 2006 Citroën C3 Pluriel. We sent her license number to police and Carabinieri patrol cars to be on alert, especially at motorway toll booths. If she's on the run, we could pick her up. I'll get a call if they arrest her. I want to interrogate her myself. I know how to break her down. Her friends say she never recovered emotionally from the motorcycle accident that ended her fashion career. She's bitter. She makes a little money with a video business but loses jobs because her personality is volatile. I'll mock her career and tell her she's washed up, and she'll come at me like a caged tiger. I'll wear her down until she breaks."

"You're tough. I've seen you work. I wouldn't want to be across the table from you. I'd spill my guts just to get you off my back."

"It's my favorite part of being a cop: breaking down low-life criminals."

"You've got to find her first."

"We will. She won't be able to hide for long. That's why I'm going back on the street today. The next forty-eight hours are critical. I've briefed everyone to be alert for unusual traffic in neighborhoods—cars or trucks driving suspiciously—and to treat any situation like it could break the case. Catch them when they make a mistake."

"Keep me posted. And don't smoke," Giorgio said with a smile. "I quit thirteen years ago. I miss it every day, especially when I get a whiff of someone lighting up on the street."

"Same here. I swear, it was the hardest vice I ever had to overcome."

"Nicotine's more addictive than drugs."

"You sound like my husband," she said with a grin.

"Get back on the street," he said. "Bust this open. We're due for a break."

* * * * *

Fabio had a difficult time sleeping. After he'd padlocked Sylvia in the cottage, he had gone back to the car and carried in the food, the pistol, and his suitcase.

His mother had left the small house neat. He put food in the refrigerator, went into the bedroom in which he'd slept as a child, undressed, and lay down. He was exhausted from the long drive and the late hour. He fell asleep but spent the night tossing and turning, worrying about Sylvia and the news about Vera.

Fabio slept late, exhausted and groggy from the late-night drive to Cornalba. He dressed, made coffee, and went outside to walk around the yard. The sun was now over the mountains. It had been two months since he'd been in Cornalba. The vegetable garden he and his mother had planted in April was overgrown with weeds. He opened the gate and walked around, pulling up the tallest weeds and tossing them onto a pile. He didn't know how long he'd be at the home, but he hoped he'd have time to get in the garden and stake the tomatoes. He had loved working in the garden when he and Luca were young. They would plant vegetables in the spring, water and weed them throughout the summer, make gopher traps, put white strips of cloth to keep birds away, and have fresh vegetables for their mother to cook when she came home late from working two jobs in Bergamo to support the family.

When Zio Gino had arrived one summer after being released from San Vittore prison, he had been anxious to do physical work—sweat in the sun and make something you could see and touch. After painting and making repairs around his sister's home, Zio Gino had torn down the chicken coop their grandfather had built when the family had raised chickens and had a large vegetable garden. All summer, they'd sold eggs and vegetables at the village market. The chicken coop had become decrepit, with pigeons roosting in the roof. It had needed to be torn down. In its place, Zio Gino had erected a stone cottage that he had designed as a single-room apartment, in which he had lived for two years.

Fabio and Luca had liked having Zio Gino around. He told them stories, kicked the soccer ball around with them, and took them hiking on mountain trails. Every afternoon, he'd wave to the boys and walk down into Cornalba to drink at the bar. Gino kept his past secret, not wanting others to know he'd been in prison as a Brigate Rosse member. Cornalba was a conservative region; local people didn't like the changes going on in Italy, especially the turmoil caused by the BR and other terrorists. Gino told the other men at the bar he was recovering from a medical condition and didn't say more.

The morning air was cool and refreshing, smelling of pine trees. Fabio sucked deep breaths into his lungs and looked down the dirt road at the rooftops of Cornalba. He knew older farmers along the road into Cornalba but hesitated to let them know that he was at the home. Too many things could go wrong. They'd bring fruits or vegetables from their gardens and might see Sylvia. Gossip about him and a girlfriend would spread like wildfire throughout Cornalba.

Fabio continued to walk down rows of tomato plants, green bean vines, herbs, and squash plants. He bent over and pulled more weeds, adding them to the pile along the fence. It felt good, being outdoors, doing a little physical work, remembering the joy of helping his mother in the garden. He spent a half hour weeding, and when he stopped, sweat was running down his forehead and his neck, making his shirt damp.

Fabio went over to the cottage and looked in. Sylvia was still asleep in the small bedroom with a blanket over her. He went back inside and made breakfast: cheese, bread, fried eggs, and fruit juice. He prepared a tray for Sylvia, took it to her bedroom door, and knocked.

"I have a breakfast tray for you. I'll unlock the door and put it on the floor. Don't come out."

After delivering her breakfast, he went back to shower and plan the day. He'd wait for her to eat and take a shower, and then he'd knock on the door and offer to take her on a walk.

He'd thought of a modest disguise; he'd wear a cap, sunglasses, and a long-sleeved shirt.

Later, he knocked on the door and said, "Sylvia, would you like to go for a walk?"

"Oh, yes, please. I really want to go. I need to get out; this place is tiny and smells funny. There's mildew and spiders, ants, and flies. Also, I'm cold. I only have short-sleeved blouses."

"I'll get you a jacket and shoes. Sandals aren't good for hiking."

When he returned, he was carrying a light jacket and his mother's garden shoes. He knocked and said, "I'll unlock the door and hand in a jacket and shoes. When you come out, turn left and walk up the trail toward the forest. I'll be behind you. Do not—I repeat—do not turn around. I'll be behind you, wearing sunglasses and a cap. I don't want you to see me. Is that clear?"

"I understand. I won't turn around. Will I be safe?"

"Yes, don't worry. I have bottled water, bread, and some fruit."

"Good."

"The trail goes up the mountain, over a small bridge, and through a pine forest. We probably won't meet anybody on the trail. But if we do, don't talk to them. Just nod, greet them, and keep walking. Understand?"

"Yes."

"Come outside and walk up the trail. I'll be behind the cottage and will come up behind you. Don't turn around even for a second. If you do, I'll lock you up and never let you out."

She hesitated. "I won't. I promise."

She followed instructions, and soon they were on the trail, a narrow path through a grove of pine and cypress trees. Patches of weeds, fallen twigs, and dried pine cones littered the path.

Sylvia bent over, picked up a twig and twirled it in her hands. She stooped again and picked up a pine cone, putting it to her nose and inhaling.

"Aaah, that smells soooo good. I miss the smells and sounds of the woods. This is like heaven to me. Thank you."

They walked up the trail without talking, hearing birds chirping in trees, breezes rustling pine branches, and the crunching of their shoes on the dirt path.

The trail began climbing along a mountainside with occasional glimpses of a valley and homes below. Across the valley, the forest reached to rocky cliffs and ridges. On the highest ridges there was a dusting of snow on the peaks.

They came to a clearing with a rocky ledge, a bench, a meadow below, and a sweeping view of the valley. Sylvia stopped and looked across the valley. "Look at that. What a view! It reminds me of Menaggio, but you don't see snow unless you take a ferry to Colico, where you can see the Southern Alps."

"Yes, I've been there. It's pretty."

"Can we stop a minute? This view is incredible. I want to drink it all in. I feel so good!"

"Sure, we can stop. Stay in front. I'm behind you."

After a minute, she asked, "Can you tell me where we are, what mountains these are?"

"They're mountains in Lombardia."

"We're near the Alps. I can tell. Switzerland is over there," she pointed north, "and Austria is over there," she said, pointing to the east. "I think I'm right."

"That's right. Good sense of geography."

They lingered for more than five minutes. Sylvia turned her head from right to left, then back again, raising a hand to shield the sun from her eyes.

"We'd better keep going," Fabio said.

"Sure, whatever you say. I'm glad we stopped. This is a beautiful place, very special. I'll remember it for a long time."

A hundred yards above them, a retired biology teacher from Bergamo, Giuseppe Mantovani, was scanning the mountainside through binoculars, looking for birds to photograph. That morning he'd seen plenty of crows, buzzards, sparrow hawks, owls, and woodpeckers. But he was looking for smaller songbirds and found a *peppola* with a faded orange breast, a *fringuello* with a pointed blue cap, and his favorite, a *upupa*, with bands of black and white feathers pointing from the top of its head in the same pattern as its wing feathers. Mantovani would enlarge the *upupa* photo and show it at the next birders meeting.

Mantovani, a sixty-three-year-old grandfather, had spent the summer after his retirement taking up birding so he could hike in alpine foothills, get strenuous exercise, and marvel at the beauty of birds. He scanned the mountainside below and saw a couple out for a morning hike. They were in a clearing, gazing across the valley, the man behind the woman, looking over her shoulder. She raised a hand to shield her eyes from the sunlight.

Mantovani admired her trim figure, narrow waist, and slim legs. Her black hair seemed a little long, with waves curling below her ears. She'd look more attractive, he thought, if her hair were trimmed. When she lowered her hand, he saw her face.

Attractive. Sensual dark eyes. Strong jaw. She held her head high as she gazed off into the distance. Probably in her early thirties, out for a walk with her lover.

Mantovani stared at her. Something about her looked familiar.

He gasped. He gripped the binoculars to steady his view. *Is it . . . her? Could it be? Is that the American woman who was taken hostage?*

Mantovani adjusted his binoculars to get a closer view of her face. Her photo had been on TV and in the newspapers for days. He had barely paid attention to the story: some shooting at Stazione Centrale, a politician killed, an American woman taken hostage. In the wrong place at the wrong time.

Mantovani moved his binoculars to look at the man standing behind her. Black cap pulled down on his forehead, sunglasses, arms folded across his chest. Why was he standing behind her?

Mantovani lowered his binoculars and reached for his camera bag. He pulled out a 400x power lens and screwed it onto the camera face. He lifted the camera and zoomed the focus on the woman's face. He snapped a picture of her profile.

"Turn . . . so I can see you better," he muttered to himself. As if she had heard him, she turned back, allowing him a full view of her face.

He snapped once, twice, three times, four times as she turned her head slowly, her lips moving, talking to the man over her shoulder.

Mantovani focused on the man with the dark glasses and cap. Hard to distinguish his face. He snapped several photos then moved back to the woman. But she had resumed walking down the trail, the man behind her. In seconds, they disappeared in the woods, swallowed up by trunks of thick pine trees and long branches.

Mantovani lowered his camera, his heart racing. *Could it be? Was that the American woman hostage? If it is, what should I do?* He could chase them, run down the trail, cross a ravine, and then go up the other side to meet them. What would he say? They'd think he was a crackpot if he told them why he'd run after them.

He knew the trails all over the valley from photographing birds all summer. It was hopeless to get another view of them. The trail they were on wound down the mountainside and looped back toward Cornalba.

Mantovani unscrewed the telephoto lens, put it and the camera back into the camera bag, and looped it over his shoulder.

He knew what he had to do.

CHAPTER THIRTY-THREE

F abio took Sylvia along another trail that climbed the mountain to the base of a rocky cliff. The vantage point allowed views for several kilometers in both directions. Cars traveling along the winding road that passed through Cornalba looked like toy cars. They were so high, they could see hawks and birds flying around the valley below them.

Fabio told Sylvia they could spend an hour there. She could walk in a small area below the cliff, sit on boulders, and enjoy the fresh air, brilliant sky, and sweeping views of the valley below. Fabio felt secure; the trail ended at that spot, and there were no trails above where anyone could see them.

They descended on trails via several switchbacks, which made it difficult to talk. Sylvia had obeyed him, not turning around to look at him, following his instructions on which trails to take, when to stop, and when to continue hiking.

When they reached a meadow halfway down the mountain, Sylvia stepped off into the grass to rest. When she heard Fabio stop behind her, she said, "I have a request, please."

Fabio wiped sweat from his brow and said, "Yes, what is it?"

"I know it sounds strange . . . but I'm lonely at night. I eat by myself every night. It's been like that for, what, twelve or thirteen days? I've lost count. Is there any way we could be in the same room to eat dinner? You don't have to talk to me, just be in the same room. I know it's a lot to ask . . . but . . . but it would mean a lot to me."

Fabio stood a few steps behind her, staring at her back, contemplating her request. She had honored his request not to turn and face him. He felt somewhat comfortable talking with her on the trail. She was his captive but had obeyed him. "Let me think about it," Fabio answered. "Let's keep going. We have another hour until we get back."

On their way down the mountain trail, Fabio thought about how he could fix dinner and have Sylvia in the house with him. His mother's home was small: two bedrooms, a kitchen with a small dining area, and a living room with bookcases, a table, chairs, and a TV on a stand.

When they returned, Sylvia went into the cottage and shut the door. When Fabio locked it, he said, "Let me see how I could arrange to have you come to the house for dinner. I'll be back and let you know."

"Thank you," she said through the door. "I need a shower and then I'm going to rest. That was a strenuous hike; we were gone a long time. It felt good, but I'm tired."

When Fabio entered the house, he took out his Albanian cell phone and called Luca. "Any word on her?" He avoided using Vera's name in the remote chance the call might be intercepted.

"No, nothing yet. We've been watching TV news and reading the papers. We haven't heard from her. She probably drove through the night, got a small hotel, and slept most of the day."

"Even when she's working, she'll stay in bed till noon," Fabio said. "She doesn't sleep well. Tosses and turns, has nightmares, lots of worries."

"Do you think she'll call soon?"

"Hard to say," Fabio said. "She was mad when she left and will probably be angry for a few days. So she might not call until she gets to Sicily."

"I called her Albanian phone earlier this afternoon, but she's not answering."

"Don't worry about it for now," Fabio said. "We can try tomorrow. Maybe she'll cool down by then. I called my contact at the charity today," Fabio said, changing the subject. "No word on the ransom yet. Something has to happen soon. I'm anxious to get confirmation so we can get rid of our friend; it's risky to keep her captive."

"How will you . . . get rid of her?"

"I've thought about it. If the ransom comes in a day or so, I could release her in a remote area on my way back to Milan. Leave her a couple kilometers away from here on a country road and give her a little money so she can catch a bus to Milan. There are a lot of remote roads in the mountains, as you know."

"Right. It would take her three or four hours to get back. How long will you stay . . . where you are?"

"I don't know. But it's quiet and remote."

"How is . . . 'your guest' taking it?"

"She prefers being here. I even took her for a hike in the mountains this afternoon."

"What? Isn't that risky?"

"Not really. I took her on the trail behind the house up the side of the mountain. She walked ahead of me. I wore sunglasses and a hat. She had strict instructions not to turn around or I'd lock her up and never let her out. She obeyed; didn't try anything funny."

"Did you carry that 'object' I gave you?"

"Yes. It was tucked in my belt under my shirt."

"Good. Keep it with you at all times. By the way, I called that 'office' you told me about, and I told them the car they were interested in probably belonged to someone looking for a job. I said a lot of men come by to look for work, but I don't meet them or know what kind of car they drive. The 'person' I talked to understood. He didn't ask anything else."

"Good. I hope it's the last we hear from them."

* * * * *

After the call, Fabio took a shower, changed clothes, and looked around the house to see how he could arrange a place for Sylvia to eat so she couldn't see him.

He carried a small table into the living room and put it behind the four-foot-high divider between the living room and the kitchen table. She could eat in the living room and not see him. He'd turn out the lights, light candles, and put them on her table and on the kitchen table, where he would eat. He felt safe with this arrangement and went out to tell her.

"Thank you," she said through the door. "When will you be back?"

"A half hour or so."

He returned and prepared dinner—a salad, bread, and spaghetti alla puttanesca—and he opened a bottle of wine. While the pasta and sauce were cooking, he put out plates, utensils, glasses, and candles. When the meal was ready, he filled a plate for Sylvia and put it in the living room. He poured wine in his glass and put a half-full bottle on her table.

Fabio looked over the room, was satisfied, lit candles, and turned out the lights.

It was dusk when Fabio went to the cottage and knocked. "Dinner is ready. Walk straight ahead into the house. I have candles lit; you'll be able to see. Turn right after you enter and go to the living room. There's a table set for you, with a candle so you can see. There's wine for you as well."

"Thank you, Leo, I'm ready. The hike made me hungry."

Sylvia followed instructions and walked straight for the house, still wearing Fabio's mother's jacket and garden shoes. She opened the screen door, turned, went into the living room, and sat down behind the room divider.

"This is nice. I like the candle. The meal looks excellent. I'm hungry. I appreciate this—my first meal with another person since . . ." Sylvia didn't know what to say. Her last meal in Milan had been their farewell lunch on Via Dante, drinking delicious prosecco. Oh, how she missed sipping chilled prosecco, sparkling and zesty. It seemed a distant and painful memory. When they had all finished that meal, they had returned to their hotel and taken a taxi to Stazione Centrale. And then Sylvia's life had become a nightmare. That last meal was too painful to talk about, and she was sure Leo wouldn't want to know.

They started to eat in silence, both uneasy about the unusual circumstances, but after a couple of minutes, the mood seemed to change. They were both more relaxed, sipping wine, eating bread and pasta, taking their time.

Then Fabio said, "When was your last meal with people?"

Sylvia held her breath. She was anxious to have a conversation about something other than her captivity. She took a breath and began, "It . . . it was in Milan. An outdoor restaurant on Via Dante that caters to tourists; you know the type. We ate under a red umbrella. It was hot and sunny. I was with my daughter and fiancé. We drank prosecco. We had pizza and spaghetti. I had tiramisu for dessert, and my daughter had gelato."

"A nice memory," Fabio said.

They were silent for a minute or so, eating slowly. Then Sylvia said, "I like the wine. I poured another glass. A Syrah, I believe?"

"Yes," he said, looking at the divider to make sure she wasn't looking over and seeing him. He was in semidarkness, the candle off to the side, so even if she did see him, he would be in shadows. He could trust her up to a point but had to be cautious.

"The pasta is tasty," she said. "I like the spices in the sauce. You're a good cook."

"I try," he said.

Fabio could hear Sylvia's fork and knife scraping her plate, the clinking of the water glass and wineglass being set down.

When Sylvia finished dinner, she wanted to linger. Going back to the stone cottage was depressing. She'd rather talk to Leo than be back in her prison.

"I . . . I don't know much about you," she started. "You've been kind . . . and thoughtful. Hiking in the mountains was a wonderful experience. I feel alive again. Thank you."

Fabio hesitated before he answered, "You're welcome."

"Can we talk more?" she asked.

He hesitated. "Maybe a little . . ." He finished the last of his pasta and sipped his wine. He wanted to talk more also but felt uneasy.

"I told you a lot about myself when we drove here. Thank you for letting me open up a bit. It felt good."

He said nothing.

"I . . . I . . . almost feel a connection to you," she started hesitantly, stumbling over her words. "It's strange . . . isn't it? What I mean . . . is . . . well . . . you've listened to me . . . not been judgmental . . . and I almost feel like I can tell you more. It's . . . it's strange. . . . I know it is. . . . I don't know what I'm trying to say."

Fabio had no idea where she was going with her comments, but he wanted to hear more.

"I guess what I'm trying to say is, I feel better here . . . in the dark . . . talking to you . . . than I would alone in that small room. I don't feel good there. Can I . . . maybe stay longer?"

Fabio felt anxious about her request but also touched by her sincerity. "We'll . . . we'll see. No promises. If you want to talk, I guess that's okay."

"Thank you."

Neither one spoke for a few moments. Sylvia sipped her wine and poured another glass. "I'm having another glass of wine. It tastes good. I feel more relaxed."

The wine was bringing back pleasant memories of the many nights she'd drunk wine with men she had loved or had slept with. She and Charles had loved to drink wine during their passionate, tempestuous marriage. She had slept with many men after her divorce, when her sexual appetite had seemed to have no end. And she had encouraged Cole to relax, enjoy wine, and be more sexually aggressive. Sylvia missed the touch and smell of men, their firm muscles, sweaty bodies, and the pressure of naked bodies coming together. She ached to be held, caressed, kissed, and fondled. She had suppressed sexual feelings for days. But during the last few hours, after taking a warm shower, lying down to rest, and now having a good meal and wine, she was feeling liberated. And alive. And female. She wanted more.

She poured more wine and felt even more relaxed. It was a wonderful, guilty feeling, drinking wine that her captor had served her. Who else could understand what it felt like to have a few moments of pleasure after being locked up as a hostage? It didn't matter. She was going to make the delicious feeling last as long as she could. It almost felt . . . wicked.

The house was quiet. Fabio looked at the divider, wondering what she was thinking, wishing he could see her face. He was touched by her openness; most women he knew were not as open with their thoughts; they tended to hide their vulnerability. Vera had been the worst; her anger would explode at unexpected times, and she had never shown the introspection to dig into the reasons for her emotions or how she could deal with that better. Anger had sabotaged their relationship, and had probably destroyed Vera's other relationships, both personal and professional.

"When . . . when this is over . . . ," she started, not sure what she was going to say, "what will you do? Will you do other violent things . . . or . . . or . . . have you learned something from this? I mean . . . has this thing you did changed you?"

Fabio was stunned. She was expressing thoughts that he had had the last few days. The excitement of the planning and execution of the bombings and shootings had been exhilarating. They were doing things to change Italy. The world. But nothing had happened except they had become criminals and were in hiding, running from the police, and not likely to escape capture. What would his life be like if they were captured? Prison the rest of his life? Most likely. A terrifying thought. They had become revolutionaries, but Fabio had seen no positive response from their actions. Did that make them failed revolutionaries? Just another gang of radical thugs? Students wouldn't write books and articles about radical thugs. They didn't have the romantic visionary view of the world like Che, Fidel, Mao, or the BR.

"I don't have an answer for you, Sylvia," he finally admitted. "It's very complicated . . . and I guess . . . unknown."

"I'm sorry," she said. "I wish . . . I wish . . . you hadn't done what you did . . . and I could have met you under other circumstances." Again, she was surprised by what she had said, but it was true. He was the only person she had talked to in many days; she was curious to know what his motivations were and what he had been like before the shooting. He didn't seem like someone who'd been a criminal all of his life. No, that wasn't possible.

Sylvia sipped more wine, not certain what she would say next.

In the end, she didn't say anything. She stood, turned around, and looked across the darkened kitchen where Fabio was seated at the table. The candlelight faintly illuminated his face, even though he was in shadows. He was looking at her, not trying to hide. His face was calm, with handsome features, dark hair combed over his head, large eyes, and almost feminine nose and mouth.

They looked at each other in silence for what seemed a long time. Neither spoke. A bridge had been crossed; she had seen him without a mask or sunglasses. He looked like many handsome Italian men she had seen at cafés, on trains, in markets, and in theaters. She'd been curious about those men, imagining their lives, loves, and dreams. For a moment, she thought Leo looked like an Italian father who should be walking hand in hand with small children.

She moved toward him and stood in front of the kitchen table, the flickering light of the candle reflecting off a profile of his face. He didn't move. Their eyes never evaded each other.

"Stop," he finally said. "I don't want you to do this . . . to see me. . . ." He reached over and blew out the candle. They were in near total darkness, with only the light of the moon coming through the kitchen window.

"Your face . . . is kind. . . . It . . . it's a handsome face."

Wind was coming down the mountain, blowing through the trees, and brushing pine branches against the roof. The wind became stronger, blowing dried leaves and pine needles down the trail, some of which flew onto the porch and against the windows, making gentle tapping sounds. When the wind subsided, the pine branches brushed one last time against the roof, and then it was still. A clock someplace down the hallway was ticking, syncopating with a slow drip of the faucet in the kitchen sink.

Fabio stood up, out of the illumination from the moon. Sylvia could not see his face anymore. She moved a step closer and reached up a hand.

"I want . . . to . . . touch . . . your face."

Fabio stepped back, but she came closer. He reached up to touch her fingers. They were warm and damp.

"No . . . ," he said, his voice a whisper.

"Why . . . why . . . not?"

"Because you . . . shouldn't. . . . We shouldn't. . . . It's not—"

"I know it's not."

The wind blew down the mountain again. Pine branches brushed against the roof.

"I'm not trying to . . . ," she stammered. "I just . . . can't help . . . I haven't . . . touched . . ." Her voice drifted off.

She moved closer. Fabio's face was still in shadows. She took her hand away from his fingers and gently brushed it along his cheek, feeling the soft bristle of facial hair, as he had not shaved for a day or two. Sylvia lowered her hand to his jaw, then down to his neck. It was smooth and warm, with cords of muscles.

"Sylvia . . . don't. . . . We . . . can't," he whispered.

She smelled his warm breath, sweet with wine, and moved to him, putting her arms around his back. She pressed her body into his, nestling her face against his chest.

Fabio wanted to push her away, but her warm, firm body with her breasts against him felt comforting. Her soft hair brushed against his chin. She had come to him out of loneliness, fear, and tenderness.

He wanted her. He had wanted her all day. He had wanted her since he had first seen her in the tiny room with the cap covering her face.

They embraced in the darkened kitchen, bodies entwined, hands caressing each other's backs.

CHAPTER THIRTY-FOUR

DAY TWELVE

Antonella's cell phone rang at 3:20 a.m. She was in the middle of a strange dream, watching a woman plummeting to earth after falling from an object that looked like an air balloon that then changed into a bus, then a tram, and then a boat. The woman looked helpless, spinning head over heels, arms and legs spread, falling from a sky with patches of blue and red overhead.

The cell phone beeping grew louder, sounding like an alarm as Antonella struggled to awaken from a deep sleep. The dream of the falling woman spinning through the sky faded as she was swallowed by a billowing cloud and disappeared, the sky turning from blue and red to yellow.

Antonella pulled a hand from under the covers and reached for the nightstand. Her fingers fumbled for the phone. She found it, pulled it under the covers, and pressed the talk button.

"Amoruso . . ." Her voice sounded like gravel.

"*Dottoressa,* this is Vittorini," said one of her agents who worked the night shift at DIGOS. "Sorry to wake you, but you told us to call if there was significant news."

"Mmm," she mumbled, opening her eyes in the dark. Her brain was fuzzy, the bizarre dream of the falling woman still fading from her memory. "I'm here. . . . Tell me . . ."

"We think we know where Sylvia is."

The fuzziness in Antonella's sleepy brain evaporated in an instant. "Where?" she asked, rubbing sleep from her eyes, focusing in her darkened bedroom on a blurred sliver of light from the streetlights coming through between the closed drapes.

"In a village north of Bergamo . . . Cornalba."

Antonella cleared her throat and pushed herself up onto a fluffy pillow. "I'm listening. Tell me more."

"A birdwatcher from Bergamo was hiking and taking photos of birds yesterday. Through binoculars, he saw two people hiking across a valley. He thought he recognized Sylvia from the TV reports."

"What time was this?"

"About noon. He started to hike back to his car but stumbled and twisted his ankle and had to limp down the mountain to his vehicle. He made it home but had his wife drive him to the hospital before he went to the Bergamo Questura. They downloaded the photos, called us last night, and e-mailed the photos to us. We analyzed them and think they match Sylvia de Matteo's photo."

Antonella tossed off the covers and sat on the edge of her bed.

"Where's Cornalba? Never heard of it."

"It's a village north of Bergamo in Val Serina, near Parco delle Orobie."

"What the hell is she doing there?"

"*Dottoressa,* I don't know."

"Sorry. I'm thinking out loud. I thought she was in Milan all along. No wonder we couldn't find her."

"Yes . . . ," Vittorini said, not sure how to respond.

"You said two people were in the picture. Who's the other one?"

"A man wearing sunglasses is standing behind her."

Antonella turned on the nightstand lamp and reached for her robe on the bedcovers. "I'll be there in an hour. Get a NOCS team ready to move."

"Yes, *dottoressa,* right away."

* * * * *

At 6:00 a.m., Giorgio's cell phone buzzed at his bedside. He bolted awake and reached for it before it buzzed again and woke his wife. "Lucchini," he whispered.

"*Buongiorno, Capo.* It's Antonella. I'm at the office."

Lucchini looked at his bedside clock. "So early?"

"Big news. We know where Sylvia was yesterday."

"Really? Where?" he said throwing off his covers, reaching for his robe, and shuffling to the bathroom so he could shut the door and let his wife sleep. Getting calls at all hours of day and night was part of his job; he didn't want his wife to have her sleep disturbed.

"A village north of Bergamo near Parco delle Orobie," Antonella said.

"Mmm. I know Orobie. Beautiful mountains and pine forests. But how did she get to the mountains?"

"No idea, but she was there yesterday. I got a call in the middle of the night from our command center. The Bergamo Questura e-mailed photos to us taken by a birdwatcher who saw her on a trail and took pictures with a long-distance lens. There was a man with her wearing sunglasses, probably a guard."

"They took Sylvia for a hike in the mountains?" Giorgio said in disbelief. "I thought she was locked in a garage or basement—not hiking like she's on vacation."

"I agree. It doesn't make sense. Someone could recognize her."

"The birdwatcher did."

"Oh, Madonna. Do you think they took her to the mountains to kill her and hide the body?"

"Let's hope not. You've got to move fast."

"I'm going to run home and get extra clothes and take a team to Bergamo to investigate. I might be there for a couple of days."

"Go. Call me when you get to Bergamo. I'll call the prosecutor immediately and make sure that the news doesn't leak this time. It would be a disaster."

"I agree. We have to keep this out of the media."

"Good luck. And be careful."

* * * * *

Sylvia woke at dawn the next morning. She opened her eyes and looked out Leo's bedroom window. The previous night's wind had tossed pine branches across the path to the stone cottage.

She closed her eyes and recalled the previous night's lovemaking with Leo. The night had rejuvenated her. Something about this remote location had given her back a part of herself she thought she'd lost. She wasn't locked up in a windowless room; she was in bed with Leo after a passionate night of lovemaking and tenderness. He had done something unexpected earlier in the day when he had allowed her the freedom to be outdoors for the first time in almost two weeks. She had relished the fresh air, exercise, and majestic views of snowcapped alps. She was regaining a sense of her former self, especially after the unexpected, wonderful sex with Leo. Things were changing. She was feeling more confident about herself and her fate. She was going to make it, somehow escape from her captivity and rejoin her family. She didn't know how, but she felt it was going to happen.

Sylvia felt Leo's warm body against her back, his slow breathing from deep sleep. She lay there for several minutes, reliving the sensuous drama of seeing him for the first time, touching his face and neck, and their first embrace.

After that embrace, Leo had taken her by the hand to his bedroom. It had been semidark, the only light coming from a sliver of moonlight streaming through the window. Leo had slowly removed her clothes, letting them fall to the floor, running his hands over her shoulders and breasts and down her stomach. He had stripped off his clothes and they had embraced, their naked bodies melting together. Every nerve in her body had felt electric with his soft touch.

She had felt aroused and had run her hands over his arms, shoulders, and bare chest. After a long kiss, he had pulled back the covers of his bed. Sylvia had slipped between the sheets and looked up at him. Their eyes had locked, and then they had embraced. He had kissed her tenderly on her forehead, cheeks, neck, and throat before their lips met in a long, passionate kiss.

Sylvia had been hungry for sex, which she hadn't had in weeks. Fabio's fingers had gently passed down her shoulders, stomach, and lower. She had ached to have him come inside her. She had willingly submitted to passion she hadn't felt in a long time. Leo was a patient lover, and he had let her anticipate every brush of his fingers over her quivering body.

Sylvia lifted the sheet, put her bare feet on the wooden floor, and tiptoed into the bathroom. When she emerged a few minutes later, she had a towel around her.

Instead of returning to the bed, she crossed the hallway and went into another room. In the faint light, she saw a small bed, a bureau, a dressing table with a mirror, a small sofa, and many framed photos.

Above the dressing table were sepia photos of Leo's ancestors who'd been dead more than a century: peasant farmers in stiff poses with drooping mustaches, wrinkled shirts, and oversized coats standing next to overweight women wearing scarves, aprons, and blouses buttoned to the top. Fathers and mothers cradled babies in confirmation dresses; they looked like cherubs with chubby cheeks, double chins, and curly hair.

Sylvia studied the faces of these humble Italians, remembering similar photos she'd seen when she had visited her father's relatives in Lago di

Piano. She felt a spiritual connection to these people who had struggled and sacrificed, devoting their humble lives to hard work, family, and the Catholic Church. Such good people, simple and honest, who'd seen their children leave Italy for America, where many had become wealthy and had rarely returned.

Family photos were arrayed in a semicircle on the dresser. Sylvia leaned down to look at one with a man and woman and two young boys. In an instant, she recognized Leo, the younger boy, about six years old, standing stiffly, hands at his sides, with soft, gentle eyes, a full head of black, wavy hair. He was standing next to his mother, a short pretty woman with wavy black hair. The father was a tall man with a gaunt look, possibly from poor health. Next to the father was another boy, about 9 or 10, who must have been Leo's brother.

On the wall Sylvia saw framed confirmation awards for Fabio Cecconi, Luca Cecconi, and a wedding certificate for Roberto Cecconi and Daniela Guzztti Cecconi. She checked the dates of the confirmation awards; Luca Cecconi's was four years earlier than Fabio's; he was his older brother. Leo's name was Fabio. She finally knew. But she was still going to call him Leo, the name she had given him when he wouldn't tell her. He would always be Leo.

She picked up a family picture taken at the Vatican. Leo looked to be about four years old. His father was holding him, and his older brother was standing between their parents. The family looked happy. They were smiling, wearing new clothes, and standing in bright sunshine with St. Peter's Basilica behind them. Sylvia smiled at the innocence of the happy family.

She walked around the bedroom, stopping in front of the bed with pillows and sheets turned back under a patterned quilt similar to what she'd seen in Lago di Piano peasant homes. Over the bed was a faded print of Christ on the cross with a Latin scripture from Saint Anselm on a scroll beneath: *Credo ut intelligam, non intelligo ut credam.*

An old family Bible with a worn cover and tattered edges was on the bed stand. Sylvia turned back the cover and ran her fingers over tissue-thin pages. Each page had two columns, with the chapters' initial letters enlarged in red ink. She leafed to the front and found a page of Cecconi family genealogy back to the mid-nineteenth century. When she picked it up to read the names, she was startled by Leo's voice.

"What are you doing? This is my mother's room," he said, standing in shadows by the doorway, a towel around his waist. "You shouldn't be in here. There's too much for you to see."

She set the Bible back on the bed table. "I'm sorry. Curiosity is one of my traits. I know it sounds strange . . . but I can feel the presence of your mother here. Is she a gentle, kind woman?"

He nodded, a sad look on his face. "Yes, she is."

"I saw her picture. She's a beautiful woman. I'd like to . . . meet her someday," she said, embarrassed as soon as the words came out of her mouth.

"That won't happen."

"I know. I know," she said, leaving the bedroom and following him into the hallway. He shut the door, took her hand, and walked back to his bedroom.

Sylvia walked across the bedroom and stood by the window, turning to look at him across the rumpled sheets on the bed.

"Last night was—" she began.

"Don't talk about it. It happened. I'm sure you're angry."

"No, I'm not. We're adults. We knew what we were doing. The circumstances . . . are bizarre . . . but that can't take away from what we did. We slept together. We made love because we both wanted to. I'm not sorry, are you?"

He shook his head. "But it doesn't change anything."

She stared at him, not sure what to say. She didn't agree with him; things had changed. But she didn't want an argument. "Okay, it doesn't change anything." It was a lie.

"I think . . . we should . . . be apart for a while," Fabio stammered. "Last night was just . . . so unexpected—"

"Yes, I agree. You need to be alone. I'll go back to the other place. I need to be alone too."

"I have to lock you up again."

She nodded. "I understand. But . . . can we go for a hike again later today? I don't want to be cooped up all day and night."

"I'll think about it. I have things to do. I need to be alone."

Sylvia dressed and went into the hallway. Fabio put on his clothes and, when he went into the hallway, he saw her standing by the door. Neither one talked as he walked her over to the stone cottage, let her in, and locked her inside.

* * * * *

At 8:15 a.m., Antonella left the Questura on Via Fatebenefratelli in an unmarked police car with two plainclothes DIGOS agents. Following behind was a Panther police car with two members of the NOCS unit trained in hostage negotiations.

The cars turned on sirens and flashing blue lights, which allowed them to navigate slightly faster through Milan to the A4 *autostrada,* which was clogged with heavy truck traffic. When they reached the Bergamo Questura at 26 Via Alessandro Noli later that morning, Antonella and her fellow officers were escorted to an emergency meeting with the Questore of Bergamo, Gianluigi Fumagalli, and the head of Bergamo DIGOS, Alessandro Vitale. After a brief introduction, the Questore left the room to wait for the prosecutor in his office.

Two hours later, Antonella was before a packed room of Bergamo and Milan police officers and DIGOS special teams who'd received an earlier briefing on the situation. On one wall was a color map of the Bergamo province. Alongside it was a screen displaying a digital map of Cornalba and Parco delle Orobie.

"I want to thank Questore Fumagalli and *Dottor* Vitale for assisting us in this investigation," she said, gesturing to Vitale. "I don't have to tell you how dangerous these criminals are. They murdered one politician at Stazione Centrale, wounded two Polfer, and took an American woman hostage. They are violent criminals, well armed, and willing to kill more police if they have to."

Antonella looked around the room, eyeing each officer. No one looked away or displayed any visible signs of fear or doubt.

"You're all well-trained and experienced. We're going to approach them carefully and professionally with the best surveillance techniques possible."

One or two nodded. Others looked ready to run from the room, jump in their Panthers, and speed off to play cops versus criminals.

"We're going in two teams. I'll have my DIGOS staff and backup in two cars. *Dottor* Vitale will lead the Bergamo team. We'll drive in unmarked cars to Cornalba. The director will have two cars set up a roadblock and check all vehicles coming from Cornalba. Others on his team will drive into the bordering villages of Oltre il Colle, Serina, Costa di Serina, and Gazzaniga," she said, pointing to the digitized Cornalba map.

"You'll be in civilian clothes. When you arrive, walk in neighborhoods without attracting attention. Your story is you're on vacation and want to hike around Parco delle Orobie. You've been briefed already. Any questions?"

No one raised a hand, and she continued. "I'll take my team and another car from Bergamo to Cornalba, find a small hotel or room to rent, and set up a command center. We'll have two snipers on each team, and everyone will be issued extra ammunition, binoculars, night-vision goggles, heat-sensitive cameras, and webcams."

As Antonella looked around at the attentive plainclothes officers, she was pleased to see four women in the ranks. She wanted one to come with her to share the rented room where she would set up the command center. One female agent looked promising: reddish-blonde curls; a trim, athletic physique; alert posture; intense eyes; and long legs spread like she was ready for confrontation.

Antonella turned over the briefing to Vitale, who listed teams and villages where they'd be assigned. He gave instructions about communication via police radios and cell phones, code words for alerting others, and the reporting chain of command to Antonella's command center.

After the briefing, Antonella mentioned to Vitale her request to have a female agent with her to share the room and be in charge of the command center. He walked her over and introduced her to the agent. "*Dottoressa* Amoruso, this is one of my finest agents, *Ispettore* Simona De Monti."

Antonella smiled and reached out her hand. "If you don't mind, I've asked *Dottor* Vitale to assign you to my team to take over the command center when I'm not there. We'll rent a room and say we're cousins taking a hiking vacation."

Agent De Monti beamed and nodded toward her boss. "Of course, *dottoressa*. I'd be honored. You have a very good reputation. It would be a privilege to work with you."

Antonella smiled and patted her arm. "Good. We'll talk more on the drive. Do you hike?"

"No, but I have a mountain bike and do yoga."

"Good enough. You're in good shape. We'll get along fine."

* * * * *

When Fabio returned to the house, he showered and made coffee. He was upset; the previous night with Sylvia had made him worried. It had been a mistake. He was furious with himself for letting Sylvia see his face. And definitely for sleeping together. That was a huge mistake. And she had seen his mother's bedroom, another mistake. He cursed himself for his lapses in judgement.

He paced around the house for an hour, clenching and unclenching his fists, drinking coffee, and watching the morning news programs. Then he called Luca on his Albanian cell phone. He wasn't going to tell him about the previous night.

When Luca answered, Fabio blurted out, "Things are fine here. How about you? I watched the morning news but didn't see anything about Vera. Anything in the papers?"

"Not a word," Luca said. "That's good; I think she's being cautious. You heard what she said about having to go to jail. She's terrified. She's too emotional to know how to handle an interrogation. She'd fall to pieces and say too much."

"I agree."

"Any news about the dough?" Luca asked.

"I'll call my contact at the charity again this morning. Hopefully, he'll have good news. I'm ready to move on, release our guest, and get back to Milan. We'll stay another night or two if things are quiet."

"Call me if you get good news."

While Fabio showered, he thought about another hike with Sylvia. The previous evening had been a shock, both Sylvia's behavior and his own desire to sleep with her. It had been a mutual seduction; they both had wanted to make love despite the bizarre situation—a captor sleeping with his hostage. He didn't think he'd been the first captor to sleep with his hostage. Their sex had been passionate, exciting, tender, and a powerful release for both of them.

But the situation hadn't changed; he was the captor, and she was the hostage. He had to be careful. The stakes were so high. He didn't want to make a mistake that could lead to being identified and captured. Sylvia had seen his face. She had exhibited trust, but what were the chances that she would not identify him after she was released? He couldn't trust her. Last night had been last night. When Sylvia was set free, she'd likely tell the police what he looked like, even reveal his name, and he'd be hunted down.

* * * * *

Antonella asked Simona to ride in her unmarked DIGOS car when they drove to Cornalba so they could talk and get to know each other. They sat in the backseat while two plainclothes DIGOS officers sat in the front. Their car led a procession of unmarked police cars, an ambulance, and a forensic van.

"Your boss spoke highly of you," Antonella began. "I told him that I would like a female officer to be with us when we went to Cornalba. He said he had a young officer who had great leadership potential. I spotted you in the briefing, and when I asked who you were, he said, '*Ispettore* De Monti was the one I was going to recommend.' Congratulations; you come with high praise."

Simona blushed and looked away before she turned to look at Antonella. "Thank you, *dottoressa*. I'll work hard to meet your expectations. It will be an honor."

Antonella smiled and reached over to grab her hand for a moment. "Good. We have a lot to do before we get to Cornalba. Let's get started."

"I'm ready," Simona said.

"First of all, I want you to be my contact to Vitale and the Bergamo officers. Your boss already knows and approves. We are going to set up a command post, in either a hotel room or a rented home or apartment. I'll tell the landlord or manager that we're part of a hiking team checking out the area for a major event later this fall, and that members will be coming to our rooms to coordinate the hikes, so no one will be concerned when other officers show up. One of us will be in the command center twenty-four/seven. I want to get out into Cornalba, look around, and be with officers if they see anything suspicious. You'll stay in the command center and coordinate receiving calls and giving orders. If and when we find them, you'll call in the snipers and NOCS team to set up perimeters."

"I can do that. I've worked on similar teams in the past."

"Good. I'm going to call my boss, Giorgio Lucchini, at Milan's DIGOS. He's very smart and experienced. You may have to relay messages between him and me, as well as orders from me to the rest of the teams. Are you comfortable with that responsibility?"

"Of course."

Antonella smiled. "I like your attitude. Welcome to our team."

Simona smiled and blushed again.

Antonella continued, "Now that we have that taken care of, tell me a little of your background. Where are you from? How long have you been a police officer?"

"I was born and raised in Bergamo. I studied law at Università degli Studi di Bergamo and graduated when I was twenty-four. I went to the police academy and won the public concourse when I was twenty-seven. I'm thirty-two now, and my rank is *ispettore*. I'm interested in working in major crimes and antiterrorism and would love to work with DIGOS in Milan or Rome. That would be a real honor for me."

"What did you do before you became an officer?"

"When I was in high school, I was idealistic . . . maybe even a bit of a dreamer. I played volleyball, studied drama and theater, and thought I'd study philosophy when I went to university. But when I was seventeen, a terrible thing happened. I was with a friend at a club one night. She went to the restroom and was gone a long time. And when she came back, she looked weird. She said she felt dizzy, and then she collapsed in my arms. When we got her outside, she wasn't breathing. By the time the ambulance arrived, she had died. I was heartbroken. I later learned that someone had given her a drug in the restroom. I was so angry that I wanted to become a police officer and fight against drugs."

"I'm so sorry to hear about your friend," Antonella said. "Drugs can cause such misery. If only we could do a better job of educating children about the dangers of drugs."

They were silent for a moment. "Tell me about your family," said Antonella.

"I have wonderful parents. My father is an engineer at Tenaris in Dalmine. My mother is a music teacher at a middle school in Bergamo. My older brother is a skipper and summer teacher at the Caprera sailing school, and when he's not sailing the world, he lives in Genoa."

"Do you still live with your parents?"

"No, I have a studio apartment in Bergamo."

"What are your interests?"

"I play piano when I have time and go to the Teatro Donizetti to see plays and opera. But I'm so busy with work now, I don't have much spare time. When I do have free time, I spend it with my boyfriend, who's a lawyer specializing in family law."

"Any plans for marriage?"

"Oh, no. I want to spend more time on my career before I get married and start a family."

"Very wise, Simona. You're a smart young woman. I'm going to enjoy working with you."

CHAPTER THIRTY-FIVE

After talking with Luca, Fabio pondered what to do that day. Sylvia wanted to go on another hike; he didn't want to stay in the house. The memory of sleeping with Sylvia haunted him, and he didn't want to stay in the house alone, with a constant reminder every time he went into the bedroom. He stared at the rumpled sheets. The side of the bed where Sylvia had slept. Her pillow with a slight dent where her head had rested.

Fabio decided they would take a hike. He prepared a tray with cheese, bread, olives, oranges, grapes, and water and took it over to the cottage. He knocked. "I have something for you to eat. When you finish, we can take a hike."

Sylvia was behind the door. "Thank you. I don't want to be cooped up here all day."

He unlocked the door and handed her the tray. "I'll be back in an hour."

He returned to the house, fixed a plate of the same for himself, and sat down to watch the morning TV news. Still nothing about Vera; only a brief mention that the Questura had not issued a press release that morning updating the case. No news—that was good.

After washing the dishes from the previous night, Fabio put on his hiking shoes, stuck two bottles of water in his pants, walked back to the cottage, and knocked.

"Ready?"

"Sure. Thanks for the breakfast. I liked the fruit."

"I know it sounds strange . . . but I want the same rules as yesterday. You walk ahead, I'll be a few paces behind you."

She hesitated before answering. "If that's what you want, I'm fine with that."

When she came out, she cast a quick glance at him. He was wearing a cap and sunglasses. She turned and started on the trail.

He followed a few steps behind. "We'll take another trail. When you reach the forest, head to the right. You'll see another trail off to the right."

"Okay."

Sylvia followed his instructions and found the new trail, a narrow path through shrubbery and wildflowers. Fabio said, "This trail is steeper than yesterday's. It narrows as you climb the mountain. It's more remote; we probably won't see anyone again."

Sylvia was wearing Fabio's mother's garden shoes and the jacket he had given her the previous day. They walked in silence through a meadow with purple, yellow, and pink wildflowers on both sides of the path. Ahead she saw the trailhead in a grove of spruce and fir trees.

"Where does this trail go?" she asked.

"After we climb for a half hour or so, we'll reach a rocky gorge near the top of the mountain. There's a waterfall in the gorge, quite beautiful. We have a steep climb ahead of us. We rise almost eight hundred meters over a kilometer."

The mountain air was cool and crisp, more so when they hiked in the shade of mature spruce trees. Sylvia watched where she placed each foot as she climbed; the trail was not groomed, and it meandered across the mountainside over rocks, tree roots, and patches of dirt still moist from morning dew.

Along the way, they talked rarely; the strenuous hike made both of them breathe heavily. Sylvia was thrilled to see wildlife as they climbed; eagles and hawks soared overhead, and furry rodents scampered across the trail to dive down holes. The higher they climbed, the more rodents she saw. "Are those gophers?" she asked.

"We call them marmots. They're all over these mountains. You might see small deer or chamois, but they stay away from humans."

After Fabio's comment, Sylvia started looking to the left and right when they came to a clearing or meadow. This hike was more strenuous, but she was energized from smelling the fresh mountain air, the wildflowers, and the pine trees. Her years of travel throughout Italy had been mostly to urban centers and tourist destinations, rarely into remote areas. Her anxieties and fears were slowly melting away. She felt more alive than she had in days.

They approached a ridge, and Sylvia climbed stones until she reached the top. Fabio said, "We're close to the gorge. Keep climbing until you reach a narrow ledge you can't see from here. When you reach the ledge, keep to your left. It's a steep drop-off, dangerous if you're not careful. Walk along the ledge until you see the waterfall below. Then stop and rest. I'll stay here below, let you have some time by yourself. When you're ready to return, climb down to where we are now and head down the trail we just climbed. I'll follow after you pass by."

"Okay. I'll do as you say." Sylvia followed his instructions, climbing to the ridge and onto a narrow ledge. When she saw the waterfall, she stopped to admire it. She sat on a boulder to watch the rushing water spilling from a rock wall and cascading into a pool at the bottom of the gorge. A mist covered the pool and rose like a fog, dampening the rock walls and juniper trees growing along the steep sides. Small, tern-like birds flitted through the mist, landing on dead limbs of juniper trees and in rocky crevasses.

Sylvia breathed in deeply, inhaling the watery mist. Feeling refreshed, she recalled again the previous night of lovemaking. What did it all mean? Things had changed for her, and she was sure it was the same for Leo. But he was remaining cautious for good reasons. She couldn't push him; she would keep the conversations light and conflict free, not ask for anything, and let him adjust to being together for a few hours in the mountains. She hoped he was enjoying this, but she knew he had a lot on his mind. He had looked worried and preoccupied earlier that morning and had said little on the hike up the mountain. But she felt that the tension and fear of the bad days were behind her.

Sylvia remained on the boulder, drinking in the beauty of the gorge and waterfall, turning around on the boulder to see another view of the valley below and the mountains on the other side. She looked down the mountain but couldn't see Leo.

After lingering on the boulder, Sylvia walked back and forth on the narrow ledge and returned to gaze down at the waterfall and mist-covered pool. She wanted to stay longer. Where were they? North of Milan, yes, but she didn't know this part of Italy. One day . . . sometime in the future . . . she might return. Under different circumstances. She'd bring Angela but not her father, because he couldn't manage such a strenuous hike. Cole could. He'd like this.

* * * * *

Two hours after they arrived in Cornalba, Antonella rented a home near the church to set up their command post. They pushed furniture to the walls and moved a table into the center of the room, where they put computers, cell phones, radios, and cameras. A large map of Cornalba and the neighboring area was propped up on chairs facing them.

Dottor Vitale and two of his officers arrived to coordinate with agents reporting from neighboring villages. Vitale and Simona marked the map with the locations of unmarked Bergamo police cars and the officers assigned. The five agents from the Milan Questura were investigating in Cornalba, walking the roads and taking the hiking trails into the mountains. By late afternoon, none had reported seeing either Sylvia or the man in the sunglasses.

"My officers are getting odd looks in the villages," Vitale said. "They've rented rooms and are going out walking to look for any suspicious movement."

"How about the roadblock?" Antonella asked.

"They've checked about fifty vehicles. Just local villagers going about their business, visiting family or friends, driving to work. The officers just say they're searching for a stolen vehicle, all routine, nothing to worry about."

"We can't expect villagers to think it's routine for long," Antonella said. "They'll get suspicious and eventually call the Carabinieri station."

"I've got it covered," Vitale said. "The closest station is in Selvino. I've talked with the *maresciallo*. He'll confirm that he knows we're in the area and that they're helping out in the investigation."

"Simona should also call him in case of an emergency. We might need more help."

"I'll do that," she said, making a note.

"We have only an hour or so of daylight," Antonella observed. "Let's talk about tomorrow. We'll have officers in plainclothes walk around like tourist and hikers. We don't want to alert anyone about what we're doing, at least for the first couple of days. We'll start early. If they're here, I'll bet we see sunglasses man first, whoever he is. If they're here, we'll find them."

* * * * *

After they returned from their hike, Sylvia went to the cottage to rest and shower. She was pleased that Fabio was going to let her have dinner in the house again. He returned around dusk and they went into the house, where he had set one table with two place settings. No candles. Fabio asked her to go into the living room to read while he finished dinner. He gave her a glass of wine, and she did as he asked. They were quiet as he prepared a simple dinner of pasta with pesto sauce, both unsure of how the evening would go. Fabio didn't want a replay of the previous night; she had learned too much about him already. He'd keep conversation brief and formal while they ate, and then he'd send her back to the cottage.

Sylvia was having similar thoughts. The previous night had been a situation that got out of hand. She didn't have the same feelings now. She just wanted a quiet dinner with some small talk, and then to return to the cottage. She knew Leo wouldn't want a conversation that would make him uncomfortable. She'd have a glass or two of wine, enjoy dinner, and then excuse herself. She had no idea how long they would be in this place. She didn't want it to become unbearable if their tenuous relationship became tense. She wanted to show him he could trust her in this confined setting. She'd be quiet, polite, and follow his orders.

Her father had counseled when she was confused or in some kind of trouble: "Sylvia, take each day as it comes. Keep your expectations low. Let time be on your side. This too shall pass."

It had been good advice. She would follow it.

Her thoughts were interrupted by the ringing of a cell phone.

Leo answered it, "Yes."

Sylvia wished she could hear the conversation, but all she heard was Leo's side.

"*Pessime notizie,* Fabio," [Bad, bad news] Luca said excitedly. "*L'hanno presa!*" [They caught her!]

"Where? How?" Leo's voice was agitated; Sylvia put down the magazine and listened.

"It's on RAI3. Pietro Besana is reporting."

"*Porca troia,*" [God damn it] Fabio cursed. He had to see the news, but Sylvia was in the room with the TV. He grabbed the remote in the kitchen and turned on the TV.

As the picture was brightening, Sylvia said. "Oh, you want TV?"

"Be quiet. I need to see the news."

". . . at a roadblock near Maratea. Suspect Vera Pulvirenti's car had been spotted in the town of Sapri, and police began a chase that lasted nearly twenty kilometers. Her car was forced off the road and crashed into a truck. When Pulvirenti began to run, police pursued and tackled her. She resisted but was restrained, handcuffed, and taken to the Questura in Salerno, where she's being questioned."

Fabio was devastated. His heart was beating like a sledgehammer against his chest. *Damn, damn, damn;* their plan was in jeopardy. Vera had not only been caught; she'd been chased and tackled by police. She had fought and resisted arrest; the police knew this was a sure sign that she was guilty. They'd break her down eventually. How long would they have before police came knocking on their doors? Fabio felt sick to his stomach.

Pietro Besana turned to face another camera. The backdrop was a blown-up photo of Sylvia that had been seen by millions of Italians.

"Oh, my God, where'd they get that picture?" she said excitedly.

Besana continued, "We have two more breaking news stories about the bizarre Stazione Centrale crime, both sad stories that affect families. One of the Polfer agents who was shot at Stazione Centrale has died. His name was Gabriele Trapani. He was twenty-seven. He leaves behind his wife, Rosanna, and a six-month-old baby girl, Angela. This is the second death from that tragic attack."

"You beasts!" Sylvia said, standing and looking back at Leo. "You killed the father of a newborn baby. Her name is Angela, just like my own daughter. How could you do such a cruel thing? He was young, only twenty-seven. You've made his wife a widow with a baby daughter to raise by herself. She'll grow up and never know her father."

Fabio was stunned, staring in disbelief at the TV. It was bad; they would now face two murder charges. The hunt for them would intensify.

Besana shuffled papers on his desk and looked into the camera. "Our last story in this tragedy is that we just learned that Paolo de

Matteo, the father of hostage Sylvia de Matteo, died three days ago from a heart attack—"

Sylvia screamed. "Papa! Papa! No! No!" She continued screaming, her hands to her mouth.

Fabio felt like he was going to faint. He put his hands on the chair to keep from falling. This was the worst news he could imagine. If Paolo de Matteo had died, his bank accounts would be frozen, and they'd never get the ransom. Everything had gone wrong, terribly wrong. He started breathing rapidly and deeply. He felt terrified, like he was going to have a breakdown.

Tears were running down Sylvia's face. Her fists were balled up on her cheeks. "My *papa* . . . is dead! He's gone . . . my *papa*! Oh, God, I can't live without him!"

Fabio didn't know what to say. Their plan was smoldering in ashes. What was he going to do with Sylvia? Did they stay at the house, return to Milan, or . . . or . . . what else? He couldn't come up with other alternatives. The news of Paolo de Matteo's death was devastating.

Fabio stared at Sylvia. He watched her sobbing, her hands over her face. A flood of terrifying thoughts raced through his brain. Was their scheme over? Would police burst through the door to arrest him? Would a fleet of police cars with sirens wailing race to Luca's warehouse? Would Alfredo and Luca surrender or get slaughtered in a gunfight if police stormed the warehouse with tear gas and automatic weapons?

Tears came to Fabio's eyes. He looked away, out the window, hands shaking uncontrollably, feeling as lost and desperate as he'd ever felt in his life.

CHAPTER THIRTY-SIX

DAY THIRTEEN

Antonella's team of three DIGOS from Milan and two from Bergamo were sitting around the table in her room, sipping coffee, eating pastries, and studying the map of Cornalba she'd marked up.

"Here's our plan," she said, checking her watch. "We leave in fifteen minutes to begin an early morning surveillance of the village.

"Volpara, you start at the south end of town. Walk along the streets and take any paths into the woods.

"Cella, you take the streets at the north end of the village and do the same—walk the streets and take paths.

"Esposito will be on the trail where Sylvia and sunglasses man were seen two days ago.

"Mastrantonio, you'll go on the trail the birdwatcher was on that day.

"Baroni will walk on the west side of the village. There are fewer homes and shorter streets; most have gardens and farm animals. We walked there yesterday and saw old couples. The homes aren't in good shape. Any questions?"

The plainclothes DIGOS officers, wearing hiking boots and backpacks, shook their heads and waited for her orders.

"When you go out, look to see who rises early. What are the villagers' morning routines? Some people will leave their homes, visit neighbors' homes, go to markets, get in cars or trucks, and leave. Some will go into the fields with their farm animals. This is a sleepy, remote village that doesn't see visitors during the week."

She turned to Simona at her side. "*Ispettore* De Monti will be here at the command center. Check in with her every hour. Give her your location and any significant details. If you spot either Sylvia or sunglasses man, don't approach.

"Call on your radios and use the code *germano reale* [mallard].Give your location and any information on how we should approach. If you see them before they see you, don't attract attention. If you see them in a car, the code is *germano reale in volo* [mallard in flight]. We'll blockade the road and not let them leave the village."

Antonella looked around to see if there were any questions.

"Everyone is armed with Glocks, tear gas grenades, and extra magazines in your backpacks."

They all nodded, touching their backpacks or the concealed Glocks in their shoulder holsters.

"I'll have a sniper rifle in my car and won't be more than a hundred meters from it. If we need it, Baroni is the best shooter, so he gets the rifle."

They all looked at Officer Baroni.

Antonella continued, "We don't know how many of them are here; it could be two or more. If we can take them without shooting, that's our first objective. If anyone pulls a gun, shoot to save your life or the life of another officer. We want to rescue Sylvia without harming her. Let's hope they don't use her as a shield; they're ruthless killers and may try to shoot their way out. Any questions?"

"What if they're in another village?" one of the officers asked.

"*Dottor* Vitale and I are giving the same orders. Whoever spots them first will alert the command center, which will call in reinforcements. We have close to thirty officers, including snipers and hostage negotiators, who can be anywhere within ten minutes."

Antonella looked around at her team. "Any last questions?"

There were none.

"Then let's go find them."

* * * * *

Neither Fabio nor Sylvia slept well; Fabio tossed and turned until after midnight. When he did drop off to sleep, he'd bolt upright from a nightmare, his body drenched in sweat. Finally he got up and walked around the house, fearing the worst, that police would be closing in soon and they'd all be arrested and thrown in prison.

Vera would likely break down under intense interrogation and reveal names and the location of Luca's warehouse. Fabio thought about places Luca and the others could escape to; they could hide out in some remote location or even come to Cornalba. But if police learned their names from Vera, they would have license numbers of cars, cell phone numbers, and bank cards, and they would issue a press release. TV news stations would break into programs with a bulletin and publicize their names and photos.

Sylvia's concerns were deeply personal: Paolo's death and worrying about her mother, Angela, and Cole. Where were they? How were they coping? Angela would be so distraught; she loved her *nonno* so much. She had great memories of her summer vacation with him, but now he was gone. She'd never again be able to laugh and go on walks with her *nonno,* poor child. Sylvia wished she could be with Angela now, hold her, comfort her in her grief. Her mother was likely so devastated that she would have to be heavily sedated. Her health had already been bad; losing her husband so suddenly would make it worse.

Fabio finally collapsed from fatigue and slept for a couple of hours. When he bolted awake shortly after dawn, he knew he had to get up, make difficult decisions, and deal with Sylvia. He worried about her as well. She was devastated about her father's death. What would happen to her now? She might fear that she would be killed; he would assure her that that wouldn't happen unless . . . unless . . . she tried to escape. But he couldn't imagine killing her. His feelings toward Sylvia were conflicted. He had fantasized about her when she was their prisoner in Milan. But they had made love their first night in Cornalba. He did have strong feelings for her . . . but she was still his captive. He couldn't let those feelings affect any decision he might have to make about her fate. They had had one night of passion, but that was all it was. One night. A passionate night. Never to be repeated.

He had to do something with Sylvia today . . . tomorrow. . . . It made no sense to keep her much longer. It was all so confusing; all of his options were bad.

He got up, fixed coffee, and stood naked in the kitchen. When he sipped the scalding liquid, it tasted sour. When it hit his stomach, he almost threw up. He was too nauseous to contemplate eating. He went into his bedroom, dressed, went to the cottage, and knocked.

"Sylvia . . . are you awake? Do you want coffee? Something to eat?"

It was quiet inside. He knocked again. "Sylvia?"

He heard a noise, then shuffling of bare feet on the floor. "Yes . . . I'm awake . . . terrible night. I barely slept. I'm so sick I couldn't manage eating anything."

"I understand. Do . . . you . . . want to shower and come over to the house? We need . . . to talk."

"Yes, we do. Give me a few minutes. I'm not functioning well."

"I'll be back in half an hour. Take your time."

He returned to the house, showered, sipped a little coffee, and turned on the TV. Both RAI3 and Mediaset made brief comments about Paolo de Matteo and the Polfer's death and reported that the Questura would have a press conference later that afternoon. The RAI journalist speculated that it was possibly related to Vera's arrest.

Fabio shuddered. Bad news . . . had she talked? Were police on the way to Luca's warehouse?

He called Luca on his Albanian cell phone. "What's happening?" he asked when Luca answered.

"Nothing. I'm watching the news. RAI3 reported the Questura will have a press conference, possibly about 'our friend.' I'm worried. What are you going to do?"

"We have to move fast," Fabio said, his voice breaking. "Leave the warehouse. Have the others go someplace where they won't be found."

"They're not here yet; I'm waiting for them. I can't leave until they get here."

"Do you want to come up here? It's quiet. We could hide a couple days until we decide where to go. Do you have money?"

"Yes, I keep emergency money in my safe. I'll wait until the others get here. What about 'your guest'?"

Fabio sighed. "I don't know . . . I haven't talked to her yet. I think I'll let her go, like we talked about yesterday."

"Are you sure that's the right decision?" Luca asked.

"I think so. Let's talk later and decide."

Fabio hung up, paced around the house, and then went over to the cottage and knocked.

"Are you ready?"

"Yes."

He unlocked the door and opened it. Sylvia looked weak and drained, still wearing his mother's jacket and garden shoes. Her damp hair was disheveled, bunched in clumps on her forehead and temples. Her eyes were bloodshot from crying.

They walked over to the house and sat at the kitchen table. Sylvia shook her head when he asked if she wanted coffee.

"I'm so depressed about my father," she said, wiping away tears. "It was . . . such a shock. I can't believe he's dead. We were very close."

"I'm sorry."

"And . . . and . . . it's worse finding out here. . . . I feel so lost. I need to be with my family. They're grieving too; it's a terrible loss for all of us. He was such a good man . . . loving . . . kind . . . a real force in people's lives."

"I'm sorry, but that's not possible."

"Why not?"

They looked across at each other without speaking. Sylvia wiped tears. Fabio opened his mouth, then closed it and looked away. "I'll . . . get you back . . . to Milan."

Sylvia read pain and fear on his face. She was overwhelmed by grief over her father's death, but recognized Leo also had profound emotions, facing possible arrest and imprisonment.

"I don't want to go to Milan," she said. "I want to go to Menaggio and see my mother. I'm sure my daughter and fiancé are there. I need to be with them."

He shook his head. "We can't do that—"

"Why not?" she protested, surprised how strong her voice was. "Your escapade—political terrorism—or whatever you call it, is over. My father is dead. You won't get a ransom. Your cohort is in jail. The police will come looking for you soon. What are you going to do, kill me?"

He shook his head. "No."

"Then what? Don't take me back to Milan and throw me in that fucking prison cell! I won't go!" Sylvia's grief had turned to anger; all the memories of the last thirteen days had made her stronger. "Shoot me if you want. I know you have a gun someplace, you . . . people always do. But I'm not going back to Milan with you."

He stared at her, surprised at how forceful she had become. Two days ago, she'd been compliant, meek, obeying him. The news about her father's death had changed her. If he kept her, she could cause problems. He would release her on a remote road and tell her how she could get back to Milan on buses. She'd have to make transfers in Bergamo; it would be hours before she'd get back to Milan. Luca could be in Cornalba by the evening, and then they could make plans for hiding out.

"I want to go to Menaggio, where my family is," Sylvia insisted, interrupting his thoughts. "I won't reveal your identity. I don't know anything about your gang. . . . I was your prisoner. . . . I didn't learn your names. . . . You kept me locked up. . . . I never saw your faces. . . . When you brought me here, I was blindfolded and tied up. I was locked up . . . here . . . wherever 'here' is. I don't know the name of this place. . . . It's in the mountains; that's all I know. That's the truth."

Fabio looked at her, wanting to believe her, but he knew it was futile. She'd tell everything once the police started questioning her.

Sylvia bit her lip, took a deep breath and said, "I'll never . . . ever . . . tell anyone we slept together."

They stared at each other in silence, knowing they had reached an impasse. Sylvia would not back down. Fabio had to agree or they would end up in a fight. Sylvia was small but strong and determined. She could strike or kick him; he could restrain her, but he couldn't hurt her. He cared about her in a way that would have seemed impossible thirteen days ago. His hostage had become his lover. And she was now demanding her freedom.

Fabio's face sagged from weariness. "I need time to think. I have to make phone calls."

She nodded. "Okay. But find a way to get me to Menaggio. I have to see my mother and daughter."

He looked into his coffee and then into her eyes. "I can drive you to Como. You can get a ferry there."

Sylvia smiled. "I know Como. Ferries leave almost hourly. When can we leave?"

"Go back to the cottage and get your clothes. I need to make a phone call."

Sylvia reached over and put her hand on his. "Look at me. I meant what I said. I won't identify you. We never came here; you kept me in a cramped cell in Milan all this time. Then someone put me in a van and dumped me out in Como. I won't say it was you. I'll say I was blindfolded and never saw who drove me."

"The police will interrogate you until they get the information they want. They deal with hardened criminals and Mafia killers. They know how to get information."

"I said what I said. I meant it. How long will it take to drive to Como?"

"About two hours."

"Then let's go soon. We'll talk in the car. I want to know more about you . . . why you did this terrible thing . . . killed people . . . took me hostage. . . . It seems so crazy. Why did you think you could get away with this? And I want to know what's going to happen to you."

Fabio stared at her, not believing what she was saying. "Why do you care what's going to happen to me?"

"Because . . . because . . . from the first day . . . or night . . . you talked to me. I hated that woman . . . she was vicious. Is she the one who was arrested?"

"Yes."

Sylvia stammered, running words and thoughts together, her emotions raw from the terror and fear and loss and loneliness and conflict of the last two weeks. "I hated her. . . . I thought she was going to kill me. But you talked to me . . . through that frosted window . . . day after day. I needed to talk, too. I don't know how I would have survived if you hadn't talked to me . . . been almost kind . . . and you fed me. Made me feel like a person and not just a prisoner. I saw your shadow and didn't know if you were tall . . . or short . . . young or old. We talked in the car when you drove here . . . and when we hiked . . . and then . . . the other . . . night . . . when . . . when we slept together and made love. . . . I want to know more about you."

"There's nothing more I can tell you. You know too much already. Don't waste your time."

She shook her head. "We have time to talk when we drive to Como. I want to know more about hard times in Italy—the desperation of people . . . the families who are suffering . . . the poor children . . . the lost dreams. Italy is my second home. I know your judges and politicians are corrupt; that's not news. But I want you to tell me more . . . what can be done to make things better. Since I was a child, my father talked about Italy and how much this country meant to him. He loved Italy. So do I. I want to do something to make life better here. I don't know what, but my heart is here."

Fabio shook his head and stood up. "Italy is lost," he said. "It's never going to recover, even if people rise up and throw out the corrupt politicians. Another group of criminals will take over and bleed away the essence of what made this a great country. It's hopeless. Something in Italian culture is a poison."

* * * * *

DIGOS officer Ernesto Baroni, a twelve-year veteran, was returning from a trail near the rocky gorge when he walked between a modest home and a stone cottage across from it. A car was parked under fir trees.

Baroni glanced at the house, slowly measuring it, and then looked over at the cottage. Both were dark, with no activity in the windows. He continued down the dirt road and turned a bend that would take him into Cornalba.

Then he heard a door shut behind him. When he reached a grove of pine trees, he moved behind them and looked back. Twenty meters behind, a woman was going down steps. She crossed the dirt road and entered the cottage.

She was attractive. She had short, dark hair and was wearing a thin jacket and rubber garden shoes. *Is that Sylvia?* His heart leaped.

Baroni raised his binoculars and focused on the cottage. In less than a minute, the door opened, and the woman walked out carrying a small bundle of clothes. She opened the back door of the car, tossed the clothes into the backseat, and shut the door.

When she turned around, Baroni got a brief look at her face.

Yes! It was Sylvia. Thinner, pale, almost gaunt. But it was she. She was alone. Where was sunglasses man? Did she have freedom to be by herself?

He grabbed his radio to call the command center. When Simona answered, he said in a low voice, "*Germano reale.* [The mallard] She's in a small house on the north side of the village. No sign of sunglasses man. He may be inside."

"What's your position?"

He gave her a general distance from the main street of Cornalba and a description of the houses at the corner of the unnamed road.

"I'm behind a tree—out of sight unless I stick out my head. She put something in a car; they may be about to drive away. I need backup fast. Proceed quietly; no fast cars or sirens."

The first backup arrived in two minutes. Officer Volpara and Mastrantonio ran up the dirt road, followed by Antonella. They spotted Baroni in the trees. He signaled them to move off the road and walk directly to him. A few meters behind Antonella came two more officers, heads low, hands on their holsters.

"The house is twenty meters on the other side of this tree," Baroni whispered when they all reached the grove and crouched next to him. "Sylvia went into the stone cottage to get clothes or something. She put them in the car and went into the house. It's quiet; no sound from the house."

Antonella leaned out and stole a quick look to survey the area. When she turned back, she said, "Quick, Volpara and Mastrantonio, go to the right into the woods," she said pointing across the road. "Approach the house but remain out of sight of the door in case someone opens it. Baroni and I will stay here. Esposito and Cella, go to the left through the trees so you're on the upside of the house in case they come out the back door."

Antonella pointed and Esposito and Cella headed through the trees, stooped over, taking out Glocks from shoulder holsters. They ran behind the stone cottage and kept moving, keeping their eyes on the front door.

An unmarked car came up the road with two officers inside. Antonella signaled for the driver to park before the bend in road. The officers gently opened and shut the car doors and ran toward Antonella and Baroni in the trees.

Antonella got on her knees and drew a circle in the dirt with her hands.

"Here's the house . . . the car . . . the stone cottage . . . trails. Mastrantonio and Volpara will be in place. We'll wait for everyone to be in position and see if they come out. I'll give them ten minutes. Then we'll approach and circle the house, and I'll go up and knock. We don't know how many are in the house—maybe three or four plus Sylvia. There's only one car. If they don't come out, we'll start hostage negotiations. Let's hope we don't have to use force. But we may not be able to avoid it; they're killers."

Baroni looked through the trees and rasped, *"Stanno uscendo!"* [They're coming out!]

Antonella swirled around and looked through the trees. Sylvia was three steps ahead of sunglasses man, who was carrying something coming out of the door. She waited for him, and they walked toward the car.

Antonella sized up the scene instantly. Sylvia had no mask. Her hands weren't tied. Sunglasses didn't have a gun; he wasn't forcing her. Strange . . . Sylvia was walking willingly without signs of duress.

Not what Antonella had expected. She grabbed her radio and spoke to her team.

"I'm approaching. Don't shoot unless I do."

She took her Glock out of its holster, stepped around the trees, and ran forward. Baroni was two steps behind on her right. They stopped in the dirt road, raised their weapons, and aimed at Fabio, who was fifteen meters from them.

"Fermi!" [Stop!] Antonella yelled. *"Polizia! Metti giù quello che hai in mano! Stenditi a terra."* [Police! Drop what you're carrying! Lie on the ground.]

Sylvia's and Fabio's heads jerked around to see two police officers holding weapons on them. They heard a sound to their left as a third officer came out of the trees, aiming his pistol at them.

"Non sparate!" [No, don't shoot!] Sylvia screamed. *"Sto bene; non sono ferita!"* [I'm okay; I'm not injured!]

"Mani in alto! Subito!" [Hands in the air! Now!] Antonella yelled, knees bent, arms extended in a firing stance, both hands gripping the Glock.

Fabio dropped his package and pushed Sylvia toward the car. She stumbled and fell to her knees. Fabio looked toward Antonella and Baroni, his eyes wide, mouth open.

Another two seconds passed without anyone moving. Fabio reached behind his back and pulled out the Glock tucked into his belt.

"Mettila giù!" [Drop it!] Antonella yelled.

Fabio raised his pistol and fired at Antonella.

Bang! Bang! Bang! Bang! Four shots boomed in the serene setting, echoing off the trees. Birds exploded from trees, screeching as they flew away.

Three of the shots hit Fabio. He spun first to his right and then to his left. He dropped slowly to his knees, falling forward onto the dirt road.

"No!" Sylvia screamed, throwing her hands up to her mouth. "No, no, Leo!" she screamed, running and falling on his crumpled body.

Antonella felt a burning sting on her left arm. She glanced down and saw a tear in her sleeve. A ribbon of blood was running down her bicep.

CHAPTER THIRTY-SEVEN

"Get back!" Antonella shouted at Sylvia, running to stand over her, pointing her Glock at the back of Fabio's head. A trickle of blood was running down Antonella's arm to her hand. She felt a burning sensation in her upper arm but ignored it.

"*Via di li!*" [Move away!] she yelled again, pulling Sylvia off of Fabio. Sylvia lifted her head, tears in her eyes, a smear of blood on her jacket.

Antonella scooted Fabio's pistol away from his outstretched arm and stood between him and Sylvia. His face was in the dirt, one cheek exposed, eyes and mouth partially open. Antonella pressed her fingers into his neck and felt a weak pulse.

She kept the barrel of her Glock at the back of his head and yelled to the officers standing in a circle around them, "Get inside the house! There might be more. Run around back; there might be another door!"

She called out to Baroni, pointing with her bloody hand to the cottage. "Look in there!"

The officers ran to the house, guns in the air, threw open the door, and burst in. "*Polizia! Venite fuori! Siete circondati!*" [Police! Come out!

You're surrounded!] they shouted, tramping through the house, throwing doors open and running from room to room.

Baroni pushed open the cottage door. *"Polizia! Mani in alto!"* [Police! Hands in the air!] The door slammed against a wall when he burst in. He was out in a few seconds. "No one inside! No back door. Only one window."

"Search the woods! Others might be hiding!" ordered Antonella.

She turned to Sylvia, who was standing next to the car. "Sylvia, is anyone else here?"

Sylvia shook her head. "No . . . n-no . . ." she stammered. "Just the two of us."

Antonella held the gun near Fabio's head and pivoted around, scanning the woods. It occurred to her that others could be nearby that Sylvia didn't know about. Antonella raised her radio in her bloody hand and called the command center. *"Ispettore* De Monti, get everyone over here! We have Sylvia. Sunglasses man is down! We need an ambulance. We need to search the area!"

"Is he alive?" Sylvia asked, her voice shaking.

"I felt a pulse," Antonella replied.

An officer stuck his head out of the house and shouted, "No one inside! Small house! We searched everywhere. The back door is locked."

Antonella scanned the woods. The officers were spread out in the forest, guns in the air, running tree to tree, signaling each other and talking on their radios as they progressed with their search.

Antonella looked down at Fabio and turned his head to see his face. His eyes were still half-open, lips parted. Blood oozed from a corner of his mouth. Antonella rolled his shoulder back to examine his wounds. Bloodstained holes in his upper body were grouped inches apart, like on a target at a shooting range. The bullets had penetrated internal organs: liver, lungs, and stomach. He was losing blood fast. Antonella's officers were good shots, thank God. If he'd had time to shoot again, he might have killed her.

Antonella took a wallet out of his back pocket and opened it. She found his driver's license and read his name: Fabio Cecconi. She studied his face again; it seemed familiar, as did his name. Then she remembered.

She raised her police radio and called Giorgio. "We have Sylvia! She's safe! We shot sunglasses man!"

"Good news! Anyone hurt?"

"I've got a flesh wound; nothing to worry about. But I recognize sunglasses! I met him patrolling a week ago. Name is Fabio Cecconi. He's down with multiple shots to the upper body. I don't think he's going to make it."

"Was he alone?"

"We're searching the area. Sylvia says it was just the two of them, but we're checking anyway; there could be others nearby that Sylvia didn't know about. Send a NOCS team to the place where I saw him; it was a warehouse near Bresso. It belongs to his brother, who has a construction business there. Check my log; you'll find Cecconi's name in my report, and you can get the address. We were investigating a Fiorino seen driving in. The others might be at the warehouse."

"Good work! I'll get teams out there immediately!"

Adrenaline was pumping through Antonella's body. The shooting had been brief and violent. Now it was quiet, except for the squawking of police radios in the woods. Antonella looked over at Sylvia, who was leaning against the car with her head in her hands.

"Are you okay?" Antonella asked.

Sylvia nodded. "Yes. . . . I'm not hurt."

Antonella glanced down at the jacket Sylvia was wearing. There was a streak of blood on the hem.

"Sylvia, do you want to take off that jacket? It's bloodstained."

Sylvia looked down and folded a corner of the jacket to cover the stain.

"No, it's okay. But I think Leo is dying."

"Leo? Who's Leo?"

Sylvia pointed at Fabio, whose eyes remained slightly open. "I called him Leo. . . . I didn't know his name. . . . He kept his identity secret."

"His name is Fabio Cecconi."

Sylvia nodded. "I saw something in the house with that name, and I heard you say it a moment ago. But I called him Leo."

Antonella looked at her, puzzled about the names. She didn't have time to question her now; that would come later.

Drops of blood were dripping off Antonella's hand, staining the dirt. The burning pain in her upper arm was getting worse, but right now she had to do her job. She'd get treatment later.

Four police cars raced up the dirt road, sending up clouds of dust and gravel. Officers burst out of the cars, Vitale in the lead, holding up his pistol.

Simona was running up the hill behind the police cars.

When Vitale reached Antonella, she still had her Glock pointed at Fabio's head. "He's not going to make it," she said. "I sent everyone into the forest to make sure there are no others. Send your officers to join them."

Vitale barked orders to his officers, who fanned out in all directions, running through brush and around trees, pistols and automatic rifles in the air.

"You're hit," Vitale said, seeing the tear in Antonella's sleeve and her bloody hand.

"Just nicked. I'll be fine."

"Forensics and ambulances are on the way. Get a medic to treat you."

"The house is empty," she said, pointing at it. "So is the cottage. I think it was just the two of them."

Simona ran up between Vitale and Antonella. Two ambulances with red flashing lights drove up the dirt road, followed by a forensics van marked with the words *Polizia Scientifica*.

Medics carrying medical bags got out of each ambulance and ran over to Fabio. They knelt to check his vital signs. They turned him over and checked his wrist and neck for a pulse. One medic slipped a stethoscope under his shirt. Sylvia stared at them, one hand to her mouth.

Antonella told Vitale, "When your officers come back, I want them checking homes. Knock on doors and make sure no one's hiding out."

Three forensics officers carrying briefcases approached Antonella and Vitale. Antonella pointed at the house. "Get to work in the house. That's where they were. Go through everything and collect evidence. Papers, clothes, cell phones, weapons. Bag it all."

The forensics team ran to the house and went in the open door. Vitale said, "Antonella, let the medics treat you."

"I will, but I want *Ispettore* De Monti to take Sylvia to our car. She's shaken up. Let's get her away from here."

Vitale said to Simona, "Do as she said. Get Sylvia in the car and stay with her."

Antonella let her wounded arm drop to her side. A stream of blood covered the back of her hand and was dripping on the ground. "It's starting to hurt. Damn, now I feel it." She grimaced and let a medic cut her sleeve with a pair of scissors. "Got anything to kill the pain? Oh, Madonna, it hurts!"

Simona went over to Sylvia, who was crouched against the car. She took her arm and helped her stand. "Let's get you away from here."

Simona led Sylvia to Antonella's unmarked car and opened the back door. Simona got in beside her and began talking to her. Antonella watched as Simona engaged her in conversation. *Good,* she thought. *I want her to warm up to Simona.*

For an hour, officers searched the forest while the forensics team collected evidence in the house and cottage, photographed the scene, and took fingerprints. They collected and put in plastic bags everything with biological evidence: combs, toothbrushes, dirty clothes, and towels. Medics lifted Fabio's body onto a gurney, rolled it to an ambulance, and drove away.

The medic treated Antonella, cleaning the wound and applying a bandage to the gash in her bicep. The medic reached into his bag and pulled out two hypodermic needles. He gave her two injections, a pain reliever and an antibiotic. He pulled a cloth sling out of his bag, slipped it over her neck, and put her arm in it.

Vitale said to Antonella, "I can take charge. Go back to Milan and get to a hospital. We have enough officers to finish the investigation. I'll call my office if we need more."

Antonella went over to Baroni and told him that she was going back to Milan and that he was in charge of the Milan DIGOS team.

"You can't drive. You've been wounded," he told her.

"*Ispettore* Di Monti will drive. I want to question Sylvia and find out what she knows about the kidnappers. We'll debrief her back at the Questura and get a formal statement. She's been through a major trauma; we'll have a psychologist check her out as well. We'll call her fiancé in Menaggio and have him pick her up when she's ready to be released."

"Yes, *dottoressa*. We can finish up here without you."

Antonella went back to Vitale to tell him she was ready to leave. "How did things work out with *Ispettore* De Monti?" he asked.

"I like her. She's a pro. I'll write a recommendation for her file. I want her to drive so I can question Sylvia before we get back to the Questura. Let her know she'll be driving back with me. Better she gets the order from you."

Vitale walked over to the car and rapped on the window. Simona got out of the car, and they stepped away for a brief conversation. She nodded and looked over at Antonella, who walked over to them. "You'll be coming back with me. I need you to drive."

"I'll be happy to, *dottoressa*."

"What have you learned from talking to Sylvia?"

"She's very upset that her father has died. I tried to calm her down. She's in shock about the shooting and keeps asking when she can see her family. Do they know she's okay?"

"I'll have *Dottor* Lucchini take care of that. I'll call him now, and then let's leave."

Simona got in the driver's seat while Antonella got out her police radio and called Giorgio.

"I'll be leaving soon. I have a flesh wound and need to get it taken care of. Vitale is in charge. Forensics is collecting evidence, and teams are searching the forest. I don't think anyone else was here. Officers will be spending the rest of the day going around the village and questioning residents about what they witnessed. We'll keep the area secure for a day or so until they finish investigating. I'm taking Sylvia back to Milan for debriefing. I'll question her in the car and record the conversation. Have you talked to the family?"

"I called her fiancé and gave him the news," said Giorgio. "They're elated and want to see her as soon as possible. They're all in Menaggio at the family villa. Mrs. de Matteo is under heavy sedation."

"When Sylvia is back at the Questura, she should see a psychologist before we release her. She's shaken up, crying, almost like she's having a breakdown."

"We'll have a psychologist ready to see her."

"Call her fiancé and have him drive down to pick her up when she's ready to be released. She might need to spend a night in a hotel and have a sedative so she can sleep."

"I'll call him right away," Giorgio said.

"I should be there within two hours. I'll call when we reach Milan."

"I'll be waiting. I want to question Sylvia myself."

Antonella got into the passenger side, and Simona turned the car around and drove down the hill to Cornalba. "We'll be in Milan in about two hours," Antonella said, turning around to face Sylvia.

"Good. I want to get out of here. How's your arm?" Sylvia asked.

"Just a scratch. It stings a bit. I'll be fine. How are you, Sylvia?"

Sylvia looked out the window, seeing Cornalba for the first time. It was just a village; they passed through it in a minute and then were in forest. She would never come back again. "I'll be okay. I'm still shaken up. When can I see my family?"

"Probably this evening. We need to question you at the Questura and get a formal statement. My boss is calling your fiancé to have him pick you up when you're ready to be released. Your family has been told about your rescue. They're eager to have you back as well."

Antonella took out a small digital recorder from the glove box, placed it on the console between the front seats, and turned it on. "I'd like to ask a few questions while we drive."

"Yes . . . I understand," Sylvia said. Her voice sounded weak, as if she'd recently been awakened from a nap.

"Can you tell me why you weren't being restrained this morning when an officer first saw you? When you were seen coming out of the house, you were walking ahead of Cecconi. You weren't tied up. I don't understand why he would let you walk around . . . or why he would let you see his face."

Sylvia had to think fast; she had to have a believable answer or Antonella would pry even deeper into why she'd had freedom at the house. She had to keep her sleeping with Leo a secret. If the police suspected anything, it could ruin her life . . . sleeping with her captor. She couldn't be seen as a Patty Hearst, sympathizing with her captors.

Sylvia held her breath and then answered. "Here's what happened," she began slowly. "This morning, when he came out to the cottage where I was sleeping, he told me that my father had died. I was so shocked that I broke into tears, bawling . . . screaming . . . I just lost it. He must have felt sorry for me. . . . He left and came back and said we were going in the car someplace. I was supposed to get my clothes together, and he would return.

"I followed his orders, and he took me into the house after I put my clothes in the car. I don't know why he took me in there or why he finally let me see his face. We were in the house maybe ten minutes. He was on the phone in another room but kept an eye on me. I could hear his voice but couldn't tell what he was saying. When he came out, he told me to go ahead of him, and I walked out. He was behind me. And then . . . and then the shooting started."

Antonella considered her answer, looking over at *Ispettore* De Monti and then back at Sylvia. "Okay, I think I understand. It was just . . . odd to see you like that."

It was quiet in the car, and then Antonella said, "Let's go back to the beginning. What do you remember from the time you were taken hostage until we rescued you?"

For a half hour, Sylvia told her story about being grabbed and dragged through Stazione Centrale and thrown into the van, staying the first night in the small cell, and spending several days in the larger room with a bathroom. She spoke in monotone, with little emotion, as if reciting someone else's story. She described how relieved she was to be driven to the remote location and how kind "Leo" had been. But she left out their having slept together.

"Tell me about Fabio Cecconi," Antonella said.

"He was my kidnapper . . . maybe their leader. I was afraid at the beginning that they were going to kill me. There was a woman in their group I was afraid of. She was angry and cursed at me. I think she wanted to shoot me herself. I got the impression Leo—Fabio—kept her from hurting me. I never saw her face. . . . She cursed me the day I was captured and the next day, but I didn't see her anymore after that. I think he kept her away from me."

"She might be the woman who has been arrested and is being questioned. Can you give me a physical description of your kidnappers?"

"No, I can't. I had a mask on every time they came into my room. After the second day, the only person I talked to was Leo. I called him that because he wouldn't tell me his name."

"Of course not."

"He gave me orders and told me to obey or something bad would happen to me."

"How many were in the location where you were held captive?"

"I really don't know. Three people took me out of the station and into the van and threw me on the floor. Someone hit me over the head, and I was unconscious for a while. When we arrived wherever it was, they put a mask over my face and put me in the small cell. I talked only to Leo. I could hear voices in the next room, but I couldn't make out how many."

"What did you learn about him?"

"Not too much, except that he and his group were fed up with the politics in Italy. They wanted to shock the country into doing something radical against politicians and bankers. As you know, my father is . . . was . . . a Wall Street banker. They were angry about the financial crisis and blamed it on the bankers and politicians. They wanted to overthrow the government, like revolutionaries. I don't understand that political philosophy; it only leads to violence and heartache. How many revolutionaries live a happy life or a long one?"

"Very true. How long were you in the location where we rescued you?"

"Just two nights. Leo drove here and locked me in that stone cottage, where I slept at night. I don't know where we were; he never told me."

"It's a village called Cornalba in the alpine foothills."

"How did you find me?"

"A birdwatcher saw you in the mountains two days ago and took your photo with a long-distance lens."

Sylvia thought about how Leo, in trying to be kind to her, had taken her on a remote trail where they'd been seen. His act of kindness had led to her rescue and to his being shot. What an irony.

"Is Leo . . . dead?"

"Yes."

Sylvia said nothing and looked out the window. Antonella watched to see if she was going to show any reaction and then asked, "Are you glad he's dead?"

Sylvia sighed. "I . . . don't know. He was kind to me. But he was my kidnapper."

"And a dangerous criminal. They killed two people at the train station."

"Yes . . . yes . . . I learned that."

"How did you learn about the two deaths?"

Sylvia thought about the question. She had seen the TV news about the Polfer agent dying and had read about the politician shot at the station from newspapers Leo had given her.

"Aaah . . . I only heard about one . . . a railway police officer who died. Leo gave me a few newspapers, and I read about someone else who was shot. A politician. I don't remember the name."

"How and when did you learn about the Polfer officer dying?"

Again, Sylvia had to think through her answer. If she said she had seen it on TV, she'd have to admit that she and Leo had been in the house together. She was uncomfortable with Antonella's probing. She didn't want to talk about her conversations with Leo and certainly wasn't going to admit she had slept with him.

"Can we stop talking for a while? I'm exhausted. Drained. I just want to forget what's happened."

They drove for about ten minutes in silence. Finally, Simona asked, "When will you go back to New York, Sylvia?"

"Soon, I hope. . . . I want to start my life again. I had time to think while I was held captive. I think . . . I'll make . . . changes in my life. . . . I don't know when I can work again. . . . I want to give my father a decent burial . . . maybe in Menaggio . . . but I can't think about anything else now. . . . I just can't. I need time to think things through."

"Take your time," Antonella said. "You've been through a life-changing experience. You may need counseling to grieve about your father's death and to come to terms with your captivity."

Sylvia thought for a minute. "Yes . . . grief. . . I feel grief and doubt." Her voice began to break. "I haven't had many doubts in my life." She paused, as if trying to pull herself together. "I feel so sad. Everything I thought about Italy has changed. I don't have a romantic view of this country anymore; maybe I'm becoming more of a realist. I have deep emotional ties to Italy. It's funny: I was an Italian American before this happened. But now . . . I feel more like an American Italian. I want to see changes in Italy, but I don't know what I can do."

"Be patient with yourself, Sylvia. The answers will come when you're ready," Antonella suggested.

Sylvia smiled. "You . . . sound like my father. . . . He was very wise."

"You'll get through this, Sylvia," Antonella said. "You're through the worst part. Everything will get better from here. Your life may unfold in ways you can't even comprehend now."

CHAPTER THIRTY-EIGHT

Minutes after Antonella's car arrived at the Questura, she and Sylvia were escorted by armed police into the building. They were taken to the third-floor DIGOS headquarters behind a vault with special security. At the end of a hallway was an interview room with audio and video devices to record meetings with suspects and witnesses.

The interview room was sparsely arranged with a two-way mirror and a wooden table with one chair on one side and five chairs on the other. Giorgio Lucchini and a team of investigators were seated across from the single chair facing them.

Everyone stood when Antonella entered the room. Antonella said, "Sylvia, this is the head of DIGOS, Giorgio Lucchini. He was in charge of the investigation and search that led to your rescue."

Sylvia managed a weak smile and took Giorgio's hand when he offered it. "We're pleased to have you back safely, Ms. de Matteo," he said, making a gracious bow. "We've had hundreds of officers searching for you. We were determined to rescue you without harm."

"Thank you . . . thank you," she mumbled, feeling uncomfortable with the men and women staring at her as if she were a lab specimen.

"Would you like some coffee? Tea? A soft drink?" Giorgio asked, motioning for Sylvia to take the lone seat across from him and the other officers. "We'd like to ask you some questions about your captivity. Your answers will help us prosecute the criminals who took you hostage."

"Yes, thank you. I would like something cold and sweet . . . a lemon soda, if that's possible," she said nervously. She sat down and glanced at the probing eyes of the officers, feeling uneasy at the stiff formalities.

"Would you like something to eat?" Giorgio asked. "We can order a meal or a sandwich."

"Ah . . . ah . . . I am a bit hungry. Maybe a *panino*. Prosciutto *cotto* and mozzarella would be wonderful. And heated, please."

"Of course," Giorgio said, looking over at an officer standing by the door who nodded and left the room.

Giorgio was not surprised that Sylvia looked pale and tired. She had lost weight and looked wan, like she might be recovering from a fever or cold. He could see the resemblance to her father: round face, gentle eyes, and a soft chin. She was beautiful but also appeared haunted by the memories of her captivity.

"First of all, I want to tell you how sorry we all are that your dear father passed away. We're sad for your loss."

"Th-thank you," she stuttered, looking down at the table. "It was a shock when I found out. I just . . . lost it . . . I felt I was having a nervous breakdown. I was in terrible shape at that time. . . . I didn't know if I'd ever live to see my family again. And then . . . to learn that he had died . . . I still can't believe he's gone."

"He was a wonderful, kind, and loving man," Giorgio said in a reassuring voice. "I spent several hours with him and enjoyed his company. The night before his heart attack, he invited me to his hotel for a drink. We smoked cigars on the balcony, and he told me about his life, his Italian heritage, and how much he loved his family. Please accept my condolences."

Sylvia started to cry. Tears trickled down her cheeks, and she reached up with the bottom of her jacket to wipe them away. One of the female officers reached across the table and handed her a handkerchief. "Thank you," Sylvia said, her voice breaking. "I'm sorry. . . . Give me a minute, please. . . . I'll be okay."

"Your jacket has bloodstains," Giorgio noted. "Do you want to take it off? We'll get you something else to wear."

Sylvia looked down, put her hand over the bloodstain along the hem, and shook her head. "No, I'm fine. It's okay."

Giorgio was puzzled by her response. He looked around the room, and his fellow officers appeared similarly confused.

Giorgio was anxious to move on with questioning Sylvia; he needed information from her before the press conference later that evening. The media would be clamoring for details about her rescue and the arrest of the terrorists. Only Sylvia could provide certain details about her capture and rescue. Giorgio didn't want the media to be critical if he was not forthcoming with details about her experience and condition. The press would accuse him of withholding information.

"Ms. de Matteo, our first concern is your welfare," he said firmly. "We know you have been under extreme duress."

The officer reentered the room carrying a tray with a *panino,* two bottles of lemon soda, a glass of water, and a small salad. He placed the tray on the table in front of her. Sylvia raised the bottle of lemon soda and took a long drink, wiping her chin when she put the bottle on the table.

"Please, take your time. You need nourishment," Giorgio said. He looked around at the other officers and said, "Let's give Ms. de Matteo a few minutes to eat her *panino.*"

Sylvia finished the bottle of lemon soda and nibbled at the sandwich. She took two bites, swallowed, and leaned back in her chair, looking more at ease. She wiped her mouth with a napkin and said, "Thank you. That tastes good. I was thirsty and hungry. It's been a long day."

"Let me know when you're ready to talk," said Giorgio.

Sylvia took another bite, sipped from the second bottle of soda, and looked at Giorgio, flashing a brief smile.

"Okay, I'm ready," she said. "Thank you for being patient. I know I need to talk to you. Deputy Amoruso said you needed to debrief me." She looked over at Antonella, who was seated at one end, her slinged arm resting on the table. "Thank you for being patient with me driving back," Sylvia said. "I know I was disoriented."

"You're welcome, Sylvia," Antonella said with a half-smile. "I'm relieved that you are safe and unharmed."

Sylvia took a deep breath and wiped her eyes with the handkerchief. "Please ask your questions. I'm ready."

"Thank you. Can you please tell me about the people who held you hostage?" said Giorgio. "How many were there? Did you see their faces? Did they torture you or cause you harm? Take your time."

For an hour, Sylvia retold the story of her capture at Stazione Centrale and her arrival at the warehouse, where she spent her first night in the small, dark room. As well as she could, she went day by day, offering details about the room, conversations with Leo, the sound of voices in the room next to hers, and the boredom of being held captive for so many days with only a few magazines and newspapers to read. She told the investigators that she had daydreamed about happier times in her life, the birth of Angela, family Christmases, summer vacations in Menaggio, learning about her Italian heritage, her close relationship with her parents, and her engagement to Cole.

The room was still as Sylvia told her story. When she finished her long monologue, Giorgio said, "You've mentioned Leo—Fabio Cecconi—many times. What else can you tell us about him?"

Sylvia hesitated before speaking. She drank more soda and took a deep breath. "At first . . . I was afraid of him . . . all of them, actually . . . but mostly him, because he was the only one I talked to. After the third or fourth day, he seemed . . . different. He wasn't cruel. Didn't say bad things. Said he wanted to make me comfortable. If it wasn't for him, I don't know what would have happened to me. I was very afraid of . . .

that woman. She was mean . . . angry. I didn't understand how she could be so angry at me; I hadn't done anything wrong. I think she wanted to hurt me—even kill me if she had a chance."

"Did Fabio Cecconi ever touch you?"

She frowned and looked over Lucchini's head. "Ah, well, let me think. . . . Yes, he did . . . when I went into the room. And when they led me out of the room on my last day in that place, he and somebody else took my arms and put me in the car. I was wearing these dark glasses they'd painted over. When I got out of the car after we had driven for an hour or so at night, he led me to a stone cottage. It was small; one tiny window and that was all."

"Did you learn details about his life . . . the others . . . who they were . . . why they shot two political officials and two police officers at the station?"

Sylvia thought for a few moments. "He told me about his group. . . . I don't know if they had a name; no one told me. I just thought they were terrorists. It was all about the financial crisis . . . Italian politics . . . corruption . . . bad judges, those kinds of issues. They hated Berlusconi and his scandals. They despised the whole Parliament and all of the politicians of the left-wing party because they were supposed to help the poor but were only protecting their own privileges. Although they were a small group . . . at least, I think they were . . . they wanted to overthrow the government. That's why they shot those people in the station. They took me hostage because I had taken pictures of them at the station. But I didn't know who they were; I just took a few pictures, and moments later, someone grabbed me and dragged me out of the station."

"Did you sympathize with their beliefs?"

"Oh, no, absolutely not. I'm against violence of any kind. It causes immense pain to the families of those who died. I was angry about what they had done but didn't share my feelings because they could have hurt me. I was sympathetic to their distress about the conditions of unemployed Italians and their families, but violence doesn't help anyone."

The room was silent. Sylvia looked at the officers staring at her without any emotions on their faces. She knew she had to keep secret the night she and Leo had made love. She was deeply conflicted about having slept with him and didn't want to give any hints about what had happened.

"I'm tired, sir. I'm sorry . . . I need to rest. And I'd like to see my daughter; I've missed her very much. Can we continue this later?"

Giorgio sighed and looked at her, disappointed but understanding. "Yes, of course. You need rest. Your fiancé is driving to Milan with your daughter, and you will be reunited with them at a hotel nearby. The media will likely be outside the hotel, but we have arranged to escort you there without being seen. We'll have guards by your room and outside the hotel. You'll be safe."

"Thank you."

"We have arranged for a psychologist, if you would like those services. It might help you begin your process of recovery. You can spend as much time with her as you like. But we would like to get more information about the details of your rescue. We'd like to have you return tomorrow morning."

She nodded. "Yes, tomorrow will be fine. I'll be rested. My mind is just a jumble right now. . . . So much happened so fast today. . . . I need to see my family and get some rest."

* * * * *

Two hours later, Giorgio, Antonella, and Vitale were waiting offstage in the largest meeting room in the Questura, which was equipped to host press conferences. The press office had warned the Questore that there would be between eighty and one hundred journalists, reporters, and cameramen from Italy, Europe, and the United States, as well as representatives from the Polfer, NOCS, and the Milan Questura.

Cables and power cords for TV cameras, lights, radio microphones, and TV boom mikes were strung snakelike across the floor. Outside, TV trucks with dishes and roof antennae were lined up on Via Fatebenefratelli, and crowds of people lined the sidewalk across the street. The sidewalk in front of the Questura had been barricaded. Armed officers with automatic weapons and bulletproof vests stood guard around the entrance.

The media inside the conference room were as restless as a crowd at a soccer stadium. They shuffled their feet, talked loudly on cell phones, made sound checks of microphones, and cleared their throats as they impatiently waited for someone to come onstage.

The small stage was crowded with a wooden table, several chairs behind it, the flags of Italy and Europe, and the banner of the Polizia di Stato in the background. Police officers stood in front of a curtain where a floodlight shined on the standard of the city of Milan and a projection screen.

Armed police wearing bulletproof vests and carrying automatic weapons stood around the perimeter of the noisy conference room, scanning the restless journalists, alert for any disruption.

At 7:05 p.m., Giorgio confidently walked out onto the stage, followed by the Questore of Milan, Vitale, Antonella, the director of the Polizia di Prevenzione, the *pubblico ministero* (public prosecutor), and the American consul general from the US Consulate in Milan.

The Questore of Milan, Giancarlo Taddei, held his hand up to shield his eyes from the bright TV lights and reached for the microphone. The others sat down in unison.

"Where is Sylvia? Is she safe?" a TV journalist shouted above the other jabbering journalists who pressed close to the stage, which was guarded by grim-faced police officers.

"Please, could we have it quiet," the Questore said. "We have an important announcement that you've all been waiting for. We'll get to the details, but first I'd like to introduce the people who will be saying a few words about the dramatic rescue early this morning of Sylvia de Matteo and the arrest of the terrorists who committed two murders at Stazione Centrale thirteen days ago."

"Did you kill a terrorist today?" a journalist shouted out.

Taddei raised his hand. "Please, no questions now. Please be orderly. We'll answer your questions after we tell you about the day's events. We have a number of people who will be making brief comments about today's dramatic occurrences.

"You will hear from *Dottor* Giorgio Lucchini, *primo dirigente* of the DIGOS, and his deputy, *Dottoressa* Antonella Amoruso, about specifics of the investigation and the arrests. But first, I'd like to introduce several officials who were overseeing the investigation."

Taddei introduced the director of Polizia di Prevenzione, the head of the police agency in charge of NOCS, and then the public prosecutor. Each made brief comments about how well the investigation had been coordinated with various police agencies and the professionalism of the Milan DIGOS. They all offered profuse praise for Giorgio and Antonella.

After statements from the police officials, the Questore introduced Giorgio and handed him the microphone. A few journalists applauded politely. Giorgio waited until it was quiet before he spoke.

"This afternoon," he began, his voice strong, "agents of the DIGOS arrested three suspects at a construction warehouse between Bresso and Cormano, just outside Milan: Cecconi, Luca; Rizzuto, Mario; and Gori, Alfredo. They were involved in the shooting at Stazione Centrale and the kidnapping of Sylvia de Matteo. Pulvirenti, Vènera, another member of their group, has been arrested near Salerno and is being interrogated now."

A slide of the four in police mug shots flashed on the screen behind the table, their faces grim, their hair disheveled. Cameras flashed at the screen.

"All of the suspects are being questioned at San Vittore prison, and we will release more information in the days ahead. They will be charged with numerous felonies, including murder, kidnapping, and extortion. We believe at this time they were the only members involved in these crimes.

"Our investigation in the case was exhaustive, with several hundred police officers involved on a daily basis. Our highly trained officers coordinated across the country and across agency jurisdictions in a textbook case of professional police procedures. Let that be a warning to any individual or group that thinks they can outsmart the resources of the Italian police."

Giorgio turned to Antonella, whose slinged arm was resting on the table. "I have special regard for my deputy, Antonella Amoruso, who was on the front line of the investigation. She went on patrols, talked to numerous suspects and witnesses, and coordinated with other agencies. We are all in debt to her for her diligent commitment to solving these crimes.

"Yesterday I received an early morning phone call from her with information that led to her leading a team that went to Cornalba and rescued Sylvia de Matteo. Cornalba is in Bergamo province, and *Dottoressa* Amoruso collaborated with the Questura di Bergamo, *Dottor* Vitale, and a team of highly qualified police officers. Together, teams from the Milan and Bergamo Questuras organized a thorough search of the village and the surrounding area, which led to the safe recovery of Sylvia de Matteo."

Giorgio turned to Antonella. "As you can see, *Dottoressa* Amoruso suffered a minor wound in the rescue. In a brief shoot out, the leader of the terrorist group was killed."

An anxious reporter burst out near the front of the stage, "Tell us about Fabio Cecconi! Who killed him? Did she?" Two police officers moved toward him, and he slinked back into the crowd.

Giorgio continued, ignoring the journalist's outburst. "This morning, *Dottoressa* Amoruso provided us with the location where we arrested the other suspects. On her daily patrols, *Dottoressa* Amoruso had been to the warehouse near the Bresso airport, where she first encountered two of the suspects but had no evidence at that time to link them to the crimes."

Giorgio turned again toward Antonella. "*Dottoressa,* would you like to say a few words about rescuing Sylvia this morning?"

Giorgio handed the microphone to Antonella. She looked out over the TV lights and the flashes from cameras and cell phones.

"Thank you, *Dottor* Lucchini. I just have a few words to share at this time."

"Where's Sylvia? Can we see her?" a reporter yelled.

Antonella ignored him. "Less than forty-eight hours ago, we received a tip from the Bergamo Questura that a person who resembled Ms. de Matteo was seen walking on a mountain trail. We examined a photo taken by a retired teacher who had been hiking that morning. When we examined the photo, we were convinced it was Ms. de Matteo. Within a few hours, we dispatched teams of investigators, officers, and a NOCS team and began a search of the area. Our attention was focused on the village of Cornalba. On our first morning of searching in Cornalba, one of our officers saw someone who he thought was Ms. de Matteo."

"Where was she? Why was she in Cornalba? Who was guarding her?"

"Within minutes," she continued, "we surrounded the home where she had been seen. When she came out of the home with Fabio Cecconi, the leader of the terrorists, we surrounded them and told him to surrender. He fired at us—I was wounded in the exchange of fire—and he was brought down by expert shots. He died at the scene from multiple wounds."

The room became hushed except for the snapping of cameras and cell phones as she told the dramatic story.

"Forensic specialists have collected evidence from the scene. We believe Ms. de Matteo had been moved to Cornalba two nights before. We returned with Ms. de Matteo this afternoon, and she has been reunited with her family."

Antonella stopped and looked over at Taddei, who said, "Now, would you like to ask a few questions of *Dottoressa* Amoruso?"

The room erupted in a barrage of questions. "When can we see Sylvia? Where is she? Was she tortured? Was she alone with Cecconi? How many times was he shot? What did he say before he died?"

While Antonella answered reporters' questions, a police officer came onstage carrying a folder. He handed it to the Questore and whispered in his ear. The Questore opened the folder and read something inside. He closed it and nodded at the officer, who departed.

When Antonella finished, Taddei stood up and said, "Thank you for coming. It has been a long day for everyone involved in the police investigation and arrests. We will have photos of the suspects and a press release tomorrow at our press office."

Taddei opened the folder. "I have received many telegrams in the last hour from the chief of police, the Ministry of Interior, the *sottosegretari* in charge of security, and high US authorities. Copies will be available in the press office shortly."

He took out a sheet of paper from the folder and held it up. "I'd like to read a message that was just faxed to me. It's from Palazzo Chigi:

"'I would like to express my deep appreciation,'" he began reading, his voice full of conviction and authority, "'for Questore Taddei of the Questura di Milano, Questore Vitale of the Questura di Bergamo, and all of the police officers for a brilliant investigation that resulted in the release of American Sylvia de Matteo and the arrest of suspects who committed the terrible crimes at Stazione Centrale.

"'Italians abhor violence and lawlessness. Our country depends upon the many sacrifices that officers in our hardworking police agencies make to keep our country safe and free.

"'Let their courage be an example for all of us that Italy will not tolerate those who want to rob us of our liberties and safety.

"'With deepest regards,'" Questore Taddei paused before he read the signature, "'Il Presidente del Consiglio dei Ministri, Silvio Berlusconi.'"

EPILOGUE

Sylvia was reunited with Angela and Cole early that evening. They talked late into the night in their suite at the Hotel Cavour, Sylvia repeating her harrowing story but leaving out the parts that would make Angela more upset.

Angela clung to her mother, clutching her hand, wrapping her arms around her neck, and telling her how much she loved her. When it came time to go to bed, Angela begged that she be allowed to sleep in the same bed as her mother and Cole. They slept in a king-sized bed, Angela between them, her arms around her mother.

The next morning, Sylvia returned to the Questura with a police escort: two male officers in front and back of her and two female officers beside her. The press snapped photos and yelled questions from behind barricades on the other side of the street. Sylvia ignored them.

Sylvia spent an hour with Giorgio and Antonella in the interview room, answering their final questions. She then had a two-hour session with a psychiatrist who offered her sedatives, but she declined.

The police escorts walked Sylvia back to the Cavour hotel. Cole and Angela were waiting in their suite, eager to leave Milan. A police escort followed them to the underground garage, where police cars were waiting to escort them to the outskirts of Milan. The police cars kept media cars from getting too close as Cole drove out of town and was able to blend with the traffic. One police car followed them all the way to Menaggio.

Sylvia had a tearful reunion with Harriet. They hugged each other on the couch, with Angela close by. Costanza prepared a big meal, and they all sat around the table, where Sylvia gave her mother a sanitized version of her captivity.

They discussed Paolo's death and the profound impact it was having on all of them. Harriet asked Sylvia where and when they should have his funeral. Sylvia said he should be buried in the Menaggio community cemetery, which they had visited on the day that she, Cole, and Angela had departed for Milan two weeks before. Just outside that cemetery was where Sylvia had seen her father for the last time.

Four days later, during a morning drizzle, Paolo was buried in the de Matteo crypt. An older uncle and aunt from Paolo's family near Lago di Piano attended. Giorgio and Antonella drove up from Milan and stood behind the family during the brief service led by a priest from Santo Stefano church, where Paolo had attended mass, occasionally with Angela.

Two days later, the family and Costanza took a rental car with a driver to Malpensa Airport, north of Milan, to fly back to New York. They wanted to avoid Stazione Centrale.

Sylvia and Angela stayed with Harriet in the family's East Side apartment after they arrived in New York. Harriet had lost a considerable amount of weight and had become more disoriented and depressed. Her doctor confided to Sylvia that Harriet's health had declined seriously since her last exam in June, before she had flown to Menaggio for the summer.

A week later, Harriet had a stroke. She was in intensive care for four days and died without regaining consciousness.

The evening after Harriet's funeral, Sylvia told Cole she wanted to break their engagement. She said she needed to be alone, rethink her life, and spend time with Angela, who, for the first time, was having trouble with her studies. Cole was deeply hurt. He asked Sylvia to reconsider and take time before she made a final decision. But she persisted, telling him they both needed to rebuild their lives without any involvement.

Sylvia's book, *Italia Ieri, Italia Oggi, Italia Domani,* was being published in the spring, but Sylvia told her editor that she wouldn't do a book tour.

After New Year's, Sylvia took Angela out of school and closed her studio. They flew to Italy with Costanza and moved into the family villa in Menaggio. Sylvia stored her parents' clothes in a spare bedroom and moved into their large bedroom. She brought few clothes from America, but at the back of the closet she hung the bloodstained jacket and stored in a shoe box the garden shoes she'd worn the day she had been rescued. She sealed the clothes they had given her after she was taken hostage in a plastic bag and kept them in a bottom dresser drawer.

Sylvia enrolled Angela in a public Italian school, Scuola Media in Menaggio. It was in the center of town and within walking distance. After just a few days at her new school, Angela returned home and excitedly told Sylvia that her Italian classmates were nice and wanted to become friends with her. "Kids in New York are so stuffy and mean," she told Sylvia. "They brag about how rich their parents are, and if you don't wear expensive clothes, they say nasty things about you. I'm glad we don't live in New York anymore."

Angela began telling Sylvia that Italian boys were flirting with her. She liked the attention, and she and Sylvia had intimate conversations about the changes that come with adolescence.

Sylvia went to parent events at Angela's school and met the families of her classmates. Sylvia invited mothers for tea at the villa and began making friends.

After her mother's and father's passing, Sylvia became very wealthy. She began making generous donations to Menaggio schools to pay salaries of teachers of disabled children. She donated to a charity in Milan, Opera San Francesco, which provided meals for the poor. Women's health care was another cause that was important to Sylvia. She consulted with doctors to provide support for poor women who might be forced to have abortions because of poverty or health problems.

After local media heard of Sylvia's return to Menaggio, they showed up unannounced at the villa. Sylvia refused interview requests and had security alarms and cameras installed. She hired twenty-four-hour guards at the gate and inside the grounds.

She asked one of her guards to take her to Como to buy a new car. She bought a new Audi A1 so she and Angela could drive around Lake Como and go to markets in Menaggio, Cadenabbia, and Tremezzo to shop for food and clothes. On shopping trips, Sylvia wore sunglasses, a floppy hat, and loose clothing to shield her identity. When shopkeepers or clerks recognized her, they respected her privacy and treated her like any other Italian mother shopping with her daughter.

In mid-June, Sylvia gave birth to a seven-pound baby boy at a hospital in Menaggio. When she brought him home, she put him in her former bedroom, which she had renovated into a nursery.

She named her young son Paolo Leo de Matteo. On summer mornings, she nursed Paolo Leo on the patio. It was a nostalgic place for Sylvia, as it reminded her of when the family had celebrated Paolo's last birthday. After dinner that August evening, she and Paolo had had a memorable father-daughter conversation late into the night about her pending marriage to Cole, her new book, and her anxiety about returning to New York. That last evening with her father now seemed so long ago . . . when she was a different woman . . . living someone else's life.

On those summer mornings after Paolo Leo fell asleep, she would put him in the bassinet and return to the patio for a few quiet moments. She thought about her future and fantasized that when Paolo Leo started nursery school, she might open an art gallery or a shop to sell antique Italian furniture. Or she might return to photography. She had plenty of time to think about her future; for the next year or so, she just wanted to enjoy their new life in the family villa.

Summer was busy for Angela and Sylvia. They took Paolo Leo for walks along Lake Como and pushed his pram onto ferries to visit Varenna, Bellagio, and Como.

On a Sunday in late December, a snowy and cold day in Menaggio, Sylvia hosted a Christmas party for Angela's classmates and their families. Costanza fixed traditional Christmas treats: panettone and *pandoro* with mascarpone cream, hot chocolate, nuts, chocolate cake, and star-shaped cookies. Everyone sang carols around the Christmas tree, which was decorated with ribbons, ornaments, and bulbs that Angela and Sylvia had bought on shopping trips to Milan. They all played tombola in front of the fireplace until late.

After their guests had gone home, Sylvia and Angela sat on the sofa in front of the fireplace, with Paolo Leo sleeping in his pram. They shared how much they had enjoyed having new friends in their home for their first Christmas in Italy.

"I'm so happy . . . but also a little sad, Mom. This Christmas is so special, and last Christmas was terrible. Both Nonno and Nonna died last year, and Christmas was so sad. But this year is the best! I love it. I just wish Nonno and Nonna were here to see how happy we are. I really miss them, especially at Christmas."

Sylvia kissed her on the forehead. "I miss them too, dear. I think about them every day. But I'm sure they're looking down on us at times like these and are happy that we've made wonderful lives for ourselves here."

"We're so lucky, Mom. I have a baby brother now. I love him; he's such a sweet baby. He's going to love growing up in Menaggio. I can't wait to teach him to speak Italian like Nonno taught me. What do you think he'll call me, Angie, *sorellina,* or *sorellona?*"

Sylvia reached over and ran her hand through Angela's long hair. "You're going to be a great sister for Paolo Leo. He'll need you to introduce him to Menaggio."

A weak cry and then a wail came from the pram. "Whaa . . . whaa . . . whaaa!"

"Mom, I think he heard us talking about him! Paolo Leo's awake. Is it time to feed him?"

"Yes, but let's change his diaper first. He's been sleeping almost two hours. Want to help me?"

"Sure, I'll push him into the nursery."

Angela steered the pram around the gifts and wrapping paper from the afternoon party and down the hall to Paolo Leo's nursery. Sylvia lifted him out of the pram, set him on the changing table, and stripped off his baby clothes. Angela opened a drawer, pulled out a clean diaper, and handed it to her mother. Paolo Leo's tiny dark eyes looked at his mother and then at his sister, who was combing her fingers through his thin, dark curls.

"I love his curly hair. It's so fluffy and soft," Angela said. "He's going to be a cute little boy, isn't he?"

Sylvia smiled. "He already is, dear," she said as she finished changing his diaper and picked him up. "Now, let me go feed him by the fireplace where it's warm. He's starved. Get a couple Christmas cookies for us and sit next to me."

"Can I play with him before he goes back to sleep?"

"Sure, of course. I'll clean up the gifts and wrapping paper while you take care of your baby brother."

Angela ran out of the nursery into the kitchen to get the cookies. Sylvia picked up Paolo Leo and glanced back at the dresser next to the bassinet before she turned out the light. On the dresser was a picture of Paolo Leo's father when he was a young boy, in the arms of his father when the family was on vacation in Rome.

Sylvia turned out the light and left the nursery.

THE END

ACKNOWLEDGMENTS

I was fortunate to have many people assist me in researching and writing *Thirteen Days in Milan*.

Bruno Megale and his deputy, Giuseppina Suma, at DIGOS Milan's Questura provided extensive guidance about investigating terrorist crimes and Italian police procedures. I am indebted to them for their support and interest in my book.

Tito Boeri, Claudia Flisi, Barbara Claren, Stefano Claren, Massimo Guidolin, Larry Gurwin, Aaron Maines, Giovanni Mastrobuoni, Giorgio Navaretti, Marco Ottaviano, Paolo Pasi, and Eric Sylvers shared their knowledge with me while I was researching in Milan in October 2012.

My editor, Pamela McManus, has been providing me invaluable professional support for 20 years. Pamela was helpful with guidance on grammar as well as story development and character background.

Elena Ciampella was my guide and interpreter in Milan. She offered valuable insights into Italian culture, politics, and contemporary life. Elena became my researcher and offered her expertise in reading early drafts, correcting my errors, and suggesting key details. She's a woman of many talents.

Pamela and Elena provided friendship and advice all along the way. It was a pleasure to work with them. I look forward to continuing our professional relationship in books yet to be written.

I consulted many sources while researching *Thirteen Days in Milan*. They included:

The Sack of Rome, Alexander Stille
(Penguin Books, 2007)

*Excellent Cadavers: The Mafia and the Death of the First Italian
    Republic*, Alexander Stille
(Vintage Books, 1995)

The Dark Heart of Italy, Tobias Jones
(North Point Press, 2003)

Days of Wrath, Robert Katz
(Doubleday & Company, 1980)

The Pursuit of Italy, David Gilmour
(Farrar, Straus, and Giroux, 2011)

Good Italy, Bad Italy, Bill Emmott
(Yale University Press, 2012)

Italian Days, Barbara Gruzzuti Harrison
(Weidenfeld & Nicholson, 1989)

Anatomy of the Red Brigades, Alessandro Orsini
(Cornell University Press, 2009)

The Moro Affair, Leonardo Sciascia
(New York Review Books, 1978)

Le polaroid di Moro, Sergio Bianchi e Raffaella Perna
(Derive Approdi Siri, 2012

Look for the next exciting international thriller featuring Giorgio Lucchini, Antonella Amoruso, and Simona De Monti of Milan's Questura in late 2014.

http://www.JackErickson.com

ABOUT THE AUTHOR

J ack Erickson is the author of international thrillers, mysteries, novels, short stories, and true crime.

He is writing an international thriller series featuring Giorigio Lucchini and Antonella Amoruso from Milan's Questura.

Erickson also writes an international travel blog, A Year and a Day. He lives in northern California with his wife.

www.jackerickson.com

ericksongypsycaravan.wordpress.com

CPSIA information can be obtained
at www.ICGtesting.com
Printed in the USA
FSOW01n0651171214
3927FS